Falling Walrus

Robert J. Wolfe

East Baton Rouge Parish Library
Baton Rouge, Louisiana

For Larri Irene Spengler.

1

"Peligroso! Quédate aquí!" shouted *el jefe* above the roar of the storm, 'stay here,' and no other spot! The boss jabbed a finger to the half-frozen ground for emphasis.

Francisco Fernández Muñoz, leaning into the freezing blasts, nodded vigorously and did as ordered, planting himself beneath the hummock's wet slope. If the boss shouted 'dangerous' and 'stay here,' then here he stayed. *El jefe* knew this awful place, Francisco didn't. Even this storm! So frigid! Not like the downpours in Chiapas, his mountains in Mexico. Where were his toes? He could not feel his boots!

The boss jerked the pack from Francisco's shoulders and threw it on the icy slope. Terrific updrafts slammed them. Dead grass thrashed like whistling whips.

Francisco bent low into the violence and shivered. He had jumped ship in Dillingham, the first sizable port after Dutch Harbor on the Aleutians, quitting the herring fleet because of the violent storms and awful sea sickness, the constant lurching and swaying of the fishing boat, even in his sleep! His stomach kept nothing down. In the mirror his cheeks stretched like hollow drums. But quitting the herring fishing for this new job was no better. He was freezing! Soaked to the bone!

The Eskimo appeared at Francisco's shoulder. He threw down another pack.

"Get the line!" the boss shouted.

The Eskimo shoved his face into Francisco's, flashing an evil, gap-toothed grin.

"Windy?" he mocked the Mexican.

1

He shoved something soggy into Francisco's freezing hands and disappeared into the flying rack with a high-pitched laugh. It was Francisco's wool cap, heavy with rain, snatched from his head by the storm.

Francisco steadied the packs as the boss extracted equipment, a thick mallet and long, sharpened wooden stakes. Electric lanterns flickered silvery sparks in the blackness. The boss hammered the stakes deep into the earth. How can he work, shivered Francisco, when the hands are dead? The Eskimo reappeared with a length of rope. The boss looped it through the stakes' heavy eyelets and passed the end to the Eskimo.

"The same up there!"

Grinning at Francisco, the Eskimo scrambled up the slope, the wet line squealing, his lantern's glow lost in the murk of rain. In a minute the rope jerked taut. The boss buckled upon a wide leather belt that gripped his middle. He slung a sturdy rucksack over his shoulder, grabbed a lantern, and shouted again at Francisco.

"Quédate aquí! Peligroso!" he jabbed his finger downwards. 'Stay here! Dangerous!'

"Okay!" shouted Francisco through chattering teeth. He wasn't moving.

The Eskimo reappeared, coiling line.

"I'm going!" the boss yelled.

The Eskimo nodded. And Francisco watched stunned as the man strode into the flying black rain and vanished as if swallowed by the earth. The Eskimo held the rope tight. A safety line, but for what?

The line went slack.

Instantly the Eskimo rolled to his stomach, pressed flat upon the sodden ground. His eyes swept the slope, eerie flashes of white defying the shadows beyond the lantern's glow.

"What's that?" he rasped with alarm.

"Eh?"

"That!" repeated the Eskimo in the hoarse whisper. "You hear it?" He grimaced frightfully and jerked his head skyward.

Francisco heard nothing but screaming wind.

"Nada," growled Francisco, swallowing his distain and mistrust. He hated this Eskimo! Always mocking him, always joking.

'*No haga preguntas, no oiga mentiras,*' his father warned Francisco, just before his departure to the Far North.

'Ask no questions, hear no lies.'

Here was the warning come to life, *el bromista*, the teller of lies. Lies to scare him because he was young and came from a poor village in Chiapas for the hard work in Alaska. Lies to trick him because he was alone and ignorant and far from home. He could not read the Eskimo's twisted face. He hated his yellow-toothed smile and high-pitched laugh and the bogey tales, horrible stories he only partly followed about ghosts. Haunted islands. The dead who would not stay dead. Stories about *el chupacabras*, the goat-sucker. Francisco knew the Eskimo lied. This was Alaska. It had no chupacabras. He didn't think Alaska even had goats, though maybe it did. Francisco knew nothing of Alaskan goats. The trickster lied about the chupacabras.

"Wait here!" barked the Eskimo. He grabbed a lantern, waved vaguely at the anchored line, and disappeared into the bone-chilling storm.

The rain abruptly turned to hard-hitting hail. Ice pebbles hammered the slope, pounding the dead grass flat beneath a bouncing white swarm. Francisco hunkered below its vengeance. The frigid rain returned, milky rivulets pouring off the pale earth.

Then Francisco heard it through the roaring wind.

A long, low, eerie moan!

Francisco's heart nearly stopped. Hugging the ground, he fumbled his cap and strained his ears, his body shaking. An icy hand squeezed his chest.

It came again, a long, low, gut-churning groan.

"*Pendejo!*" cursed Francisco weakly. Damn that jokester!

The Eskimo materialized from the storm, sliding on his back off the slick hummock. His eyes bulged wildly. He clutched a rifle to his chest.

"You hear it?" he rasped.

"No!" shouted Francisco, filled with sudden anger. "*No oigo nada!*"

He was through with the tricks! He grabbed at the rifle stock and pulled.

"*Nada! Nada! Nada!*"

At that instant, a dark shadow rose from the storm above them.

Francisco froze and stared upwards, open-mouthed.

The shape grew from the black clouds, a great swell above the hummock blasted by the squall. Huge! Monstrous! It perched, slickly glistening in the light. Slowly it turned, swaying from side-to-side in a strange dance, surveying them. Its throat rumbled a deep, menacing growl. The vibrations rattled Francisco's teeth. And then, to Francisco's horror, the chupacabras pulled back on its haunches. It bared fearsome fangs and lunged!

The Eskimo jerked the rifle free from Francisco's grasp. He rolled, aimed from his gut, and yanked the trigger. The blast shattered the air.

Francisco stood planted, right where the boss had put him, wide-eyed with shock. The ghostly mass took him.

The Eskimo spun frantically.

Francisco was gone!

A challenge exploded above him. He dove aside to hug the ground, chambered a round, and set himself in the whipping wind. There! This time he took aim. Fired! Chambering another, he fired again! And again!

Into the roar of the storm they resounded, sharp staccato blasts, snuffed to small pops.

Swallowed up.

Carried off by raging wind.

2

"They don't believe our stories!" the old woman huffed angrily.

The boy shied from her, sunk among the remnants and half-worked fabrics. Still, he listened.

"They happened way back! But they don't! We tell it because they happened!" She waved a hand as if swatting troublesome flies. "That noseless kalla'alek! And Cuniq!"

Gasping for air, she grimaced defiantly at invisible doubters in the cramped sewing room. It was a frightful broken-toothed grin, wide and fixed as she labored to breathe.

Alexie would not sit with her on the old sofa. She scared him. He settled astride the broken rocker, wrapping a leg around an arm. It tipped perilously and nearly pitched him on the spool case. Over-correcting, he rocked backwards and almost dumped upon the converted treadle.

Kalla'alek.

That meant a shaman, a conjurer of ghosts. He liked to be scared by stories of kalla'aleks.

"Gave up… gave away his power."

"Up a… what?" the boy nervously yelped as the rocker tipped again.

"Cuniq! He gave up his power to that noseless devil! Beyond the great bay where they sent him to hunt, he threw it away and he lived!"

Noseless devil.

Alexie had heard something about this from Christof, the goofball at school who taped up his nose like a pig to tease classmates.

The old woman scowled at him. Her chest wheezed and popped. He was sitting now. She saw he was afraid, like all boys his age get afraid of old scolds, elders who shout from deafness, ugly like herself. And that was good. He should be afraid. He was young, unprepared, and the world filled with dangers he knew nothing about.

"We tell it because they happened!"

"Cuniq," Alexie whispered the alluring name, the hunter who gave away power to a devil.

"Like a great, great, grandfather to you... way back! At Kodiak... where we lived before the Aleuts, way back! That was our home before the Russians came on the ships... before the Aleuts chased us here... before the Great Death."

Alexie checked the open door. His mother worked in the next room cutting half-dried fish for jarring, the sockeyes and chums his father had caught in the rough waters of Prince William Sound before the last storm. Alexie had helped to pull them from the nets, pitching them on the deck, whipped by rain. He examined the shrunken elder on the sofa, his great aunt who sometimes stayed with them, wrapped in a heavy Pendleton, heaving for air, lungs ruined by tuberculosis and cigarettes. She no longer watched him. Her eyes had moved to a shadowy edge of the room, looking beyond the walls where the wind whined off the sound.

"Russians and death and broad-sailed ships..."

She spoke with a slow certainty, taking her deep breaths, remembering, translating in her head from the Sugstun to English for the boy who hardly knew his Native language, assuming the cadence from that other time, before television, before schools, before even this village where they lived. She would not water it down. She would not sanitize or simplify or apologize for the violence, because it all had happened.

"Russians and death and broad-sailed ships... they came, driven by storms, each with the other. And the Sugpiat began dying, our people, the real people, driven from the shores of our home... Sitkinak, Tugidak, Kodiak, Afognak... dying like fish on sand beneath the moon, too many to count! Before his own birth it began, the Russians and ships. But Cuniq knew. Like a great, great, grandfather to you, he felt it inside of him here, hot with a fire that burned inside of him, on that seal rock in the haunted sea, because he was dying too!"

At the edge of sight, she saw the boy shudder with nervous excitement, imagining seal rocks in haunted seas. He hugged his knees, pushed back into the broken chair for warmth, afraid but unable to leave, wanting more. She remembered how it was for her when she first heard the story. It was like that. She hadn't slept that night, trembling on her cot at the hunting camp, recalling what was told, over and again. She could never forget how it went.

She would tell it to him now. She would tell it to him right.

Because it all happened.

Way back!

Cuniq's story.

Her own story.

His.

3

The storm blew itself out. Its remnants covered the shore. Squeezing his eyes to the brisk morning air, Tooluyuk surveyed prospects, ripped and cast upon the sand. The beach stretched into the far distance like a winding silver highway. It smelled with the thick pungency of fresh bull kelp. He sat easily at the back of his skiff, steering the noisy Johnson one-handed, piloting with an unconscious grace through the low swells, smoking a bent cigarette with wet fingers.

The storm had come in hard from the North Pacific, gaining strength, jumping the Aleutian chain. It tore across the Bering Sea and pounded Togiak Bay with left-hook winds and high surf. The fury drove all the boats to shelter. Commercial fishing stalled. The huge commercial herring fleet with its entourage of tenders, processors, and spotters ran for cover at Dillingham, the nearest port hours to the south, hunkered down for two days of fury. The storm's trailing winds, still packing power from the North Pacific, finally passed during the night. The herring fleet frantically prepared to race back to the bay to complete its fishing frenzy.

But Tooluyuk had beaten them. He departed from Togiak in the early dawn, as soon as the winds quieted and the pale skies cleared. A faded goose-down jacket guarded his wiry frame against the morning chill. A stainless-steel Thermos with strong dark tea brewed by his wife kept his insides warm. In the long half-light of spring, he observed other boats like his leaving the village with the early dawn. A pair of young hunters he knew took off west, partnered in hopes of catching a few more seals in the choppy bay. The Bavilla family headed upriver to work on a new fish camp, their old site lost from erosion during breakup. And he spotted that troublesome bootlegger Ignatius Smart, stranded in Togiak by the storm, finally leaving town, pushing north for Goodnews Bay with his illicit pickup from Dillingham.

Undoubtedly they had seen Tooluyuk too, pointing his skiff south along the shore of the bay. They probably guessed where he was going, doing what people like him often did after storms.

'Go look, be first,' his grandfather had taught him long ago. Yup'iks with foresight and energy always searched beaches after storms.

Storms left bounty. They brought gifts from places too deep or too distant for people to reach, at least old men like Tooluyuk. The storms cast up spruce, cedar, and hemlock, logs stripped smooth of bark by the waves, tossed like polished bones of giants on the muddy flats and pea-gravel beaches. In these treeless reaches of the Bering Sea, large logs were welcomed gifts. Who had money to buy the sturdy beams for a fish-drying rack? Who could afford the stove oil for heating a home during winter? Not him. He looked for these necessities from the sea. By mid-morning he had found and claimed several large spruce logs. He affixed strips of red cloth to their gleaming trunks to mark them for later retrieval. Other salvagers who saw his tiny rags would leave his logs alone.

Storms also dredged up food. The waves that churned the shallow bay laid a banquet along the shore. Tooluyuk loved the delicacies, the special seaweeds, the crabs, clams, and mussels, the odd sea cucumbers and snails that experienced foragers knew to be edible. Already this morning he had filled two plastic sacks with beach food. When he returned, he would distribute his finds among the home-bound elders.

This storm had cast up thick mats of kelp, wide and meandering along the beach. Here and there among the weeds poked flotsam snatched from the decks of other seafarers, broken Styrofoam containers, a rubber boot, Japanese glass floats, and fragments of nets. Once after a storm he had found an intact fiberglass dingy, perfect for holding the red skeins of roe at fish camp when his wife cut salmon. Another time he found a kit of miniature tools in cunning waterproofed lacquered boxes, inscribed with a Hokkaido address. He mailed the boxes back. Somewhat later he received a thank-you note printed with tiny pink-on-green wood-block flowers, delicately inscribed from an inked brush by the dentist of a Japanese village. It gave him joy, remembering it. Tooluyuk judiciously combed the beach for surprises like these, steering and smoking and enjoying the cool spring morning.

The beach turned black and rocky. Tooluyuk motored down and drove carefully. The skiff approached the bay's southern capes where fingers of basalt extended into the sea. He maneuvered the boat by large rocks near the surface, cautiously guarding the outboard's lower unit. In the shimmering distance he spotted the island named Qayassiq, 'place to go in a kayak,' called Round Island by the kass'aqs. It was one of several nearby islets rich with sea life.

His people hunted from these rocky points in the short winter days. They searched for issuriq, nayiq, and other seals in the shore-fast ice shattered by the cape. At the village the bay froze for miles offshore. But at the rocky cape, the sea ice broke open nearer to shore. People and seals had lived here for centuries because of these special conditions.

In line with these thoughts, a low hump appeared on the rocky beach. Tooluyuk smiled and powered down. He veered the boat toward it. A convention of gulls and ravens scattered, screaming insults as he landed and stepped ashore. Stretching his old limbs, he strode toward the dun-colored mound, chest high and nearly as long as his boat.

He grinned.

Asverrluk.

A beached walrus. Dead on the rocks.

Tooluyuk offered a silent thanks. The morning's search was now complete.

After a quick inspection, he set to work with tools from the boat, his ax, a saw, and a stout knife. He worked fast and efficiently, puffing a cigarette as he butchered, beads of sweat cooling his brow in the light breeze. He filled heavy-gauge trash sacks, five-gallon plastic buckets, and a large galvanized washtub in the boat's bottom. An audience of gulls surrounded him. They anxiously watched, in some way aware that their luck had improved too.

After an hour, he was finishing up. He had stripped the prized skin and blubber from the top of the walrus, filling the entire washtub. This was what people desired most, the rich fatty skin. Several sacks also bulged with select cuts of meat undamaged by the storm's pounding, a rib section, and the liver, heart, and kidneys. He washed the purplish intestines in the frigid salt water, working a rock inside along its full length, squeezing with both hands to clean out the black contents. He coiled the loops into a compact pile in the skiff. Good eating. In a wet burlap sack he placed the flippers. His wife would beam when she opened it. These were her favorites. He opened the stomach for clams to eat, but found it empty. The animal had died hungry. Finally, tired and satisfied, he secured the cargo in the boat.

As he stretched canvas tarps, the sea birds converged on the bare carcass stripped for easy dining. They screamed and fought though it held days of feasting. It was then, over the querulous clamor, that he heard it. A low roar came off the sea. He shielded his eyes. Stainless steel flashed in the sun. A shining vessel hydroplaned along the shore, skipping atop the swells with thrusts from powerful jets.

Tooluyuk recognized the boat by its sound long before he saw it clearly. He was Yup'ik. Though his homeland in southwest Alaska was vast, his people were intimate and nosey. A neighbor's equipment was as noteworthy as family members. Most Yup'iks could identify boats at great distances. This proved to be a useful skill for finding (or avoiding) particular owners. Even children could do it. Tooluyuk, who was no child, knew the sound of this boat and wondered if the morning's good luck was about to change. He resumed securing tarp lines.

The jet boat came directly toward him. It beached a stone's throw off. A deafening stillness followed the shutdown of its engine. Two kass'aqs stepped out, removed ear protectors, and smiled. One of them, a paunchy man bulked in an orange floatation vest, pushed at the sky with an exaggerated wave. It was Darryl Thomas, an agent with the wildlife refuge. Tooluyuk had met him before. He did not know the gangly, bushy-haired boy who trailed behind, a head taller than Thomas.

"How's it going, Afcan!" the agent shouted as if to defeat the cape's silence.

Tooluyuk nodded at the greeting.

"Eddie, this is Afcan Tooluyuk, an elder from Togiak, still doing, uh… the traditional subsistence lifestyle. Afcan, this is Edward Cummings. He's just come on board with the refuge."

"Nice to meet you, Mr. Tooluyuk," the new hire grinned, gently taking the elder's hand and pumping once. The newcomer had learned the local handshake.

11

The fresh young face towered above his. Tooluyuk smiled into it. Unavoidably, he looked straight up the boy's nose. Oh, an absurd nose! Kass'aqs had big noses, but this was the greatest nose he had ever witnessed up close. The nostrils stretched like coin slots in a piggybank, like the great beak of a payiq. That was it! The fresh-faced kass'aq was like a payiq, a long-nosed, shaggy-headed merganser duck!

'Beak Boy,' Tooluyuk chuckled to himself.

"You've been hard at work! What have we here, a walrus?" The agent's voice boomed like canon as he strode to the carcass. Gulls scattered.

Darryl Thomas began a close inspection. Young Eddie Cummings fidgeted beside Tooluyuk. He wanted a closer look too, but some propriety held him beside the Yup'ik elder.

Tooluyuk observed the government agent examining the walrus and felt guilty. Customarily, Yup'iks enjoyed chance meetings. In this case, Tooluyuk wished he'd loaded faster and gotten away. He chastised himself for the uncharitable thought. Unfortunately, the agent's behavior confirmed his low expectations. Hunters normally enjoyed relaxed chat over hot drinks, swapping news, exchanging observations that might improve a hunter's luck or save a traveler's life. Darryl Thomas did not chat. He lay prone on the rock peering beneath a shoulder. What was he doing? The strange behavior made Tooluyuk mildly uneasy.

Darryl Thomas straightened up.

"Let's get samples and pictures from this one too," he directed his young charge. With a sheepish grin, Eddie hurried to the jet boat for equipment.

The agent approached Tooluyuk, wiping his hands on a rag hanging from his canvas pants.

"Doing some beachcombing, hey?"

Though he spoke to Tooluyuk, the agent's eyes fixed upon the skiff with its covered buckets, sealed trash sacks, and battened tarps. They bored holes.

"Yes," replied Tooluyuk, who could not help but follow his eyes, wondering what they were trying to see. When they abruptly turned on him, Tooluyuk suppressed an urge to jump.

"Did you happen to notice the other two, the ones toward town?" the agent asked, waving that direction. He carefully watched Tooluyuk's face.

Noticing this, Tooluyuk held his face completely still.

Why would Darryl Thomas ask me this? Why is he so intently watching my face?

Tooluyuk took a moment to work through the puzzling question. There were two other walrus carcasses between here and town, a large adult and a mid-size juvenile, both males, like most summer walruses. Tooluyuk had encountered them earlier that morning while canvassing the beaches. They were resting above the storm line, clearly visible along the route he took from the village to the cape. Darryl Thomas was asking if Tooluyuk noticed. Yet, it was obvious Tooluyuk had noticed. He had put his boat ashore to check them. His boat's marks would be clearly visible, his footsteps sunk in the wet sand. The signs would still be there because of a receding tide. How could Darryl Thomas not already know this?

Tooluyuk considered how to answer the obvious question without insulting the asker. Maybe, reasoned Tooluyuk, maybe Darryl Thomas didn't want to appear to presume that Tooluyuk took that route this morning. Why, he didn't know. Or maybe they quickly passed the carcasses and had not gone ashore to inspect them. But that made little sense because he said to that boy, 'let's get samples and pictures from this one too.' No matter how he analyzed it, the question 'did you notice the others' remained perplexing. Nevertheless, not wishing to rudely ignore him or insult his intelligence, Tooluyuk decided it safest to give a direct answer.

"Yes," Tooluyuk replied.

The agent watched his face a few more moments.

"You didn't take anything?"

This question in what was becoming an interview made Tooluyuk wonder if he had missed something when he stopped to check the carcasses earlier that morning. Maybe this was the point of the questions. Darryl Thomas had noticed something. He was preparing to tell him about some oddity he had missed concerning the other walruses.

"No," he replied with some interest, wondering what the agent had observed.

"Why not?"

This next question was very unexpected. Why not? What a ridiculous question!

Is this an ignoramus? Didn't the agent know anything?

It was obvious why he took nothing from those walrus carcasses. Didn't the agent stand beside them? Didn't he walk on the footprints?

Stupid questions! How can the stupid be spared?

Tooluyuk nearly frowned.

Sand.

The beaches were sand!

That was the reason.

The walrus had tumbled in sand before being cast ashore. Grit was forced into every wrinkle and crease of the skins. Recovering edible blubber from such carcasses was nearly impossible, even internal meat and organs without great effort. He had considered it but decided instead to push ahead in case there might be something on rock toward the cape. There had been.

Tooluyuk worked hard not to insult.

"Sand," he said.

A light dawned in the agent's eyes.

"Ah!"

Darryl Thomas walked a few steps, mulling something over. Beak Boy snapped photos of the butchered walrus. The agent's voice assumed a deeper, formal tone.

"Mr. Tooluyuk, you didn't happen to salvage any ivory, did you?"

The question was clear and polite. It was now Tooluyuk who received the epiphany. Ah, that's it! Ivory! Of course, here's the reason for all the questions. He'd begun to wonder if what some said about refuge workers was true... they were paid to pester people. Tooluyuk knew that wasn't correct. Refuge workers weren't paid pests. This was just ivory talk.

"No," Tooluyuk replied, now secure with the conversation.

He and the agent stood together in silence watching Eddie take tissue samples. The young refuge worker filled transparent vials with pieces of skin, fat, muscle, and hair. The boy worked with precision, carefully labeling each tiny bottle. Tooluyuk watched with interest. He wondered what would be done next with them and for what purpose. But when Darryl Thomas broke the silence, ivory was still the topic.

"Well, I expect you know that all ivory must be tagged by an authorized agent within thirty days. I know the last tagger quit in Togiak. The nearest tagging station is at Dillingham. But Mr. Cummings and I are authorized for ivory. We can tag it while we're in town."

Tooluyuk nodded. He understood. He'd tell others when he returned, if he remembered. They resumed watching Eddie.

Eventually, sneaking one last long look at the tarps covering Tooluyuk's boat, Darryl Thomas strode to the walrus where young Cummings wrapped up.

"If we're done, we should be getting along."

"I'm done."

"Okay. See you later, Afcan!"

Darryl Thomas waved broadly.

"Nice to meet you!" shouted Eddie with a grin.

They shoved the jet boat from the rocky beach. It rumbled to life and roared away. Tooluyuk watched the craft disappear behind the near point.

As he pulled his own skiff free, Tooluyuk replayed the conversation, the series of odd questions from Darryl Thomas. Kass'aqs at times acted strangely. And English was not his first language. He thought he had got it right. But it was still puzzling.

Why did Darryl Thomas keep asking about the ivory?

It was obvious why he took no ivory.

He really didn't think Darryl Thomas was stupid.

Tooluyuk looked behind him to the beach with the butchered walrus, trying to resolve the oddness of those questions. The gulls and ravens fed on the carcass, dwindling specks in the distance. He reasoned it out.

This walrus left by the storm had been dead for some time, at least two days. The others toward town were the same. Two days. That was easy to observe. Darryl Thomas and that boy had inspected the carcasses. They took pictures. They took tissue samples from each. Of course they saw that. Two days dead.

Further, and of course much greater significance, when the storm put them ashore the carcasses had no ivory to give.

That was obvious. There was no ivory to salvage.

Because the walruses had no heads.

They were headless.

Surely they noticed that!

Tooluyuk was stumped.

How could anybody salvage ivory from a headless walrus?

It was not possible.

The elder shook his head at the puzzle.

He took the outboard's stick between his legs and lit a cigarette, watching the submerged rocks and near point. He guessed he just didn't understand kass'aqs.

With a yelp he threw the cigarette!

His driving hand jerked, killing the boat's progress. The skiff rocked and swayed, riding the wake as if frightened to choose a course.

Tooluyuk leaped to the stern. Stretching high above the outboard, he intently scanned the rocky point ahead, balancing with the swells, shielding against the glare. A growing dread filled him. He reclaimed the pilot's seat and engaged the outboard. Reluctantly, he pointed the skiff toward the beach.

Securing anchor, Tooluyuk waded ashore. He forced himself to walk the rocky strand. Gulls screamed at his approach, scattering at an outcrop.

Yes, there it was.

It lay partly hidden upon a shelf.

The birds had shown him.

Partway up a low cliff, the waves had tucked another carcass. A tidal pool partly covered it within a shallow cleft. Storm-cast remains. Bare skin glistened in the morning light.

Tooluyuk gave a pained sigh.

A naked man. A corpse.

Here was a gift from the deep he had hoped never to find. But someone would be glad he had.

The sea had stripped it of clothes. The torso was thick, slightly bloated, and savagely mangled. Arms and legs twisted in disturbing directions. The storm had wrenched loose every joint, jerked hard, and crushed the body between powerful hands.

Reluctantly, he inspected more closely.

A kass'aq. Young.

Tooluyuk didn't know him.

He was a stranger, a visitor from outside… maybe one of the seasonal workers who came with the herring boats, washed from the deck while fishing. It sometimes happened.

Tooluyuk looked again to make sure.

Yes, a strange young kass'aq.

He had never seen him before now, not in Togiak, not at Dillingham, not anyplace he had traveled.

Of this he was certain.

Despite the pecked-out eyes.

Unlike the walrus, this one still had his head.

4

"Russians, death, and broad-sailed ships…"

The Aleuts came too, churlish slaves of the Russian masters, skeletons of a robust people, ruined by the Devil's trade. The Aleuts wrecked and stole from the people. And when everything was taken, they lusted for more. They demanded the pelts of sea otters, ermines, and foxes. Musky castor from the glands of beavers. Yellow-veined ivory. Glistening pokes of seal oil. Quotas of dried meats and hides of any sort, scraped, smoked, salted, stacked, bundled, recorded in endless ledgers, and carried off in their deep skin boats. And always they lusted for more.

The Devil's trade.

The Russian priests named it. For in exchange came fevers, fluid-filled lungs, and corpses. Abandoned hamlets. Dying slaves. Orphans. Skins for death, proved that night by Cuniq on the seal rock in the haunted sea as the twilight failed… because he was dying too. He was a mighty hunter, the best of the seal hunters, like a great, great grandfather to you… a fire burned inside of him here… dying too.

Cuniq sprawled on the rock, fighting the dreams that fool the mind near death. He had fallen by his kayak, his paddle beneath him, his hot cheek pressed to the cold stone. He faced his last kill, the harpooned seal… an isuwiq staring into his eyes. She stretched alongside him like a lover in the gentle rain. Mist gathered on her soft neck, beading into clear droplets on the fine hairs. At their appointed times, they slipped down the gentle slope of her cheek and ran atop her long unblinking lashes, cascading over her open gaze.

Cuniq watched the sadness fall.

She weeps for me.

She was my mistake, but still, she weeps for me.

He was overwhelmed by remorse for all the mistakes in a world of needless deaths… for the Sugpiat, his people who suffered on his far island, for the poor isuwiq tethered to the line, for himself, a conscript to the Russians, dying on a seal rock in a haunted sea.

'Go with hope,' Cuniq spoke to the seal with his mind, offering a small comfort. 'You die near home. You know the way back. But how will I find it?'

He had lost the way, long ago.

Cuniq heard a sound. Below the flattened ear pressed to the stone, it came up from inside the rock. Running. A gentle splish-splash, splashing up into his ear. The running sound gave him a location, a bearing on the seal rock where his body burned with fever. He moved his eyes from the seal, a slow effort, and saw Uyuluk, the scar-faced Aleut who partnered with him in the kayaks. The running sound had stopped and Uyuluk stood there apart, tight shoulders askew, tensely poised, deathly afraid.

'Yes, always turned halfway,' Cuniq recalled from a remote distance. There was never much in Uyuluk but fear. It was all panic now on his pox-scarred face. The contagion that struck the company and took them, one by one… it froze Uyuluk halfway. And with this Aleut there was only one thing that counted. He moved to preserve that now. He turned and splish-splashed away.

'Calm yourself,' Cuniq's mind reached out. 'There's nothing left to fear from me, another dying slave. Fear the sea lion! The uncleaned bones cry vengeance!'

He knew Uyuluk flew back to the killing ground. But he'd find no solace in that place, all slaughter and waste, smoky fires and piles of ripped and salting skins. Cuniq's burning thoughts swirled with those fires. They burned with the smokes of judgment and retribution, the confusions of the hot swinging censers of the Russian priests, the heavens and hells of the Russian chants…

'Their hells, not ours.'

Cuniq heard his grandfather's quiet voice through the confusion, reminding him.

'We are real people. Not Russians.'

His grandfather took his hand. He gently led him down the sooty passage of their home filled with the smoky fragrance of seal oil lamps and dried salmon and damp earth. Cuniq had been lost but his grandfather's hand, rough, strong, and gentle, had found his. He pulled him down into the dark ciqlluaq, took him underground, the sod house pounding with drums of pale shining men, singing, stoking the hot coals in the central pit, naked and sweating.

Oh, his lungs burned! His insides felt on fire!

His grandfather pushed a plug of shaved wood between his teeth.

'Breathe through this.'

The sweat began. The fire consumed his inner poisons like the purest oil. Bitterness poured out!

'Never fear them,' his grandfather whispered in the dark of the ciqlluaq. 'They possess many things, but not your life, never your death.'

'We die like slaves,' Cuniq dissented, shocked he argued with his grandfather.

'Don't even bother to grasp for it,' the elder scolded.

'It was for skins, Grandfather!' he desperately countered, overwhelmed by guilt and fear... not for himself, but Puyangun. She was pregnant. When threatened by the Russians, he had abandoned her.

'It was the quota of skins, Grandfather. They made us hunt. I did it for Puyangun. I went to save Puyangun!'

His grandfather said nothing.

'We searched for the skins,' Cuniq pleaded, 'for the haunted rocks, the place of the kalla'alek!'

The kalla'alek.

That noseless devil.

The skin hunters searched the old haul-outs first. They found them empty, left bereft by kills. So the overlord pushed them like slaves around the peninsula, across known boundaries and into the great bay. They paddled the boats for days. And finally in the evening mist, the rumored rocks appeared like ghosts, apparitions in the fog at dusk. The company was terrified to find them. The crew muttered, doubting, rocking in the skin boats.

The overlord ordered Cuniq in first, followed by Uyuluk. They had the kayaks. If the kalla'alek waited there on the haunted rocks, the kayaks were expendable.

Uyuluk shook when he stepped ashore. His sealskin pants dripped urine. Cuniq's heart pounded. He expected devils. They found only sea lions, a large haul-out for sea lions.

Then the slaughter began... the driving, clubbing, and flaying.

The fever followed. It took the crew like they took the sea lions, punishing them, one by one, finding him on the seal rock, lost and far from home.

Skins for death.

The Devil's trade.

All for smoking fires and salted skins... and in Cuniq's heart, for love.

He had done it for Puyangun.

For her unborn child.

5

Mel Savidge was livid.

Having just learned of the herring meeting (starting immediately!), she marched swearing through Fish and Game. The idiot secretaries in Sport Fish were gabbing and Mel overheard, purely by accident.

How does Sport Fish know about emergency herring meetings when I don't? Sport Fish doesn't care shit about herring. Why am I even working here? I'm a fucking freak in the system, an anthropologist in Fish and Game... that's why they treat me like this!

Today was a circus at headquarters, especially in Subsistence, her unit that handled fishing and hunting in the villages. She juggled multiple emergencies, running madly from crisis to crisis. The first was caused by an idiot State Trooper who cited an Inupiat elder for killing a brown bear for food at a spring camp in the far northern region. State regulations didn't recognize the traditional hunt. The trooper seized the bear and the hunter's gun. His region was furious about the citation and called the Governor, right up the street. The Governor's office called Fish and Game to do something... crisis number one.

Then a fisheries biologist closed a salmon stream on Prince of Wales Island. The runs weren't strong enough for subsistence fishing, he claimed. This was after the managers had allowed a near-record catch by the offshore commercial fleet. Angry fishermen threatened to fish anyway, regardless of emergency closures and incompetent biologists. The villages had to eat. That was crisis two.

Then the lost snowmachine. Her staff in Fairbanks called sheepishly to say the department's snowmachine was discovered 'lost' from its usual storage in Barrow. No one knew exactly when it disappeared. Some teens took it joyriding last winter, maybe, and abandoned it without fuel, somewhere. There might not be enough snow to drive it back, depending on where it might be outside Barrow, if they found it.

And Mel was just acting! She covered for the real director of the Subsistence Division who had been snatched (like the snowmachine) by the Governor's office for some political mischief regarding rural-urban policy. Mel juggled the crises on the fly, improvising solutions until the real director resurfaced. The emergency meeting on herring was the fourth crisis of the morning.

Mel stomped into the second-floor conference room. The conveners stared like she was some lost child.

"I'm here for the meeting," she flatly declared, claiming a spot before anybody could object.

The chair of the meeting appeared to be Derby Peters, a snotty special assistant to the commissioner. Momentarily flustered, he searched the table for reactions to the fait de accompli. He found mild amusement and stony indifference to Mel's entrance.

"Okay. This is Mel Savidge for the Subsistence Division. Everybody know each other?"

Mel surveyed the assembly. Yeah, she did know everybody... all but one. She knew Fred Hendricks and Bud Jerkins with Commercial Fisheries. Their division managed the herring fisheries. The emergency was about herring, so here they were. She knew Jeffery Means who worked for the Board of Fisheries, the outfit that made fishing regulations. Cathy Waterson, Commissioner's office, was note taker.

Finally, in the middle of this pack, sitting like king on a throne, was a disgusting shock... Philip Elsberry!

Elsberry was a smarmy marine mammal biologist.

What was he doing at a herring meeting in Juneau?

Mel had had run-ins with this jerk for years at the university. He was a sexist, arrogant blowhard and closet racist, heir of the old guard from territorial days. He preyed on students. His most recent conquest had been expelled from school for underage drinking when it seemed Elsberry might finally get caught. He was a backstabbing bastard who bore careful watching. Why was he here? She thought he was off somewhere in the Chukchi Sea, abusing whales.

"I don't believe we've met," said the one stranger on her immediate right. "I'm Sgt. Harry Combs with Public Safety."

They shook hands. A badge flashed on his blue jacket.

A fish-and-game cop... what sort of herring meeting have I stumbled upon, with Elsberry and a cop?

"Okay," Derby Peters started again. "We've called this meeting because of events in Bristol Bay. The request came from Philip Elsberry with the university. It's a scoping session. That's the commissioner's expectation. Our purpose today is to get details. And Dr. Elsberry has expressed interest in floating ideas about regulatory solutions, if there are things that need to be fixed. Okay? Let's keep it brief and on target. I've another commitment at noon."

"Thank you," said Elsberry. "I'm glad we could all meet at such short notice..."

"Excuse me, Phil," Derby interrupted. "It may be best if we first had a short summary of the herring fisheries from Commercial Fish. Fred?"

Elsberry's face tinged red. He nodded curtly and shuffled some papers.

Yep, put him in his place right off, smirked Mel. The big boys are shoving already. Derby's top dog, calling the shots. Commercial Fish is next. Phil, it may be your meeting but you're at the bottom of the heap today. You should know all about this. It's just like those rutting bulls you get off on watching, bellowing to hump the harem.

"Thanks, Derby," replied Fred Hendricks. "We're happy to participate in any meeting that may involve our herring fisheries. I'll turn it over to Bud here. He's been tracking them and knows more details than I do."

That's because you don't know shit about the herring fisheries, thought Mel, except what others tell you, sitting in your fat office. Time to pass the ball.

"Uh, yeah," grunted Bud Jerkins, opening spreadsheets with thick fingers on his laptop.

Mel knew of Bud, a veteran in fisheries management. He'd worked his way up from fish tech to area biologist. Not your usual polished guy at headquarters, all rumpled and awkward at meetings. But he knew fish. That's why he was here. He's the kind of guy she'd hit up if she had to know something in a hurry about herring. If he'd tell her anything. He probably would. He looked okay, though someone should press his shirts!

"Uh… what are we talking about here? All the districts or just Bristol Bay?"

"Togiak and Security Cove," said Derby.

"Togiak," corrected Elsberry.

"Okay," grunted Bud, reviewing his laptop. "Yeah, we had good herring this year in the Togiak subdistrict. A little late, but a strong run. A good show of five and six-year age classes, what we expected. Same at Security Cove up the coast. Lots of interest from buyers. Above average prices. Good roe content. Let's see, we took 50 metric tons at Togiak and 15 metric tons at Security, both near the upper pre-season guidelines. So overall, solid fisheries, better than the five-year average. We're looking to expand, but not too fast, depending on recruitment of four-year olds. We'll know more about that by next year."

Then he was done. Par for the course, thought Mel, short, to-the-point. He'd covered timing, the catch, the age of the fish, the quality of the roe, and the sustainability of the fish stock, all the things fish managers were trained to watch.

"Some fun with that storm, eh Bud?" said Hendricks jovially, like one in the know.

"Bit dicey," mumbled Bud.

Mel had heard about the awful storm. And she heard the understatement in Bud's reply. Fishing the Bering Sea was a hazardous occupation. Big storms and big money were a deadly combination, the stuff of reality shows. This year's storm had been big.

"We was watching it," said Bud. "It came up quick. We got in two openings before it hit and everybody had to run."

"You got to play hero, right?"

"Well, some guys stalled out," said Bud, looking embarrassed. "We gave 'em tows."

Saved their asses, thought Mel.

"Everybody worried the runs were done," Bud continued. "But they weren't. After the storm we opened again and made the quota real fast. Then everybody moved to Security Cove and did it all over. But that's the next district, so I don't go."

"Good," Derby Peters jumped in, working his wristwatch. "Sounds exciting."

Philip Elsberry drew a breath. But Derby turned his eye on Mel.

"All right, Ms. Savidge, what have you got for us?"

Mel gulped. Well surprise again. Let's keep Phil dangling. Let's hear from Subsistence Division who wasn't even invited to the meeting. Of course, she had absolutely nothing to say. She had only a general idea of how things worked out there. The commercial fleet followed the herring runs going north along the coast in spring. It was a roe fishery. The eggs went to Japan where roe could be big money. The carcasses probably got ground into oily fish meal, but she wasn't sure. Maybe they got dumped. She knew that herring was important subsistence food for some Alaska Native villages north of Togiak, as essential as salmon. The big mobile commercial fleet threatened small local boats. That's why she was damn sure not going to miss an emergency herring meeting that might impact villages. But as for Togiak, a Yup'ik Eskimo village above Bristol Bay, she hadn't a clue. She couldn't raise any of her staff. So here she was, caught flatfooted. She could bluff and make up something. She decided to play it straight.

"Thanks, Derby. I've nothing to add right now. I'm here to listen. I may have a couple of questions later on."

An acceptable recovery, Mel thought. Fred Hendricks smirked. He thinks I'm an idiot. Yeah, yeah, I'm as stupid as you without my staff. You're an asshole!

"Okay, then. Phil, what have you got us here for?"

Philip Elsberry finally had the floor. He puffed up.

Have to be the biggest guy in the room, don't you Phil? Puffer-fish syndrome. Makes your fat face look even fatter.

"Thanks, Derby," began Elsberry. "First, I'd like to thank everyone here for being so willing to meet on such short notice. The issue is only a week old. The quick response shows what everyone knows about Fish and Game, how fast the department can address new issues, especially compared with federal agencies, as I can attest from personal experience."

Ugh, groaned Mel. Spare us! What butter-up crap. She almost rolled her eyes.

"I also want to say a personal thank you for the professionalism I've always encountered in Fish and Game. I get efficient responses to requests for information, even within my research area on marine mammals that extends beyond the state's expertise. It's always a pleasure to work with people here."

Careful, thought Mel, your smarmy brown-nosing is sounding downright condescending. God, he's worse than I remembered. Okay, Phil, that's over with, time to lay the turd.

Elsberry paused strategically and moved to point.

"That's why I wanted to contact the department quickly regarding the issue. I knew you would want to hear of this in-house, before it becomes public, or elevated to some higher federal level."

That caught everyone's attention. Bad publicity and federal meddling worked like cattle prods in Fish and Game. Bad publicity meant phone calls from upset legislators, or worse, some legislator cutting your budget. As for the feds, everyone bashed the feds in Alaska. The federal government was the outfit the state loved to hate, even while gorging at the federal trough.

"The concern is illegal walrus hunting on Round Island by herring fishermen," said Elsberry, laying the turd on the table.

Illegal walrus hunting?

Mel now listened hard. She saw the sergeant beside her sit straighter in his chair, listening carefully too. Round Island was a walrus haul-out. Mel knew it was near Togiak, probably near the herring grounds. How close she didn't know. Maybe right in the middle. The island was a state-run sanctuary.

"I believe new evidence is about to come out," said Elsberry. "It's not conclusive by any stretch. But it's consistent with what we've suspected for some time. Herring fishermen come ashore on Round Island when fishing is closed and kill walrus. They kill them during the slack time between fishing periods."

Mel watched the table. Fred Hendricks and Derby Peters sat poker faced. Bud Jerkins frowned, staring down at his laptop, shaking his head. He's not buying this, thought Mel, our man who knows the fishery. Or else, he's not liking what he's hearing. Sgt. Combs jotted notes.

"Now, as you all know," said Elsberry, "Round Island is part of the Walrus Island Sanctuary, established to protect the haul-out. It's closed to the public. So coming ashore during downtimes is the first problem. That's illegal. Second, killing walrus is prohibited under federal law..."

"Except by Alaska Natives," blurted Mel, and then cringed because of her patently bad manners. Elsberry eyed her coolly.

"Yes, as Dr. Savidge says, except for Natives, killing walrus is prohibited under the Marine Mammal Protection Act. And for Natives too, if wasteful. So that's the second problem, fishermen killing walrus, presuming the hunting is by non-Native fishermen."

Was that a good presumption? Mel didn't know.

"Finally, and most important I think, disturbance like this threatens the haul-out. It drives walrus away. Walrus are a threatened species. Conditions get progressively worse for them. Sea ice is shrinking. Round Island is the last land-based haul-out. The others are gone because of this kind of harassment."

"Now how's that?" said Bud Jerkins, coming out of his sulk. "Nobody knows why those other haul-outs disappeared. That was a long time ago."

"Are you blaming fishermen for that too?" said Hendricks.

"Whatever the cause, they're gone," Elsberry shot back. "Only Round Island is left. It's exceptional. That's why it needs protection."

"Uh, Dr. Elsberry," asked Sgt. Combs politely, looking up from his notes, "what is this 'evidence' about to come out, if you can tell us?"

"Certainly. Three dead walrus washed ashore after the second opening," replied Elsberry.

"That don't mean nothing," muttered Bud, mostly to himself.

"How is that 'evidence'?" asked Sgt. Combs.

"They were headless. Killed for ivory. They washed ashore near the south capes."

"Where's that?" asked Mel.

"A half-dozen miles from Round Island. The timing of when they were found and their condition strongly suggests they were killed just after the second fishing period."

"How could that be?" challenged Bud. "There wasn't no time. The big storm chased everybody out. Who'd hunt heads in a blow like that? That don't make no sense."

Mel watched this exchange with increasing interest. She began scribbling notes.

"Well, you have to be pretty dumb," replied Elsberry. "And they were dumb. A body washed up too, a half mile from a walrus. He was a Mexican national working off a herring boat. That did make the local news. The headless walruses haven't, yet."

Mel wrote, 'body washed up' and 'three headless walrus' in her notes and quickly looked around for reactions. Bud Jerkins really shook his head now.

"No, no, we all heard about that," said Bud. "He was working on the *Ema Louise*. But he went missing before the first opening. They thought he'd gone home. He wasn't even working the second opening. Nobody knows what happened to him. But I know the *Ema Louise* sure didn't visit Round Island after the second opening. There wasn't time and you'd be crazy to try it."

"First or second opening, whatever. It was headhunting," replied Elsberry matter-of-factly.

"Do you have a report I could have on the dead walrus?" asked Sgt. Combs. "For my commissioner?"

"An unofficial one," replied Elsberry. "It's my personal copy of the preliminary field report from the refuge staff who found them. It's mostly pictures and scientific measurements. But you're welcome to it. I've got it here."

"It don't mean nothing," muttered Bud.

"I'm looking at the clock and seeing time's running short," Derby jumped in, recognizing the signs of disintegration. "We've all heard the allegations about headhunting before, Phil. As you can see, there's some skepticism about its connection to the herring fleet. However, we do appreciate the heads up, or I guess in this case, heads off." He chuckled.

What a cretin, scowled Mel.

"We'd also like a copy of the field report while you're making one for Sgt. Combs," continued Derby. "In the interest of time, maybe you could move to your proposal. Except for me, no one here has heard it."

Elsberry was looking for his field report on the headless walrus, obviously irked by the exchange with Bud Jerkins and Fred Hendricks. He found it, gave the report a little shake, and passed it to Cathy Waterson, the secretary.

"Yes, good, thank you," he said, collecting himself. "Protecting the haul-out is paramount, I think we can all agree. Therefore, I'm suggesting, this is tentative you understand, just a pre-concept at this stage, a proposed change in the management of the herring fishery in Togiak Bay. One possible adjustment is prosecuting the fishery quickly in a single opening. Instead of multiple open periods with dead time in between, the fishery would be done in one period. Everything caught at once. Then closed. Second, the rules prohibiting herring boats near the sanctuary would be expanded to create a bigger buffer. With these changes, there'd be no incentive to hang around after a closure and raid the sanctuary. The fleet just moves up the coast to Security Cove. Enforcement can nail any offenders hanging back."

Mel scribbled and watched simultaneously, a skill she performed with anthropological aplomb. She was in her element, detached as a participant observer, watching another fish-and-game blowout. She loved it. She noticed that Cathy Waterson, the official note taker for the commissioner's office, had hardly moved her pencil, looking bored. What a twit, Mel thought, this is a great meeting. Mel noted gleefully that Bud Jerkins was a volcano ready to explode. He did.

"That don't work! You'd wreck the fishery. Or you'd wreck the herring. You can't fish it in one period. You'd overshoot the quota. You'd get green herring. That's just stupid!"

"It could work! You could make it work!" Elsberry shot back, apparently forgetting that this was a 'pre-concept,' a term Mel had put in her notes. "What's more important, the last walrus haul-out or piddling eggs for Japan?"

"Okay, okay," said Derby, putting a halt to it. "Okay, I think we've got the proposals. Right, Catherine? You got them? Good. Phil and I talked about these ideas a bit before the meeting. I think we agreed that this is a scoping session. A logical next step is to pass the ideas along to each of the commissioners. I'll brief mine, and Sgt. Combs, I know you'll brief yours in Public Safety. And Jeff, as Board staff, you can alert the chair of the Board of Fisheries about the issue. Ultimately, it's the Board's call. The Board may want to take it off-cycle. But that remains to be decided. All right? This has been productive. Anything else before we break? Uh, Mel?"

Derby shot her a poisoned look that plainly said, whatever it is, make it snappy. Mel thought this might not be the best time, but it might be the only time, so what the hell.

"Thanks, Derby. I want to raise one additional concern. And that's how any proposed changes in fishing rules or closed areas might impact subsistence fishing for herring at Togiak. We should keep that in mind as we examine this issue. That's all. Thanks."

Mel looked around. Fred Hendricks and Jeffery Means had completely ignored her. Bud Jerkins had listened, stone faced. She saw an irritated Elsberry take a quick breath. He fairly spat the last volley.

"We'll keep that in mind, Dr. Savidge. But for the record, and so you may know, there is no subsistence herring fishing at Togiak!"

With a sour look, Elsberry gathered his papers and shoved them in his brief case. Fred Hendricks and Bud Jerkins were already out the door. Derby Peters, seeing the meeting had adjourned itself, quickly fled for his noon appointment.

"Nice to meet you, Ms. Savidge, or is it Dr. Savidge?" said Sgt. Combs, shaking Mel's hand again.

"Dr. Savidge, but I go by Mel. Nice meeting you too," she said with sincerity and watched everyone exit.

Mel gathered her own notes, organizing her thoughts. 'No subsistence herring fishing at Togiak.' What a load of crap! That jerk! A major spawning run in their bay, and nobody eats herring? We'll just see about that!

Holding this thought, she marched from the conference room, juggling crisis number four in her head.

As she approached the stairs, the detestable Philip Elsberry stood, fidgeting for the building's tiny elevator to open. What a lazy asshole! It's a two-story building. Can't he walk down one flight of stairs? Shit, he's seen me. Now I can't avoid him without looking like a wuss.

"Well, Phil, that was fun," she said breezily, marching past.

"It's always fun around you," he sniffed curtly. He positioned his back to her and jabbed the down button.

"At least it wasn't 'the Natives' this time," baited Mel.

"Well then," he sneered happily, "I'm glad what's convenient for me is convenient for you."

He stabbed the down button again.

Mel stopped.

What's this sneaky bastard up to? 'Convenient for him, convenient for me?'

"What's that mean?" she challenged.

Elsberry didn't answer. She wormed around to stare him down. Elsberry worked to ignore her. Exasperated, he finally shot back.

"Come on, Melinda. Get real."

"What. Real about what?"

She waited, insisting on an answer.

"The headhunting!" he finally exploded.

"The headhunting?"

"The headhunting by Natives. Everyone knows about it."

Mel stood firm, obdurately signaling that she wasn't taking this.

"For the drugs! Cocaine! Meth!" And he smiled, 'there, you've finally made me say it.'

"What? Where? Round Island?"

"Where not?" he laughed scornfully.

"That's bullshit! That's malicious crap!"

"If you say so."

"Walrus get hunted for food and you know it. It's subsistence hunting!"

Elsberry shook his head dismissively.

"Subsistence hunting. There's no real subsistence anymore. It's all about money. Handouts. Poaching. Drugs. Everyone knows it. But publicly, you can't say it. You can't call a spade a spade anymore. You can't blame Natives for anything."

The elevator popped open. Elsberry entered, turned, and fired his parting shot with an oily grin.

"But commercial herring fishermen? They're easy."

The doors shut in Mel's face.

Mel ran to her office, fuming. She shouted and worked her phone.

"Cheri! I need the files on Mac Cleary!"

"Okay!" Cheri shouted back.

Mel's office sat kitty-cornered to Cheri, the administrative assistant. They usually talked by shouting. This disturbed no one because lowly Subsistence Division was crammed in a cul-de-sac of the Fish and Game building, formerly the back row of the end wing of the seats of the defunct Taku Twins movie theatre. Juneau's entertainment was now Fish and Game.

"Hello?"

It was Jeff Hall on the speakerphone, his voice echoing from Anchorage as if from a distant planet. As head of the southwest region, Togiak herring fell in his district.

"Jeff? It's Mel! I tried you earlier."

"I just got the message. Sorry. I was out."

"I tried Dillingham too."

"Yeah, nobody's there. They're setting up the salmon survey. You might find somebody at Manokotak."

"I could have used some help. I got sucked into an emergency herring meeting. I looked like a complete idiot."

"A herring meeting?"

"Togiak herring. Called by the assistant commissioner. Listen, Jeff, I really can't talk right now. Do you know Philip Elsberry?"

"That's the whale man? Uh, sort of, not well."

"I do. He's an egotistical jerk. I've never trusted him. He asked for the meeting. I don't know what he's up to, but it's nothing good."

"What's this all about?"

"Headless walrus. Three washed up. Elsberry claims the commercial fishermen did it between openings. He wants regulations to eliminate dead time. And a bigger buffer. You hear anything about this?"

"Well," said Jeff thoughtfully, "maybe. Where was this?"

"Togiak Bay."

"It's the first I've heard about those walrus. But ivory hunting, you know that issue has been around a long time. It's not something we get involved with. The feds do walrus. I've heard those accusations about herring fishermen and Round Island. So this is near Round Island?"

"Six miles away. Who's been saying that?"

"That's a state sanctuary. Permits to visit are issued out of the Dillingham office. So we hear gossip."

"Is it true?"

"About fishermen killing walrus? Who knows? Maybe. I don't think anybody really knows."

"There was a dead fisherman. Did you hear about that?"

"No."

"He washed up with the walrus. A worker from Mexico, crewed on a herring boat."

"I hadn't heard about that. That's too bad. What happened?"

"Drowned I guess. Elsberry says he was headhunting. Listen, Jeff, what do we know about subsistence herring fishing at Togiak? Will new timing or buffers in the commercial fishery impact the subsistence fishery somehow? We might get asked."

Jeff was silent for a moment, thinking.

"We don't know much about herring at Togiak. We've never had funding for that. We've got some information but it's spotty."

"You've got one chart showing that people take herring. I couldn't find anything else."

"We've never really studied herring."

"Look Jeff, I know your staff is completely booked. Your staff would be great for this. But I know they're booked."

"They're doing salmon surveys."

"Do you know Camilla Mac Cleary?"

"Who's that?"

"Camilla Mac Cleary. Called Mac, her middle name. Camilla Mac Cleary. She's on the register and looking for work. I met her last week. She's here in Juneau right now. She looks pretty good."

"I don't know her."

"Anthropology major at Berkeley. She's done everything but write the dissertation. She's taking a break. I think she needs money. We could hire her as a non-perm or on contract and send her to Togiak, a quick look to discover what's up with herring."

"To Togiak? A new hire? Alone? Uh, that's kind of sink or swim, don't you think?"

"Yeah, yeah. But she looks good. She can't be stupid."

"What's she done in Alaska?"

"Nothing."

"Why's she up here?"

"She's taking a break. She's on the register and she's here."

"Togiak's not the first place I'd send someone new."

"I don't trust Elsberry. He's out to screw somebody, you can bet on it. If we're going to be players, we've got to find out about herring. If Mac Cleary doesn't work out, well, at least we tried."

Jeff fell silent. Mel knew he was thinking that a screw-up by Mac Cleary in Togiak was his problem, not hers. He came back on, resigned.

"If she talks with elders, she'll need a translator."

"Yeah."

"My staff can't help her. Maybe Bristol Bay Native Association has someone," his tone suggesting the association probably didn't.

"I've thought about that too. I think I know somebody. Ever hear of Nicholas John?"

"No."

"He's at the university in Fairbanks."

"A student?"

"Yeah, Nick John, anthropology program. He's from the Yukon Delta, speaks Yup'ik. They've got him translating oral histories or something. I think we can steal him for a project."

"I've never heard of him. Is he any good?"

Mel had noticed Nick during a lecture. His graduate advisor said he was great, except for a few things… like classes, deadlines, and paper.

But he sure knew Yup'ik. And boats.

And he always needed work.

Mel grinned slyly.

"Perfect."

6

Nicholas John spread his hands in disbelief.

It was a rising red tide.

Blood... filling the cups of his palms.

Wincing, he clenched his hands into fists against the bloody flow. Scarlet drops rose between his fingers, pressured up, an artesian swell. He grimaced, squeezed even tighter, and squirted! Dark rosettes flew, splattering fish in the bottom of the boat.

From the stern, his grandmother watched the absurdity, saying nothing.

Mortified, Nick grabbed for rags jammed by the outboard. More blood flew. He numbly found them crusted black with oil.

Without a word, the old woman shook her headscarf free.

Nick accepted it with acute embarrassment. He wrapped his hands, plunged them into the channel, and rubbed, envisioning the enzyme detergent he'd need to rid the scarf of the marks of his stupidity.

Pulling out, he inspected. Several ragged wounds slashed across the fingertips of his right hand. Miraculously, the left hand was unscathed.

Nick gave the net an accusatory look. It stretched across the bow of the skiff, half-pulled from the river. The culprit protruded through the mesh, a cuukvak, snaky and flat-headed, snagged by a fin. Its toothy mouth grinned wickedly.

Stupid! He'd fallen asleep picking the net and jammed his hand into the mouth of a northern pike!

His grandmother observed without comment. He'd offered to check her net as a favor. It was easy work for him, an excuse to get out on the river and away from the village. Seventy-two years old, his grandmother continued to put out gill nets, an activity she'd done each spring since childhood. Over a lifetime her knuckles had grown gnarled and arthritic from such work. She still could do it, but Nick knew the cold water made her hands ache. So he offered to help. She came along, an inspiration and silent remonstration, watching her grandson christen the boat with blood.

The mishap came from sloppiness. The first nine fish he had pulled from the net were sheefish, the variety his grandmother wanted. The tenth was this grinning pike, the lower Yukon River's equivalent of the Nile crocodile except with sharper teeth. In a mindless stupor, he didn't notice. He'd grabbed its gills and shoved his fingers into its mouth. Thank God the pike was small. He imagined his obituary had its mouth been any bigger.

'Nick John Dead. Wrists Slit.'

The wounds throbbed. He winced at the next idiot prospect… slime infection. He saw himself medevaced to Bethel with swollen hands, ballooned fingers awaiting broad-spectrum antibiotics or amputation.

Nick knotted his bloody fingers with the scarf. He groped beneath the seat. His good hand found the food bucket. He fumbled free an energy drink, warm in its silvery can. He popped it left-handed, leaned over the side, and drenched his bloody fingers with fizzing yellow-piss, silently screaming.

He plunged into the channel again.

The wounds came up degreased.

That's how you did slime infection.

He sealed the mess with waterproof surgical tape from the emergency kit.

The swallows played throughout. Of course. They didn't mind the mishap. They flashed white and blue around him, enjoying the foolishness.

Skilled as dragonflies, the sleek birds performed loop-the-loops and high spirals in the air above the boat. Then they plunged to the river, feeding off the surface, exhilarating free falls to snatch its skittering bugs. They missed the water by inches in dangerous exits controlled with the flicks of feathers.

The daring acrobats performed for Nick.

That's what he thought.

Their holes pocked the mud banks.

Every spring the river drew them back.

Seeing the dance of shadows on the water returned Nick to the broodings preceding the pike mishap, random thoughts of college physics, a class barely completed, errant musings about pulls of gravity, dense singularities, time-space distortions, and their relationships to his own miserable circumstances, his annual sojourn home and dismal prospects. It was a blend of disparate, reinforcing materials, the way his mind worked.

Like the bank swallows, Nick returned each spring. The river drew him too. This was the pause between academic torture and a summer grind of paid work, between his digging into debt at school and his futile attempts to climb out. His home on the lower Yukon River was small and remote. It offered few paid jobs. Expatriates like him sought employment elsewhere. This summer he had reluctantly agreed to transcribe oral histories for his anthropology advisor. He would work in some dim chamber beneath the university library in Fairbanks. He'd hate it.

Before the underground plunge he came home, his annual appearance. He couldn't prevent it, inexorably drawn like a comet falls toward the sun, pulled close by irresistible forces. He braced for the short flip. It was the shove that got him moving again, re-energized for the rest of the year. Or, he brooded, it was the flip that kept him from getting anywhere, trapped in an endless orbit.

His village stretched along a bent finger of the Yukon River, its sluggish flow nearly sealed by sediment from the main river. Descending to the narrow airstrip, he would search the rooftops of its tiny houses. He remembered each place. Reconnected them with names and histories. Relived events. Replayed the dark rumors. He felt the resurgence of anger. The ostracism. Abuse. The stirring of old feelings that had matured during his absence, awful possibilities, new capabilities of what he might now accomplish. And with the anger, he felt the fear. The fear of getting too close... the fear of his own burning... a bright flash, a quick incineration, a puff of substance re-fused with the source.

It had happened to many.

Nick located a glove beneath a seat. He pulled it over the damaged hand and returned to work, dragging the net atop the prow and picking it of fish. This was the simple part, he realized. The anthropology texts at school had it wrong. The books emphasized the physical harshness of the Far North, the climatic extremes, the seasonal privations. By comparison, all that was easy. The hard part was living with those you should love.

He slipped the net from the boat. It fell to the river with a splash, its meshes sinking beneath the float line, rearranging to work with the current for this old Yup'ik woman whose family needed to eat. The afternoon's catch was fourteen sheefish and one toothy pike. His grandmother used to scold him... don't count the fish! The kass'aqs always counted. Counting decreased them. Don't count! Nick always counted.

He pulled the outboard to life and settled beside it, guiding the boat back along the slough, floating on softness in the fine afternoon light. The gray hairs on his grandmother's uncovered head fluttered with the wind. She watched the river's courses and waved a hand vaguely, the merest of gestures. Nick turned right, deflected into a side channel. It meandered among willows, hidden, hushed, and abandoned. A cleared spot appeared. He powered down and coasted to a place on the cut bank where a broken heap of earth had collapsed into brown water. He jumped ashore and tied to the roots of an alder, bent and toppled, its bottom undermined by time, its branches swallowed. He helped his grandmother up. She stood at the clearing for a long while, just looking, blinking in the sunlight, remembering. Then she wandered toward a low mound among the alders.

Nick went another direction. Pushing through willows, he found a narrow grassland thick with flowers and insects. It arched inland, the remains of a bend in the slough, an old oxbow cut off from the river, filled by sediment and overgrown with grass. The level walk was easy and hot, sequestered from the river breeze. The grass swished between his knees.

He used to help with the grave. But sometime back he had stopped. He never knew her, he told himself, his own mother, the young girl buried at camp. As a child he called his grandmother aana, 'mother,' because the old woman had raised him as a son. At some point he became aware of his other mother, buried here, not at the village. The grave was an outcast... like him. He walked with this thought along the dried-up channel. He left the simple tasks to his grandmother, culling unwanted plants, pulling erect the tiny white fence, resetting the nameless wooden stake.

Giddy swallows found him walking. The birds dipped and circled, round and round, eating the bugs he attracted from the grassland. The swallows filled him again with astrophysical mysteries. He knew he pulled them in. He drew bugs, the bugs drew swallows. He had no problem imagining such attractants, the grips and pulls of suns, dense bodies, distant birthplaces, invisible glues that bound the fragments that composed all living things. He could easily imagine them. They surrounded him, enveloped him, constituted him, entirely unseen yet credible because of their effects, or rather, unimaginable effects without them. Things would simply fly apart, everything bonded to nothing. Subatomic forces formed flesh. Densely-packed suns held planets. Such invisible attractants were entirely plausible.

His grandmother was a prime example. She constituted the singular mass that held the family together, an aunt and an uncle in separate households, two cousins, and himself. This wisp of a woman bound them. Without her, they would fly apart. Eventually this would happen. She would die. The family would fission. But for now, she held them. The food cache was at her house, the family's fish rack, the smokehouse, the steam bath. Major meals and celebrations happened there. At seventy-two, her pull was strongest, her will firmest, her knowledge most secure. In his social constellation, she was the densest star, a power from age and experience, an attractant that drew and held. Nick accepted it easily.

But this afternoon, before the pike mishap, Nick had brooded on how the great forces worked... by distorting space-time itself. This seemed incomprehensible. He visualized gravity around a dwarf star, a distortion of space-time, deep wells curving down to meet the dense center. Mass did not just attract, it deformed, twisted, and reshaped. Objects fell toward dense masses like marbles spiraling around narrowing drainpipes. Nick chewed on this. Invisible forces were easy to imagine, but distortions of space-time were imponderables. He looked around him at the flatness of the meadow, the river channels stretching outwards toward the Bering Sea, the low tundra banks covered in dwarf shrubs, sedge, and grass. Where were the deformations? His eyes were entirely blind to the twisted distortions beneath the order of the world.

He watched the swallows spiraling around him like errant planets, snagging the mosquitoes and black flies his body attracted. Could a swallow sense the hills and valleys of space-time compressed and stretched by the embedded mass of objects? Did swallows navigate a flatness of space in the air between South America and the Subarctic, or did they fly toward their birthplace like a marble down a chute? Once the swallows launched on the annual migration, was navigation as simple as falling? At birth, when a swallow emerged from the membrane between worlds, did it leave a dimple pressed into the space-time fabric, some deep well marking the point of emergence, the origin of the swallow's life joining the dimensional planes? Perhaps some residual was left like a lump of scar tissue, a birthmark, the beginning and endpoint of a swallow's life.

Nick didn't know.

The swallows dipped and ate. Maybe the swallows didn't either. They just found their birthplaces automatically, effortlessly, year after year, not knowing how or why. Like Nick's own homecomings, they were simply and inexorably drawn back.

Nick heard a swish in the grass behind him. He turned to see his grandmother, slowly approaching.

"How did you find me?" asked Nick.

She pointed upwards at the air and smiled.

"Oh yeah," said Nick, seeing his swallows.

The old woman turned back toward the river, wending her way through the grassland. Nick trailed behind, watching how slowly she moved. The swallows came with them, dipping and shining in the sun.

Nick drove the boat unhurriedly, thinking nothing more of physics, just absorbing the still beauty of the afternoon. Rounding a river bend, the village moved into view. The faded blues, reds, and browns of its small houses peeked among leafing willows bright with the green of spring, tips already puffed white and yellow with seed. He diverted up another side slough and maneuvered among parked boats piled with fish totes and salmon nets, all smelling of sweet sunbaked mud and decayed peat. He ran the boat ashore, scattering a clutch of short-legged sandpipers. A four-wheeler and trailer sat beneath the skeleton frame of an old fish rack. Children played on the riverbank beside it. They ran with joyous squeals, disappearing into the willows.

Nick helped his grandmother from the boat. He noticed the problem with the small trailer as he unloaded the catch. It sat detached from the four-wheeler. That's not how he had left it. Those kids… why would they unhitch the trailer?

As he hefted it to the coupler, he found the cotter pin missing. In its place, a nail had been pounded, sealing the hole. Pure mischief! Not kids… some mean-spirited vandal with a spike and hammer. Nick's grandmother shook her head.

"I'll fix it later," he muttered.

His grandmother nodded and sighed and touched his shoulder. She climbed on the four-wheeler, engaged the engine, and drove off toward town. He watched her dwindle, wheels kicking out small hunks of wet earth. Nick found the family's wheelbarrow in the old smokehouse beside the rack and began loading. The children returned to watch him work. They solemnly examined Nick's bandaged fingers, taking turns opening and closing the pike's toothy mouth, learning from his mistake. Then they took off at a happy run. Nick covered the fish with damp burlap and began the slow push into town, his anger smoldering.

'Do nothing,' her touch had said.

Along the muddy path the old village came first, its run-down houses in slow tumble. Scattered and deteriorating, they were occupied by unmarried singles, stubborn reprobates, and local miscreants, a sort of village overflow. Its people found it convenient to keep separate from the rest. Nick himself chose to sleep here in the family's old cabin. His grandmother now resided at the new village in a pastel-colored box perched upon pilings above a gravel pad, one of many boxes uniformly set in multi-colored rows, a subdivision designed by some outside architectural firm. Nick preferred the dark log cabin, smelling of fish and dried pelts.

"Hey! Ninja!"

The oily bark came off from the side, a smoky doorway with slouching shapes. A veiled insult. A challenge.

'Do nothing.'

"Hey! Ninja!"

Nick John kept pushing the wheelbarrow.

"Where's that little trailer?" it mocked.

The heckler laughed with a dry hacking cough.

Nick continued on, staring straight ahead.

"Hey, Ninja! What's wrong with your hand? Did you get bit? Did he bite you last night? Where did you put it? Did he bite you?"

More laughing, hacking.

Somebody peered through curtains. It looked like Nita. Fifteen, Nick recalled. No, sixteen this past winter. Sweet, shy Nita, peering from the window of the tormentors. Haggard. Strung out. Nick hated them even more. That's how it begins. The burning. The incineration. It had happened to many. It would happen to many more.

He'd find Medea. She'd know what to do.

A plump youth in wide overalls rode into view, bouncing down the trail on a four-wheeler, a toolbox in his lap. Freddy... his younger first cousin on his aunt's side, a mother's sister's son, almost like a brother to Nick. He stopped beside the wheelbarrow, his lower lip working snoose.

"They're looking for you at City Office."

"What for?"

Freddy spat and shrugged. He engaged the four-wheeler and headed off to fix the hitch on the wagon.

In the subdivision, Nick found the right boxy house in the lineup. He transferred fish to a galvanized tub beside the cutting table. His grandmother appeared with an ulu and bucket.

"I saw Freddy," said Nick.

The old woman nodded. She began rinsing the table. His work on the fish was done.

Nick strode toward the City Office. A rectangular unit at the center of the village, the office sat upon thick pilings for the floods at breakup when ice clogged the main river and backed water up the slough. With the only public flush toilet downtown, it was a common destination for visitors. Nick paused at the entrance, overcame an ill-defined reluctance, and mounted the metal steps. A ragged hole punched halfway through the front door. Someone had tried to enter with a sledgehammer, or an ax, probably in the middle of the night, angry and drunk. Cheap door, thought Nick.

He pushed inside and found the middle office, a cramped cubicle paneled in wood veneer, door opened to the hallway. Its broad thermal window overlooked a pond with tall rushes and grass. Dabbling ducks made it home this late afternoon. He knew who he'd find beside that window at work at a steel desk, and there she was, Hannah Pete, the city administrator, young, friendly, and intimidating.

"Hi," swallowed Nick.

Hannah looked up, unreadable.

Nick felt his stomach clench.

"Hi," said Hannah.

Her eyes narrowed slightly. A careful smile? Irritation?

Nick had known Hannah since childhood. They'd grown up together. But more recently he'd seen her for short snatches only. He studied in Fairbanks, she in Bethel. After a two-year diploma, Hannah had accepted one of the few full-time jobs at home, the city administrator, a position of considerable responsibility, overseeing the passage of money in and out of the city government. She wrote grants to procure it and watched how it got spent. She was reliable, sharp, and no nonsense. City finances had rarely run so smooth.

Hannah made Nick nervous. He thought he knew why. He and she were married... sort of. This was not the entire reason, or even the main reason, but it was surely part of it.

Like everyone, Nick possessed several names, bestowed at birth or acquired during life, Yup'ik and English. Some were of people recently deceased. Hannah did too. One of Nick's namesakes had been married to one of Hannah's during their great grandparents' generation. That meant they had been husband and wife. At some point growing up, Nick became aware of this special relationship. He got teased about it, gentle off-hand one-liners, 'there's your little wife,' 'there's your sweetie.' He'd look up and see Hannah, this small girl. Undoubtedly, she'd been teased similarly. They'd been friends throughout, despite the banter. But recently, she gave him odd looks and veiled displays, like this afternoon's half-smile.

"Somebody said somebody was looking for me?" said Nick.

Hannah studied his face like a mind-reading gypsy before dealing the cards. Nick wondered what she saw. His idiocy at the gill net? His anger about Nita? His discomfort with little wives? Her long fingers found a pink office slip. Nick half expected her to put it to her forehead to pronounce an answer to his question. Instead, frowning at Nick's bandaged hand, she passed it over. There was the name of his university advisor, a telephone number, and a time.

"He called about nine," she said. "Try him tonight."

Nick waited. That was it from Hannah. Nick suspected his advisor had said much more. His advisor was a blabbermouth, a hard guy to shake off the phone, especially when he called at the village. But Hannah sat like a fox. If she knew more, which she probably did, she was waiting for Nick to ask. This seemed like a needless extension of his discomfort.

He sat down.

"Did he say what about?"

He noticed Hannah's eyes, distinctly almond shaped. Was that eyeliner?

"Your summer job."

"Oh, yeah?"

"Transcribing interviews... that's horrible work," she said matter-of-factly. "It's bad, even with those foot pedals." She pulled long, jet-black hair from the ivory beads that dangled from her ears and raised her heavy eyebrows above those almond eyes as if to say, 'I've got all the time in the world.'

"You've transcribed files?" Nick asked, surprised.

"Of course I did. In Bethel."

Nick didn't know this.

"I used to hate the sentence fragments," she continued, "you know, when the speakers start and then stop, start and then stop, over and over and over, until they finally get a sentence going. I never knew what to transcribe. I mean, who wants to read junk like that? The Yup'ik speakers are embarrassed to see their mistakes on paper. I used to cut the junk out and hoped that no one noticed."

"Uh, yeah, I do that too," Nick allowed. "Well, unless they pay by the page."

Hannah smiled broadly.

"They always paid me by the job," she replied, "even when it took me hours and hours to transcribe a bum recording. By the hour, I figured I earned more waiting tables because of tips."

"Huh. I've never figured it out like that," offered Nick, "uh, you know, by the hour, not the tips. I'm maybe not so good at tip work."

God, did I just say that? He felt his face flush.

But Hannah smiled again. She rotated the notepad on the desktop, considering something.

"The person you're working with, what's she like?"

Nick thought he misheard.

"Uh, okay, I guess. But you know, he talks a lot. But he's okay."

Hannah looked puzzled.

"Adkins... the guy who called," said Nick, waving the message slip.

"Oh," said Hannah, disappointed.

There was a long awkward pause, long even for Yup'iks who enjoyed well-timed silences. The easy conversation about transcription was over. Nick didn't know what had happened. Did he say something wrong?

"So you'll be leaving again," said Hannah finally.

"Yeah."

"I hope it's not too boring for you," she said flatly. "I mean, it can't be much bigger than here."

Nick sat confused. What was Hannah saying? Compared to this place, Fairbanks was huge.

"To me, it's big. But I feel like a squirrel, you know, a ground squirrel, stuck in that basement."

Hannah again looked perplexed.

"Basement? What are you talking about?"

"The basement of the library."

"Library?"

"In Fairbanks."

Hannah shook her head in exasperation.

"No. No. Not that job! Togiak! I hope you're not bored in Togiak."

Nick was completely lost.

"Togiak?"

"Togiak," she enunciated clearly, as if speaking to a dog.

"Togiak?" Nick repeated weakly to himself.

"The place you'll be working… with Camilla Mac Cleary!"

Huffing with annoyance, she grabbed papers at random and stormed off.

Nick hadn't a clue what had happened.

7

Qeng'aq crouched among the rocks that overlooked the camp of strangers. Other warriors crouched with him, their bodies wrapped in hardened skins, poised to follow. They watched the cruel waste with shock and anger. Tengeng had discovered it, a boy hunting from his kayak. The sea lions charged the water, milling with confusion. The stampede nearly threw him into the sea, Tengeng laughed. So he investigated. That's how he found the camp.

They brought the news to Qeng'aq. They always came to Qeng'aq. By the fire pit in the qasgiq, he deliberated with the elders, bending their thoughts on the problem of the strangers who killed sea lions for skins.

'The world is getting squeezed from the bottom and top, north and south, qec'issuun, like a clamp,' an elder said.

'The north doesn't matter,' said another.

Qeng'aq knew what that meant. Qeng'aq himself was a refugee who came from the north, many years before. He fled to this place and found asylum. The elders said not to mind, to welcome the northern refugees, bring them in.

But the southern strangers were different. They came secretly in the dark from beyond the great bay, hiding in the mists. The animals fled before them. They herded and clubbed, brought waste and sickness. The old people predicted it, long ago. Strangers would come to trade and to take for trade without permission or consideration. The world was gripped in a powerful clamp, north and south, top and bottom, compressing, compacting.

'Nothing flows through a floor compacted by many feet.'

Qeng'aq understood. The animals could not pass between worlds with such damage. Hunger and death faced the Yup'iks.

They sent messages for the armored warriors to gather. They paddled in fog, guided by waves and currents to the sea lion rocks. They awaited his sign.

As he watched the camp of strangers, Qeng'aq wondered about this. Why did they wait for him?

'You were chosen,' the elders told him when he was young. They pointed to Qeng'aq's face. He was marked for this purpose. 'The tuunrat pity you. The spirits give you power. You survive. You are meant to lead others.'

Qeng'aq doubted this as a child. How could strength come from weakness? A violent feud had destroyed his family. Boys playing darts started it. A dart struck a boy's eye. Furious, the father grabbed the boy who threw it, stabbing his. Both eyes. That excess started it. Families fought families. His was attacked at fall camp. They captured Qeng'aq last. He cried, helpless, and they laughed at him. They chose him, a witness to their ferocity. All who met the orphan would know their cruelty. They led him to the river.

'The rest of your people went that way,' they lied, pointing downstream. 'You'll find them that way.'

'Where?' he sniffled.

'That way. There. It's simple. Just follow your nose.'

They gouged out his nose, tossing it in.

But he lived.

Just a boy, all alone, he followed the coastline. He found new people. They named him Qengailnguq, 'the noseless one,' or simply Qeng'aq. 'The Nose.' They told him that his strength came from tuunrat, the spirits who had helped preserve him against the cruelty of his enemies. Years later, the elders proved right. Men followed the damaged orphan with confidence into battle, the noseless warrior, a demon from whom enemies fled.

Qeng'aq carefully observed the camp. Three skin boats rested at the killing ground, tipped as temporary shelters. They resembled large angyaqatak, the open hide-covered vessels the Yup'iks used for hauling goods, four men to a boat. The company also had two kayaks, narrow, closed-hull, single-person craft with distinctive prows, made like sleek arrows. But the kayaks had left for the seal rocks.

Fourteen men in all, but with two missing. Large men, well equipped, fierce-looking, good fighters, Qeng'aq did not doubt. He absently massaged the bridge between his eyes, rubbing together his thoughts, forcing down an aura rising in his mind, a stirring of odd sparking blocks, images he didn't want just now, right before battle. But five of the men looked sick or hurt. They had not moved from beneath the over-turned boats. Four men worked at skinning, their weapons near at hand. They had skinned all morning, piling ripped hides for scraping and salting. Carcasses lay wasting at the edges. They labored like stooped old men at an unending toil. A tenth man watched sea lions that swayed and roared among staked lines where they had been driven, held bunched in nervous knots for clubbing. And two men moved at the guard near the shore, vague shapes passing in and out of sight, watching the sea. But the sea was not the enemy. The guards watched the wrong horizon.

The mist deepened into heavy fog. The watchmen disappeared. All was shadow beyond a spear's throw. The moment had come.

Qeng'aq gave sign. The Yup'ik warriors slipped noiselessly from the rocks. The bowmen took the front, descending the slick basalt. Qeng'aq slipped out to follow, bearing a heavy spear. His mind blazed with colorful sparks only he could see. The fog that had hid the invaders now hid the avengers. He strode freely without bothering to crouch. The whoosh of an arrow and a muffled cry told Qeng'aq the engagement began. They would release this grip on their world.

* * *

The fires burned out. The fever lifted. Mists vanished. Cuniq opened his eyes. His grandfather had foreseen it. He had not succeeded dying.

The seal regarded him with unblinking eyes, brown irises etched with the finest strokes of light, a clarity he had not known for weeks. He knew where he was. He stared into misfortune. He lay beside a tidal pool on a seal rock at the edge of a distant sea, a conscript of the Aleuts, sick at heart, and far from home, caught like the tethered seal. It was a painful assemblage without release. He could find no way free.

At length he returned to the immediate mishap... the seal. It came to him what he must first attempt to do.

Cuniq willed himself upright. He came up weak and stiff as if rising from a hard night's sleep. The fever had soaked his clothes. He felt chilled and light-headed.

He splashed his face from the tidal pool. White flashed beneath him. His grandfather's pendant... it had come loose and slipped off. It flickered just beneath the surface.

'Your luck,' Talliciq had said, presenting the ivory bauble before the journey.

Cuniq reclaimed it from the pool, tied the cord around his neck, and silently addressed its maker.

'I must try this thing, Grandfather, though you've warned against it.'

With an effort, he staggered to the kayak. From its frame he freed his sturdy knife set with the iron blade. He wobbled to the seal, knelt, and felt along the stomach, still warm. This seal was strong. She held on to life. Such strength would be rewarded.

"I'm sorry," he whispered. "You are my mistake. I didn't see how high you swam in the water. You swam like a male to me."

With a steady hand, he drove the blade. Skin and blubber split. A grey ball rose through the cut. He reset the point a half-finger's depth and sliced again. Bloody water welled around his hands. He reached within and found the compact form, pulling it free. Severing the cord, he washed the small bundle near the kayak, infusing the pool with a pink blush like dawn above his far home. He thought of Puyangun and her baby. The child would be born soon. He might never see them. And he remembered his grandfather's warning.

'Never bring one to life. You are not the mother.'

But with his fingertips, Cuniq pushed on the small chest, push and release, push and release. Abruptly, the animal woke. It twisted in his hands. Small eyes opened into his.

"I'm not your mother," Cuniq declared solemnly to the newborn seal. Then he smiled. He had not smiled like this in a long while.

He wrapped the pup within the folds of his gut parka and launched the kayak.

"I'll come back," Cuniq reassured the spirit of the seal that lingered to watch.

He angled toward a rocky point. He had found the rookery yesterday, crowded with seals. Pupping had peaked. He came ashore near its edge.

The haul-out moved with congested confusion. Hundreds of seals filled the rocky strand. Newborn pups huddled beside their mothers, sleeping or nursing or bawling for food, struggling amid the mass of kindred. Underneath the noisy milling, new pups got squashed, bitten, and assaulted, jostled by braying adults pushing through the crowd, smashed by yearlings still chasing mothers for milk. Angry adults tossed them rudely. In the tumult, mothers called for lost pups, shouting, threatening, and defending their offspring. Abandoned pups cried for missing parents momentarily gone to quarrel or to feed in the ocean. Seabirds preyed on the unguarded at ragged edges. Ravens, jaegers, and gulls picked among the dead.

Cuniq spoke aloud to the pup in his parka.

"It will be hard. Be persistent."

He studied the crowded beach, identifying groups, discrete clusters, and pairs of mothers and pups. He searched the mass for a long while. Finally he found what he needed inside a nearby group, a young mother just returned from feeding, wet from the sea. She moved with frantic desperation. Barking ferociously, she charged marauding birds from her spot where her newborn pup lay, limp, crushed, and pecked, a luckless victim of the first cruel days of life.

Cuniq filled a bailer with seawater and sea grass and took up his spear. Holding the pup close, Cuniq boldly stepped into the rookery. Seals scattered, turned, and roared in defiance. His spear foremost, Cuniq poked his way through a shifting passage toward the mother who defended her lifeless pup. She faced the newest threat, roared, and gave ground.

Cuniq knelt at her spot. Cautiously watching the mother, he unfolded the pup from the parka. He picked up the dead pup and rubbed them together, back to back, front to front. The mother bellowed. She feinted a charge and retreated before the spear. He placed the living pup at the mother's spot and stowed the lifeless carcass in his shirt. Finally, he emptied the bailer, dousing the pup in seawater and weeds.

"Be persistent."

Cuniq quickly stepped away. At the rookery's edge he turned to watch. The mother had returned to her place. She hovered suspiciously above the small pup, wet like her, covered in sea grass. She nosed it roughly. The tiny seal nosed back with all its small strength, weak, hungry, and cold. This was the critical moment. The mother lifted her head and looked around. The area had recovered its normal disorder after the intruder's exit. She glared, temporarily ignored by other seals and winged marauders. Cuniq watched her begin to clean the pup. She picked off weeds and tossed them aside. The pup weakly protested, ineffectively lunging at her great nose. Finally she lay down.

He could not see it, but Cuniq knew. She nursed.

The pup had found its mother.

* * *

Qeng'aq strode on the killing grounds among the carnage of stripped carcasses and squandered lives, enemies caught by surprise in fog without an organized defense. All lay dead among the ripped hides. None of the Yup'ik avengers was hurt. He examined each of the slain. They numbered thirteen, including the last casualty, a pock-marked man from a kayak. After the main battle he had appeared, stood amazed to find strangers, and bolted for the beach. A harpoon dart struck him in the back, launched by Tengeng, the hunter who had first discovered the camp. When Tengeng saw what he had accomplished, he wept. He had never before struck a man.

The sparking in Qeng'aq's vision faded. He felt the light-headedness that presaged a fit, a condition that plagued him even as a youth. His companions eased him against a rock where he rested with closed eyes.

The sparking formed into blocky shapes that floated before his eyes whether open or closed. A fuzziness wrapped his thoughts. The sparking blocks gave way to a deep-water dream of corpses pulled within powerful currents. Death swirled about him... men, women, and children, all with protruding bones, spirits exposed, sucked by the rips and swept out to join the dead beneath the sea. Wild creatures swam with them. Spotted seals, bearded seals, belugas, grey whales... bodies and creatures caught within a great vortex.

'Call to the walrus!' a voice charged.

So he called.

The walrus heard on their island fortress. But they could not reach him.

'Call to the walrus!' he heard the voice again.

So he called to the walrus in the deep. They heard his call. But they could not reach him.

'Call to the walrus... the end is near!'

In desperation, he called for help from the sky.

They heard him. And the walrus began to fall. They plummeted from the sky, one after another, falling and falling and falling...

He awoke surrounded by his warriors. They sat with him, waiting, feigning indifference. But the newcomers from more distant camps looked unnerved, uncertain of the terrifying leader who had collapsed entranced after battle.

"You were not gone long," a companion said.

Qeng'aq shook his head clear.

"I've seen what we must do."

He deployed them. Some went to collect the slain, to arrange them in the large skin boats and pull them beyond the bay. He told them to swamp the craft where the currents would sweep the wreckage to sea. Nothing should wash ashore.

Others he directed to gather skins and salvage meat from the carcasses.

"Let nothing waste," he declared.

But no fighter who killed a man should eat of it or directly use the skins. All would be given away to others.

The men set off for their tasks. No one questioned. Most were eager to leave the unsettling shaman. While they labored, Qeng'aq sat propped against the rock, pondering the troubling vision. He examined and re-examined without success the starved people whose spirits had been sucked into the sea. And the walrus, falling from the sky, one after another...

What could this mean, falling walrus?

It was Tengeng who woke him, the boy nearly spilled in his kayak by sea lions, the boy who wept for an enemy.

He whispered by his ear.

"The last kayak... it comes."

8

The drone of the Twin Otter laid throbbing pedal bass to the industrial rock in Nick's earbuds. The slow, low pulse of the plane's powerful engines rose and fell with the music, a blend of fuel and air and huge blurred blades beside Nick's head, a consistent growl driving the wings against the streaming air, 'waaah WAAAH waaah WAAAH waaah WAAAH,' supporting the blast of lyrics.

'Kinda like a cloud I was way up in the sky and I was feeling some feelings, you wouldn't believe…'

Exactly right.

Nick John cracked his eyes.

What did the pilots hear on their fat headsets while they flew the Otter? Weather and air traffic control, he supposed.

Nick leaned and poked the co-pilot.

"Try these!" he shouted above the roar.

The co-pilot nodded and stuffed in Nick's earpieces. He listened and smiled.

"Nine Inch Nails!" Nick shouted.

The co-pilot nodded again. He knew the group. He offered his own headset. Nick cupped it against an ear.

'…on the BUMP top of the world lookin' BUMP down on creation…'

The Carpenters.

Worse than weather.

Nick smiled weakly, returned the co-pilot's headset, and plugged back to his own. The lyrics ranted.

'I was way up above it, I was way up above it, now I'm down in it…'

Exactly right.

Way down in it.

In an unexpected turn, Nick found himself winging his way to a village he'd never seen, to join a project he knew nothing about, to work for a woman he'd never met. Somebody named Mac Cleary. He'd been 'hijacked.'

If he consented to be hijacked.

"How would you like to work in Togiak?" his graduate advisor had proposed over the phone when Nick called back. A 'summer alternative' documenting subsistence herring fishing instead of translating digital sound files. It would be good experience conducting ethnographic research. He'd work for Fish and Game.

Nick had checked his ears. Fish and Game?

Work for the enemy?

"It pays double transcription."

At which Nick decided that what he told Hannah Pete was correct. Transcribing narratives in an underground library was a waste of a good summer. Catching salmon on a sunny beach at Togiak... that sounded much better, especially as it paid double, even if it meant fraternizing the enemy.

Fish and Game.

'I was way up above it, now I'm down in it...'

The first leg to Bethel took most of the morning. Now at mid-afternoon he flew above the Kuskokwim River heading west toward the Bering Sea. The area he skimmed at eight hundred feet was a flat alluvium of wet tundra. A thousand lakes shimmered with light among rich green rills pushed between meandering sloughs. Long bending rivers entered from snowy horizons off the left wing.

This was the Yukon-Kuskokwim Delta, the vast homeland of the Yup'iks, his people, a place known to few outside of Alaska. He had calculated its size once... eighty-eight thousand square miles, an unspoiled natural expanse rich with fish, birds, and land animals, a hundred scattered villages, ninety-five percent Alaska Native, a people never conquered or displaced. It would rank twelfth as a separate state.

Not bad for a bunch of Eskimos.

He watched its beauty pass beneath him.

Here we do what we want.

He nodded with pride.

When we know what we want, he amended.

Frowned.

As if I knew what I wanted.

He quit the messy regression.

He had gone to see Medea his last night home. He went as he often did, seeking her counsel. She had known him from the start. What should he do about his tormentors?

"They persecute you because you're different," she said.

Her grin was frightening.

"What do you want to accomplish?" she asked, slipping beside him on the worn sofa, putting her arm through his.

Nick didn't know.

"To prevail," she answered for him.

Yes, that, at the least.

"Then wait," she whispered beside his ear.

"Don't see her," his grandmother warned. "Medea Okitkun is dangerous."

Each competed for him.

"There is time," whispered Medea. "When you come back, when you are really back, then…"

She left it unsaid. Her lips brushed his cheek, offering what she hoped he might want beyond counsel. He did not take it. He had never taken it. He did not know what Medea offered half the time.

So he did as Medea and his grandmother advised. He did nothing, departing quietly on the early plane. If prevailing against his adversaries was what he desired, he could wait.

He watched the rivers pass beneath him.

At the moment what he desired most was Goodnews Bay. The Twin Otter ran late.

Togiak wasn't in the Yukon-Kuskokwim area. It lay on the seacoast in the Bristol Bay region, south of ancient ranges that ran east to west off the wings. That region was another homeland for Yup'iks, an expanse of inland mountains, broad bays, and freshwater lakes. Togiak was a sizable village, over eight hundred people. Nick had never been there. He was eager to find what it offered.

No direct flights reached Togiak from his area. Travelers normally flew east from the regional hub in Bethel to Anchorage, back west to the regional center at Dillingham, and then north to Togiak, a long circuitous journey with inconvenient overnights. Nick despised Anchorage. There had to be another way. He phoned around and reached a city clerk at Goodnews Bay, a village west of Bethel. A fishing boat would leave for Togiak the next afternoon, she said. If he could get to Goodnews Bay, he might be able to hitch a ride. Nick asked the clerk to get word to the captain.

This flight was an afternoon milk run between villages. With every stop the Twin Otter dropped off mail, supplies, and passengers. Nick watched the movement of people and goods. At Eek a frail elder on oxygen deplaned. A four-wheeler waited for him at the airstrip. He climbed into its bucket trailer atop green oxygen tanks and rumbled away in a dusty cloud, an old man coming home to die. At Quinhagak, the next village stop, a family of four deplaned with piles of boxes, the spoils of a shopping trip to Bethel. It was cheaper than the local store, even with the airfare.

Nobody got back on. The plane felt empty.

Other than Nick and a plump woman, a trio of soldiers lounged at the back of the plane beside the cargo bay. They wore baggy black-on-green camouflage fatigues and tall laced boots carelessly shoved into the aisle. Most villages possessed national guard units. But these weren't guardsmen. Local guardsmen were your cousins who trained for a little money and excitement. These three soldiers were outsiders. They had the look of warriors trained to slit throats. What were they... Special Forces? What were they doing on this milk run?

Nick caught a soldier staring.

"Hey! What's this place?"

"Kuinerraq," replied Nick.

"What?"

"Quinhagak village. Where are you headed?"

"Newenham."

A sour-faced companion punched the soldier. He glared threateningly at Nick as if their destination were classified. He looked mean and angry, like a pit bull spoiling for a fight.

Nick turned away.

Ugly bastard.

With a roar of engines, the plane took off.

Newenham.

Nick knew the name. Anyone who listened to weather reports did. Forecasters gave weather for 'Cape Newenham to Dall Point,' a section of the coast. Nick vaguely knew that Cape Newenham stuck out into the Bering Sea. He always supposed it had a weather station. Three military men in combat fatigues suggested other things happened there too.

The Twin Otter banked inland. The muddy waters of the Kuskokwim mouth receded. A mountain spine grew beyond

Nick's window, a substantial ridge standing above the coastal plain. The plane steered directly toward it. Nick frowned. He studied the long rock wall pushed from the lowlands... a virtual rampart. The plane angled toward a narrow gap in its cliffs.

The co-pilot with the fat earphones sat rigidly erect, a hand with a death grip on a front stick, another on knobs above his head, intently watching the fast-approaching wall of rock. Nick saw what was coming. He jerked out his earpiece, cinched his lap belt, and grabbed his seat.

WHOOSH!

Rocks slashed by the windows like knife blades. The bottom fell out. The plane dropped off an edge.

WHACK!

Hard air hit with an underhand slap. The Twin Otter shuddered. The plane bounced and settled. The engines resumed their monotonous drone. In the cockpit, the pilots did high-fives. They successfully threaded the needle.

Turkeys!

He hated flying with turkeys.

The vista opened. The sea appeared directly ahead. A beautiful sparkling bay budded off the gray waters like a pale-blue heart. Goodnews Bay. Twin spits of white sand pinched it from the sea. The sight was breathtaking. It was worth the trip, even if he missed his boat. Nick spied Platinum, a tiny village on the farthest spit. He craned his neck and found the village of Goodnews where a silvery river entered the bay. That was his stop. He wouldn't be going to Platinum.

The plane descended to the strip. With a surge of engines, it spun around in a spray of gravel and cut power. Nick and the plump woman deplaned in the thick silence, passing the soldiers who still sat against the trussed cargo. While the pilots unloaded, a battered truck came racing up the runway. It skidded to a halt in a dusty cloud. A breathless youth leaped from the cab.

"Nicholas John?"

"Yeah."

Nick tossed his backpack and boxes into the truck bed. So did the woman. All three squeezed into the cab. The driver roared off.

"Where are we going?" asked Nick.

"Boat," the young man breathlessly replied.

But the truck veered from the water. It shot up a short hill into the village and careened to a stop at a weathered storefront. The driver leaped out.

"Gas!" he beckoned.

Nick chased him through the store's narrow aisles. A stocky clerk with wide suspenders lounged atop a beat-up counter, perusing a catalog of engine parts.

"Nicholas John," the driver announced.

The clerk's finger found a yellow slip beside the cash register and shoved it toward Nick. It was an invoice scrawled with a thick black marker, 'one drum, fuel.'

"Gotta go," urged the driver.

"Where's it at?" asked Nick.

"Loaded," said the clerk.

From his backpack Nick pulled a packet of travel requests used by the university. He flipped to the top slip and scribbled the amount and location.

"What's that?" asked the clerk.

"State TR."

"I never seen that for gas."

"Better than a check," joked Nick.

"The manager don't like checks," said the clerk, looking uncomfortable. "You don't have cash?"

"It's business. The State will reimburse you."

"Is that like a purchase order?" the clerk asked, twisting his head to read as Nick scrawled his name.

"Yeah, just like a purchase order," said Nick, being agreeable.

"The manager don't like purchase orders. They take forever to clear."

"Yeah, they're slow," said Nick, peeling off the top copy. "Mail this to that address and they pay."

The clerk took it doubtfully. He held the thin paper up to the light like funny money, wondering if this was his termination slip.

"Come on," called the driver, disappearing out the door.

Nick followed him into the cab. The truck spun its wheels and shot down a dirt track toward a dock at water's edge. Several boats moored in muddy shoals. The largest among them was a sturdy wooden skiff. It was built on the open skiff design but with a broad beam and a small plywood cabin at mid-ships. Dual ninety-horsepower Mercury outboards hung off the stern. Home-built, shallow draft, wide beam, probably good in heavy seas and shoals, Nick surmised. A couple of fishermen could sleep on this boat, crammed in that little cabin. This was something rarely done in his village.

Three people hurried at the dock. The man in charge was a wide-set Yup'ik in brown hip-waders rolled mid-thigh down his jeans. A skinny preteen boy untied and threw lines. A high school youth, balanced on the rail, took Nick's boxes and pack. The airline agent roared off with the truck.

"Let's go," said the captain.

Nick hopped aboard. The high school youth pushed them off and swung aboard too. With a practiced touch, the captain started the engines from a stern console and eased the boat from shore. Water was leaving with them. That was the hurry... a falling tide, draining the shoals. Extensive mud flats formed on each side of the skiff as the water receded. But they had left in time.

The boat snaked through a tricky channel where the river entered the bay, its sinuous bends sinking beneath the surface, hidden in subtle shifts and shimmers of color. Nick knew he would run aground in seconds, stuck in mud until the next high tide. But this boatman would not get stuck. There was confidence in every turn at the helm, a quarter turn here, a slight adjustment there, back and forth, keeping to the center of deeper water. Even the two boys could take them out. They attentively watched the series of turns.

Nick leaned against the cabin and enjoyed the ride. It smelled of the sea. A group of ghost-like gulls joined them to cross the bay. Soon they passed through the sand spits at the bay's mouth and swept into the open ocean. Nick watched the Otter take off across the bay. It banked left to follow the coast.

"It won't stop at Platinum?"

"Not today."

"Nicholas John," Nick said, holding out a hand.

"Harry Coopchiak," the captain replied, shaking it. "That's my boy, Cornelius." He nodded at the preteen who grinned at Nick, eager for new company. "And that's my helper, Herbert Small, my sister's son."

Herbert nodded with pride. Introduced as 'helper' conferred status, a partner with his uncle.

Harry relinquished the wheel to his nephew. The youth opened the throttle toward a distant point. The village of Platinum quickly passed on their left. A dirt track briefly followed the coast before disappearing into bare hills. From a stainless steel thermos, Harry poured coffee into mugs for Nick and his nephew, taking his own from the screw lid. It was scalding black and freshly brewed.

"My sister," Harry explained.

Salt spray washed them as Nick looked upon new horizons. This was great. It was rarely better than this.

Nick knew he descended from a maritime people. There was the sea in the blood of every Eskimo. His own village lay many miles inland, its houses strung like beads along a bend of the Yukon River. But the sea sustained it. Runs of salmon came from the sea on west winds. Their carcasses brought food and nutrients from the distant water. Rain came from it, flowing cold and sweet from rooftops to fill their wooden barrels. The sea drew the hunters every spring and fall for the seal hunts. The Yup'iks could never live without seals. Life emerged from beneath its flat surface, rising for them like the living beat of gut drumheads capturing the dancers celebrating its bounty in winter. Here on the surface of that world, Nick's body felt more alive than anywhere else. He felt content with himself like he could never feel hemmed inside a village or city. Nick looked at the youthful face of Herbert Small, confidently guiding the boat toward the distant point. He saw the peace there too.

Three 55-gallon drums of fuel bounced in the front of the boat. Apparently, Nick had paid for one of them.

"How far to Togiak?"

Harry Coopchiak threw a hand vaguely southward.

"Forty miles for a bird, but for us, one hundred and twenty, a long run around the cape. But we'll stop for supper."

Harry's boy, Cornelius, settled across from Nick. He began the questions they all were interested in. He shouted above the roar of the outboards.

"What's your name?"

"Nick John," he shouted back.

"Where do you live?"

"Yukon River. Kuigpagmiu."

He waited to see if the boy would know what that meant, Kuigpagmiu, 'a person of the Kuigpak,' the Big River. Nick wanted to be known for that. The Big River. The small boy understood. He was impressed.

"But I go to school in Fairbanks," said Nick, notching it down, discomforted by his own boasts.

"How old are you?"

"Twenty-three. How old are you?"

"Twelve. You married?"

"What? I'm too young to be married."

Cornelius considered this and frowned.

"My cousin's married. She's younger than you."

"But she acts much older."

Cornelius grinned at this foolishness.

"Why are you here?"

"To get to Togiak."

"Why?"

"My advisor told me. Get to Togiak for work!"

Cornelius didn't know anything about advisors. He waited for more. So did the others.

"I'm supposed to meet somebody named Camilla Mac Cleary. Do you know her?"

Cornelius thought a moment, looked to his father and cousin, and shook his head. The name meant nothing to him.

"I'm supposed to learn about herring."

At the word 'herring,' Cornelius whirled on his seat, pointing ahead.

"We get herring there!"

Nick looked, though he didn't know what he was looking for. A steep coast rose into a good-sized mountain, the last of the Kuskokwim range as it disappeared beneath the waters of the Bering Sea.

"On that mountain?"

Everybody laughed.

"Security Cove, just up there," said his father. "We pick the eggs in there."

"Bird eggs?"

"Herring eggs. We get bird eggs around the corner. The cliffs are full of eggs. Gulls. Murres. All kinds. You'll see. We climb with ropes and buckets."

"Sounds dangerous."

"It's okay if you go slow."

Nick had never done this, crawling up a cliff to gather eggs from bird colonies. There were no sea cliffs on the lower Yukon.

"I'd like to try that sometime."

"Maybe you could go with him," Harry nodded at Herbert, who had a twinkle in his eye. Good, thought Nick. He had a standing invitation to get bird eggs off a sea cliff. The summer job was getting good already.

"But better go soon," said Harry, "maybe they're already finished."

"You get herring eggs, what… on kelp?"

"Kelp is good."

"To sell?"

"Not here, too much commercial."

"Too much?"

"It gets crazy."

"How do you do it?"

"Between openings. We rake the kelp at low tides, or after commercial fishing is closed, when it's covered with eggs. But now we mostly stay away. They don't want to buy our fish."

"Why not?"

"Long story."

Nick nodded his interest. He opened his supply box for salmon strips, passing them around. He settled comfortably to hear the story, chewing on strips, sipping the fresh coffee.

"You know herring," said Harry Coopchiak, gesturing toward the rocky coast with a piece of dried salmon, "good oil, good food for seals and whales and salmon. That's what they eat, you know. Oily herring. We eat it too, but not so much as them. We get other kinds of fish… king salmon, sockeye salmon, trouts…"

"Trouts?"

"What they call the char that spawn up the rivers."

"Oh yeah. We don't get that kind."

"The herring spawn in all these little rocky bays, especially Togiak Bay and Security Cove. Big runs. The herring here was the last to get sold in Alaska. I remember when the first buyers came to Togiak. They said they would buy our herring. I was his age, working for my father. We fished that first decade, caught it with short gillnets, sold to the buyers. That worked good. We got money from that. But it didn't last. Big seiners moved in, boats from Petersburg, Wrangell, Bellingham. Everything changed. The outside boats put out long purse seines, surround entire schools of herring. The processors suction it straight from the water with vacuum hoses, tons of fish from a single set. After that the fishing turned crazy, more outside boats, shorter periods, spotter planes… hundreds of tons caught in minutes.

"You can't compete with that. The buyers couldn't be bothered with us anymore. They only bought from the seine boats. Millions of dollars get sucked from our bays by outsiders, shipped to Japan. All we can do is watch."

"Huh!" said Nick with disgust.

Harry patted the skiff.

"But we still got salmon."

"This boat's for that?"

"I helped my father build it. One of the first Togiak skiffs. Good design."

"Is that overrun too?"

"Not like herring. We got lucky. Salmon went limited entry. We hold most of the permits. Only boats with permits can fish. But it's got problems too. Prices keep going down. We earn less and less. The fish farms are killing us."

"Yeah, same with us."

Nick knew this problem on the lower Yukon. Fish farms had proliferated elsewhere, mostly in Canada, raising salmon cooped up in pens, colored red with food dyes, and kept alive with antibiotics. Farming produced a mushy, tasteless, industrialized product, nothing like wild salmon. The glut of farmed salmon drove down prices everywhere. It undermined wild salmon caught in western Alaska, among the few remaining sustainable wild fisheries anywhere, fisheries that helped the Yup'iks to survive as traditional peoples.

Someday everybody would be working for giant food conglomerates producing crap on assembly lines, absorbed by agribusiness.

The boat passed Security Cove, the small bay where Harry's family used to rake kelp for herring eggs between commercial openings. Steep cliffs framed the long open cove. Just weeks before a fishing frenzy by outside seiners had siphoned up tons of herring from its waters. This afternoon the bay looked pristine and undisturbed.

Harry regained the helm.

"Cape Newenham, up ahead. This turn can get tricky. Lots of wind and currents."

On their left a jagged mountain rose two thousand feet from the sea. The near shore bristled with rocks. Seabirds soared and screamed. A stiff wind buffeted the deck.

Harry cautiously steered farther offshore.

Suddenly, WHOOM!

Something blasted the boat. Everyone ducked as it blew overhead.

BOOM!

Nick jerked around, following a fleeting shadow. He found it as it banked sharply up and over, vanishing behind the cape's ragged edge. Fast and low... like a stub-winged missile, flat black and without markings, huge dual fuel tanks flamed off its rear.

"What was that?" screamed Cornelius.

His father pulled the steerage right. He moved the skiff even farther offshore.

"Newenham," he growled.

An airstrip emerged from behind a rocky ridge, creeping up the base of the mountain. A complex of low buildings hid at its far end. At this distance there were no signs of people, no indications of activity.

"What's Newenham?" shouted Nick, watching the lone installation pass.

"Air station."

"For what?"

"I don't go there," said Harry sourly.

"What was that?" asked Herbert, searching the sky.

"I never saw that one before."

Nor had Nick. But he knew what it was... a plane designed for speed and destruction.

They nervously watched the mountain.

The black missile didn't return.

Rounding the cape, the outside coast of Newenham unveiled with spectacular grandeur. High cliffs rose from the open ocean. Great swells crashed against the rocky walls unleashing plumes of spray. Colonies of birds billowed from every crease and hold. They filled the air with shifting clouds of black and white. Large flocks of black brants thrummed the air, racing in long, low, v-shaped formations. Vast mats of murres and other seabirds undulated upon the ocean's surface.

Dolphins joined the boat. They rose and fell alongside like sinewy serpents. Sea lions and seals arrived too, escorting the skiff, boldly surfing its wake.

"What kind are they?" shouted Nick.

"Issuriq," Harry replied.

"Spotted seals?"

"Harbor seals."

"Huh," said Nick. They resembled seals off the south mouth of the Yukon where he hunted. But issuriq designated spotted seals where he lived. There were no harbor seals off the Yukon mouth.

The boat left the spectacular cape behind. The coastline briefly leveled, then lifted again. They approached a second, smaller cape jutting into the sea.

"Cape Peirce," announced Harry. "Nanvak Bay. My auntie camps in there."

The captain deftly guided the boat beneath the cliffs of Cape Peirce. With an expert's ease, he found the entrance of a tidal chuck where a river formed a bay before joining the sea. Harry negotiated a series of shallow bars and entered the bay. He pointed the boat toward a shore with low dunes. Children appeared running along the water's edge, shouting and waving. A dog barked. They anchored and ferried ashore with the skiff's dingy.

Nick stretched his legs on the sand. A large canvas wall tent luffed with the breeze above the grassy dunes, set high on a broad wooden platform. Smaller side tents fluttered around it. A substantial rack constructed of driftwood logs stood nearby, packed with drying meat and fish. Wood smoke filled the camp with a sweet fragrance. The camp smelled just like those along the lower Yukon River, two hundred miles to the north. Nick felt right at home.

Fred and Millie Coopchiak greeted them at the tents. 'My aunt and uncle,' said Harry. This week, three grandchildren from Togiak stayed with them at camp, scampering about like the pampered in paradise. An older girl, tall and lean in jeans and a baggy kuspuk, caught Nick's eye, Lydia, an adopted daughter of the Coopchiaks, about Nick's age. She had a sweet familiar look, big eyes, ruddy cheeks, and prominent ears that poked from thick blowing hair. She smiled at him without a trace of shyness. He smiled back.

The racks held salmon, seal meat, capelin, and flounder, drying in the breeze. From Goodnews, Harry Coopchiak delivered boxes of whitefish and generous cuts of sea lion packed by his sister, adding to the camp's store of food. Nick contributed some sheefish, pulled from his grandmother's net the day before. The faces of the elders glowed with thanks for the gifts of food.

In minutes, the travelers sat on blankets inside the wall tent. Stew simmered on a cast iron stove. The grandchildren romped like puppies as the visitors got served. Nick felt like a celebrity. Lydia brought him a hot mug of tea and sat to the side to watch him eat. He had to catch himself from sneaking looks, an evasion she seemed to enjoy.

In the presence of elders, the conversation switched from English to Yup'ik. Nick was introduced as Kuigpagmiu, a visitor from the Yukon River. Fred Coopchiak asked why he traveled to Togiak. Nick explained the herring project, admitting he knew little about it. He was here to learn about herring.

"We saw a missile!" Cornelius interrupted.

"A missile?" Lydia smiled.

"It almost hit us!"

"Some kind of plane that looked like a missile," said his father. "Black. Two engines on its rear. Going fast. The pilot blasted above us at the cape, way too low."

"What was it?" asked Lydia.

"I don't know," growled Harry.

"Military," said Nick.

"Military?"

"It looked like that to me. Three soldiers in camouflage were on the Twin Otter flying to Cape Newenham. What happens there? I thought Newenham was a weather station."

Fred Coopchiak looked unhappy. Nobody spoke. Was the air station classified?

It was Millie Coopchiak who finally answered.

"Usviilnguq." Crazy person.

Fred nodded in agreement.

"They play games," grumbled the elder. "They are always playing games out there. We hear about it. We see it. Games against the Russians. They send planes from Kamchatka. Interceptors meet them from Galena and other bases. They meet three miles out to challenge each other, Russian pilots, American pilots. Who will fly closer? Who will turn first?"

He spat angrily into a coffee can.

"Like reckless children," said Milly.

"Like reckless children," Fred agreed. "What happens when something falls?"

"We are right beneath it," said Milly.

"This camp, that boat, right beneath it! There's no reason for games. The Cold War is done. It was over long ago."

Fred drank his tea in disgust.

"What about that missile plane?" asked Lydia.

"I have not seen that one," grumbled Fred. "It does not surprise me. Many things disturb that place. You have seen it. Many things."

On the horizon a bank of clouds dimmed the light. The tent fell into shadow. A dog whined outside. The conversation paused. Fred Coopchiak lit a lantern hung from a ceiling spar. It hissed with a soft pulsing light. The tent acquired black edges. The eyes of the grandchildren grew larger. Lydia's ears glowed like translucent shells.

The elder returned to the blanket.

He watched a corner of wavering shadows. His speech assumed the cadence of a practiced narrator. He began a story.

"There was a young woman, a kass'aq," the elder waved his hand southward. She lived where there was an old mother with two sons. The eldest of the sons worked hard, but the youngest was useless. That family always came up short. We know about that because the eldest son came to Cape Newenham to look for gold to help the family. Before he left, he married that young woman. He said to her, 'while I am gone, watch my mother, watch her with my brother.'

"That's how we met him. He worked above Nanvak Bay. Oh! How excited he was that day he came to our camp! 'I found it! I found it!' That's what he said, many times. 'I found it!' But what he found was too much for him alone. He had to get help. So he left Nanvak for his home. When he got there, he found his mother had died. And his wife... she was pregnant.

"He took his brother aside. 'Come back with me. I need your help. What I have found is too much for me alone.' So they came back together, back to Nanvak, the brothers and the woman. They put their camp at the confluence where the two rivers meet before entering the bay. The brothers worked in the hills. The woman watched the camp.

"But that brother, he was useless. It began with him. He could not work. He could not even sleep. He shivered beneath his blankets, cold and afraid.

"His brother's wife would scold him. 'You have to work!'

"'There's something down there!' he told her.

"'We will starve if you don't work!'

"'But there's something down there!'

"So she said to her husband, 'I'm lonely to watch the tents. Today I'm going too. I'm going up with you.' That day she said that, she did go too. She walked with them to that place in the hills where they worked.

"But it was the same. The brother was useless. He refused to go down the rope into the hole. He shook with fear.

"'There's something down there!' he said to them.'"

The elder paused for tea, clearing his throat. He looked around the tent.

"I wondered, what could be down in that hole?"

No one in the tent guessed.

"A carayak?" he whispered.

The children's eyes grew bigger. A carayak was something like a ghost, a monster.

The old man resumed the tale.

"The eldest laughed at him. 'There's nothing there! Look, I'll go down first.' They tied the rope to him. He went down first, climbing into the hole. When he got down, the rope went loose. Then suddenly, it jerked! The rope jerked! Like holding a fish, she said. The rope jerked! They heard him scream!

"'Go down!' she shouted.

"But he could not move. He shook with fear.

"'He's your brother!' she shouted.

"But he could not do it. He just shook.

"'I'll go myself!' she said and she took the rope.

"That shamed him. That she would say, 'I'll go myself'... that shamed him. He took the rope himself. He took the rope and the light and went down into the hole after his brother."

The lantern hissed.

The elder shook his head.

"They never came back. She called above the hole where they had gone. Nobody answered. They never came back. She could not go down. She had no light. They had taken the lamps. She could not go down without a lamp. It was black. She had no light to see. That's what she told us.

"We found her in the hills. She wandered like a person in a dream. Something went wrong in her mind. We looked for that hole. We never could find it. That place where they worked, it was gone like it never was there. We looked and we looked, but we never found it.

"Some say her husband closed it up, after killing his brother. After killing his brother for fooling around with his wife, he closed it up to hide it. I don't know. We never found it."

"Some say it closed itself," said Lydia.

"We never could find that mine. We never found those brothers."

The story was done.

"What happened to that woman?" Herbert asked his cousin.

"They took her away," said Lydia. "We don't know what happened to her. We don't know what happened to that baby."

Everyone sat in silence, pondering the strange affair. What had happened in the hole? Where was it? What had been in it?

A dog barked, breaking the spell.

Harry Coopchiak stood and stretched.

"It will be dark when we reach home."

"Stay! Stay!" the children begged.

Millie Coopchiak presented boxes of food from camp with instructions about its distribution in Togiak. They loaded the boat and left on a rising tide. With Harry Coopchiak at the helm, they glided from Nanvak Bay on black water, the camp twinkling in shadow.

In the long dusk, Harry opened full throttle on a calm sea. He knew this reach well.

They passed an island called Hagemeister.

"Used to have reindeer," Harry said to Nick. "Belonged to a herder in Togiak."

"What happened?"

"Fish and Wildlife bought him out. Shot them all. Said they were 'too skinny.'"

"Huh!"

"Good thing the government's well fed."

Nick laughed. He zipped his jacket against the chill and watched the long island pass, mulling over Fred Coopchiak's story. Stories that elders told conveyed lessons. Sometimes not. They left it to the listeners for the deeper meanings. If you were smart enough, you were meant to get it.

"Do those hills have bears?"

"Lots."

Nick considered that. The carayak of the story might refer to a brown bear. Maybe the brothers had dug into a bear's den while prospecting. A mother bear had killed the brothers to protect her den.

"Are there mines up there?"

"Did you see that road out of Platinum? That's where it goes. That's why they call it that."

"Oh, yeah," said Nick, of course, 'platinum.' A platinum mine.

"There are lots of private claims back there. It's federal wildlife refuge now, but the State fights to keep them open. Somebody is always poking around, looking to get rich."

"Do they?"

"Not that I've heard."

"Do they bother the camp?"

"What?"

"The prospectors that poke around to get rich."

"Sometimes. Mostly it's Fish and Wildlife that's always bothering them."

"Why?"

"To close the camp. They're always pestering us to close our camp."

Nick chewed on it.

Newenham, strange and paradoxical… a spectacular cape, placed far from the rest of the continent. No one should even know about it except the animals that used it, and the Yup'iks who did too, hunting, fishing, gathering from its cliffs. But Newenham attracted others… commercial seine fleets that sucked ripe herring from its small bays, prospectors who looked to get rich from platinum and gold, pilots playing war games above it, federal refuge managers pestering the camps of elders… a powerful attractant, a dense singularity bending the world, sucking others to it, yet invisible to him. He was entirely blind to it. Passing the spectacular cliffs, he saw none of the distortions, felt nothing bent or twisted, only a richness of life on windswept seas, blowing fresh to his heart.

The low sun broke from the clouds. Lights rippled off the water. In the glow, homes shined along a bluff like a row of teeth on a curved jaw.

Togiak.

They had made it.

They skirted a sandy beach crowded with skiffs and entered a slough behind the village. Harry slowly motored past parked boats and fish-drying racks and glided to a spot used by his family. With a surge from the outboards, he drove the boat onto the bank. A truck waited by an empty fish rack.

"Where can I take you?" asked Harry.

"When is the last flight from Dillingham?"

"About now."

"Can you take me to the strip?"

They loaded the truck. Harry drove a muddy track onto noisy gravel that headed toward the airstrip. A small commuter plane appeared from the south. The plane touched down with a whisper, turned at the strip's end, and rolled to where several vehicles waited. Harry pulled alongside them.

The pilot opened the plane's door and pulled out the step. People came off lugging bags and babies. Nick examined each one, looking for somebody with the name of Camilla Mac Cleary. He didn't know if she might be a Yup'ik or not with a name like that. A tall male kass'aq stepped out, dressed in an Australian bush coat opened at the neck and dragging the ground, a bulky backpack riding high on his shoulder. He scanned the small crowd like a hungry gull. Another kass'aq followed, a lanky boy with short black hair about Nick's height in blue jeans and loose cotton shirt. Nick took another look. No, a boyish girl... long lashes, a grim mouth, a face as pale as death. She too carried a pack.

Nick moved forward.

"Camilla Mac Cleary?"

She focused her dark eyes uncertainly on him, brows furrowed. The eyes tried to smile and failed.

"Nick John," he said, extending a hand.

"Oh, yeah," she said with a catch of breath.

She took his hand in hers and slightly pumped.

"I'm pleased to meet you," she whispered.

Then she dropped her pack to the ground, turned aside her boyish head, and vomited, just missing Nick's foot. Recovering her slim erectness, she wiped her mouth with a wrist and wobbled.

"Sorry," she smiled weakly. "You can call me 'Mac'..."

And she promptly collapsed.

Nick madly grabbed for her armpits.

The tall kass'aq in the bush hat leaped over, grabbing hold from behind, helping to keep the swaying girl upright. To Nick's surprise, he was laughing.

"A bit tipsy, eh Camilla?"

"What?" asked Nick.

The stranger smirked.

"Too much for one flight, don't you think? Why don't you come along with me."

Supporting an arm, the stranger directed her toward a green truck parked at the edge of the field. Nick helped from the other side. Camilla stumbled between them. About a dozen steps along this course, Camilla suddenly straight-armed the stranger, shoving off like a boat from a pier, throwing her weight onto Nick. They nearly fell in a heap. Harry Coopchiak jumped in.

"What's going on?" demanded Harry with the authority of a ship's captain.

"Camilla Mac Cleary," said Nick. It was all he could think to say.

"Gawd, I'm so sorry," apologized Camilla, clinging to the bulky captain. "I can't... I need to sit..."

She spoke with the voice of a person near a faint, an athlete at the end of her race. She didn't sound drunk to Nick. Or smell it. Harry glared darkly at the tall kass'aq who stood to the side with a bland smile. In this face off, the bush-coated stranger stood taller, but Harry considerably broader and thicker.

"She's welcome at my place," he said to Harry.

Harry closely examined the girl's face, ghostly white, drawn, and young. Without a word, he steered her a different direction, toward his own truck. Nick assisted again. They eased her into the middle of the front seat where she sprawled, eyes shut. Cornelius flattened his nose against the rear window, following events from the spare tire. Nick found her bags and boxes and piled them around the two boys. Harry turned the truck toward town. Nick saw that the tall stranger watched for a moment, lost interest, and went back to his own affairs.

"Where are we going?" asked Nick.

"My sister's."

They bumped down the gravel road. Camilla seemed almost asleep.

"You know that guy back there?"

"Yes."

That seemed to be all Harry was going to say. But Nick waited. This was a Yup'ik village. He knew more would follow.

"Works Round Island. Thinks he owns it," muttered Harry in disgust.

Harry maneuvered the truck into the driveway of a weather-beaten house perched along the bluff overlooking the bay. A scruffy dog barked greetings, straining his chain beside a mound of gill nets. Warm lights shone behind curtains. A door sprung open and children hopped down the wooden steps and grabbed the dog's collar.

Nick saw enough time to cast a final question.

"What's his name?"

"What?"

"The guy from Round Island?"
"Philip Elsberry," was the flat reply.
"Elsberry?"
"Doctor Philip Elsberry."

9

Cuniq paddled in the half-light of the extended dusk. He stroked wearily, drained by the night's fever. His kayak carried meat, fat, and skin from the seal. He had saved everything except the bones and guts, pulled into the water in proper respect. He hoped the seal would choose to return again to pup on the rocks. And when she did, he hoped to be someplace far away, free of the Russian traders. The sun had come out while he worked. He dried his sealskin clothes, drawn inside out and laid on the pebbly beach. He napped with the warm spring light on his face. Now it grew late. He paddled warm, dry, but fatigued.

As he approached the wide beach of the sea lion's island he looked for Uyuluk's kayak. What would the Aleut say when Cuniq suddenly appeared? Cuniq guessed he would say nothing, pretending nothing had happened, that he had not abandoned his sick partner. He did not see it or the other skin boats. He was not surprised. They were pulled inland, hidden from view.

As Cuniq stepped from the kayak to the beach, he felt it.

Something was wrong.

No sound of penned sea lions. No voices. No butchering. Only the shush of the water on gravel and the thin cries of ghostly terns as they soared and fell to the sea. Cuniq waited, listening to an ominous still. He cautiously freed a heavy spear from the side of the kayak, holding it at ready above his elbow. Here the short beach rose steeply. Beyond, the islet leveled toward the cliffs. Standing at the low tide, Cuniq could not see over the last rise of the rocky bench. So he waited by the kayak, listening to the eerie silence, feeling his pounding heart.

On the gravel beach hidden by the rise, a party of Yup'ik warriors lay on their stomachs. They could not see what Cuniq was doing. Instead, they took direction by hand signs from a man positioned behind them, who took his direction from Qeng'aq, their leader on a rocky vantage. No signal had been given. Qeng'aq watched from the cliff, reassessing the strategy. He planned on surprise to avoid hurting the men. But the moment for surprise had passed. The last of the intruders had not stepped into the trap. This one noticed something. He stood by his kayak with his spear ready. Qeng'aq wondered what he had noticed. Probably the lack of sentries.

Qeng'aq waited. He watched for the intruder to get back in the kayak. That would put him at a disadvantage, sitting, spear down, craft near shore. He could be killed during the launch. Qeng'aq waited for that to sign the attack. But the man did not do it. He just stood at alert with his spear, facing the beach. The man looked prepared to fight. He was outnumbered. Still, a cornered warrior might hurt many before dying. So Qeng'aq waited.

With his heels in the water, Cuniq furiously weighed choices. The longer he waited, the more he learned. The sentries set to watch the beach had not appeared or hailed. The company was gone. They had packed up and gone. He now stood alone on the islet. But even the sick men? Had they recovered, like him? If not, then there was danger over the rise, just beyond a short bowshot.

Cuniq's body woke. He found himself trembling. If he pushed forward, he was surely dead if an enemy hid over the rise. If he jumped in the kayak, he might survive. But he would present a lingering target for the enemy. There was a third improbable choice. At this low tide, the beach dropped steeply behind him into deep water. He might dive into the sea before the enemy arrived, hiding behind the kayak, kicking the boat from shore. The kayak might be punctured. But it would stay afloat. With enough distance, he would attempt a deep-water entry and flee. He did not know where their boats were hidden, but he'd have a head start. His kayak was fast. He had food and water. Of these choices, the last seemed the most unexpected. Improbably rash, it might work if boldly executed. However, there was an impediment... his clothes.

Watching from the cliff, Qeng'aq was dumbstruck by the man on the beach. He was kicking out his legs in some outlandish dance. He moved like the clownish buffoons at mid-winter feasts. With his spear in his armpit, he leaped above the strand with wild high kicks. What was he doing? A leg kicked hard and a legging came free. Another leg kicked. The man's pants flew to the gravel. He stood in shorts and calf-length boots with white legs flashing. How comical! Qeng'aq laughed. The man tucked the short spear between his legs. With one practiced tug, he yanked the gut parka over his head, throwing it on the leggings. Now Qeng'aq understood. This crazy dancer was not crazy at all. He was going to swim!

With a hard shove of the kayak, Cuniq dove into sea.

Qeng'aq signaled the relay. Attack!

The icy water shocked like a heavy blow. He stroked underwater... one, two, three, four, five. He surfaced, located the kayak, gave it another hard shove, and plunged again. One, two, three, four, five. He heard muffled shouts from the shore. A projectile pierced the water to his left. He reached the kayak. Grabbing its prow he kicked to one side, placing the craft between him and the attackers. Thunk! Thunk! Arrows hit. Here the effort stalled, the kayak turned sideways to the beach. Foosh! A harpoon dart missed his head. He kicked backward, lying under the stern, tugging the kayak straight. Thunk! One, two, three, four, five. The men continued shouting. He was getting out of range.

Cold gripped him. It was exhausting. The night's fever had weakened his body. He willed himself through the frigid water. He was losing coordination and strength. He needed to board.

Reaching up from the stern he found the tailing edges of the rear racks, lashed with lines and equipment. Gripping with both hands, he kicked and pulled, lunging like a breaching whale. He launched directly in line with the narrow craft. If he hit off center, the kayak would flip.

The front of the kayak rose steeply from the water as he yanked skyward. He grabbed for the center well. The nose fell with a vengeance. WHAPPP! The kayak wobbled violently, but did not flip. He was aboard, prone on the tail, gripping the edge of the well, shivering with cold. He had to keep moving, get the kayak farther from shore. Commanding his arms, he dragged himself forward. The kayak wobbled with each move. He twisted, trying to enter the well without capsizing.

Qeng'aq watched this display of nerve and skill from the beach. He had sprinted from the cliff in time to see the perfect stern entry. An admirable feat! Qeng'aq felt honored to observe it. His warriors also watched, entertained by the show. They no longer cast spears or shot arrows. Their adversary had outsmarted them. True, he lost his shirt and pants, but the escape was superb.

Qeng'aq saw the boatman struggle, his movements slow and exaggerated. He fumbled to disengage a paddle from side ties. Cold, thought Qeng'aq. His body was barely working. And though far off, he was still a target.

Qeng'aq called for line and a toggling point. He armed a darting shaft and set them in a throwing board. Running, Qeng'aq launched the missile. The dart and line arched high. It came down, almost vertically.

THUNK!

The point pierced the prow.

A lucky cast!

You are brave, boatman, but you are caught like a seal.

Cuniq felt the missile hit. The frame splintered. The toggle point set. The boat jerked its nose toward shore.

He had to break free.

Cuniq rose from the well and leaped for the cord. This time, he launched off center.

The kayak flipped.

Cold swallowed him. Cuniq frantically kicked and broke for air. Something strangled him. He jerked violently. He was noosed by some trick or magic! Blindly, he grabbed at the chokehold and held on. Frigid water rushed. He couldn't breathe. His lungs burned, nearly to bursting.

Breaching, he collapsed upon gravel, half-blinded, gasping for air. It fell upon him, falling from the sky. A hideous face! The kalla'alek!

It grabbed his throat.

Qeng'aq knelt beside the choking boatman and reached among twisted lines and knots that entangled his throat. A cord came off the man's shoulders looped among white hardware fashioned of thick bone. Qeng'aq fingered it. It was ivory, a pendant. A harpoon point protruded from its center. A dart cast from the beach after his own had skewered it. The point struck mid-center and sheared off, leaving its shank at the amulet's middle. The dart and amulet had fused. The warriors pulled the boatman ashore by the harpoon line snared around his neck.

Lucky boatman! You should be speared. Or drowned.

The smooth ivory slipped within his fingers like something alive. Its wet polished surface flashed with sun.

Qeng'aq fell to both knees and covered his eyes.

Images flared, searing the dark.

Four great animals!

They circled the point, one following another in a chase around the center as if sucked in a vortex tighter and tighter.

He knew them instantly.

The falling walrus!

He shoved it into gravel.

* * *

Cuniq waited for death. He shivered on the beach, hugging himself for warmth. His kayak was pulled beside him, pocked with small holes, arrows and darts recovered. It had not been touched.

Why he was still alive? Why did they delay?

Warriors surrounded the hideous kalla'alek. They listened spellbound as the demon talked. It was almost intelligible to Cuniq, a dialect close to his own, dancing beyond comprehension.

He didn't doubt what would happen. They would kill him. The company was killed already. Why did they delay? Did they plan his torture?

The speech stopped. The warriors broke apart and the demon approached. Cuniq saw it was no monster. He was a man with wounded face. A dark hole took the place of a nose. A line coiled about one hand. His grandfather's pendant swung from the other. The warrior displayed both and asked something.

Cuniq examined the pendant. A broken harpoon point poked through the hole drilled at its center, trailing the harpoon line. The point and pendant had joined. This was how they snared him. With the line they had hauled him ashore.

Cuniq shook his head. He hadn't known that a dart had skewered the amulet.

The warrior asked another thing, something about the pendant. He didn't know how to reply, so he answered simply.

"My grandfather made it."

77

The noseless warrior understood.

He gazed to the far horizon. He turned back to Cuniq, pointed at the engravings on the pendant, and asked about them. It was something about walrus. Cuniq gave the same answer.

"My grandfather made them. He carved the walrus."

Not knowing why, he pushed the pendent to the warrior.

"I give it to you. It's yours."

The noseless warrior stepped back, amazed.

He turned to others gathered around him. He lifted the amulet and loudly declaimed, something about walrus and dreams and danger. Men began to mutter and shift uneasily. Something profound was happening.

Suddenly, the noseless warrior jumped. He displayed a knife. He turned to Cuniq and boldly swung. Cuniq stiffened for the kill. With a upward stroke, the warrior severed the cord joining point to line. The warrior lifted the pendant for all to witness and put it on. He coiled the harpoon line as everyone watched and shoved it into Cuniq's hands.

An exchange.

Cuniq understood. For his grandfather's pendant, the coiled line. A trade.

He would live.

Tears sprang to his eyes.

Puyangun!

He would see her again!

At that perfect moment, a warrior lifted his bow. He swung around fast. Sinew whistled. Light exploded, a brilliant sunburst, swallowed by black.

Qeng'aq stood above the stranger, crumpled on the beach.

There was great mystery here. Inexplicable forces. Uneasy portents. Yet Qeng'aq was certain… his visions were bound to this boatman. The strange visions were somehow linked with the ivory amulet and the person who made it. It carried the walrus. He had first dreamed them. Now he wore them on his neck, carved in ivory.

'Call the walrus.'

The vision commanded it.

They came.

They fell from the sky.

A mystery.

The souls of his starving people, sucked out to sea… he called for help and they came and they fell.

The boatman's grandfather made the amulet. Who was he? A powerful angalkuq? Its power had pierced his mind. Did he send it to him? Why?

He didn't know. What he did know for certain was that the walrus came first as a vision, then carved on ivory. Walrus had never been his spirit helper. He knew little of walrus. He must act carefully, respectfully.

His warriors waited restlessly. Despite the slaughter, perhaps because of it, fighters still lusted for blood. It might be difficult to save this last boatman.

He turned to them again and spoke openly. He told them about the vision. He told them of its connection with the stranger and the prudence of sparing the skilled boatman who delivered the gift from a great angalkuq from the islands to the south. Sent home alive, the boatman would tell others of the ferocity of the Yup'iks. This would help keep their lands free of intruders.

Most listened. Some grumbled.

Qeng'aq called for Tengeng, the boy nearly spilled by the sea lions, the boy who had wept for an enemy. He took him aside.

"Tow the stranger beyond the bay. Release him to the sea. Don't overturn the kayak. Leave water, food, tools, and this."

He pressed the trade into his hand, the coiled walrus line. He took Teneng's arm and drew him closer, whispering by his ear.

"Listen to no one else."

Tengeng nodded, staring into the black pit of Qeng'aq's childhood, seeing only marks of honor.

Qeng'aq considered the boatman a final time, sprawled unconscious on the gravel. The bearer of the mysterious gift would wake on the open sea, borne by currents away from the land of his enemies.

"You are a person with luck. A person like you will have no trouble finding home. Tell your grandfather this. Tell him, I wear the walrus."

He touched it at his neck.

He nodded with respect.

And strode for the cliffs.

10

Camilla Mac Cleary prayed for elephants. Sumos with meaty hands. Falling pianos. Balled tightly on the narrow bunk, she prayed for anything to crush her senseless.

Pain ripped her head. Deep beneath an eye, a pulse of agony released with every heartbeat.

God, what pain!

She had never felt such pain!

Knees flexed, elbows up, she gripped her face and squeezed. The agony eased momentarily. She held until her hands failed. Throttled pain erupted. Her insides roiled on an overwhelming flood. She blindly groped for the pan, sprawled off the lower bunk, and desperately swallowed.

Don't let me puke. Not in the bunk. Don't let me puke.

She hung in the dark holding the vomit and prayed for something, anything, to crush her senseless.

Children whispered. They were shushed.

Somebody knelt beside her. A damp cloth wrapped her neck with a heavy coolness. Light fingers stroked her short hair. A gentle touch.

Winnie Friendly.

She whispered distractions as she worked fingers through her hair, spoke about her children, spoke about the names bestowed by the missionaries on the Yup'iks. Some were 'friendly'... her husband's family's name. That's who she was. Winnie Friendly. The irony wasn't lost on Camilla. She'd taken in the stumbling, vomiting stranger.

"Winnie's really a Coopchiak," Nick John said before leaving, as if this explained everything.

The gentle voice spoke with a lute-like quality, each sentence a song.

"Still feeling sick?"

Camilla nodded beneath her fingertips.

"I made tea."

Camilla nodded again. Bring it with elephants.

Moments later the alcove smelled of grass.

"Medicine," said Winnie.

Camilla got levered up. Blindly, she received a hot mug. Something blistering hit her mouth, bitter, a remedy to fix the problem with the anthropologist. Let it be poison. She choked, downing a scalding mouthful. She lifted the mug and ironed her eyes, searing pain with pain.

"More."

Camilla quaffed and sputtered and relinquished the mug. She clung like a sparrow to a reed. Winnie held her for a long while. Then she eased her to the mat on the narrow bunk in the semi-dark. She instructed the children in Yup'ik, a whispering of code. Again, Camilla felt fingertips gently probing her head, cool touches and taps like raindrops on scorched canvas, insistent drumming on a burning canopy as the bitterness spread.

Things had gone wrong, fast.

Way wrong.

She should get help. Get help now.

Now! Get up now before it's too late!

Get up!

She was too weak. Her body failed her. Too messed up. Physically. Emotionally. Ache after ache. Unstoppable agony. Unstoppable tears.

Panic swelled.

She'd waited too long.

Run!

She was so fucked.

Voices muttered beyond the chamber.

For God's sake, get up and run!

But the pain… she couldn't stop the pain, couldn't stop the crying, filled to bursting. Absolutely fucked.

He spoke beside the bed.

"We're here."

"No."

"You knew we were coming," said another.

"No," she whimpered.

"So it's time."

"Please… no."

"Don't make this harder."

"Oh God! Please… no!"

"It's time."

"Don't take her!"

She jolted awake.

She lay in semi-darkness on the narrow bunk, alone, in silence. There was nothing… nothing but blurry grey.

Nothing.

No pain. No sound.

Nothing.

She was too weak to move.

Too tired to prevent it.

Her eyes shut in the murky pit.

She fell again into dreams.

11

Nick John stood beneath the water tank. It rose in the twilight four stories above his head, round and ominous, an empty cylinder of thick planks surrounded by rusted forklifts, derelict cranes, and stacked crab pots whose webbing sighed in the wind, abandoned monuments from another time. A door yawned at its side like a cave. A man blocked it crosswise, his shoulders jammed against the frame, mud-clotted boots shoved off the wooden stoop.

He held a bottle at his gut.

Seeing Nick, he jerked up, angry and alarmed.

"Where are you from?" he rasped.

Nick dropped his backpack cautiously.

He could not see the shadowed face.

"Airstrip."

The man saw the wet boxes and laughed scornfully.

"Liar…"

Nick frowned, said nothing.

He waved the bottle toward the black water, spat against the tank, and growled.

"You came with Coopchiak."

Nick squared for trouble.

"Yes, that too."

"Where are you from?" the man demanded.

"Yukon River."

Nick stared beyond him into the hole.

"It's locked," the man growled.

"I have the key," said Nick.

They waited, eying the other, neither speaking. They challenged the other to speak next. The hot silence lengthened, grew worse, insufferable. The man shrieked as if burned.

"Don't bother us!"

"I don't."

"You come to make trouble!"

"No trouble."

"That's what this place is for… people who make trouble!"

"That's not me."

"You have the key!"

Nick snarled. The man was drunk.

"Why do you even come?" the man whined.

"To sleep. Let me sleep."

The man set his boots on the stoop. He leaned toward Nick, tensed, a pulled bow. His voice turned savage.

"I know who you are… you fucker."

"You don't know me," said Nick, angry.

"You've come again to make trouble."

"No, no trouble."

"To go around and bother us and not even know the trouble you make!"

The man lashed out.

"Go away!"

"No."

"Go home!

"No."

"You don't even know! When it all goes wrong from what you are doing, you don't even know! Go away! Go home! You don't even hear what they tell you! Who you work for! Why you are here! Nothing is what you thought it was! Just go away! Before we all suffer!"

He bolted into the dark.

12

Cuniq woke with a blast of spray. His kayak listed dangerously, a sliver driven on escalating violence. Wind howled off the crests of ocean swells. He instinctively reached for the paddle. His hand found it lashed in place on the deck's edge. He dug the blades side-to-side, cut into the swell, and pulled the kayak into a cresting wave. Up he surged on a wall of water, up and over, falling down the other side. He quickly adjusted, stroked left and right, pointing the kayak into the howling wind.

Cuniq shook his head for answers.

Where was this?

What was this storm?

How was he here?

A wall of water surged from his left. He charged to meet it, twin blades driving. He climbed the steep face and glided down the back slope. The kayak's prow, carved for the open ocean from a dense spruce knot, cut deep into the swell, splitting its force, stabilizing the craft. Cuniq's people knew the shape and power of waves. They were people of the North Pacific. The northern sea churned up swells like the high surf of home.

"Keep us safe," Cuniq sang to the storm.

It could hear.

"Keep us safe."

He struck forward with rapid strokes to meet the next swell, cut deep into its side and then over. He soared off in brilliant spray.

He was now fully awake. He found himself dressed in his own clothes, covered by his seal-gut raingear as if outfitted for an ocean voyage. The spray skirt was drawn expertly around him, sealing him within the kayak's well.

Who had done this?

Cuniq struggled for answers as he maneuvered over a succession of swells. He remembered the noseless warrior, the threat of death, the joy of reprieve, and a blinding flash. Here he woke in a storm, secured in his kayak. All its gear was lashed in place, everything as before, except that a harpoon dart protruded from the splintered prow, small punctures in the kayak's top shell had been patched, and a coil of line was attached beside the spray skirt... the walrus-hide line traded for the pendant.

A blast of wind struck, driving him sideways.

WHOOSH!

The storm instantly muffled in freezing gray.

He was underwater.

Cuniq rode with it. He revolved, hanging within the kayak's well. He felt the momentum pass its lowest point. Reaching toward the surface on the leading side, he flicked a blade down hard, sustaining the rotation. Up he rolled, emerging into sounds of fury.

He beat on the leading side, stopped the roll, and pulled back into the wind, cutting into the face of the next wave that fell like an avalanche. Up he sliced and down. He was back on top, adjusting with the wind, this time the victor in its deadly game. The roll had taken scarcely five heartbeats. He blinked back the spray and licked brine from his lips.

The storm was building. The light failing.

"Keep us safe," he sang to the storm.

A blast hit him. This time he was ready. The kayak skipped airborne and settled hard. A blast hit again, launching him above the highest crest.

Lightning slashed.

The horizon froze with light.

Water filled the frozen sky!

The sea rose like a massive flexing tree. A column of water reached into the clouds. Spray ejected from countless branches off a twisting trunk, pummeling the angry waves. It was a gigantic spout moving on a tidal bore. Debris churned in its base, sucked down and spit up in a vicious grind.

Lightning slashed through it.

The giant roared.

"Help us!" Cuniq cried.

He drove a blade to turn and instantly flipped. Under the water he rolled. He flicked skyward and surfaced, his back to the charging monster.

Frantically, he paddled. The wind pushed. But the massive wave was faster. The surge caught him. Up he rode the wave that built to join the waterspout. He dug with all his strength. The kayak teetered on air, fell, and surfed the steep face. The wave grabbed the tiny craft, shifted its course, and lifted again. He moved sideways and upwards, gripped by irresistible forces.

He frantically leaned and paddled to keep atop the wave, pointing with the rotation, desperately fighting the suck of the inner pit. Wind whipped left and then right as he rode a complete turn. Debris circled with him, great logs, massive stumps, and thick trailing kelp swept up by the spout's passage.

A bristling snag erupted beside him. Desperately, Cuniq struck his paddle full against it, holding the kayak off. The snag vanished beneath him.

On the second turn, the wave released more debris… the company's boats! Ribs splintered, skins torn, sinew joints groaning, the monster spit them up. One, two, three, the wrecks erupted from the depths. They circled the spout with him like stones of a bola, bound and breaking within a centripetal grinder.

The men came up too. Crewmen popped here and there amid the swirling column. They swam with him, pale bodies stripped of clothes, flickering within the vortex, shining like new-born creatures racing toward uncertain ends. They came abreast and joined with him to complete the circuit.

Cuniq fought to stay atop.

He could not close his eyes to the horror. He could not even speak. He desperately stroked and prayed.

Keep us safe… keep us safe…

His mind prayed it.

Wind whipped through another turn and eruption. A kayak blew up from the depths. For an instant it stood on its tail, foundered in the wave, and caught, slowly moving in the turn. His partner's boat. It swung alongside, a skeletal frame with shredded skin, gaining speed.

Riding its top, strapped to the well, Uyuluk the Aleut flopped. His dull eyes were open, searching paths to follow. This time, he seemed to say, this time I won't leave you.

Uyuluk grabbed the lead.

He turned, listed broadside across Cuniq's bow, and beckoned.

A blast of wind hit.

Cuniq blew off the wave like refuse.

The maelstrom disappeared behind him into the dark.

Its roar grew fainter and fainter.

Cuniq shook as he stroked.

Keep us safe. Keep us safe.

All through the passage of night.

Keep us safe.

Day came. The storm blew unabated. Its winds pushed northward within unending rows of whitecaps, driving farther into the northern sea. Cuniq struggled to stay afloat, stroking throughout the long day, unable to sleep, weakening. By dusk, he was finished. He could no longer fight.

The storm had beat him.

With the twilight it appeared, a dark shape that bobbed among the swells. It skulked beneath the cresting waves, traveling with the wind, moving closer like a languid dolphin.

Cuniq saw it, long, straight, stripped smooth, the width of an outstretched hand, a tree undercut by flood in some upland forest, washed from land to sea.

He closed and snagged it.

In the swells he labored. He lashed harpoon shafts draped athwart the center well. Bound them to the frame. Crossed spears to hold them rigid. Then collapsed into the well, shaking with fatigue. Fixed to the tree, the craft now had two hulls lashed together, kayak and outrigger. It would not flip. He rechecked each knot, secured his paddle, closed his eyes, and fell unconscious.

The storm howled in anger. It blew all the night and day.

Rotting icebergs appeared with the dusk.

Cuniq woke to cold. He moved in shattered ice, a realm of slush, rind, and cakes. Scudding fog hid the half-frozen sea. Temperatures fell. Cuniq broke out mitts to save his hands. His prayers took shape in the air.

"Help us," he called to the sea.

But the currents pushed north.

"Help us," he called to the wind.

But the winds blew unabated.

"Help us," he begged the ice.

He heard them, soft and distant, huffs and groans and bell-like tolls, coming from the ice. They grew louder. Finally he spied them. Dark heads rose and fell on slushy swells.

Walrus.

Females moved among the drifting floes.

A harem heading north.

Cuniq stowed his mitts. He cautiously loosed the probe with terminal spike, the last free shaft on the kayak. He looped the butchering knife around his wrist. And he waited, tense and alert, the pole at his chest, resting on the central well.

A low moo voiced from the fog to his left. A deep-throated huff burst from the front, something larger. Cuniq's kayak moved within them, riding the wind. A groan came from behind. The herd surrounded him.

"Help us," he prayed.

It came from the rear. A massive head lunged from the water with a roar, white tusks flashing. Cuniq swiveled in the well and stabbed. The probe caught the snout before it hit the kayak. He pushed down hard. The bull backed off and sank. Heads shot up from the depths at his right, roaring. Cuniq swatted them, driving them under.

A deafening roar bellowed at Cuniq's elbow. A huge bull launched from the sea, long tusks slashing. They speared the log. The craft shuddered and groaned. Caught in the lashing, the bull thrashed to tear free. With a two-fisted swing, Cuniq drove the knife down, straight through an eye. The violence nearly ripped the blade from his hands.

The frame groaned and sagged. Cuniq yanked the knife free and frantically sawed at the thick neck. With a snap, he severed the spine. The huge body came free and sank to the inky depths. Cuniq reclaimed the probe. But the attack was done. The herd had scattered.

Above bristling whiskers, the eyes of the great bull had closed. The walrus slept, its head upon the log. Tusks as thick as Cuniq's arms curved into the lashing. Beside the mounted head, the bundle of walrus-hide line trailed into the sea, the trade from the noseless warrior.

Cuniq stared amazed.

In blowing fog he set to work. He freed the great head. Skewered its thick cheekbone. Affixed the rawhide line. And dropped it overboard.

The head sank.

Cuniq played out line, singing as it slipped through his hands. The line grew short. The heavy head hit. It dragged and caught. The kayak swung around.

The gale screamed. The line grew taut, tied at the prow. White rapids beat against the craft. But it held, anchored by the bull's head, set by thick tusks to the seabed.

It did not break.

Cuniq cried.

His tears fell to the sea.

He thanked the walrus for its gift.

He wept for his grandfather.

For Puyangun.

The winds raged for days. The storm tried again to take him. But the walrus did not fail. It would not let go.

Finally, the anger ended. The winds fell and shifted. The currents ebbed and turned.

It was done.

Cuniq loosed the tree.

He freed the head and line.

To each he gave thanks.

And he struck south… for home.

13

When she woke, there was nothing.

Sweat soaked the mattress. The pan lay tipped on the floor.

Through wet lashes, her eyes traced a river of whorls in the wood above her.

Time frozen in a tree.

She feared to move, to reawaken it. She searched without moving… searched for the pain. But it was gone. There was nothing except a faint echo inside her head, a fuzzy blur like the afterimage left by a flash behind the eyes.

That and a dull ache, lower down.

That inescapable thing.

She placed her fingers upon her skinny midriff and carefully pressed.

Nothing. A declivity sunk by gravity.

The awful nothingness.

"You woke up," piped a voice.

Winnie Friendly stood in a hallway framed in gray light. Children peered from behind, mute as moths.

"Yeah," Camilla weakly replied.

Winnie knelt by the bunk and put a hand on Camilla's forehead. She gently smoothed the skin between her brows.

"Last night… really pinched." She drew out the word 'really.'

"Yeah, pinched," said Camilla, risking a laugh.

Winnie laughed cautiously too.

For the children, that was sufficient. They squealed and scrambled to reclaim the bunk, one on top, one beneath, pushing aside the worries that had filled the house last night because a strange kass'aq lay in their room, sick and in pain. Camilla swung her legs to the floor.

"Are you okay to sit?" asked Winnie.

"Yeah."

"You were so sick."

Camilla leaned over and moved her head like a turtle. The pain was truly gone. Even the furriness faded.

"I thought my head was going to explode."

"Something... on that plane," ventured Winnie.

Camilla considered it. She'd rushed to make the flight in Anchorage. Her head had felt strange. The terminal's food smelled overpoweringly bad. She ate nothing. Then she met Elsberry. Same flight. Dr. Philip Elsberry. Doctor Lothario. All the smarmy moves. He bought drinks on the plane, ordered for them both without asking. She barely sipped it.

"Something on that plane," Winnie nodded with certainty.

Not likely, reasoned Camilla. Elsberry was a first-rate slime ball, but he wouldn't have messed with her drink, would he?

"A headache. I've never had a headache like that."

"Poor..." said Winnie with sympathy. "Like Edna Smart."

"Edna Smart?"

"When the outboard caught her hair."

Winnie jerked her fist like pulling a plug from a bottle.

"She gets headaches?"

Winnie nodded.

Camilla appraised Winnie Friendly, pulling hair from a boat engine, her round face burnt by the outdoors, crescent eyes watching cautiously, her life molded, without a doubt, by experiences far beyond Camilla's. To her, Camilla was the oddity, the interloper from unknown places, unrequested, sick and potentially dangerous, like plague. She had taken her and nursed her through the night, a mother with her own charges, placed at risk. The boy and girl climbed the bunk like it was a new toy because the stranger sat on it. Camilla's throat grew thick. A tear strayed down her cheek. She took the woman's hand.

"You are so kind, thank you," blurted Camilla. "I'm such an idiot. God, I almost threw up in their bunk!"

Camilla laughed at the absurdity, wiping her eyes with a palm.

The tears astonished Winnie.

The night had been long and scary. After the last plane her brother had arrived with food boxes and a strange kass'aq. He dumped her on Winnie. Her brother always did things like that. He always chose to bother her over his own wife to minimize obligations with his in-laws. He hated his in-laws.

'Take her yourself,' she wanted to say. 'You've got a big house. You've got money.'

She felt like saying that. But she didn't. Winnie's husband said nothing. It wasn't his brother asking favors. It was up to her.

"What am I going to do with a kass'aq?" she asked him. "What's wrong with her? What if she dies?"

"She's not going to die," said her brother.

"What about that one?" she suggested, nodding at the other rider, a strange Yup'ik. "Why doesn't he take her?"

"He's renting the tank," her brother said.

So she got the puking kass'aq.

In her life, Winnie knew kass'aqs. There were the teachers. They rotated through town and told students how to behave. They kept to themselves and fled when the term ended, eager to leave. Or the big boat captains who appeared each summer as the teachers left, strutting around town, buying fried chicken and frozen steaks from the co-op store. Or the drifters who abused local girls. There were always a couple of them. Or the preachers who circulated like bad colds, making trouble, driving wedges between families. Or the doctors who worked off their college debts, learning from their mistakes at the clinic. Yes, Winnie knew kass'aqs.

'I'm such an idiot. I almost threw up in the bunk!'

She took her hand and cried.

This skinny kass'aq with the too-short hair, head upside-down in a bucket, called herself an idiot and held her hand. She still held it, tears coming down her cheeks. Her strange, long fingers wrapped around her own. Winnie remembered back through the teachers and captains, the doctors and the drifters and the no-good preachers. Of all the kass'aqs, this was the first to thank her, to take her hand, to apologize with embarrassment, to sit and to cry.

'I'm such an idiot.'

Camilla wiped her eyes.

So did Winnie.

"Are you hungry?"

14

Puyangun felt the first splash trickle down her spine. She moved quickly. Reaching back, she grabbed the infant tucked inside the folds of her parka and lifted. Out came the baby over her head. She held him at arm's length to the cold clean winds, her precious child, naked, pudgy, and wrinkled. Unceremoniously yanked from the cozy dark into the brisk air, the baby's sphincters instantly closed. He howled at the indignity. Puyangun giggled. Thekla laughed too, watching her cousin's baby, squalling and reddening, hanging by his dimpled armpits, legs bunched toward his shoulders. They waited out the little muscles. Finally the urine squirted free, watering the breezes with a silvery spray.

"Good baby!" Puyangun praised.

She nosed his fat ruddy cheeks. She kissed his tiny penis clean. She put him to a breast for a quick suck, then tucked him again inside her parka, warm and secure against her naked shoulders.

Thekla watched with approval. Puyangun was a good mother. Despite the family's hardships and the harsh Russian overlords, Puyangun had blossomed into natural motherhood. Her breasts swelled with milk, unlike many half-starved mothers in the relocated settlements. Her baby grew fat and strong and had not been ill. He screamed lustily in the cold air. He quieted quickly at the breast. A true prize.

The Russian lover, angry and withdrawn, had even returned. He had not abandoned her completely. Despite the ambiguities, he noticed the prize, the healthy baby boy whose flawless skin seemed white enough, at least for now. He felt the

94

stirring of pride, or reawakened lust. Puyangun retained her beauty. Small gifts reappeared at her sod house with Puyangun's mother. Entreaties. Preludes to his moving hips. Would her cousin acquiesce? Sugpiat babies darkened later. Now was the time.

It would not be easy, Thekla knew. Puyangun pined for Cuniq. She anxiously waited and watched. The Aleuts took him away to hunt for skins to cover the trading boats. During his absence, the Russian had coerced her. Hard choices. Even so, it was the moody Russian who had found himself ensnared. When her belly showed, he counted, consulted, then raged about the pregnancy, how the child was not his. In her final months, he had disappeared, holed up with the monks at St. Paul's harbor. Now he resurfaced. He saw the prize. And the gifts resumed, left with Puyangun's mother.

Thekla knew what she herself would do. A woman chose living lovers. A mother chose partners from rich houses, not poor ones, or better yet, a rich Russian. This first child, not fully this or that, might not achieve it, but the next would, freed from servitude, born for privilege. That's what mattered, your children. They counted more than loyalty to old affections. That's what Thekla had learned as a child, listening to her mother's bitter crying, abandoned and alone with despair. That's how a family survived.

Her sleepy baby secured, Puyangun resumed cutting fish. Thekla knelt with her, slitting sockeye bellies. They saved the orange egg skeins and fat brown livers for soaking. Guts they tossed in piles for the dogs. With their broad lunate knives they scored the red flanks for the drying racks. They worked fast, watching for unfriendly eyes. They should not be noticed cutting these fish. The Russian lover would be furious.

The salmon came in secret, a gift to Puyangun's mother from Talliciq. This in itself was of little consequence. Talliciq was an old man in the village, a fisherman at Toothed Water, a wizened elder skilled in healing. The Russians let the old men alone to fish, unmolested, unrecorded, and untaxed. The elders kept the village alive. They fished for women like Thekla's mother, bereft of men, dead or conscripted for work. An elder like Talliciq could give food to whomever he wished.

Giving was not the peril, but the gift's meaning. Talliciq normally gave little to Puyangun's mother. Her family had no close connections to his. But Talliciq was the grandfather of Cuniq. After Puyangun gave birth, suddenly sockeye caught by

Talliciq arrived at Puyangun's mother's house. The gift affirmed a new link between families. It acknowledged a great grandchild.

Puyangun's mother accepted the food. It indicated nothing, she sniffed. She played both sides, wanting the fish but also the rich Russian. Talliciq, astute and cautious, knew of the moody lover. So the fish were delivered at night. And Puyangun and Thekla feverishly worked to cut them, hidden by the trees. The Russian shouldn't discover the gift.

Thekla's nieces and nephew arrived, their faces shining with fish oil. They hopped about, eager to help the conspiracy. They ate bits of salmon belly as rewards. Puyangun laughed at their fishy faces and loaded their packs with the last salmon cuts. Bent low with fish, the children scurried off to the drying racks. Placed at a woody edge of the settlement, the racks hid from the beach where the Aleuts patrolled. The salmon would dry several days. A smolder of willow and alder would give a hard, dark crust and delicious smoky flavor.

The first salmon catch of the season, drying on the racks.

The first of many racks... 'God willing.'

Puyangun pondered this as she walked with Thekla. The Russian priests of St. Paul's harbor who prayed and worshipped there, the robed hieromonks who swung the smoky censers, they always said this. The racks would fill... 'God willing.'

She walked with both arms clasped behind her back, her hands cupping the round bottom of her baby. It delighted her to hold it. The small bottom bounced inside her parka with every step. It felt so tiny now. It had not felt small during the delivery, twisted wrong, tearing her apart.

The Russian priests said it during the long and difficult delivery. The baby would live, 'God willing.' Puyangun would live, 'God willing.'

They asked for her confession.

'In preparation,' they said. Confessions brought heaven closer. She should confess her sins to the heavenly Father. This was the God of the Russians. This was the God who, if the monks spoke true, withheld fish from starving people, or killed unborn babies... 'willing it.'

Why would a father do this?

To show humans their need, to draw them closer to Him, said the priests.

'Their gods, not ours,' whispered Talliciq, the old man who gave her fish. 'Russian ghosts' he called them. Gold-leafed pictures of dead patriarchs shined above rows of votive candles within their chapels. The priests prayed to ghosts.

God did not withhold fish from people, Talliciq told her. The fish themselves decided how to return each year. If the fish did not come, this was because of what humans had done or failed to do, hoarding, wasting, or despoiling the fishing places. God did not kill babies or cause stillbirths. It was a mother's poor diet, or lack of rest, or weak lungs, or coughed blood. It was jealous rivals or malicious shamans they hired. Not God.

She believed the old man. Such things made more sense than 'God willing.'

Despite her fear, she had not confessed. The monks left unhappy. And her baby was born, strong and healthy, yelling for all the village to hear, even the deaf old women. This was the baby asleep on her back with the tiny butt and bruised feet. He kicked his way out.

Her Russian disagreed.

Aleksei Stepanovich Petrovskii trusted the priests.

Puyangun knew he was an intelligent man.

The priests were educated, he told her. Aleksei would choose to spend more time with cloistered monks than with the company, if he could. They were devout and dedicated, like his family in St. Petersburg far to the west, over the seas and empty taiga, months of travel by road and broad-sailed ship, one now anchored at St. Paul's harbor. The monks trained at Valaamo, an island near his family's home. As a child, he loved to hear them sing. Compared to them, the workers in the company were vile louts. An afternoon with the Valaamo monks was worth a month with any of them. Especially the hermit, he said. He was so holy, the hermit lived in a cave. He slept with a board for a blanket. She had seen the hermit once, hairy, emaciated, clothed in filthy deerskin. Aleksei went to the monks whenever he could to talk, drink, and argue. He laughed at Puyangun's surprise.

Yes, they loved to drink and argue.

The priests influenced her Russian, Puyangun perceived. And for her benefit. Aleksei was moody, impulsive, often despondent, occasionally angry. Without warning, he had turned dangerous. He saw her belly and raged. The madness shocked her. He fled to his priests. He disappeared like a wounded bear goes beneath a tree. This had saved her. She rarely saw him after her sixth month.

Now he had emerged, the bear after winter, strangely changed. He came first to her mother, renewing his gifts. Her mother accepted as before. Then he came to the sod house unannounced, looking on her at the hearth fire as she nursed. He stared at her like the priests did their icons, silent, transfixed, at the baby, pale white and asleep on her brown nipple. He seemed caught by an unabashed affection, some unassailable adoration.

His face shined above the fire.

A glowing face.

Like a golden ghost.

It made her shiver.

15

Nicholas John found his boss too late. He had missed breakfast. Camilla Mac Cleary chatted with Winnie Friendly over nearly-empty plates. Two unrestrained children romped about them in the kitchen. Pancakes... no extras in sight. Winnie poured him a consolation cup of coffee.

Nick had slept in the water tank. It was the strangest room he had ever rented, a water tank in an old service area among weathered storage sheds, electrical generators, and stacks of idle crab pots. The town's clean water facility made it obsolete. Somebody had converted the tank into locked storage units, topped with a makeshift room for travelers without options. Lit by bare bulbs, stairs curved up the inner wall to a heavy wood door. Beyond was a single unit stinking of creosote. It had no windows, no views, no nothing except a cot, rough wood floors, bottled water, and metal rungs up a wall to an escape hatch in the ceiling. Forty bucks a night. Exhausted, he collapsed on the cot and slept, fitfully dreaming of stack fires and shadowy thugs who threatened him. He ate breakfast on its flat roof overlooking the village, squatting on blistered tar-paper, chewing dried fish, tasting creosote with each bite.

Camilla had done substantially better.

Winnie's kitchen smelled of baked bread and coffee.

Still, the night had been dry and quiet and he had provisions. Nick knew Fairbanks had spoiled him. He looked for eggs, bacon, and muffins to start each day, fixed by somebody else.

Nick cautiously eyed his new boss, the boyish girl sick on the airstrip. She appeared a bit better today. Just a bit. She looked inordinately thin in faded jeans and loose cotton blouse, its billowy sleeves partially pulled above her elbows. She was pale to translucency. Blue veins trailed up her inner arms like vines up a trellis. Set against the ghostly pallor was hair as black as a Yup'ik's but cropped unreasonably short, a prisoner's cut, shorter than his except for tresses draped behind her ears. Her puffy brown eyes, thick with lashes, peered from some inner place as she nursed her coffee, a presence both in and out of the world.

Who was this? A lost penitent from a convent? Some tormented soul in slow dissolution? Why self-destruct on the Bering Sea?

"Are we working today?" asked Nick guardedly.

He hoped, somewhat, the answer might be 'no.'

"I'd like to," said Camilla with a sudden doe-eyed innocence, her inner gaze instantly affixed on him. "Do you think we should?"

"Uh, I guess," said Nick, unprepared for the question, wondering about his options.

Camilla stuffed the last bite of pancake into her mouth and chewed thoughtfully. Nick watched her lips move, puffed, like the soft skin beneath her large eyes. Nick caught Winnie watching him watch Camilla's lips.

"Are you working for her?" asked Winnie dryly.

Nick knew what she was thinking.

"We're working together," answered Camilla quickly, wiping the lips with a wrist. "Like partners, right?"

"Uh, right," replied Nick on this as yet unnegotiated point. "But, I think Camilla's like the boss. Right? I don't know what we're supposed to be doing."

"Herring," said Camilla.

She quickly dug into a bulky backpack for a one-sheet prospectus. Nick read through it. 'Subsistence Herring Fishing in Togiak, Alaska.' It confirmed what his advisor had said by phone… interviews about herring.

"Who's the mayor in town?" asked Camilla.

"Huh?" asked Nick.

"We've got to get permission."

"Permission? For what?"

"I don't want to interview without permission."

Nick frowned. He didn't see why he needed permission from a mayor to talk to people. He already had talked with Harry Coopchiak about herring on the boat ride over. He had talked with Harry's aunt and uncle at their fish camp, learning about air stations and mines. They both were talking to Winnie Friendly over coffee right now. Camilla chewed her pancake.

"I don't think we've got a real mayor," said Winnie cautiously. "I think, maybe we're between mayors."

"Between mayors?"

"Maybe there's an acting mayor at the city office, acting like mayor."

"Well, then maybe we'll see him," said Camilla, adopting Winnie's doubtful tone.

"Wilson Bavilla."

Camilla wrote the name in a notebook. "And we need to talk to the tribe. Who's tribal chief?"

Winnie looked at Nick, puzzled.

"She means the chairman, the president, whatever it's called here, of the IRA council," said Nick.

"Oh, the traditional council. Why do you want to talk to him?" she asked Camilla, surprised.

"For permission to survey."

Winnie looked dubious.

"Do you know who that is, the head of the traditional council?"

"Yes," said Winnie doubtfully. "But I don't know if he'll want to talk to you. He kind of doesn't like kass'aqs."

"Oh," said Camilla.

Boots clomped outside. The outer door opened, more steps, and a loud knock. The oldest boy ran to the door. A tall kass'aq stood in the entryway, an Australian bush hat shadowing his broad tanned forehead.

"May I come in?"

Winnie stood up in shock. Two kass'aqs in her house at once! This had never happened before.

"Philip Elsberry," he said, gently taking her hand. "I wanted to check on Camilla to see if she's doing okay."

Elsberry turned to Camilla.

"Are you okay? You looked pretty green last night."

"Much better, thanks. Nicholas John, you may know Philip Elsberry? We met on the plane."

"Pleased to meet you officially," said Elsberry, shaking Nick's hand and taking a chair. Winnie kept standing apprehensively.

"I'm heading out," said Elsberry. "I thought I'd check before going."

"To Round Island? You're going today?" said Camilla.

"This morning." He quickly checked his wristwatch.

Nick appraised the tall kass'aq. He sat with such confidence he had chased the host from her seat without even noticing. Nick remembered what Harry Coopchiak had said about Elsberry.

'Thinks he owns it.'

"What's Round Island?" asked Nick.

"Walrus haul-out, part of the sanctuary, thirty-five miles that way," Elsberry waved carelessly.

"What do you do out there?"

"Research."

"Philip and I talked last night," said Camilla. "He's the reason for our herring project, it turns out."

"Well, not me," Elsberry gave a self-deprecatory chuckle. "The reason was headhunting by herring boats."

"The proposals came from you, right? A larger buffer around the island, and a single fishing period."

"Protections for the haul-out," smiled Elsberry, "new rules to create disincentives for commercial fishermen to poach between periods."

Elsberry sat smugly like self-appointed royalty. He seemed pleased the conversation had centered on him. Nick didn't much like it. And he had never liked the word, 'poach,' too often used to mischaracterize subsistence hunting. He noticed Elsberry's eyes straying down Camilla's loose blouse. What a pervert.

"You see them?" said Nick.

His eyes jerked up.

"What?"

"The poaching."

"No, not me," readjusting his gaze, irked. "That fishery ends before we set up camp. There's no one on the island when they fish for herring. That's the problem. They sneak ashore and kill walrus when nobody's there. The larger buffer will help air patrols spot the violators. Any boat within the buffer gets busted whether they're caught on the island or not. The single fishing period removes the temptation to poach during dead time."

"If nobody sees them, how do you know it's the herring boats?"

Elsberry frowned at him.

"Public Safety has suspected them for years. Black market ivory to China… the drug trade… nasty stuff."

"A worker got killed," said Camilla to Nick.

"What?"

"A herring worker drowned, a Mexican national. They found him washed ashore."

"With three headless walrus," Elsberry smiled, lifting fingers. "The current runs from the haul-out to Right Hand Point where he was found. They were working the storm."

"They?"

"Well, who else escaped with the heads?" Elsberry snickered.

Nick snarled at the insult.

"So they busted the boat?"

"No," sniffed Elsberry. "The boat got away."

"The boat claimed it wasn't involved," said Camilla. "It had a good alibi. Its engine quit. Fish and Game towed them to Dillingham."

"So they say," dismissed Elsberry. "Poachers jump ship to hunt. I'm not saying all herring boats poach. It's the renegades that jump and hunt."

Elsberry turned to Camilla, finished with Nick. Nick felt Camilla watching. He wasn't going to let Elsberry end it like this.

"How many are out there?"

"What?"

"Walrus on Round Island."

Elberry studied Nick and decided to answer.

"The counts vary. Fourteen thousand… down to several thousand now. We do the counts. Round Island is the last haul-out. It's imperative to save it."

"They pup out there?"

"No," Elsberry scoffed. "They do that on ice. The cows go north with the ice pack. Only bulls stay behind."

Nick felt the insult again. He knew little about walrus. He'd never hunted them.

"Why?" growled Nick.

"Why what?"

"Stay behind?"

Elsberry momentarily foundered.

"Dominance," he said, recovering. "Dominant males go north. Non-breeders stay behind."

Elsberry put his back to Nick.

Asshole, thought Nick. That didn't even make sense.

"Dominance? How many then?"

"What?"

"Altogether... walrus in the Bering Sea?"

Elsberry looked annoyed.

"Altogether? Two hundred thousand. That's going down too, if you want to know."

Camilla pulled Elsberry's sleeve.

"How big are walrus, the ones you study?"

Elsberry returned to her, suddenly smiling.

"Think of walrus like a car. An adult male walrus weighs as much as your car. A ton-and-a-half of power, fit with tusks a yard long. When he moves, you'd better too."

Nick hardly listened to this bragging. He was working it out. Equal births of sexes meant one hundred thousand males and females each, more or less. With fourteen thousand males on Round Island, that left another eighty-six thousand males traveling north with the pack ice. Elsberry's explanation didn't make sense. They couldn't all be 'dominant males' going north.

"So eighty-sex thousand males go north," Nick interrupted. "Fourteen thousand stay on Round Island. Why them? That doesn't sound like dominance to me."

Elsberry looked at him cross-eyed.

"That's why we do our research, to answer questions like that."

What a bombastic jerk! Elsberry pretended to know so much about walrus, and maybe he did, but he couldn't admit he didn't know why some walrus stayed behind.

"And what's the big deal, anyway?" needled Nick. "Three dead walrus out of two hundred thousand... that's nothing, biologically, right? The bodies don't waste. They feed the clams that feed more walrus. Biologically, nothing's wasted, and somebody uses the tusks."

Elsberry inflated.

"It's a sanctuary! No one should go there!"

"You go there."

"To protect it!"

Elsberry abruptly stood.

"I'm glad you're better, Camilla. If you need anything, let me know."

He offered a hand to Winnie, who looked scared.

"It was nice to meet you," he said stiffly.

Without acknowledging Nick, Elsberry clomped out.

"Jerk," Nick muttered hotly.

The house fell silent.

Nick noticed Camilla and Winnie looking at him.

Even the kids.

"Uh, Nick?" Camilla said carefully.

"Yeah?"

She looked serious, apologetic.

"Later today, when we meet the mayor and the tribe, if that happens, maybe… uh, I should do the talking?"

She lifted her dark eyebrows.

Suddenly, the serious face melted.

She began to laugh.

She laughed so hard, her hand flew up to cover her mouth.

The children converged. They jumped on her arms, pulling to find her teeth. She wouldn't let them.

She playfully wrestled.

Gave them big hugs.

And she flashed Nick a warm smile.

16

Grand designs filled him. Striding in heavy mud toward the accounts building, he arrived at his final decision about the Company. He was finished with them. He would return to St. Petersburg, and with a shocking prize. Like wind behind sails, the power of divine will drove men's lives. True men opened to receive it. Such was God's plan for him.

The ship would leave from Kodiak with him aboard, Aleksei Stepanovich Petrovskii. And at his side, Puyangun, the Koniag princess drawn from the wilderness. He'd present her to St. Petersburg, scandalous and perfectly right.

A shocking prize.

And he'd present Dmitri Alexeyevich Petrovskii, his son, born in Russian America, Aleksei the father, Puyangun the mother. Such a shock! It would be a declaration, a demonstration of God's vision, civilization and nature, born for greater things than each alone.

His accomplishment would astonish. Scandalize.

God willing, he would advance the monk's cause.

He'd challenge those who treated Russian America as an open chest for plunder, its peoples lower than peasants. With the Metropolitan's help, he'd catalyze inquiries and indictments. Moscow would be forced to amend the Company's failed charter, sweep clean the corruption, and order relief through the Holy Church.

Relief for Russian America.

Aleksei shoved aside the heavy doors of the Company. They were hewn from a single yellow cedar, set with leaded glass from Vladivostok, symbols of power and refinement.

Aleksei saw through them. They were the ornaments of pretenders, greedy merchants scrabbling for status on the backs of the enslaved. They rooted for wealth like hogs, a caste lower than the people they brutalized. Did the merchants really think beaver pelts could buy status in St. Petersburg?

Aleksei strode past them with contempt and entered his office, gold with light from the heavy panes. He gave no greeting, no glancing acknowledgement. He was done with them. He was done with this post. He prepared his final accounts. Within the week, he'd leave for home. At his side, he'd bring Puyangun and the child, upending all of St. Petersburg.

Aleksei opened the thick ledger. He turned the vellum pages, inked his pen, and worked the columns, finalizing dates and numbers and trades, recording the entries of profits and costs... sea otter pelts, fox pelts, walrus tusks, fur seal hides, beaver pelts... the unsavory pillage.

He grimaced.

He had not begun this way.

Loneliness began it. And lust.

The monks had named his sins. His high station made him worse than the rest. He had fallen farther. In despair, he fled to their dark cells. Slept on rock. Starved. The monks remonstrated his weaknesses. Ministered with kindness. Disciplined. Corrected. Instructed. He prayed. Studied. Argued. They lifted him up, offered new ways for seeing and understanding.

All the Company sinned.

This was the Devil's trade. The Natives suffered its wages. They were like children, said the monks, Nature's ignorant children. How could it be otherwise? Untaught, they knew nothing. Trapped by the Company's greed, corrupted with it, they suffered and died. The Church held the Company accountable. Russia must accept her responsibilities. She must protect the children of the new land.

He saw it now.

When he first discovered Puyangun, her face was innocence. She shined like an unblemished spring, her body without stain or infirmity. So beautiful, she drew him.

Like the Company, he selfishly took.

He nearly went mad.

It was his punishment, that fearful swell above her spread of legs, from her young belly the first deformity. It sent him reeling. The miserable crones cackled and named Cuniq, a seal hunter conscripted by the Aleuts. It goaded him to frenzy. He raged, insane with jealousy. He strode among the sod houses, blind with vengeance. He would have killed her. God's grace found her missing.

He fled to the priests, to the cloisters, to strict penance and holy mercies, a death to self and a reawakening.

There were many Godly paths, the monks counseled. Some were broad, others narrow. For the few, God reserved the narrow paths, hard and pure.

The pain he felt affirmed it. His was the hard.

He re-inked.

Final accounts.

A journey home.

Aleksei set down the pen, his tool in the sinful rape. He laid his head upon his arm and wept.

Large tears squeezed from blinded eyes.

Beneath the leaded glass, they pooled on the velum page like pus from a wound.

He would give up much.

He wept resolved.

God was merciful.

17

"This is great!"

Nick walked with her, amazed at Camilla's enthusiasm, despite the morning's failures with the mayor and the tribe. Definitely not typical. He felt the eyes of Togiak on them. They were the day's curiosities, strangers afoot in town.

Children called at them.

"Who are you?"

"Camilla," she smiled.

"What about him?"

"Nick!"

"Is that your boyfriend?"

They ran off giggling.

Within the week, all the town would know of them, the subject of conjecture, the stuff of gossip.

"You didn't answer her question," joked Nick.

"What really counts... to children, eh?"

Nick laughed.

"We're not so scary to them," said Camilla.

No, not to kids, only to mayors and tribal presidents. Bad meetings, yet Camilla looked more enthused than she had all morning.

"Oh, the view!" she exclaimed about the gleaming bay. "The houses are great!" she effused. "Hello good boys, aren't we handsome!" she praised dogs chained and staked. Their shaggy tails wagged to be recognized.

No, not typical.

Nick grudgingly concurred. Togiak was a nice place. It passed his high standards. Tidy homes stretched along sandy ridges between the wide bay and a slough. A substantial clear-water river flowed from distant mountains with runs of sockeye, Chinook, coho, and char (so said Harry Coopchiak). Seals, walrus, migratory birds, and herring frequented the bay. The uplands had moose, caribou, brown bear, beaver and fox. The air smelled wonderfully fresh. The sand gave a spring to the step. Nick saw why Togiak had become a sizable place.

That morning, Nick let Camilla do the talking, first with the acting mayor, then the president of the traditional council. He was happy to do nothing. He wasn't going to sell a project for Fish and Game.

Camilla politely introduced herself and Nick. In quiet, unemotional tones, she explained why they came to town, to interview households for a report about herring. The information might prove useful for identifying potential impacts of proposed rules in the commercial herring fishery. She hoped the project might receive endorsements from the city and the traditional council. She spoke respectfully and professionally. Then the sparks flew.

"Not doing so good, eh?" she concluded after the second failed presentation, the last with Wasky Evon.

"It's not your fault," Nick said truthfully, won over by the honest effort. "They respect you, but as soon as somebody says Fish and Game…"

"He told us to leave town!"

"He didn't," said Nick, recalling that part of Wasky's speech.

Wasky Evon, the round-bellied, hot-headed president holding the traditional council chair, hadn't wanted to talk to them, just as Winnie Friendly predicted. But Wasky's wife had let them in the house. Wasky was stuck. He sullenly listened on the living room couch. The whole while he glowered at Nick. His eyes seemed to accuse him… how can you work for the enemy? After Camilla's presentation, he railed against the continual harassment of hunters by federal and state agencies, lectured Camilla about Native rights, and stomped from the room. Then his wife brought out poached char, a fine afternoon treat. She was interested in Nick and Camilla, especially Nick from the lower Yukon.

"Nobody will talk to you," said Camilla. "You might as well go home. That's what he said."

"But he didn't tell us to leave," Nick interpreted. "He can't order us around without a council resolution."

"Is he right?"

"What?"

"Nobody will talk to us?"

"He hopes nobody will talk to us."

Camilla stopped to admire a rack of drying salmon.

"How long do they hang?" she asked enthusiastically.

"Depends," said Nick, feeling uncommonly brilliant beside her. "If it's windy and dry, less than a week. More if it's wet."

"Then they go into a smokehouse?"

"For another couple weeks."

"They smell great!"

She grinned, fully aware of her goofy behavior. Definitely, not typical, decided Nick. And she was right. The rack did smell great. Nick wondered at his reaction to this. Why did it matter to him that this silly outsider enjoyed Togiak? But it did. He felt good about it.

They strolled through a neighborhood with newer homes, interconnected by boardwalks, finding the health clinic, a single-room building tucked among weathered offices. Here was the third scheduled meeting of the day. They might find an ally at the clinic, said Winnie. And they did.

Theresa Manumik, the village health aide, welcomed them, her intelligent eyes sparkling with interest. She was short and plump and filled a scarlet kuspuk trimmed with gold brocade, round as a red potato. She served hot tea while Camilla described the project, interviews with a sample of households, if she could locate a household list.

Theresa proclaimed she'd gladly help. The clinic had a household list, regularly updated. She immediately located the list on her desktop computer to print a copy.

"Herring is a super food," declared Theresa as she worked. "Good fish oils. Iron. Kids love the eggs. They pop when you chew."

"Yeah?" said Camilla.

"We want kids to eat nutritious foods. We want them to practice good eating habits. But kids these days beg Mom for soda pop and fried chicken and sweets. That stuff's bad and expensive. The traditional diet is what's best for us... no heart disease, no diabetes, no tooth decay. Junk food is killing us!"

Theresa looked pointedly at Nick like he was personally responsible. Nick nodded his agreement, saying nothing about his own fast food habits in Fairbanks. He silently wondered about Theresa's pneumatic figure. That wasn't from eating fish eggs. He considered the waif-like Camilla, perusing the household list. Why was she so thin? What didn't she eat?

Food... essentially that's what the herring project was about, Nick realized. It was a food study, kids getting herring eggs over soda pop. The project might be important after all. Theresa Manumik was correct, of course. The Yup'iks had succeeded with traditional foods for thousands of years. If the outside boats now scooped everything from the Bering Sea for the Japanese, what would Yup'iks eat? Pizza? Would Yup'iks become consumers for the food corporations?

"Right, Nick?" asked Camilla.

"What?"

"Our meeting with the mayor was... uh, not so good."

"He didn't say no."

"Oh, that Wilson Bavilla, he should be strangled!" said Theresa.

Nick recalled that dismal meeting, just before Wasky Evon. Winnie Friendly said Wilson Bavilla was 'acting like mayor.' He didn't act very convincingly. Nick had never seen such a fidgety official. Bavilla jiggled throughout Camilla's presentation, watching a clock.

He couldn't help them, Bavilla finally declared, shooing them off like bothersome jays. It was impossible to convene a quorum of the city council, he claimed. Everybody was too busy, fishing and hunting and working. No doubt this was true, but Nick concluded Bavilla, the public servant, feared the public he served. Controversy terrified him. Bavilla wanted nothing to do with Fish and Game. He didn't want to be seen with them.

"I hoped to get a statement from the city or tribe supporting our project," said Camilla.

"You don't need them," said Theresa. "Your project helps people, because it helps subsistence. Tell them that. Everybody supports that."

"You think so?"

"I know so," said Theresa.

Here by contrast was a non-prevaricator, a woman of action, observed Nick. Theresa Manumik, barely in her twenties, knew what benefited the public health. She should be the acting mayor. Maybe she would be some day.

Theresa caught Nick looking.

She smiled back.

Nick quickly looked the other way.

18

Talliciq's shoulders ached. He rested the net and stretched his sore back. The river roared behind him. Three bright-eyed boys watched. They squatted proudly on the river's edge, waiting, their wet packs before them. They'd been at it most of the morning, playing 'qayam-yua.' They were tired, but they loved it, ready for more. The boys knew they were important. Talliciq couldn't do it alone. Only they could do what must be done.

Talliciq took up the dip net. He slowly hoisted the long pole over the rapids, carefully balanced barefoot on the wet rocks, perched below the falls. The pool boiled white. Greens and reds danced amid the billowing spray unleashed by the falls as it poured through the jumbled rocks, sharp as teeth.

Toothed Water.

A story lay behind it... the great battle between a giant and a warrior. It created the rapids and the lake. He had taught it to many boys in his lifetime. Poised with the net, Talliciq surveyed the steep slope that rose above them. An ancient slide came down there. It had blocked the river, erecting a rock dam, creating the lake behind. That made this place special. Sockeye salmon needed lakes to spawn and rear. Without that ancient quake and rock fall, this stream would have no sockeye salmon. That ancient battle had benefited the people.

Talliciq knew these rocks and the rapids that spilled from the blue lake, every sluice and slippery foothold. Few knew them as well as he did. This was his fishing place. For generations, his family had fished from the boiling pool at the foot of the rapids. Here the sockeye salmon congregated to rest, conserving their strength, building their courage before jumping the falls. They knew the challenge ahead. Like Talliciq's family, the salmon people had used the lake for generations. They knew the dangerous rocks and spillways better than Talliciq, better than even his grandfather, a great shaman who seemed to know everything.

The salmon always rested before jumping. As they rested, Talliciq's family fished. He himself had fished for the past week, though not with a dip net. He had fished with a long-poled gaff, much easier when the fish were milling. A short seine net was easier yet. But a seine required at least three men to drag it through the turbulent pool and haul it ashore filled with fish. In these hard times, such a workforce could not be mustered. So Talliciq used the gaff. A skilled fisherman perched on rocks above the pool could snag enough sockeye to fill a small rack in a morning's effort.

In his grandfather's time, when Talliciq was the bright-eyed boy, the fishing was almost like a party. So many people congregated with the sockeye. The pool was his family's fishing place, but when asked, they said yes to others. Only in poor years with few fish might they say no. The men fished and the women cut and the children romped along the grassy clearing. There were storage pits and fragrant fires and lean-to shelters. Time had erased them. The forest grew over the old racks, fallen and hoary with moss. Now, this place was hardly known and rarely visited. Talliciq came. Cuniq came. Before he was taken, Cuniq fished with his grandfather. Talliciq missed him. Now a few boys occasionally came, boys who Talliciq cajoled into work disguised as play. When Talliciq died, then who would come?

Talliciq swung the pole carefully. He aimed for a particular place where water spilled between large sharp boulders. He knew the boys eagerly watched. The eyes of children absorbed everything. They learned what they saw the first time. From this single morning, they already knew this was the one place remaining, the one waterfall left. A fish jumped, a flash of brilliant silver. It surged into the torrent, flapped its tail unsuccessfully, and fell back. Talliciq's net swung. The salmon missed. He heard a hiss behind him. The boys were holding their air. Talliciq laughed.

Talliciq rested the pole on a rock sticking from the pool to ease his aching arms. He'd never seen that rock before in all his life. That's how low it was this summer. No rain. The pool was half its size. Toothed Water still had its teeth but little water, shriveled to shallow falls between a jumble of stark granite slabs. Only this single cascade fell strong enough for the salmon to try. But Talliciq knew it was not enough. This year the rock barrier that made this place special was impenetrable, made so by the inexplicable drought.

This had happened before. All things seen by people today have happened before, Talliciq knew. In his own lifetime, he had seen this many times, though never this severe. Sometimes rains failed, rivers failed, and fish failed to spawn. Then the people suffered. Not immediately. Today, fish were easy to catch, trapped in the pool. But eventually they suffered. After four or five years, the sockeye would fail to return from the sea. That was their cycle. Several years of drought might destroy a place for the salmon people. They left to go somewhere else. Then the Sugpiat left too, abandoning the hungry place. Talliciq worried. This was the drought's second year. But his grandfather had taught Talliciq about these events. He had learned what to do.

In his youth, the shamans helped. Rains failed for reasons. The old shamans divined the causes. A man abused his wife. Families feuded overlong. A boy burned seagull feathers. Menstrual blood touched the pool. The problems got corrected. Set straight. Resolved. But in these hard times, the people were forgetting. The old shamans were nearly gone. The Russian priests were ignorant about rain, rivers, and salmon. The hermit had learned. But as for the other monks, even these young boys squatting on the bank knew more. That's why the Russians had people hunt for them. They were like untaught children from bad families. In these times, Talliciq wondered why any rains fell, there was so much trouble. What he showed these young boys, he had learned from his own grandfather at Toothed Water.

A bright flash exploded from the pool. Talliciq jabbed the net, set his feet, and pulled hard. The pole bent and bounced, nearly throwing him into the boiling water. Leaning against it, Talliciq swung the net toward shore.

"Qayam-yua!" he shouted.

The boys jumped too. One readied his pack. The others grabbed the thrashing net, water flying. Talliciq vaulted ashore. Between the boys who steadied its frame, he reached into the net and pulled the salmon free. A fat female. A large fat female. The broad smiles showed the boys saw too. Talliciq quickly laid the salmon into the one boy's pack. The other boys threw in the green moss and drenched their companion in river water, laughing.

"Qayam-yua?" Talliciq asked.

The eager boy nodded, 'yes!'

"Go!"

Off the boy sprinted. Up the trail he ran, hauling the fish-filled pack. The two boys jumped and cheered.

Talliciq hopped to the rock platform. Another fish flashed. His pole bent. He struggled across the treacherous stones to shore. A second boy readied his pack. The fish was placed, another fat female.

"Qayam-yua. Go!"

The boy raced up the trail. The last boy, too excited for his bladder, ran a few paces and pulled down his pants to urinate. By the time he was through, Talliciq hauled over the third salmon, a large male, red and hook-nosed. Talliciq was glad. The women needed men in the lake. The last pack took him, doused with wet moss.

"Qayam-yua! Go!"

The third boy raced away, yelling, trying to overtake his teammates.

Talliciq sat to catch his breath. He rubbed his calves. The morning breeze cooled his sweating face. He pulled back his wet gray hair. It cooled his neck. He was happy. With those fish, his old body had finished. Tomorrow, they'd work again. The boys agreed eagerly. They loved this game. And it was a game. 'Qayam-yua!' Talliciq laughed. He named it after a story he once heard from an old northern Yup'ik while trading skins at a lake on the mainland, high in the mountains. Talliciq traveled when he was younger. He was brave back then. They had walked to a place where people gathered to trade, the long, deep lake back in the mountains. Home of marmots. That old Yup'ik told a story about salmon. He told how the sea salmon found their way home, back to the freshwater streams of their births, the streams they had left when they were fry no bigger than a thumb. The kayak people helped them, the old Yup'ik said, 'qayam-yua,' kayak people. Little kayak people helped them upriver. So Talliciq named the young boys that, qayam-yua. They helped the sockeye home.

The first boy would be now just arriving with his fish. The run was that far, a bending, uphill path between the river and the forest, overgrown, but still easy to follow. In places, the boys must jump boulders with packs on their backs. A misstep broke a leg. It was a challenging game, a true effort. The swift runners put a live fish into the lake. No boy wanted to present a dead fish. Each ran fast!

So far this morning, all the fish had lived. The boys said it. They were good runners. In the old days when runners outnumbered packs, a runner reaching the lake threw his emptied pack into the river at a particular place, where a square rock tilted sideways. This route allowed the pack to be carried safely downstream through the torrent's teeth, over the fall where Talliciq dipped. On any other route through the rapids, the teeth swallowed the packs. Retrieved from the pool, the pack was readied with another fish on a different boy and sent up the trail before the original runner returned. But today, it was three packs and three runners, made and trained by Talliciq. No need for floating packs.

Talliciq's eyes caught movement. It was the slightest of a shadowy flicker across the water. The bear. Talliciq waited. There he was, that old man, on the far side, coming out of the willows where Talliciq watched. The bear was grizzled like Talliciq himself. He knew this old bear. And the bear knew him. They had fished from this pool for many years. Out of courtesy, Talliciq rose, picked up the dip net, and moved back. Farther from shore, he sat again. The old bear watched. Moments later, he ambled into the frothy pool. The water surged around him, chest deep, a moving rock in the roiling white. Instantly a fish appeared in his mouth. With a headshake, the bear emerged.

He always fishes better than me, with only his mouth.

He told the three boys. 'You may see a dark one,' leaving the name unsaid. 'Don't worry. That one won't hurt you. He knows you're helping the sockeye people. That helps him too. Yell as you run. At the blind bends, yell. Then he knows what you're doing.'

The bear pinned the flopping sockeye with his great paw. He stripped it clean of flesh. Leaving the bones, he mounted the bank and vanished into willows.

Going home, like me.

Talliciq gathered the gear. He started down the trail toward the sea and the kayaks. The paddle home would be with the tide. He walked slowly, suddenly very tired. Coming behind him, faint but growing louder, he heard laughter.

Three happy boys. All the fish lived.

19

Pain filled her.

And loathing.

She had meant to find other accommodations. But the agony descended.

Winnie insisted she stay put. She carved out an alcove in the linen closet for a makeshift bed. Camilla collapsed inside, tortured by pain in the muffled dark, her mind struggling through the day's work. So hard! Her head pounded like a ship's engine. The low ache began with the acting mayor. By dinner, she had trouble with her performance. She felt nauseous. Winnie noticed her wincing at the light, her brows 'pinched.' She sent her to bed with a hot water bottle.

She had not done too badly, considering she shouldn't really be there, couldn't really feel normal. But she was... had to be. She had learned from hard experience long ago that anthropology was half performance art, carefully managed presentations to strangers to worm into personal lives for contentious goals. She could do it as well as any. Today's performances were excruciating because of the pain. But they were necessary, sufficiently successful, which was what mattered. She had gained an important ally in Theresa Manumik, the health aide. She had acquired the household list. This was essential. Her meetings effectively neutralized the acting mayor and the president of the traditional council. They shouldn't pose immediate problems. Let them lurk on the sidelines, tied up in their own knots. And she'd made headway with Nick, her balky sidekick, conscripted and wary. He'd begun to swing over. He almost looked forlorn leaving her in

Winnie's care. She'd have to be careful with Nick. She didn't need complications.

God, what pain! What was it? Some goddamn neurological meltdown?

She said a silent prayer of thanks for Winnie Friendly.

I'll light a candle for you, I promise I will, just for the dark hole and water bottle.

Fucking performance art.

Tomorrow, Nick was secured even if she stayed incapacitated. He had his assignment. He'd learned a lot about herring from Harry Coopchiak on the boat ride to Togiak. He'd write it down, commit it to paper. She'd given him the formats. If he could write half as well as he observed, his notes would be dynamite. She muttered another silent prayer of thanks for Nick, a helpmeet really smart and deeply conflicted and therefore eminently malleable. She'd found a key to him early, his need for affirmation. It was good enough. He'd pull his weight. But she should be careful. Don't overdo it, no complications.

God, was she fucked!

Her fingers found her belly, flat and sunken. She pressed until it hurt.

The tears came welling up. She cried while the blackness swallowed her, taking her down once more into the pit where the nightmare waited.

They were coming for her again. Calling her.

Once again, she was way too fucked to run.

20

"Puyangun!"

The Russian's voice carried up the slope, foreign, off-key, like a strange birdcall. She spied him, her Russian, striding toward the fish rack.

She nursed the baby on the dry needles near the rack where she helped to smoke the fish. She and her baby watched the smoldering mix of alder and willow, the white waves of smoke gently rising to cover the hanging red salmon. Now and again she sprinkled water on the wood to defeat small flames whipped by the breeze. The wood should only smoke. It was slow, lazy work. She wove a basket as she watched. When the baby fussed, she nursed him on the warm earth, smelling the sweet fragrance of pine and wood smoke and fish, and thinking. She thought about Cuniq. More than anything else, she wished to see him again. And she thought about the Russian. And here he came calling, striding up the hill, as he had done yesterday, and the day before.

He smiled to see her. His sad pale eyes disappeared into moon-shaped slits. That made Puyangun happy. He should smile more. Something in a deerskin bag bounced at his hip. He stood above her, hat in hand, his fine blond hair a sun-lit halo. From the bag he pulled out a spruce hen, freshly killed. Several spruce hens. He set the bag by Puyangun, leaned his gun on a tree with the hat, and stared at the sleeping infant.

"*Kharosho*," said Puyangun, thanking him in her spare Russian. Aleksei had learned no Sugstun, unlike the monks who spoke it well. If not with Russian words, nothing got said between them.

Puyangun gathered the sleeping baby and held him up. Aleksei took him gently. Cradled in his arms, he gazed into the pudgy face. He stares like a drunk, thought Puyangun, like he's swallowed too much tobacco, oblivious to her, the smoking fire, everything but the baby. She had panicked for nothing when he found her at the fish rack. He never noticed Talliciq's sockeye. His eyes were only for the child.

Her mother would rejoice to see the gift of spruce hens. That made Puyangun happy too. Her mother seemed better with the Russian back. He was a source of fresh food. High status. Puyangun sighed. That was good too. Women like her mother struggled. So few men remained to hunt, gather fuel, protect the houses. Old men mainly. Her mother did not have even them. She had no men left. She received charity from others, second or third distributions of food going around. It was enough, though barely. All of Puyangun's life, things had been hard. Her mother's family had fallen far.

"So rich, we once had slaves," her mother proudly declared, remembering times before the Aleuts and Russians.

The family was once rich... so many men, women, and children. Deep slits along her mother's ears once hung with rich ornaments. Faded tattoos across her mother's chin, cheeks, and forehead proclaimed her wealth and status. She had been a great beauty.

"Every young man looked," she would boast.

Then she would fall silent, her face vacant, her mind staring inward, remembering.

The Great Death did it. Big men, commoners, slaves... they all died, like fish cast up by the storms. Whole families destroyed. Her mother lost almost everyone... uncles, brothers, sisters, nephews, and at the end, her husband. After the catastrophe, the Russians arrived. They relocated the remnants to this place, closer to the company traders and the priests. It happened when she was a child. Puyangun had no pierced ears for ornaments, no tattoos on chin or forehead, no marks of wealth and status. Her face was empty, the face of poverty. Her mother was ashamed to look at it.

Puyangun checked the smoldering wood. White wisps drifted on the gentle breeze, caressing the gleaming flanks that dripped with oil. Puyangun missed Cuniq. Her insides ached for him. Of everything, Cuniq had been her greatest joy. Cuniq drove the sadness from her house. A skinny girl, she noticed him, an older boy across the bay. Of that crowd, Cuniq was fastest, smartest, friendliest. Everyone said so. He had trained to become a great hunter, a good provider. Cuniq's family had suffered too. His parents were gone. But the family was never displaced, never relocated. The bay had been his family's home for generations. He had brothers and sisters, even a grandfather. Oh, how the family was envied! Puyangun could not believe it when it happened. Cuniq had noticed her too. They said he had lost his head. She was just a skinny girl, a family without people.

"How could it happen?" her mother asked.

Puyangun didn't know.

Why hadn't the Aleuts returned? She ached for Cuniq's arms, the smell of his clothes, his heaviness between her thighs. When the Aleuts took him, Cuniq knew she carried his baby. 'When the cranes return, so will I,' he vowed. Then they took him. It devastated her mother. She cried continually. She stopped working. She sat in the corner of the house, moaning. She wouldn't speak, wouldn't look up. She moaned for days.

Then the Russian appeared.

Puyangun turned on the dry needles. She looked at her baby in the Russian's arms. Tall. Fair. Moody. 'Rich and important,' they said. When he walked through the village that first time, he saw her sitting by the house, splitting willow roots, bending them into skeins to trade. She didn't like him. His pale eyes looked strange.

Soon after, things arrived at her mother's house, delivered by others, sent from the company town where he stayed. A bundle of dried cod... 'from that Russian,' they said. 'Take it,' her cousin Thekla flatly declared. At the time, the household's stores were nearly gone. Then came herring, partially dried, and then a whole poke of seal oil. Other things came too... a necklace from the white ear bones of the halibut, delicate wings strung among blue beads. And once, eight horny crabs... like giant red spiders! Thekla laughed at Puyangun's open mouth. She'd never seen crabs before. She had to ask, 'are they cooked?' And then, oh my! Three caribou! They came from the mainland. Never had she seen so much meat on the floor of her small house. She sent out children with pieces for every old man and widow. Then she sent pieces to every other household in the village. 'Who gives this?' they asked the children. 'That woman and her daughter,' they replied, eyes down. Caribou meat! What wealth was this? Things came back with the children, gifts for the caribou. Dried salmon. Tobacco. Thread. Puyangun didn't know what to think.

She had been curled up alone with Thekla, she remembered, weeping in the dark beside a mother who wouldn't speak. Cuniq was gone. She was pregnant. The stores of the house were exhausted. How would they survive? She was curled this way when the first bundle of dried cod arrived. 'Take it,' Thekla had said. And Puyangun took it. She took it, knowing what she did. Not because of Thekla, not because she said to take it.

Puyangun's mother revived. It was the seal oil, when that poke came inside. She smelled it. The smell revived her, retrieved her mind from where it wandered. She ate a bit of dried cod with the oil. And then she bathed. Puyangun walked her to the steam bath, supporting her frail arm. Puyangun washed her mother's hair and combed it out, long and nearly all black. Puyangun cried combing it out. She cried because her mother had come back.

Finally, the Russian came himself. That day he carried a small wooden barrel of berries. Puyangun's mother let him in. He crawled through the entry and set the barrel beside the hearth. He sat between them. He talked. He spoke in Russian, polite and serious. He was hard to understand. Puyangun's mother fed him. Going out, he said he'd come again, maybe tomorrow. And the next day when he came, it was Puyangun who let him in. Her mother had left to stay with friends. That's how it was.

Now he was back again, holding her baby, a boy who grew fat from her milk. Puyangun was the envy of the village, suddenly desirable, a young woman with a healthy boy baby, a true celebration. She showed what she could accomplish. She was proud... and embarrassed. 'Of course the Russian returned,' said Thekla, knowingly. 'Such a fine baby!' He brought spruce hens today. It was moose meat from the mainland yesterday. The first day, he brought trout and a bundle of blue flowers, given to her mother.

He was always quick with her. He took his pleasure on the furs above the sunken hearth pit. Afterwards, he'd talk. She always listened. No matter when he came for her, afterwards he'd stay to sit by the fire to talk, long discourses like the elders in the maqiwik. He talked about trading, or the priests, or his home in St. Petersburg. He spoke of many things, sometimes loudly, sometimes softly, at times angrily. She'd always listen carefully, completely, though his words were hard to follow. 'The Russians are strange people,' Thekla said. Puyangun tried hard to understand him. He was moody, struggling with emotions and desires, endeavoring for things Puyangun could only imagine. He spoke unlike anyone she'd known. And sometimes after his long speeches, he'd come on her again. The second time, he was always slower, gentler.

But not now, not this time… coming back after the baby's birth, he was not the same, not himself. He barely spoke. He sat with her, quietly holding the baby, as he did today. He sat subdued, almost sad. He gave no angry speeches, no long discourses that jumped between people and places and things. Only his eyes spoke, a new kind of strangeness. They spoke of yearnings, sad adorations. And he had not touched her! This was the other change. Today was the third afternoon. Still he just stood. He was there, yet missing. To Puyangun, he seemed almost like her mother, moaning in the corner of the house, lost somewhere in her wandering mind. Or like her Cuniq lost to the western seas. Oh, how she ached! How lonely it was.

"Sit," said Puyangun simply.

She took the sleeping child. She tucked him inside the cradle pack, sheltered in the shade.

"Sit," said Puyangun again more gently, looking up to her Russian, standing separate and lost to his old self. As she said it, she pulled on the hem of her summer dress. It was a light shift of soft blue cotton made by her mother of cloth from the Russian. Puyangun pulled the hem up her slim bare legs. Drawing his eyes into hers, she leaned back on her elbows. She lay on the dry pine needles fragrant with wood smoke and pulled the hem above her naked thighs.

"Come," said Puyangun, this time for herself, lonely and aching.

Aleksei's body stiffened. His eyes fixed on Puyangun's legs. They winced with sudden pain, and as quickly, filled with the sadness of a man bereft of all human things. His lips twisted and froze with some immeasurable regret. His hand rose to adjust an imagined clasp at the neck. It drifted to the top of his empty head. Haltingly, he stepped to the tree, like a child learning to walk, finding the hat and gun. When he finally spoke, almost inaudibly, something broke within her.

"I'm going."

From the frozen mouth the words twisted.

"It's good as we are. You will see. Just as now, as we are."

He raised three fingers.

"Three more days."

Then he lurched away down the hill.

Puyangun heard his steps fade. But she didn't watch. She turned toward the fish rack. From below, it seemed that she had turned to check the smoke. She looked for wind-whipped flames. Or, she turned to the baby, to see that he slept within the pack beneath the trees. But that was not why she turned from the Russian.

She turned to hide her weeping.

21

Nick found Camilla too sick to work. She hid in the semi-dark of the alcove fixed with a narrow bed by Winnie, nauseous and in pain.

"Can you work without me?" she asked, apologetic.

Nick assured her that he could.

He would start the surveys. And he would write up what Harry Coopchiak had told him about herring during the trip from Goodnews Bay. He had everything he needed to start.

Camilla thanked him and pulled a pillow over her eyes.

Nick sat at the kitchen table, wondering about her. She seemed fine yesterday. Aloysius Friendly appeared, Winnie's husband, a commercial fisherman and general purpose craftsman. He took an instant liking to Nick.

"Come every day to eat," said Aloysius, sitting for his second breakfast. He had already been out working.

"Okay," grunted Nick through a mouthful of smelt fried with onions. They tasted wonderful.

"Yeah, they're pretty good," said Aloysius, laughing heartily, taking some for himself.

As Nick ate, Aloysius showed him a series of snapshots of boats owned by his family, arranged in a photo album, from turn-of-the-century rowboats and half-horse kickers to his current Togiak skiff. Nick grunted in appreciation. The pictures illustrated the sweep of history on the Bering Sea. Technology changed, the fishing remained.

He pointed to his father sitting in the bow of the plank rowboat, a funny cap on his head.

"Before motors, they spent all day rowing," said Aloysius.

"What do we do with all the free time?" joked Nick.

"Fix them," said Aloysius, pushing from the table.

He was off to fiddle with a finicky engine. He waved goodbye to Winnie and clomped out the door.

Nick watched the fond farewell. Here was a solid union. Nick wondered if he'd ever know one. He took more smelt.

"What are you doing today?" asked Winnie.

Nick pointed to his household list.

"Surveys. Then write up my notes from your brother."

"My brother? You surveyed him?"

"We talked coming over from Goodnews. I'm supposed to write it down before I forget. And then," said Nick happily, "I'm heading over to your family's camp at Nanvak Bay. Herbert Small is taking me egg hunting."

"Egg hunting?" said Winnie doubtfully. "It's too late for eggs."

Nick shrugged.

Winnie sighed wistfully.

"We never went yet."

Nick nodded sympathetically. She missed her family's camp, an exceptionally good place. Nick wanted to see it again. And the exotic, attentive Lydia.

"Maybe Camilla can go," said Winnie, brightening at the thought. "She'd feel better at camp."

"Yeah, maybe," muttered Nick.

* * *

The spray rose in clouds from the great swells that crashed below. Nick climbed the sea cliff, Herbert Small leading the way. It was dangerous and exhilarating, but it wasn't hard. The rugged rock, seamed and shattered, had weathered into complex handholds and ledges allowing an ascent if taken slowly. Cutting palms on rough outcrops was the chief danger. Nick looked above him at Herbert's boots, then down at the crashing surf. The boat rocked on the swells forty feet below. Camilla had come along with them to Cape Peirce, eager to see a fish camp. Her nausea had dissipated. She chose to remain with the elder Coopchiaks at the tents to learn about herring. Lydia looked longingly after Nick and Herbert as they left for the bird cliffs. She wanted to come, but she stayed to help translate for Camilla and her grandparents.

Herbert wasn't searching for eggs after all. It was too late for eggs, he said. He was after dead puffins.

"Dead puffins?" asked Nick.

"Their beaks," laughed Herbert.

Herbert had an Alutiiq friend, a dancer, met at the last convention of the Alaska Federation of Natives. He needed new dance rattles. Dried puffin beaks made the best sound. Herbert said he'd get some.

For the first hour, Herbert and Nick had climbed among low-lying rocks used as roosts by puffins, murrelets, and guillemots. Clambering upon the lower roosts, they found the remains of dead birds, caught in cracks above the waves. They stuffed two-dozen tiny puffin bodies into a trash sack.

"I'll cut off the beaks later," Herbert shouted above the surf.

"Good idea!"

Now Herbert led Nick straight up the cliff. He wanted to show him something special. He wouldn't say what. Birds scattered from their path, soaring angrily around the intruders in great shifting curtains. Nick followed carefully. The salty wind cooled his sweating cheeks. The boat rocked in the white foam far below.

"Here!" shouted Herbert.

Nick scrambled over a knife-edged lip and squatted at the mouth of a small recess that shoved into the rock wall, sheltered by overhangs. It formed the entrance to a cave.

"Look inside," said Herbert.

"How far does it go?"

"Not far."

Nick's eyes adjusted to the shadows. Bones lay just inside the narrow mouth among debris from old nests. Hefty bones. And a jaw with massive teeth, squat and yellowed.

"Wow!" said Nick.

It was a brown bear skull.

Herbert grinned.

"How'd it get up here?" asked Nick.

"I found it last year."

"Did it fall?" Nick craned his head back, trying to glimpse the top of the cliff.

"There's no way up from the other side. I tried it."

"Somebody put it here?" asked Nick.

"Look," said Herbert, pointing further into the recess.

On the floor lay bundles of weathered bones tied with rawhide, hardened by time, among scattered chips of flint, knocked from ancient tools. Further mysteries. Somebody put the bear in the cliff with the bundles.

"Wow," exclaimed Nick again.

"Come on," grinned Herbert, starting the downward climb.

Nick took a final look at the bones. People had been using these cliffs for generations, he guessed. Why someone would do this, Nick didn't know, placing a bear skull in a crack of a bird cliff fifty feet above the crashing sea. Herbert probably wasn't the first to discover the secrets of this crevasse. He followed after him, leaving the remains to awe the next generation of egg gatherers.

They motored into camp in the early evening's calm. Camilla and Lydia waited for them on the beach like old friends. Lydia ran into the surf, laughing, and helped to pull the boat ashore.

"Let's go up," she said, pointing behind her.

"Okay," grinned Herbert.

"Where?" asked Nick.

Lydia smiled slyly.

"Cape Peirce," answered Herbert. "It's got a great view."

"You coming?" Nick asked Camilla.

"Of course," she said, a glint in her eye. The boat ride to camp had cured her, she claimed. She patted her backpack. "Water, binoculars, berry buckets. We've been waiting for you guys."

The trail up Cape Peirce from the Coopchiak's camp skirted a sandy edge of Nanvak Bay. Tall grass sighed in the soft breath of the evening, swishing between their knees. Driftwood half-buried in the sand cradled crops of beach greens and seedy sedges. Herbert, the youngest, took the lead. Lydia walked beside Nick. Camilla followed last. They mounted a rise between low dunes and stopped.

"Walrus!" gasped Camilla.

A group of walrus rested in a sandy saddle, right in the path. They glowed cinnamon brown in the evening's light. A large male lifted his head to assess the newcomers. His nostrils twitched and flared. He could smell them. He huffed, immediately rose, and shuffled toward the bay. Camilla watched fascinated. He moved quickly for an animal the weight of a car. His hind flippers rotated beneath him to become another set of feet. He ratcheted down the face of the dune on front and back flippers like a practiced quadruped. The walrus reminded her of the bats that walked on land using wings for front legs, a surprising skill for fliers. This walrus was a sea creature. Yet he could amble nimbly across the land.

"He's fast!" whispered Camilla.

"They can run as fast as me or you, if they want to," Lydia whispered back. "Give them lots of room. If they get angry, they spit rocks. You always find rocks inside them."

Another walrus lifted his head, huffed, and did likewise, lurching for the bay. Abruptly, the whole group woke, rose, and followed.

"They're big!" enthused Camilla.

"They always hang out in here," said Lydia.

"Sleeping," said Herbert.

"That's why we've got biologists," said Lydia glumly.

"Biologists?" asked Camilla.

"That way." She motioned vaguely. "It used to be just us."

"What are they doing here?" asked Nick.

"Spying," said Herbert.

"That's what we think," said Lydia. "They say biology. But we think they're spies."

Herbert walked up the saddle vacated by the walrus. A faint trail rose on the far side going up the back of Cape Peirce. The path wound steeply along a ridge covered in crowberry, bearberry, and dwarf shrubs. They took it, climbing higher and higher. The wind began blowing. Lydia's shell ears turned red in the brisk air. The vistas improved with every rise. They came to another path that entered from the left.

"That comes up from the other side, near the biologists' camp," said Lydia. "We'll go this way. Watch out. It gets steep."

Shortly the group stood on a vantage high on the top of Cape Peirce. Wind whistled around them. Seabirds whirled below. The hill tipped over and fell downward in steep green slopes that vanished in dizzying vertical drops. The views were magnificent. Directly to the southeast they could see Hagemeister Island, the place that once had a reindeer herd. To the northwest they saw the great mountains above Cape Newenham. Inland, reddish hills rose toward mountains that gleamed silver in the distance, the headwaters of the great rivers. They took turns with the binoculars. No boats plied the waters that evening. They stood alone in the world at the edge of the great sea with only wind and birds for company.

"I'm cold," said Lydia. "Come on, Nick."

Lydia took Nick's hand and pulled him back down the trail. Nick went without complaint.

"We're taking the other way," she shouted to her cousin.

"Walrus," murmured Herbert to Camilla. He pointed directly below to a crescent beach peeking beneath the cliff.

Camilla took the binoculars and focused below her. A group of walrus rested on the narrow beach.

"They always come here?" she asked.

"Not always."

"I thought Round Island was the last haul-out," said Camilla, repeating what Philip Elsberry had said many times. Herbert shrugged his shoulders. Then he pointed out something toward the salt chuck around Nanvak Bay. Camilla swung her glasses along the edge of the bay and saw them. Men. One. Two. Three. They walked among the brush and disappeared.

"Miners," declared Herbert.

"Miners?"

"Yeah."

"What are they doing?"

Herbert shrugged again. Camilla guessed he was unused to talking with strangers like her.

"Are they prospecting?" she asked, passing back the glasses.

"Looking for gold, I guess." He followed them for a while. "Let's go get some berries." He found food containers from his pack.

He and Camilla walked slowly back down the slope, zigzagging among the stunted shrubs, gathering crowberries. They were last year's crop, sweet, nearly fermented, and sagging in their skins. The bugs found them working, gnats, whining mosquitoes, and biting flies. The wind couldn't reach the cape's backside. They swatted and sweated to fill the containers. Toward the bottom of the slope, Camilla spied tents in the distance. It was the biologists' camp. Herbert saw them too and motioned to go the other way. He shouldered the pack with its berries and began walking. He wanted nothing to do with biologists.

"I'll catch up," said Camilla.

"Okay!" he shouted.

Camilla sat on a lichen-covered rock with a breeze against the bugs and scanned an empty horizon, alone with her thoughts. Herbert reached a rise. He turned to check on his guest and found her through the binoculars. She sat with the stones looking toward the far mountains in the late evening light. Tears flowed down her cheeks.

* * *

Nick lay against Lydia in the grass, staring into her fair face. The edges of her ample mouth smiled. Her large eyes were half closed, thick with lashes. She slowly leaned forward and they kissed again, softly brushing parted lips, feeling the silkiness, the warm moist breath, the touch of noses on reddened cheeks chapped by wind. Nick closed his eyes. He burrowed closer against her, their legs wrapped together. She laughed and reached lower. He grabbed her hands, trapping them between their shirts.

"Not now," he laughed and opened his eyes into hers.

So large. Beautiful. Uncanny. Familiar.

"Why not?" she laughed lightly and feigned a struggle.

Nick didn't know why not. The deepest parts of his body ached. So did hers. It was wonderfully beautiful and strange, because it was all sweetly familiar. In the back of his mind was an odd sensation that this had happened before. They were reliving, repeating, reawakening.

"Wait," he whispered again, brushing hair behind her beautiful ears.

Lydia pulled away and put on a pout.

"Is this how it is with Yukon boys? They worry and wait?"

"Maybe it's girls who should worry and wait," he teased back, stroking the ear. "Who knows what they are like?"

"How?"

"What?"

"How are they like?"

"Oh, the Yukon boys," he gave a wry smile, "they like money."

"Money!"

"Girls with lots of money."

"Money," said Lydia with disgust.

"Rich women, plump old rich women, the ones they call cougars... rich old women with pots of money and blue chip stocks and Hawaiian beach condos. That's what they are like."

Lydia pulled further away, pouting more.

"Well, too bad for them."

"Why?"

"Even you stay long enough, you will not know. The girls here aren't that way! They know what is real... what is best... the nukalpiat, the good hunters, generous, always giving, dressed at the feasts in fine parkas, the good hunters from families with good names."

With a wave, she dismissed his jeans and cotton shirt.

They lay apart in silence. Nick heard her breathing, her eyes nearly closed. She meant for him to go next.

"Well, too bad for them... and for me, because where I live... it's the big city, a hard place for good hunters. How could they ever know? I'm generous with nothing to give, a hunter with no place to hunt, just a poor orphan... raised by his grandmother for the hard life and all that comes with that, the good and the bad."

With a burst of laughter, Lydia grabbed his arms, wrestling him into the grass.

"Then we are matched!" she laughed. "I'm an orphan too! My grandparents raised me, but they taught me only the good!"

She kissed him.

Nick kissed back.

His mind reeled pleasantly. He saw what was happening. He was falling under the spell of this fish camp beauty. He was becoming bewitched by Lydia. She arched her back above him and stared into his eyes.

"You're beautiful," whispered Nick.

"So are you."

They joined for another kiss. Their hips moved together. Lydia's hands reached lower. This time Nick didn't stop her.

A cheery voice called from the distance, light and ironic.

"Nick! Lydia!"

"Shit!" whispered Nick.

"Don't move," Lydia gasped, smothering his body with hers lower into the grass.

"Nick! Herbert says we've got to go!"

"Stay!" hissed Lydia into Nick's ear.

Nick rolled and sat up, dumping Lydia on her back. Camilla stood a stone's throw away, pretending to stare elsewhere. Lydia sat up too.

"Sorry guys. Herbert wants to go. It's getting late. He said to find you."

Lydia giggled and whispered something in Nick's ear, something about Camilla... 'she's nice, I like her,' or was it, 'she's nice, do you like her?'

He felt his face flushing.

"How'd you find us?" asked Nick plaintively.

Camilla pointed to the air above them.

"The buzzards."

Swirling above their grassy nest, whirling in ecstatic dodges and pirouettes, flashed the giddy swallows.

"Your tuunraq," teased Lydia.

She nosed his ear and spoke fondly into it.

"We will never need Pik."

* * *

They pushed off from the Coopchiaks' camp in the extended twilight, a band of silver lighting the way to the far horizon. Gentle waves shushed against the boat. The scrap dogs barked on the beach. 'Come again soon,' Lydia pleaded into his face before he boarded, bestowing a parting kiss. Nick watched her form fade into the dusk with a heavy longing and strange discomfort. Camilla looked away in the bow. A faint smile etched her mouth. Or was it a hint of pain? Lydia faded. Camilla remained, an angular sprit pointing the way to dark waters. Her short black hair fluttered in the wind.

She leaned back and pressed something into Nick's hands.

"Look," Camilla whispered, indicating a place on the shore where lights shined.

Nick found he held binoculars. He focused on the shore. A light from butane lamps illuminated a wall tent pitched on a rise above a narrow beach. Nick saw men working a fire smoldering in a grate. One smoked a cigarette. Another cooked. A third stood ramrod straight, looking out into the bay, staring directly at their boat with his own field glasses. The man lowered his. Nick gasped.

"What?" asked Camilla.

"Nothing," said Nick.

"Miners," declared Herbert from the stern, directing the boat through the narrows and into the swells of the Bering Sea.

Nick sat back and pondered the day's events, the early interviews and note taking at Togiak, the afternoon's ride to the Coopchiaks' camp, the search for puffin beaks and the bear skull mysteriously cached in the cliff, the breathtaking views from atop Cape Peirce. His aching body pressed against Lydia's. Her soft lips against his. 'Come again soon,' she had whispered and kissed him goodbye. And this final sight through the binoculars, men on the beach, one smoking, one cooking, and one watching their departure, ramrod straight in a work shirt, a sour hard-chinned face with an unforgiving expression Nick had seen before and had not yet forgotten.

It was the commando in camouflage and tall black boots, the commando scowling from the rear of the plane because Nick had dared to ask a comrade, 'where are you headed?'

Newenham.

Nick was sure about few things in life, but he was sure about this one.

Those weren't miners.

"Nick?"

Camilla's voice pulled him back.

"Yeah?"

"What's Pik?"

"What?"

"Mosquito coils!" Herbert shouted from the outboard. "For mosquitoes!"

Camilla thought it through, what Lydia had said in the grass.

"Oh, yeah."

She gave Nick a warm smile.

22

Cuniq unlashed his war bow.

His hand found an arrow.

He hid within the alders on the hillside, watching through narrowed eyes. He was too far to see well, too far to hear voices. His breath came roughly, not from the jog on back trails to arrive in secrecy, but because of the enemy on the knoll, standing above Puyangun.

The Russian.

It took his breath away.

Here was the keeper of records, the man who had driven him almost to his death. Here was the Russian who had forced him to join the Aleuts with threats about Puyangun.

He was placed wrong. His enemy held the higher ground. He carried a heavy gun for killing bears, a gun for battle.

The shot was too long.

The Russian reached to his side. He presented something to Puyangun... a sack. He leaned the weapon against a tree. Cuniq rose off his knees. He could charge the knoll.

Puyangun lifted a bundle.

The Russian took it.

Cuniq froze. A baby! His heart pounded.

Wait... watch...

The Russian cradled it.

Puyangun took the baby back, put it somewhere beside her. He couldn't see. She was low to the ground. Now the Russian put on his hat. He took up the bear gun, said something. He turned and strode down the hill's backside.

Cuniq unclenched the bow. His hand had cramped from the arrow. What was happening here? The Russian held the baby. Puyangun took it back. He walked away.

Cuniq rolled to his feet. He sprinted down the slope, hidden by alders. He saw the hated Russian enter willows. Cuniq moved to intercept him. He ran with the bow and nocked arrow, plunging into the willow patch, breathing deep for battle. The willows ended. He skidded behind a mossy rock and peered cautiously over.

Below him, sod houses peppered the shoreline. The Russian strode toward beached boats at the water's edge, his back to Cuniq, still too far for a bowshot. Aleuts lounged around them, seven or eight men in Company clothes, some with guns across their shoulders. Seeing the Russian, they readied a boat. Cuniq's breathing slowed. He watched a boat push from shore with the Russian and several men. They vanished in the glare toward the outer point, the direction of the Russian town.

The enemy was gone.

A few dispirited dogs staked at the village margins watched the boat depart, too listless to stand in the midday heat.

The other Aleuts remained. Two moved along the main path winding among the sod houses. They disappeared behind storage caches near the mudflats. Others lingered with the boats. Cuniq knew them. And they would know him. He was the conscript assigned to a kayak in the party sent for sea lions. They'd greet him with deep suspicion. Where were the skin boats? Where was the Company?

Cuniq withdrew into the willows.

His arrow found its sheath.

His bow found its place across his back.

The Russian must wait.

* * *

The ancient maqiwik where the old men bathed rose from the earth at the village edge. Roofed with thick turfs of grass, it formed an indistinct mound among the undulating tussocks. Thin white plumes of smoke drifted above it in the twilight.

Inside, the fire pit glowed a dull red. Its heat rose and fell in sluggish waves upon a planked platform. The hot air felt thick on the skin, smelling of cedar and sweat.

In the hot silence, a shadow emerged from a black hole near the fire pit. It quickly shed clothes, searched among the bark containers blackened with pitch, and found a plug of pine shavings. It took a place among the old men, hunkered beside the glowing pit.

Each man sat in his own hot pool on the cedar planks, worn smooth as glass. Rivers of sweat ran off the old shoulders. Scalding drips collected on brushy bows and trickled down the wrinkled necks and hunched backs. Skin flowered red with ruptured vessels among old bruises and scalds, the camouflage of lifetimes of burning.

"So much!" the newcomer exclaimed.

The old men grunted in agreement.

The maqiwik fell quiet, the silence of shared suffering.

Time moved slowly.

The fire died to thin coals.

Without a word, a man produced a long pole. He poked at the ceiling and adjusted the smoke hole to tease in a breath of fresh wind. He added wood to the pit and prodded a flame for light. The fire pit danced with bright flames.

Another man passed out wooden vessels. A third ladled hot water. With much sloshing, the bathing commenced. After final rinses, the bathers reclined comfortably on the platform for drying.

"I'm home," announced the newcomer.

The first words spoken.

Immediately Cuniq felt foolish. Of course he was home.

The old men grunted anyway.

"I'm glad," affirmed Talliciq.

His favorite grandson was home again.

"I did not see the boats," said an old man.

"I came alone."

The elders cocked their ears for more. They knew the Russians had sent out a party for sea lion skins, yet here was Cuniq alone.

"I beached at Toothed Water... too many Aleuts."

Someone passed around a pouch of tobacco. Each man shoved a black wad beneath his lower lip. They sucked and waited, cooling beneath the cracked skylight.

Cuniq began the story they wanted, addressing the flames.

He told of the journey westward, the empty haul-outs, and the unfilled quota of skins. He told of paddling through the narrow straits into the northern sea, goaded by the overlord. He described the company's fear on finding the haunted

138

islands in the fog, then the sea lion drives, the wasteful skinning, and finally, the fever that struck the men, one by one.

"The wasteful suffer," grunted one.

"The uncleaned bones cry out," said another.

Cuniq described his mistake, harpooning the pregnant isuwiq, how he revived her pup and found a new mother.

The old men chuckled. Talliciq frowned. But Cuniq caught a smile at the corners of his mouth.

Then the disaster... the missing sentries, his failed escape, the noseless demon, and waking on the sea. He told of the unnatural storm, the dead company, and the ghost boats. In detail, he described the walrus attacks, the great bull's head embedded in the outrigger, and the sea anchor that had saved him.

"Good," an elder said.

Finally, Cuniq described the journey home. Sea birds took him to land, islands in the territory of the Aleuts. He skirted desolate shores with empty hamlets, devastated by the Russians. He crossed the strait to the homeland and beached in secret at Toothed Water. Taking back trails, he found Aleuts lounging with guns.

Here Cuniq ended.

The old men considered the journey.

"They are all dead?" asked one.

"They swam with their boats."

"The other kayak too?"

"That too."

"They have all gone beneath the sea."

"The Aleuts will see him. They will ask why that one lives."

"They will want revenge."

"If they find out."

"The Russians will let them."

There was silence again. The maqiwik grew cold. A bather began dressing. Everybody followed. The old men departed, one after the other, all but Talliciq, alone with Cuniq.

"Grandfather," said Cuniq tenderly.

"Yes," Talliciq smiled at his lost grandson, now returned.

"At the drying racks, I saw Puyangun. She did not see me. I saw a baby."

"Puyangun's baby," smiled Talliciq. "It came out a boy."

A boy!

"And at the racks, the Russian," said Cuniq. "The one who keeps the books. He held the baby."

Talliciq frowned and spoke cautiously.

"My grandson, this is dangerous. You will hear about that Russian, how he fed her mother. All winter, he fed her. Before the birth, he left them. He was angry. Now he's back. Now that it's a boy, he is back."

Cuniq flushed with jealousy.

"But the sockeyes you saw," said Talliciq, "on the rack watched by Puyangun, they came from Toothed Water. Puyangun dries the sockeyes from Toothed Water."

"Ah!" said Cuniq.

His grandfather's catch. Talliciq was feeding Puyangun.

"The Russians take what they want," cautioned Talliciq.

"They cannot take what isn't here."

"The Aleuts make them strong."

"I will not die like a slave."

Talliciq sat in silence. Finally, he spoke.

"The company is surely gone under the sea. That noseless warrior sent them there. All of the company but one. All but you."

Cuniq nodded.

"The Russians will learn of this. The elders are right. The Russians will ask, 'why?'"

Cuniq grunted.

Talliciq waited.

"My grandson, why?"

Now it was Cuniq who sat in silence, pondering the puzzle.

"I don't know why," said Cuniq. "They left me in my kayak with water and food. When they pulled me from the sea, they argued. They found the point in the pendant. I gave it to the noseless warrior. He spoke of dreams and walrus. I couldn't understand him. What was it about? I don't know. A warrior clubbed me. I woke in the kayak, left with water and food."

"What do you mean, the point in the pendant?"

"The pendant you made, a harpoon dart hit the center. They joined. That is how they caught me."

"Huh! Let me see."

"I gave it to that demon. I gave the pendant to him."

"Ah!"

So that was why. The noseless warrior had accepted it as a gift, not plunder. He let Cuniq live. A pendant for a life.

"That was a good pendant," said Talliciq with a wry smile, "but that good?"

They both laughed.

"I came back for you, Grandfather," said Cuniq with deep affection. "I came back for Puyangun."

They embraced.

"Stay hidden," cautioned Talliciq.

"I will prepare at Toothed Water."

"Remember, Puyangun has a mother and cousins. Stay hidden. Be patient. Wait while I learn of things."

"What things?"

"I do not know. That Russian who keeps the books is not himself. Since he came back, something is wrong in his head."

"What?"

"I do not know. Wait while I learn what he is thinking."

"Who knows what Russians think?"

"Wait."

* * *

A mirror!

Puyangun held it by its edges.

Her mouth hung open and Thekla laughed.

Puyangun's mother laughed too, giddy. She moved ceaselessly among the gifts from the Russian stacked on the mud-packed floor... cloth, iron pots, knives, dried fish, a seal poke, and more. She weaved in and out in a nervous dance.

"Such wealth!"

She caught her breath and tried to speak. She could only say it again.

"Such wealth!"

She sat on the floor to let her heart catch up.

Puyangun had never held a mirror.

She stared at it in disbelief.

"That's you!" proclaimed Thekla.

"Me?"

"Come outside!"

She pulled her cousin into the sun.

"Look," Thekla ordered.

Puyangun looked in the full light and gasped.

This was her face?

It looked like... like... her mother! Younger! Hair thicker, blacker. Skin smoother. Nose smaller. The face in the mirror looked like her mother. And Thekla! It was a version of Thekla too!

"This is me?"

Thekla snatched the mirror from Puyangun. She held it in such a way that both she and Puyangun could look together.

"Is that me?" demanded Thekla.

"Yes!"

"Then that's you!"

Puyangun stared at the reflection, awed.

Every detail clear, set before her eye, like she'd never seen before.

"I… I look like you!"

"Yes! And I look like you!"

"And I look like… my mother," whispered Puyangun.

This was her mother's face, except the skin was young and smooth, the chin smaller, rounder, and unblemished, the forehead clear and unlined. Just like her mother's face except… empty. A face of poverty. A face of disgrace.

A face her mother could not look at without shame.

A face that drove others away.

"Thekla."

"Yes?"

"Send for Uukuk."

"Uukuk?"

"Have them say, 'bring your needles.'"

Puyangun held the Russian's mirror closer, resolved.

This night she would come, Uukuk's back to the fire, her thick fingers at her throat, her rabbit heart beating, the pit ash needle pricking, blood oozing.

Pain and tears.

Then tomorrow.

A new sun.

When I look in you…

She spoke to the mirror.

I will not hold my shame.

23

Camilla took the rough path toward the beach.

The sun glared off the water painfully.

She had somehow missed Nick.

Yesterday they interviewed households. Another round was scheduled today. Maybe he sat among the boats working on fieldnotes. He was not in the rented water tank. She couldn't blame him for that, it was an abomination. The creosote burned her eyes when she searched it to find him. How could Nick even breathe?

She escaped for air. Too late.

The pain erupted.

She had finally put a name to it.

Migraine…

The poison in her brain. This was what plagued her.

A string of migraines.

She'd never had them before. Not one.

Camilla surveyed the empty stretch of sand. Beach grass blew in the gusts between abandoned skiffs. She squinted at the over-bright sea. Faint islands shimmered on its rim like dancing watermarks on rice paper. The Walrus Islands. The farthest lump was Round Island where the Lothario worked.

The light cut like a knife blade.

The smell of the tank had triggered it.

Shielding her eyes from the glare, Camilla weaved through knee-high brakes of grass toward the boats. Nick might be crunched beside them. That was where he had worked yesterday.

She shut her eyes to the agony and stepped off the path, stepped wrong, something soft, squishy, concealed beside the trail. She twisted and fell.

A dog!

Its oily coat unleashed a cloud of gnats.

Camilla gagged and rolled, choking on flies, cracking her eyes to blood. She retched.

Pain hammered her. She stood, nearly blind, and stumbled toward sandblasted sheds.

A dead dog gunned down on the beach.

Something grabbed!

With a yank, she jerked free, flew sideways, and slammed into wood.

"Sorry!"

The snatcher hopped.

"Sorry! Sorry! Sorry!"

"Gawd! I'm gonna puke!"

"Here! Sit here!"

Camilla collapsed on an upturned spool emptied of cable. She hunched, holding her guts while the world pounded. The snatcher bobbed and weaved.

"A dog's dead out there!" she choked.

The dance stopped.

"Shot!"

He abruptly vanished.

Run!

Some part of her screamed.

Run for it!

The rest refused.

Let him shoot you.

He reappeared, a shadow beside her.

"I know that dog."

"It's shot!"

"Yeah."

The dance began again.

The nausea ebbed. She squinted through pain at the dancing man. Sweat dripped down his face. So nervous, he sweated. She saw no guns.

"Do I know you?" she gulped.

The dance stopped.

"I was looking for you. You're her, right? That herring girl?"

Anthropology. Performance art.

She painfully extended a hand.

"Camilla... Mac Cleary."

"Wassulie Evon."

His palm was slick with sweat.

"Yeah, Wassulie... nice to meet you. But I'm really sorry. I feel like crap. Total crap. My head's ready to explode. I want to barf. I almost lost it with that dog."

She willed her eyes through the painful light.

"You don't look so great either."

Abruptly, springs released. The jiggling frame unhitched. Wassulie slid to the ground with a sigh, a heap of sand and broken shells from a thousand years of storms. He leaned against the sun-bleached shed and rubbed sweat across his brow. This was no mad stalker or dog killer. This was a nervous kid, barely free of high school.

"So what's up, Wassulie? Herring? That's why I'm here... herring."

It was all of the project's preamble she could muster.

"No, no... not, uh... herring."

Camilla waited. The hammering lessened. Thoughts lengthened. Wassulie's tremors began again. He struggled like a puppet jerked by strings.

"Not herring, it's uh, for the, uh... Ouija board!"

With a final jerk, he conquered the shakes.

"Ouija board?" Camilla thought hard.

"The Ouija board... the teacher..."

Where was her pack? An inviolate rule of fieldwork was proving true. You never had your stuff when you needed it. She focused past the pain.

"What teacher?"

"Ms. Wickhauser... high school."

Wassulie Evon's face abruptly brightened.

"Debra Wickhauser, New Jersey. By New York. Yeah, by New York City! Everybody likes her. Because she loves to teach. She picked us... she picked Togiak."

Wassulie began laughing.

"Her parents think she's crazy. That's too far away! Too dirty! Anything that's not paved is too dirty for them."

Camilla studied the mercurial affect. It was obvious. The boy was smitten. Wassulie Evon adored the teacher from New Jersey.

"But it's not her parents. No, not them... it's the... the Ouija board!"

He frowned, stopping to remember.

"What Ouija board?" prompted Camilla.

"For the class... yeah, she always did things like that, for the class." He said it defensively. "With her own money, you know, to challenge the group, to get us to think. Everybody worked hard. They took the Challenge Camp. Did you know that? First place at Challenge Camp."

"She sounds great."

"Yes!"

"Why a Ouija board?"

"Because we found it in a book."

"In a book."

"We said, 'what's that? What's a Ouija board?' We didn't know. 'A game with a dial that answers questions,' she said. But we didn't get it. So she got one. She brought it back so we could see. That's all."

"Yeah, a board everybody could see... what happened?"

"She got fired."

"What?"

"They played it. The girls played it. You know, they asked it questions. The dial moved. It answered."

"That got her fired?"

"They said they were messing with things they shouldn't mess with."

"Huh!"

Wassulie looked at her desperately.

"That's why we need you," he pleaded. "You're like a teacher, right? You know about Ouija boards. You can explain it to them, it's a game, it's not about... you know..."

"Who? The school board?"

"Yeah," he said hopefully.

The nausea had subsided.

Camilla waggled her head.

She could move without throwing up.

The school board fired a teacher for a Ouija board.

For dabbling in séances? Was this something traditional? Some traditional view about séances? Wassulie wanted Camilla to speak up for the teacher.

Was the school board operating from a set of traditional beliefs? Or maybe the school board knew full well about Ouija boards, a kid's game that mimicked a séance. Board members used the issue for other reasons. Fresh blood on the faculty. Factional in-fighting. A struggle between local and district boards. Or, maybe it was an effort to cut short the infatuation of a student with a New Jersey teacher.

"I don't know."

"You could talk with them?"

"I don't know," she said gently. "This sounds complicated. I do know about Ouija boards. But I'm new around here. I mean, it just seems really complicated from what little I know."

"Yeah," said Wassulie.

"I don't think the school board would have much reason to listen to somebody like me. I'm new. I know nothing about the school or anybody on the school board. And I work for Fish and Game. I'm the herring girl."

"Yeah," said Wassulie, face falling.

"I'm sorry about your teacher."

She touched the young man's knee.

Tears shimmered in his eyes. Gusts whistled through the sheds. He looked out to sea. The wind took them like flying jewels.

Wassulie eased up, brushed his pants.

"Got to go," he whispered.

"I'm sorry. I hope things work out somehow."

He moved toward the beach.

"The dog's that way."

"Yeah."

"Why would somebody shoot him like that?" Camilla whispered, half to herself, still fighting the nausea.

Wassulie looked at the grass-covered dunes.

"Got old, I guess."

"What?"

"I guess that dog got old."

He gave her a sad smile, shrugged helplessly, and vanished.

24

The old man Talliciq waited.

The rough clearing was much as he remembered. But there were changes. The hermit had been busy.

The clearing was larger. At its center, the potato garden had expanded, carefully trenched and covered with seaweed. A planked shelter without windows had been erected nearby. Missing trees had provided the lumber. The cave looked the same, a black hole in the cliff at the back of the meadow. A fire burned near its mouth though the day was hot. The hermit crouched beside it, lean, barefoot, and draped with deer hides. Unkempt hair flowed around his shoulders. A bristly beard covered his face. He looked like a wolf guarding a lair. Somehow, he knew about visitors before they arrived.

"Are you coming? I'm starving!"

The hermit shouted in flawless Sugstun.

Talliciq shouldered his sack and crossed the clearing.

"What can I do with these?" complained the hermit, pulling fresh sockeye from Talliciq's bag.

Talliciq smiled good-naturedly.

He knew the hermit handled fish as well as anyone.

The hermit immediately selected two from the sack. He carried the rest into the cool cave. Returning with a knife, in short order he split each fish, skewered the flanks on blackened sticks, and planted them by the fire. He rearranged the burning wood and adjusted a wind screen.

Returning to Talliciq, he sat. In silence, they watched the fish roast. Oil sizzled. Its piquant aroma filled the air.

"More potatoes," remarked Talliciq in Sugstun, breaking the silence. He pointed to the expanded garden.

"Because they keep stealing them!" complained the hermit in the same language. "But those monks won't steal any this year. No rain! They have shriveled to nothing!"

Water buckets beside the terraced plots suggested this probably wasn't so, despite the hermit's complaints. Hauling water was hard work. But someone was doing it.

"Your new house?" smiled Talliciq, nodding at the planked structure.

"They built a school! They want me to teach children!"

The hermit rotated the skewers. He disappeared into the cave. Shortly he emerged with wild radishes and several leather pouches. He placed the radishes on a cedar board laid between them. He lifted the skewers and slipped off the fish. From a sack came sea salt. He dusted the roasted sockeye. With nothing but his fingers, he dug into a fish, licking moist, salty flakes from his fingertips. Talliciq did likewise. They ate the sockeye and radishes in silence, enjoying the other's company in the warm afternoon.

The hermit gathered up skins and bones and guts and tossed them on a compost heap across the clearing. He stirred with a pronged stick.

"That smart one will find it," he grumbled.

Talliciq nodded. Bears had noses for salmon bones. The hermit kept no dog. Without a dog, he probably fed lots of bears with his compost.

The hermit dug into another pouch. He extracted shriveled wads of black tobacco. He shoved some into Talliciq's hand and the rest into his cheek. Talliciq did likewise. Bitter juice joined with the oil from the fish. His head lightened.

The hermit pulled a smoky glass jar from the last pack. He poured clear liquid into wooden cups.

"No," protested Talliciq.

"Take it," snarled the hermit.

Talliciq did. The hermit took his own.

"To pests!" the hermit toasted.

He tossed his down and stared at Talliciq.

"Don't insult them!"

Talliciq reluctantly drank. Fire flared out his nose. He choked. The hermit laughed and poured more.

"Take it!"

They drank again. The hermit poured once more and leaned on an elbow. His face glowed from the salmon, tobacco, and drink. His eyes smiled.

"Now we can properly talk," he declared.

Talliciq's head had numbed. He knew the hermit's drinks. They came from potatoes. They erased memories, purged stomachs, and provoked fights. He held the third cup without drinking. He tried to clear his burning throat.

"Wait!" the hermit scowled. "Something for nothing! Those monks, that school, the pests who come to bother me! Always the same, something for nothing!"

The fire popped with oil from the gift of sockeyes. Talliciq sat bemused. He would play the hermit's game.

"Something for nothing!" the hermit growled again, angry at Talliciq's good humor.

Talliciq just waited.

The hermit nursed his cup.

"When will it rain?" the hermit finally demanded.

Unfounded complaints. Toasts of pesky bears. Now the weather. When will it rain? What kind of a question was that? The hermit had turned silly. Talliciq's face said as much.

The hermit rudely pointed.

"You know! You know that you know. Where is the rain! Are my potatoes ruined?"

The hermit scowled frightfully.

Talliciq gave in. He waved toward the ocean.

"You know that bird with the hooked beak?"

"Which bird?"

"The black one, the small seabird with a beak like this?"

He crooked a finger by his nose.

The hermit nodded sullenly.

"When they fly from the west... when they come in like clouds... they will pull it behind them."

"Humph," grunted the hermit, considering this.

He sipped his drink.

"How soon behind them?"

"That night."

The hermit nodded.

"But cover them with more than that," said Talliciq.

The field had a thin layer of kelp.

The hermit reached for the jar. He refilled his own cup, offering none to Talliciq. He leaned back and stared at the plot and the glimmering sea, not a bird in sight.

The answer sufficed.

Talliciq cleared his throat. He had earned his own question.

"There are many kinds of men," he began. "Big men. Common men. Slaves. Real people. Aleuts. Russians. Good men... bad..."

The hermit nodded, listening.

"One kind counts. He marks in books. Every day, he counts, marks, hardly noting the sun, counting with books. It must be hard for a man, even a Russian."

The hermit sipped his drink, waiting for more.

"Hard on that person's mind," said Talliciq.

He stopped, sucked tobacco, and stared at the cloudless horizon. They sat together, thinking.

Finally the hermit spoke.

"That man... he comes from St. Petersburg, far to the west of where your hooked beaks fly, beyond the sea. St. Petersburg... that is a great city. His family is rich. You cannot imagine it. Estates. Servants. Power. Those families teach their sons to count. They teach them to count what they possess. When they are finished, they send the sons across the seas to count what others possess."

Talliciq closed his eyes to listen.

"St. Petersburg... the home of the monks, the potato thieves. They live on Valaam, an island near St. Petersburg. That man who counts, he adores the monks because they sing. When he was a child, he heard them. Now he sits with them and argues. The monks work on him. He is a son of a rich family, a rich benefactor. They work on him bit by bit... to drag his head from the ledgers he marks so he can see the poor he robs."

The hermit waved back and forth.

"The ideas fight inside him."

He checked if Talliciq was still awake.

"The monks pull hard. Now he finds he mistrusts what he once treasured and treasures what he once mistrusted."

The hermit's oily thumb caressed a cheek.

Talliciq saw and understood... Puyangun.

"That will drive men mad," said the hermit.

He poured himself another cup.

"Greed will drive men mad," agreed Talliciq, watching the hermit drink. "Yet, even madmen dream. Even madmen plan."

"Especially the mad! Dreams contrived by the Devil! Satan loves the mad."

"So others suffer."

"Yes, so others suffer." He now understood why Talliciq visited with a sack of fresh sockeyes. "And that one... he dreams of home."

He leaned closer. He reeked of drink.

"He leaves us soon to sail back to St. Petersburg, back to his rich family, back to his beloved Valaam, the monks he plans to join. He will take holy orders... to suffer! Don't look surprised. He wants to suffer! And like you say, he will make others suffer with him."

"Who?"

"A woman and child he plans to take."

"Is that possible?"

"What?"

"Holy orders and a woman?"

"Bah! The orders allow it. Some marry. Others don't. It rests with the vows."

"A monk... with family, with children?"

"Not children. That is not his plan. One child only. He will swear a vow of celibacy."

"Celibacy?"

Talliciq did not know the word.

"Married in the heart, not in the flesh."

Talliciq considered this. It seemed perverse.

"What woman would accept this?"

"It does not matter," the hermit waved. "He goes to St. Petersburg. Can a Real Person live in St. Petersburg? Can fish survive on land? The vow will prove easy to keep."

The hermit drained his cup and stood.

"Prayer calls. I will pray on this. Join me!"

Talliciq shook his head 'no.'

"Then pray out here."

At the cave's mouth he smiled at Talliciq.

"God works through us, my good friend!"

Then he disappeared.

Talliciq felt sick.

The hermit's horrible drink!

He closed his eyes. The world spun. He tried to stop it. He concentrated on the spinning ground. It only increased.

Round and round and round...

Like a whirlpool.

He shut his eyes completely. He gave himself to the whirling. Faster and faster he flew, the spiral tightening, down and down and down...

To the single point where all things began.

A fierce wind howled.

Black hair billowed.

A young woman walked, her hair flying atop the baby she carried. With every step, the pack she carried grew... larger... larger...

The meadow exploded! A swarm of gnats swirled around her, riding the wind... higher... higher... with every spin growing... larger... larger... until they filled the sky.

A screaming mob of petrels.

The storm was here.

25

"Hey."

It came from the shadows.

Not a 'hello' or 'hi' as Camilla heard it. Not a 'cama-i' or 'waqaa,' greetings Nick had taught her. It was 'hey,' a near inaudible huff of air, the impersonal greeting of the urban street, the college campus, the drug corner, delivered sub rosa, a monosyllable, a carefully-nuanced expression of nonchalance and disaffection, a who-cares-about-it greeting.

In Berkeley, Camilla knew the proper response... its apathetic echo.

Some part of Togiak was trendy. Or disaffected.

Nick's hands found his pockets. His head lowered, eyes tucked beneath the bill of his cap, the universal defensive slump, the hunch that minimized self, obscured facial cues, and protected the solar plexus.

"Hey," he responded.

The greeter emerged from the shadows dressed in solid black, hollow-cheeked and grinning, teeth a-kilter in swollen sockets. He twisted the top of a plastic trash sack.

"Baskets?"

The sack lifted a quarter inch, a bare shift from neutral, the blasé anti-promotion of a Goth street vendor, a 'here it is but it's no big deal.'

Nick eyed him and said nothing.

"What have you got?" asked Camilla.

The Goth leered. He untwirled the sack, reached inside, and drew out a basket the size of a grapefruit. A lid neatly plugged the top hole. He gave it to Camilla.

"Nice," said Camilla.

She passed the basket to Nick.

The Goth's eager eyes followed the transfer.

Nick was less impressed. He had seen scores of grass baskets like this one. His own aunt made them. Occasionally he was enlisted to collect the beach grass. It was built from a standard design for the tourist trade. The weaver had worked a butterfly motif around the side with dried seal gut dyed blue and red. It was compact and symmetrical. Tightly woven. Good grass. Overall, well made.

Nick passed it full circle.

"There's more! Come on!"

The stranger returned to the shadows. His back somehow beckoned.

"Ruffs. Earrings. Come on!"

Mildly annoyed with herself, Camilla found the stranger's come-on worked too well. She felt compelled to follow or look rude.

Nick felt no such obligations. But he'd come to see Togiak. Here was a guide to its fringes, a mysterious black shadow. He liked fringes. With a puckish smile, Nick followed. Camilla came too.

At a ragged edge of town they found his place, a decrepit tilted cabin. Its log frame had listed and surrendered long ago to the freeze-and-thaw of the tundra. The walls sunk into the earth like a sinking ship.

A heavy door opened into a half-buried living room. Windowsills rested at ground level. Sheets of aluminum foil pressed over wavy panes of glass blocked the summer light. The inner gloom resolved into a clutter of open boxes, scavenged electronics, and stacks of CDs. An electric guitar leaned on a wooden butter keg. A walrus gut drum sat atop animal pelts beneath a life-sized Kiss poster of a clown with an adder's tongue. A dusty table held workings of antler, ivory, and bone amid drills, files, and awls. A sweet atmosphere filled the den, an aroma of cured skins, smoked fish, and illicit drugs.

The Shadow cackled as he searched boxes.

"Baskets," he proclaimed, handing several more to Camilla of various styles and quality.

"You make these?" she asked.

"No," he smirked.

From a cardboard box he produced dangling earrings strung with porcupine quills and colorful beads. He held a striking red-and-gold pair beside Camilla's cheek and laughed.

Her ears weren't pierced.

Nick found a box of fur hats. He tried on a beaver-skin cap the color of chocolate. Its shaggy flaps swallowed his head.

"Hot!" he gasped.

The Shadow laid thick hides at Nick's feet, beautiful mottled skins of reindeer, commercially tanned, coarse haired and backed by supple leather.

"Good in winter. Warm on the bottom, even when on top!"

The Shadow looked between Nick and Camilla and grinned.

"Where are these from?" asked Nick, ignoring the innuendo.

"Nunivak."

Semi-wild reindeer roamed Nunivak, almost like caribou. The hides probably came from Mekoryuk, thought Nick, the island's only village.

The Shadow pulled an elaborate fur ruff from another box. It was pieced from wolverine, wolf, and silver fox, backed by royal blue cotton broadcloth. He draped it around Camilla's shoulders. Camilla had never felt such elegance against her skin. The frosted highlights shined brilliantly with her black hair. For a long moment, both men stared, transfixed by her fur-framed face.

"Good for frostbite," said the Shadow, his eyes at the tip of her nose.

"None of that in Berkeley," said Camilla dryly, pulling it off her long neck.

"Berkeley!" the Shadow barked. "Hippies! Drugs! Rock and roll!" He grabbed drumsticks from the worktable and pretended to drum.

"You carve?" asked Nick.

"Just starting," said the Shadow, momentarily subdued, sounding unsure. He lifted a work in progress from the tabletop, an ivory cribbage board with scrimshawed foxes and birds.

Nick examined the etched and inked animals. It was good work. He nodded approval.

The Shadow smiled relieved, caught himself, and recovered the anomic leer.

Nick weighed the ivory in his palm.

"Walrus?"

"No."

The Shadow rummaged along a wall. He came up with a substantial tusk. It gleamed with creamy satins and browns. He hefted it to Nick. Mammoth! The cribbage board was made from a section of mammoth tusk. The raw piece Nick held would be worth thousands of dollars to a carver. Where had the Shadow acquired it? Where had he acquired any of this stuff?

The Shadow reached beneath a bench and pulled out a smaller chunk. It glowed lemony. He set it beside the mammoth tusk.

"New ivory," he proclaimed, pointing to the yellow-sheened tusk. "Old ivory," he pointed to the brown.

Camilla moved closer for this lesson. The old ivory came from a prehistoric elephant recovered from the tundra, the new ivory from a walrus. Both were ivory, both beautiful, but they looked substantially different. Different animals. Different times. She rubbed the new ivory and found it slick and strangely warm, the first raw walrus tusk she had ever touched.

"Round Island?" she asked.

The Shadow's eyes instantly shuttered.

He leaned back to study Camilla through the slits.

Camilla seemed not to notice. She lifted the walrus tusk and rubbed her cheek with it, smiling at its smoothness.

"This is from a walrus, right? From Round Island? Is that where you hunt?"

Nick winced.

Camilla was crazy. No hunter would answer that question if true. She had asked him if he broke the law. Didn't she know that? She had pitched it conversationally, made it seem innocent and reasonable. But she was a stranger employed by Fish and Game, the overseer of the sanctuary, the oppressor.

Nick saw the Shadow struggle.

"That place is closed," he muttered.

A dodge. A non-answer.

"Closed?" echoed Camilla.

The Shadow offered nothing more.

"But if it's closed, how can a carver get ivory?"

She pitched it sympathetically, as if she supported carvers everywhere. Then she waited, a white porcelain angel.

The Shadow hunched like a hounded wolf. He worked hard to categorize the conversation, trying to weigh consequences.

Camilla presented enigmas. He hadn't met anybody quite like her. He was trying to figure this out.

"There's ways they can find it," he answered.

Like illegal hunting, thought Nick. Black market trades. But he didn't know how carvers did it.

Camilla chatted innocently on.

"Somebody told me, uh… the herring boats hunt on Round Island. Somebody with the Feds, you know, they told me the herring boats hunt between periods?"

Nick's jaw almost dropped.

How can she bring that up here? Can't she see how tense this guy is? The cabin reeked of money and illegal drugs. The girl had balls. Or she was really stupid.

Camilla smiled at the Shadow.

"But maybe that's all just… government bullshit."

It was like the sun breaking from clouds.

The Shadow began to hoot. He laughed like this was the best punchline ever.

"Yeah! Yeah! Government bullshit!" he howled.

Camilla laughed with him.

The Shadow plucked the ivory piece from Camilla's hand.

"They think they're so hot. They think they know so much. But they don't know shit!"

He shoved it beneath Camilla's nose.

"Look there. Does that say Round Island?"

Camilla examined the piece, eyes nearly crossed.

She read slowly…

"Uh… Made in China."

The Shadow almost fell over.

Made in China!

He hooted hysterically. He danced around his newfound friend, fingers waggling. He snatched the guitar from the butter keg, punched switches, and played a wild riff.

Camilla clapped with delight.

Nick watched the transformation, astounded.

Camilla began naming rock groups.

The Shadow knew them all. He played.

Nick did too. He found the drumsticks to pound rhythms.

Beers materialized. Candles got lit.

They jammed in the buried grotto.

The sound was amazing.

Jerome Paul… that was the Shadow's name. Originally from Quinhagak village, he told them, up toward the

Kuskokwim. After that he had lived in Dillingham. Anchorage. Fort Richardson. Kandahar. And a few other nasty places, care of the U.S. Army. Sweating from the guitar work, he pulled a velvet pouch, thumb-jammed a soapstone pipe, and lit some hash. Nick shared it with him. Camilla declined. In his most recent incarnation he was a trader, a carver, and a musician. He played at the high school dances when not blacklisted by the village.

Nick commiserated, drawing on the pipe.

Blacklisting... he knew all about that firsthand from his own village.

They smoked like long-lost buddies. The pipe passed back and forth.

"I heard something about that," said Camilla.

Jerome relit the pipe.

"What?"

"Blacklists. I heard something weird about that. Blacklisted because of a game."

The Shadow inhaled.

"Yeah?"

"At the high school where you can't go, a high school teacher from New Jersey got the boot. Her students played a game... played with her Ouija board."

Camilla offered nothing more.

Jerome smoked. Camilla waited.

Nick waited too. What was Camilla talking about? Ouija boards?

"No! No!" coughed the Shadow, emptying his lungs.

"No?"

"No... that's... not why," he coughed. "Not cuz they played with her Ouija board. If they just played with her Ouija board... nobody would give a shit if they just played with her Ouija board."

"Yeah," agreed Camilla easily. "Who'd care about that."

Then she waited again.

Like a Yup'ik, she waited. It was as if she had lived in a village all her life, thought Nick, watching and wondering, taking another hit off the pipe, how patiently and silently she waited, not like any kass'aq he had ever met.

Slow-drifting smoke filled the room.

"Because... like it wasn't," the Shadow finally said, hunched a bit lower. "It wasn't. Nobody would give a shit."

Camilla drew closer and nodded.

"It wasn't," she echoed. "Wasn't really... playing."

And she waited some more, a porcelain statue.

The Shadow peered around the gloom, checking dark corners, ill-defined landscapes in the candlelight, an underground den that had sunk lower yet, half in smoke and light, swallowed by the earth.

"Cuz you don't play like that," he whispered. "Everybody knows, you don't mess around like that."

"Yeah," whispered Camilla. "You have to be careful."

The Shadow nodded.

It was slow-motion.

The words came so low and slow, Nick wondered who had said them.

"Let the dead stay dead."

Nick's foggy brain registered the warning.

Camilla's deathly face flickered in and out with the guttering candles. The Shadow seemed only half there.

Then he was swallowed.

26

She dreamed.

A storm above an angry sea. The water rose in twisted spouts that rained like a giant's tears. She had dreamed this before. Her hand groped and found her baby snuggled safely by her side.

A deluge fell. Winds screamed.

Within a thundering crash she heard a voice.

It called her name, over and over again, like a summons to join the storm...

'Pu-yan-gun! Pu-yan-gun!'

She struggled.

"Puyangun."

She jerked awake.

Wind whistled above her. Rain poured through the smoke hole, pounding the fire pit, splattering clouds of ash and dust. In the dark, a shape knelt over her, dripping wet. A hand rested on her leg. A familiar voice gently whispered.

"Puyangun."

She lunged into his arms.

"Cuniq!"

They toppled in a frantic embrace. His clothes were sopping. She didn't care. They smothered each other.

A baby cried from the bedding.

"Don't squash him!" she giggled.

She reached within the furs, pulled him out.

Puyangun presented him to Cuniq.

"Essequyuk, your father."

"Essequyuk," Cuniq whispered.

In awe, he took his son. He gently kissed his nose with his own. He pulled Puyangun to him, holding her and the baby together.

"I've come back," he said huskily.

She began to cry. He did too.

"Hush, listen. There's no time for this now. We have to go. I've come for you, your mother, my grandfather. The boats are ready. We go together. Others can follow."

"What are you saying?"

"We must escape. This place is death for me now… and also for you, for all of us. We must escape it now or it will destroy us."

"Escape?"

"To a better place, a place free of Russians and Aleuts."

"Where?"

"To the east. I know where. I have cousins there, a new place to survive, all of us."

"When did you say?" asked Puyangun, sitting erect.

"Now."

"Now?"

She looked up to the smoke hole, pouring rain. She looked around the sod house filled with trade goods and gifts. She thought of the fish rack with sockeye, incompletely smoked, her Russian, coming after three days. She looked at Essequyuk, cradled by Cuniq, her lost lover, soaked from the storm.

"I'm ready," she said.

A voice croaked from the corner.

"Who is that?"

Puyangun's mother sat up from her furs.

"What's this noise?" she rasped. "What's this water and smoke?"

"Go fix the hole," she pushed on him. "It's Cuniq, mother! He's back! He has boats. We're going on a trip."

"Going? What are you saying?" she sputtered.

"You too. We're going east to visit his family. A good place, a place without Aleuts."

The smoke hole closed. The rain ceased its pouring.

Cuniq crawled back inside as Puyangun lit the oil lamps. Cuniq nodded to his mother-in-law, saying nothing. His mother-in-law did not nod back. She scowled. He dragged in wet skin bags and a carrier.

"To pack," he said. "I have food. We walk to the boats. We carry everything."

"What's this?" Puyangun touched the carrier.

"The baby."

"It's so big," said Puyangun, lifting the frame, twice the normal size. "It will swallow him."

"Grandfather made it big, sturdy, for a wet journey."

Puyangun examined it in the flickering lamps. Cuniq moved closer. He gently cupped her chin and turned her face to the light. Sooty lines fell down her cheeks beneath each eye. Fine needle points, densely spaced, traced swollen paths. Tattooed marks radiated beneath her lips, bursting like rayed light beneath clouds.

He looked into her large eyes.

"You're beautiful," he huskily whispered.

They kissed long and without shame.

* * *

The kayak beached in the downpour. A skinny boy pulled its nose onto the gravel. Water streamed from his gut parka. His face glowed red from the salt spray and wind. He looked frightened. Gripping his belted knife, he jogged between the skin boats toward the Company's buildings and stumbled upon a sentry. The Aleut seized his thin arm.

"What do you want?"

"The bookkeeper," he gasped.

Aleksei Stepanovich Petrovskii picked at his morning meal. Wind blew through opened doors. Watchmen entered with a boy dressed for the sea, dripping from the storm. His hand was glued to his knife.

"He asks for the bookkeeper," the sentry smiled.

Aleksei swung his legs around to face the trembling boy.

"What do you want?" he said sternly.

"They left," the boy stammered in Russian.

"Who has left?"

"That old woman."

"Who?" asked Aleksei suspiciously.

"That old woman. 'Find the bookkeeper,' she said. 'Tell him that Cuniq took us.'"

Aleksei's face swelled.

"What?"

"Cuniq took us."

"Who said this?" demanded the Russian.

163

"The old woman," repeated the boy, "the one who sent me. And her daughter."

Aleksei stood like an enraged bull.

"Where?"

The boy suddenly straightened. He puffed out his chest and proudly gripped the knife's ivory handle. The old woman had given it to him.

"I can show you."

* * *

The downpour slackened. The spruce thrashed with wind.

They were soaked from the overland journey. Puyangun carried the baby on her back, screened from weather by the gut-covered pack. Her mother struggled behind her, unused to walking. She carried nothing. Thekla came last with a large rucksack. Cuniq strode in front, a large bag across his shoulders. He took them by the back trails. Puyangun heard the roar ahead.

They broke from the forest. A gray lake stretched before them. Its surface boiled with whitecaps. Water poured through rocky chutes straight across their path. The rapids seethed, barely contained within the narrow outfall. The roaring flood rushed to find the sea.

"Old Man Crosses!" Cuniq shouted, naming the ford. "We cross here!"

Throwing down his pack, he tied a line to a tree leaning into the spray. People appeared on the opposite bank. Puyangun saw Talliciq, the old man dressed for weather. Two boys stood beside him. Cuniq secured the line to his waist, hoisted his pack and weapons, and stepped onto the granite spillway.

"Hurry!" shouted Talliciq, his voice thin above the roar.

Hopping rocks, Cuniq came to a pole wedged near the center of the outfall between great tilted slabs. He attached the line to the pole, jumped a gap, and hopped rocks to the far shore. Talliciq took the line's end and fixed it to another tree. Cuniq threw his gear down.

"The lake's rising!" shouted Talliciq.

Cuniq nodded. He rapidly worked his way back across the ford. He took the baby's pack from Puyangun and shouldered it. He began across. Puyangun gripped the line and followed. She stepped onto the first rocks. They were slick with rain. The river roared between, a hundred falling sluices, the top of the great rapids tumbling to the pool at Toothed Water. From rock to rock she deftly jumped. She saw that the water was rising, covering steps with a watery film. She reached the center pole and looked back. Her mother and Thekla waited in the blowing wind. Puyangun looked ahead to see Cuniq on shore with the baby. She jumped the gap. The water rushed around her feet. It was hard to stand. How would Mother make it?

"Cuniq! Get Mother!" she yelled.

Cuniq came leaping back, wormed around her, and worked across the ford. Puyangun carefully jumped her way to the far bank. She turned fearfully to watch. Cuniq gripped her mother's waist. He pulled her over the crossing. Thekla followed with difficulty. He bodily lifted her and jumped between rocks. Puyangun's heart leapt with every jump. Their feet were nearly under water. But the three arrived. Thekla and Cuniq pushed the mother up the bank. He immediately turned to go back for the last pack.

"Leave it!" shouted Talliciq, grabbing his arm. "Ready the boats! The strait is sheltered. The wind may shift. We can make the first island before dark."

Cuniq reluctantly nodded, grabbed his pack, and disappeared down the trail while the women rested. The path was slick with mud. A slip would send him into the raging torrent. Other footprints preceded him, tracks made by the boys who Cuniq saw earlier with Talliciq. The rain began again. The roar of the water was deafening. He arrived at Toothed Water, white and turbulent. He'd rarely seen it like this, filled to overflow by giant cascades. He stopped abruptly and stared across. Something moved. He shielded his eyes. A large bear edged along the willows, paws nearly in the water.

"Careful, Old Man," said Cuniq. "No fishing today."

The bear disappeared up the brushy slope. Cuniq continued along the broadening stream to the ocean's edge. Four craft were tethered on shore, three kayaks and an open skin boat. The boys sat among supplies. They smiled at Cuniq.

"Another," said Cuniq, throwing down his heavy pack.

He began loading the boats, feeling uneasy.

Where were the others? What was taking them so long?

He directed the boys how to finish and strode briskly up the trail. Well past the pool, he heard the first scream.

* * *

165

Following the Sugpiat boy, Aleksei Stepanovich Petrovskii broke from the woods above a seething lake. The Aleuts came out too, nearly falling down the steep incline. Breathing hard from the run, the boy pointed proudly to the ford. He had led them well over the back trails at a jogging pace. Aleksei looked upon the outlet of a great lake. Water fell with a mighty roar.

"Old Man Crosses," the boy declared.

Across the narrow outfall, Aleksei saw her. Puyangun! And the mother! He waved his arms.

"Puyangun!" he shouted.

She didn't hear. Her back was toward him. The wind blew away his voice. The boy pointed to a path leading down through the woods. Aleksei bulled along it, jumping and slipping in the muck. The Aleuts followed. He emerged at the crossing, shouting.

"Puyangun!"

He heard the screams. Puyangun was screaming.

The ford was a seething spillway over half-hidden rocks. Two women battled across it, knee-deep in the surging flood. Puyangun screamed, desperately gripping a pack on her mother's back. The mother, nearly lost in water, held to a line with both hands. The old woman was trying to cross. The pack on her back held the baby!

"I'm coming!" he shouted.

Aleksei gauged his footing, grabbed the line, and stepped into the flood. The surge nearly knocked out his feet. He gripped with both hands.

"Hold the line!" he yelled at the men.

The Aleuts grabbed and held it taut.

Aleksei plunged ahead, leaning his full weight on each foothold. Rock by rock he moved until he arrived at great tilted slabs halfway in the torrent. He gripped the center pole and leaned over the gap.

He grabbed the old woman's pack.

"I've got it," he yelled.

The old woman instantly lost her grip. Her hands left the rope. Her body swept off the rock. She dangled from the pack frame, the flood rushing around her. Aleksei gripped one side, Puyangun the other.

Like a doll, the old woman bounced on the surface of the waves. They fought to keep hold. Then her frail body turned and slipped from the pack.

She disappeared into white.

Puyangun wailed.

At the far bank Cuniq appeared.

Puyangun! The baby!

He grabbed the line and leaped onto the sunken path. He forced his way across the raging torrent.

Aleksei pulled the pack.

"Jump!" he shouted.

"No!" wailed Puyangun across the rushing gap, holding tight to the frame.

"Jump!" shouted Aleksei again, yanking harder.

"No!" shrieked Puyangun.

What was she doing? Why won't she jump? She would kill them!

Aleksei stared at her across the gap through freezing spray. He shrieked with rage. Her face... it was a horror! A corruption of soot and blood! Mutilated. Defiant. Terrible!

He was too late! She was ruined! Like all the others!

Her perfect face, destroyed!

By that... savage!

With a vicious snarl, he ripped the frame from her grasp.

Puyangun screamed and fell into the flood.

Cuniq lunged and blindly grabbed. His fingers hooked her hood. She went under.

Water knocked out his feet. He dangled one-handed from the line, holding the hood. He scrabbled desperately in the flow, found rock, reset his feet, and hauled Puyangun from the flood. Gripped to his side, he struggled against waves to the far bank. Someone grabbed and lifted. It was Talliciq. Thekla knelt on shore, hysterically sobbing.

The gulf heaved with waves. Cuniq and Puyangun stared across it. The Russian had the baby's pack balanced high atop a shoulder. His armpit held the rawhide line. He leaned against the flood. The river surged nearly to his waist. He struggled for his next footing. Step by slow step he gained his way in the rushing ford.

On the far bank, somebody ran.

Aleuts waved and shouted, their words lost in the roar.

Suddenly, they split, scattered like leaves in the storm.

A massive brown shape erupted from the forest. It landed on the rocky ford, back to the flood. It turned this way and that. The Aleuts converged with spears.

The grizzly stood and roared.

"No!" shouted Aleksei.

The old bear whirled about and leaped, falling full onto the raging spillway, planted like a new rock in the torrent. Water swelled around him. He moved to cross and stopped.

The Russian blocked the way.

They were face-to-face in the flood.

"Go away!" screamed Aleksei.

The grizzly claimed a rock.

Aleksei backed a cautious step. He teetered in the violence, clutching the line beneath his arm. The bear took another step. A shot rang from the bank, splashing beside them.

"No!" shouted Aleksei.

He slipped backwards another step, feeling for footholds. The bear moved too, matching him, rock for rock.

Aleksei desperately looked left and right and behind. It was impossible! The river was too strong! He would be swept away. His face turned livid with anger and fear. He waved with the baby's pack high above him, bellowed like a mad beast, viciously challenging the bear.

"Go! Go! Go! Go away!"

The bear launched.

He caught the Russian between powerful arms.

Aleksei screamed. The line snapped.

The bear surged on his hind legs across the rocks, standing upright, pushing the Russian before him, jaws closed on his face. Locked together, they embraced in a horrific dance.

A massive wave hit. They lifted entwined, momentarily floated, and swept over the crest.

Puyangun wailed.

Thekla screamed and pointed

The baby's pack... it was still there!

It pounded at the flood's crest, snagged at the tip of the pole at the ford's center, nearly submerged by the rising flood. Puyangun fell to the ground sobbing. Cuniq swayed helplessly, frantically searching for some way to reach it.

Talliciq grabbed Cuniq's shoulders. He jerked him around, wrapped his hands around Cuniq's head.

"Qayam-yua!" he shouted.

Cuniq's eyes went blank.

"Cuniq! Qayam-yua!" he shouted.

He turned him downriver and shoved.

The old game!

"Go!" commanded Talliciq.

Cuniq leaped.

He raced down the trail, jumping, skidding. He rounded a bend and nearly slipped, vaulted, landed, and raced again. His heart pounded. His lungs burned. His feet set in the mud faster than the last.

He burst from the woods into the sodden glade.

Toothed Water!

Something spit from the seething teeth!

Without slowing he dove into the turbulence. He stroked in froth toward the teeth. Diving under, he resurfaced. Sucking air, he dove again, blindly grabbed, and flailed toward shore. Gasping, ears roaring, he hauled the pack out.

Frantic, he tore the gut covers. Wet furs! He ripped them apart. A blanket, soft and dry.

He fell back hard.

Black eyes, round with surprise, looked out at him. Eyebrows puckered. Then a tiny mouth smiled.

Puyangun stumbled into the glade. Cuniq was on his knees, arms around the pack. She ran to him and cried out with anguish and joy. She reached within the frame.

They hugged it together, rocking and weeping.

Finally a gentle hand touched her head.

Talliciq, the old man.

"It's time," he whispered.

He took them up.

They found the boats, packed and ready.

Two boys waited for them.

Beyond, a sheltered sea.

27

Nick fumed.

Fatty herring!

Camilla lectured, sheltered beneath the abandoned skiff.

Wind whistled above their heads off the bay, blocked by the boat and storm-cast logs. Their notebooks fluttered with blowing sand. Beach fleas bounced on the pages like errant punctuation.

"Okay?"

Nick hadn't been listening.

"Sources. Referencing them. Identifying who said what."

Nick almost scowled. He knew this already. Camilla knew he already knew it.

But the notes didn't show it.

His notebook was as ratty as Swiss cheese. To call it a shorthand was generous. His records stunk. Nick knew this too. He hated fieldnotes.

Endless minutia!

But the spotty shorthand worked for him. He could read the entries. Details weren't lost to him. His cultural tradition valued what people said. He remembered. Just because it wasn't written down didn't mean it was forgotten.

Camilla's lecture irked him, her compulsive culture that had to capture spoken words on paper to make them real, to give them validity, to transform them into 'data.' That devalued oral traditions. It privileged the written word and the lawyers who used it to steal from Native people.

Paper ruled in San Francisco.

Not here. Not the Bering Sea.

Hunters knew what paper was good for… starting fires.

"The note on fatty herring…"

He'd been drifting again.

"The 'who' is as important as the 'what,' agreed?"

Nick nodded, reluctantly.

"So this entry about two kinds of herring, 'regular herring' and 'fatty herring,' who told you that?"

Nick thought back and remembered the interview. Well, not exactly an interview, more like chat.

"Bingo Woman."

"Bingo Woman?"

"Yeah, Wednesday night."

"You went to bingo? Somebody said this at bingo?"

"Yeah, Bingo Woman… put it down."

"Who's that?"

"Short, purple kuspuk, missing tooth."

Nick pointed to his lower right first molar.

Camilla waited.

"Glasses."

Nick made goggles with his fingers.

Camilla suppressed a smile.

"Okay, we can put 'unidentified female.'"

"She's not! I can identify her."

"Nick, I know you could recognize her if you saw her again, but the notes can't say 'purple kuspuk and glasses,' you know? That doesn't help anybody but you. How many women wear purple kuspuks and glasses in Togiak?"

"I'd know her," grumbled Nick.

"Okay, 'unidentified female.' So why is there this taxonomic distinction between 'regular' and 'fatty' herring?"

"They dry differently."

"You know this?"

"She said it."

"Okay, good," said Camilla, entering that point, missing from the entry. "How do they dry differently?"

"I don't know."

"She didn't say?"

"They started calling numbers."

Camilla stopped writing. She gave him the eye.

Nick was figuring Camilla out. Camilla disliked to say anything negative. But she didn't have to. She used the eye. It said it all.

"You don't talk when they call numbers! It's dangerous!"

Camilla stifled another smile.

"They take over whole tables, spread out their cards. When they start calling numbers, you stand back. Whop! Whop! Whop! The Bingo Ladies hit them like flies. If you talk, wham!"

He swung an imaginary stamp.

"A hole in your head!"

Camilla covered her mouth.

She isn't as serious as she pretends. When she laughs, she hides her teeth like a teen. Cute.

Nick caught himself.

This was his boss.

The sunlight abruptly dimmed. Shadows fell over the notebooks. Heads peered over the boat and the log.

"Heard laughs all the way in town."

A mustache and a necktie...

"Don't move. We'll come around."

Nick knew instantly.

Cops.

They never ask.

He checked his stuff for anything to hide. In the village, it was birds. You always hid the birds. Nobody knew if they were legal. In college, it was booze.

Camilla shut her notebook. Nick flipped his shut too.

"Cama-i!" smiled a stocky, mustached Yup'ik. He offered his hand to Camilla. "Andrew Sipary. This is Lieutenant Cooper."

"Camilla Mac Cleary and Nicholas John," said Camilla. "Are you officers?"

"VPSO," said Sipary.

"Alaska State Trooper," said Cooper stiffly.

Nick frowned. A village cop and a state trooper.

What was going on?

Sipary fit Nick's stereotype of a village cop... young, polite, and (he'd bet a beer) new. Nick didn't like cops. But he sympathized with the Village Public Safety Officers. They were understaffed, underpaid, and undervalued. If they worked in their home villages, they faced the daunting problem of policing relatives and friends. Most attempted it bravely, then quit from the stress. Everybody howled when their local man quit, even though they had caused it.

"I was just joking," Sipary grinned. "I really didn't hear you laughing. Somebody said we could find you on the beach."

"Please join us. Coffee?" asked Camilla.

"Sure," said Sipary, flopping beside her.

Lt. Cooper, a badge on his jacket, looked for a seat without seaweed. He wore the necktie.

"You're local?" asked Camilla, passing the thermos.

"Yes," said Sipary, serving himself.

"Anchorage," grunted Cooper. "You're Fish and Game, that right?"

"That's right," said Camilla easily.

"Well, I'm... uh... university, Fairbanks," said Nick.

"And I'm from UC Berkeley," said Camilla. "But yes, we're doing a project for Fish and Game. Maybe you've heard about it, subsistence herring fishing because the rules for managing commercial herring may change in the district. We're doing interviews for a report."

Sipary sipped and listened, entranced by the outsider.

Lt. Cooper stared too, jaw stiff.

"Yeah, everybody says you're spies," laughed Sipary.

Camilla smiled. Cooper didn't. Neither did Nick. He cringed. The gossip was right. They were paid spies for Fish and Game. That was the glum reality. He needed more coffee.

"Well, it's research. Maybe there's a distinction," said Camilla.

Lt. Cooper cleared his throat.

"Ms. Mac Cleary, that's the reason we wanted to talk to you. And you too, Mr. John. You're studying herring, right? Herring fishing around the Walrus Islands?"

"Yes," said Camilla. She had just said that.

"So what you find, I'm interested to see it."

Camilla stole a quick look at Nick.

"Of course. I think the report is scheduled for December."

"December?"

"If we stay on track."

Lt. Cooper eyed the notebooks on the sand.

"Nothing before that?" asked Sipary. "We hoped you might have something we could use earlier than that."

Camilla shot Nick another look.

He had nothing to give back. He didn't know what was going on.

"Well, it's hard to say. Why?"

Neither officer replied.

Sipary looked nervously at Cooper.

He's deferring to the trooper, saw Nick. The Lieutenant is in charge of whatever this is.

"I'm collecting information on herring fishing," said Cooper, "actually an event with the boats, me and Officer Sipary. You're talking to folks about herring, yes? So the things you come across might fit with what we're doing."

"I see... an investigation of some sort."

Cooper said nothing. But Sipary nodded.

Nick's stomach sickened. What was this all about? Was he supposed to spy for the troopers too?

"Well, you are right, we are collecting data," said Camilla. "The study findings will be available in the final report, due in December. And like you, I'm sure, as we work up the findings, we will be mindful of sources. Public Safety has confidentiality rules too, I expect."

"Confidentiality rules?"

"Ours are designed to protect key respondents."

Cooper's eyes narrowed.

"Are saying you won't share sources with Public Safety? You'd withhold information? What for? To protect violators?"

"Oh no, no... the confidentiality rules apply to everybody. Before we start a survey, we have no idea who is doing what."

"Like illegal harvests?" growled Cooper.

"I think what I'm trying to say is that our interviews with herring fishermen are voluntary. Respondents voluntarily consent to answer our questions. There is nothing to force them to talk to us. The State needs the information for herring management. So it's in the State's interest to assure privacy in order to get accurate information. Without it, you know, some people might choose not to talk to us."

"It's the State's interest to enforce existing law," Cooper growled. "It's essential for fishery management too. Public Safety has a right to access any information the State collects, including sources."

"Well, of course, I expect that may be true," replied Camilla, "and there are channels for that, right? I'm new to all this. Does Public Safety submit requests to Fish and Game for information?"

Cooper's face went red.

Sipary watched anxiously, mustache twitching.

Nick did too... Camilla was stonewalling Cooper. And Cooper was getting pissed.

"But I completely understand your position," said Camilla, suddenly chatty, pouring herself more coffee. "You have an investigation of some sort, chasing leads that might go cold.

And we both work for the State, don't we? Just different departments. In fact, now that we've met, I've been thinking, you might learn things of interest to us too. I don't see why there couldn't be the possibility of informal exchanges, consistent with department standards, of course."

"Exchanges?" snarled Cooper warily. "Of what?"

"I don't know. I'm not sure. Our project has just begun. Maybe yours has too. I guess we can't really say unless we know how our inquiries connect and all that. But if we shared our interests now, we might be able to keep our ears open later. You know, ask that additional question we wouldn't otherwise?"

She turned to smile at Nick.

"Is that right, Nick?"

What the hell is she up to?

"Uh, yeah... maybe."

"Lieutenant? Officer Sipary?" asked Camilla.

The trooper's jaw relaxed a notch.

"Yeah, well, actually we may be further along than you," said Cooper, still frowning. "But informal exchanges sometimes work."

"Who likes bureaucracies?" laughed Camilla. "So, Lieutenant Cooper, Officer Sipary, what's this 'event' you're looking at? Something about herring, yes?"

Her face radiated innocence.

She's playing the cops, just like she played the Shadow, saw Nick. Cooper saw it too, but he was considering the setup. His jaw assumed a professional angle. He had decided. He would trade.

"A death," said Cooper. "We're investigating circumstances surrounding the death of a fisherman, an undocumented worker in the herring fishery."

"A murder?" said Nick.

"Maybe... maybe not."

"We heard about that, the Mexican national who washed ashore," said Camilla. "You probably know that our project grew out of that? You didn't? Allegations of walrus headhunting by the herring fishermen lead to two proposed changes in herring regulations... a bigger buffer and a single fishing period. That's how our study got started, to look into effects of the proposed new rules on subsistence fishing."

Cooper nodded, obviously pleased to learn something new. The State's herring project was connected with his case.

"But I thought he drowned. It was an accident," said Camilla.

"Probably was an accident, but the autopsy came back… confused," stated Cooper.

"He was shot," said Sipary.

"Shot?" said Nick.

"That isn't generally known and shouldn't be yet," said Cooper, scowling at Sipary. "He might have been shot. The body was beaten up badly by the storm, stripped of clothes…"

"Hole," Sipary said to Nick, pointing to his left side.

Cooper scowled again.

"Something entered," said Cooper, "maybe something jabbed through by wave action, pushed completely through. A stick might go in and stay, or rip out the same side that it went in. Not like that. Whatever went in came out the other side."

"He didn't drown," said Sipary.

"He didn't?" said Camilla.

Cooper looked ready to scream… Sipary was messing this up. "His lungs were dry," growled Cooper. "He was dead before he had a chance to drown."

"From the side wound," said Nick.

"That shouldn't have killed him. It was superficial."

"Then what did kill him?" said Camilla. "If he didn't drown and wasn't shot to death, what killed him?"

Cooper sat glaring.

Sipary's mustache twitched nervously.

"He was… crushed," said Cooper finally.

"Crushed?" said Nick.

Cooper pushed his hands together.

"Crushed. Rib cage, crushed. Lungs, squeezed tight. No air, no water. His neck, snapped. His skull, cracked like a walnut. That's the best way to describe it."

"Before he could inhale water," said Sipary.

"Huh!" said Camilla.

"Crushed," said Cooper.

"How?" asked Nick.

Cooper eyed Nick coolly.

"If we knew that, would we be sitting here with the fleas?"

28

Someone sang a death song.

The keening came from the dry grass, a piteous entreaty to unseen spirits. It was the orphan. He yearned to join the dead.

"Shhh!" Tengeng commanded.

The death song stopped.

Someone coughed raggedly.

"Shhh!"

Tengeng watched the frozen sea.

The cough repeated, smothered by a hand.

"We're dying," Tengeng whispered to the ice. "Listen to us. Listen to how we die."

There was a soft crack.

A black head broke the surface. Water smoked.

Tengeng held his breath. The black head disappeared in a thick ring of slush.

"Call them, Qeng'aq," whispered Tengeng, this time to the camp. He projected his great need.

They will hear you, Qeng'aq. Call them up. Call them out.

The sea ice stilled.

No wind moved. No bird sounded.

The black head appeared again from the ice. Another rose behind it. Ice rumbled dully. A large body heaved itself through the rind toward the beach, huffing clouds of smoke in the freezing air.

"Wait!" whispered Tengeng.

The orphan moaned.

Qeng'aq, call them up. They hear you.

He prayed with undiminished faith. He was the shaman's eyes. The shaman's ears.

He had found Qeng'aq alone in the camp, broken and defeated. Qeng'aq's son lay in the corner of the pit house, dead, grotesquely bloated. Qeng'aq had failed to save him. Like the little girl everybody loved. Like all the others who had died, person after person, all too sick to flee the outbreak. The son had stayed to help. So he too lay dead. Qeng'aq refused to move from the house. He would not leave the son he had failed. Tengeng found him collapsed by the cold hearth, covered with devilish lice. His son had died three days before.

"Leave me," Qeng'aq hoarsely whispered, too weak from starvation, too defeated by the sickness to even raise his head.

"There are walrus," Tengeng spoke by his ear. "We see them. They swim offshore."

Qeng'aq said nothing.

Tengeng gathered wood and began a fire. He grabbed the furs covering Qeng'aq's son and dragged the body from the house. Qeng'aq didn't move, didn't care. He was ready to join his son. Starving dogs circled as he pulled the corpse beneath a brush shelter. He broke the supports and collapsed the roof. Frustrated, angry, he threw rocks at the hungry pack.

"Go! Go! Go!"

They slunk off whining at this end of affairs.

Tengeng reentered the house and knelt by the hearth beside Qeng'aq. He set water in a cup near him. He pressed a small piece of moldy salmon into his hand.

"Help us, Qeng'aq," he begged.

Qeng'aq didn't lift his head.

"Help us. There are walrus swimming offshore. Call them up."

Tengeng heard sounds. Hard voices. He grabbed his spear and scrambled outside.

Three men in winter clothes entered the encampment, ragged, unwashed, staggering. Tengeng recognized them. All had lost children, wives, siblings, friends. The last little girl to die, the favorite of the village, the one Qeng'aq had failed to save, this was her father, the tattered man propped by a lance. It kept him from falling completely over. They stared with over-large eyes through gaunt masks of stretched skin. Tengeng planted himself at the entrance.

The men watched warily. No one spoke.

A raven perched on a bare willow above them. It croaked like a stone plunked into water.

"Where's that man?" the tattered one rasped.

"Gone," said Tengang.

The man eyed the thin trail of white that escaped the smoke hole. His companions saw it too.

Tengeng reached into his pouch and withdrew a small bundle, the last of the moldy salmon. He walked over slowly and handed it to the man on the left, an old acquaintance from what was once a thriving village, now abandoned, filled with ghosts.

"Eat," he whispered. "Take this and eat."

The man immediately opened the package, gnawed a bite and passed the hard fish to his companions, who did likewise. Tengeng stepped back, his spear at ready, watching the old salmon disappear.

"There are walrus," said Tengeng. He nodded toward the shore. "Help us catch them."

Two looked anxiously to the sea.

"Where are yours?" the tattered man wheezed. He stared at the pit house behind him.

"Gone," said Tengeng.

"The lake?" asked another.

Tengeng shrugged. He didn't know.

He had sent away his wife and child as the epidemic rose in frightful proportions, killing everyone weakened by famine. All the fish and animals and birds had disappeared from the earth. 'Run from it,' he told them. 'Run for the mountains.' He did not know if they had run in time. He kissed them both, his baby and his wife, Qeng'aq's daughter. They dutifully ran, taking dogs and the last of the food. Qeng'aq's son had stayed behind to help. A collapsed hut now covered his body. Qeng'aq stayed too, tirelessly visiting the sick, singing, praying, and ministering to the dying.

The tattered man sank to one knee. He began to cry, a soundless, open-mouthed shaking. His companion touched his shoulder.

"There are walrus down there," said Tengeng again, pointing to the bay. "Help us."

The companions lifted up the tattered man and led him away, not toward the shore, but toward the frozen river, tangled with willows, stiff and stripped of life.

"Quyana," one rasped.

'Thank you.'

Tengeng reentered the house. Qeng'aq sat nibbling the moldy salmon, wheezing through the black cave of his nose. Tengeng flopped beside him.

"Help us."

"I can't," wheezed Qeng'aq.

"You can."

"They've left me."

"No."

"Look around," he declared, waving a hand, shaking his head at the ghosts of friends, friends' children… his son.

Tengeng placed a thick finger to Qeng'aq's chest. He tapped something hard tucked just under the skins. The ivory amulet.

"Call them."

Qeng'aq slumped. He stared into the pit's flames.

"They will hear you," Tengeng pleaded.

"All right," Qeng'aq whispered.

Tengeng placed his arms around the old man's shoulders, a man of power and greatness, a man he loved.

"They will save us," Tengeng declared. "They will save your granddaughter."

He left his father-in-law staring into the fiery pit, seeing beneath all things.

He would call to them.

"Wait!" whispered Tengeng sharply.

The men knelt in the grass, watching the great walrus lumber to the black beach. The men nervously crouched, doing as Tengeng ordered.

The huge bull sniffed and huffed. He could smell them. But he shook his head and continued further ashore.

Another walrus rose from the slush of the sea, shaking its large neck. It followed. A third, fourth, and fifth emerged, jostling shoulders in the smoking air. They came too.

Tengeng watched amazed. The walruses walked unperturbed. They gathered in a knot around the leader and collapsed on their sides, closing their eyes to the cold.

Tengeng sprang from hiding. The men did too, charging with spears, blocking the monsters' escape. But they died as they lay, in a group, hardly moving, hardly protesting. The large bull was last. He rose and puffed his proud chest to receive the lance. When it was over, the only sounds were men, weeping.

* * *

Tengeng toiled into camp. It smelled of burning. Sooty clouds rose above the bare willows. He broke into the central clearing. Three ragged men stared at a mound of smoking slash that struggled to burn. At their feet, face into the dirt, stretched Qeng'aq. A lance protruded stiffly.

The tattered man's spear.

It had entered his back.

Tengeng slumped.

Hope left him. His heart emptied of all except sadness. This was how a great man dies, calling walrus to help the people, too weak to move, lanced in the back. The tattered man stood beside the smoking reek, shaking violently. The two positioned beside him, spears at ready.

Tengeng dropped the sack from his shoulder. He reached inside, pulled up thick liver, reddish-brown, slick and dripping. The men's eyes grew round at the bloody hand.

"There is food on the beach," he said flatly.

Without a word, the men with spears rushed from the smoldering fire for the beach. The tattered man opened his mouth to call them back and squawked like a bird. He collapsed, grievously shaking, a piteous, unrelieved anguish. He rocked on his knees, weakly mouthing, over and over.

"Burn him. Burn him. Burn him."

Tengeng came to him.

He placed a bloody hand on his head.

Whispered from his aching heart.

"Come."

He gently raised him up.

"There's enough for all."

29

The speakerphone crackled in the clinic office.

Camilla and Nick listened with the door shut. Theresa Manumik, now fast friends with Camilla, was happy to loan the old phone. More reliable than a mobile. They could use it to conference. The hollow voices of Mel Savidge and Jeff Hall echoed in the ether.

"How's it going out there?" asked Jeff from Anchorage.

"Okay," said Camilla. "We've found places to stay, compiled household lists from the clinic, and started interviews."

"Did the city and tribe approve it?"

"We briefed the mayor and the tribal chair. But it's impossible to raise quorums. Everybody's fishing or working."

"Yeah, that happens."

"How are you doing, Nick?" asked Mel from Juneau.

"Okay," he grunted.

"We thought it was time to call in," said Camilla. "We need a consult."

"About what?" asked Mel.

"We're getting good stuff. Herring is not a staple, but it's caught and eaten. Some families gather herring eggs on kelp. It's looking like the proposed changes in the commercial regulations aren't likely to affect subsistence patterns."

"Good," said Mel. "Good to know."

"But everybody's unhappy about outside boats. They want the commercial fishery to be local."

"We can't do anything about that," said Mel. "That's commercial rules, limited entry, and a bunch of other crap.

There's nothing we can do. It's the Board of Fisheries who deals with that. Or Limited Entry."

"The fishermen know that, don't they?" asked Jeff.

"They're getting screwed," said Nick. "The outside boats fish right in front of town for Japan."

"And there's nothing we can do," said Mel. "They've got to go to Limited Entry or the Board of Fisheries or to their government reps to pull some political strings. If that's why you called, there's nothing you can do. Apologize to them and direct them to Limited Entry."

"Well, there's something else, the main reason we called," said Camilla. "A state trooper wants our fieldnotes."

"What?" exclaimed Mel.

"A Lieutenant Hyde Cooper out of Anchorage. He's investigating the worker who washed ashore, Fernández, the Mexican fisherman who died, how his death connects with herring and Round Island walrus."

"That's not what you're there for," said Mel.

"How'd this come up?" asked Jeff.

"They approached us, Cooper and a VPSO named Andrew Sipary. They found out about our interviews. They want to know what we're hearing."

"We can't do that," said Mel.

"About what?" asked Jeff.

"We can't do that!" said Mel. "Those goddamn troopers know better than to ask that! We've been down this road before. They'll bust people we interview. Kiss your project goodbye. Our notes have got to stay confidential. Public Safety knows that!"

"Well, Cooper is investigating the worker's death because it was strange."

"Strange how?"

"He was crushed… broken neck, lungs…"

"Broken neck?" said Jeff.

"What's so strange about that?" said Mel. "He was killed in a storm. Storms beat the crap out of you. I've seen it. A body stuck in rocks gets pounded. Broken neck? That's nothing. Where's this Lieutenant been? The guy drowns and gets pounded."

"He didn't drown. That's what Cooper says."

"Huh!" said Jeff.

"No water in his lungs."

"So what? I've seen that too," scoffed Mel. "This poor slob in Nome blows out the back of his boat. Bolts sheared off the console. His head hits the transom going off. They found him dead in his float jacket, his lungs completely dry. The cold water had paralyzed his diaphragm. He never drew a breath. Suffocated, head above water."

"Huh!" said Jeff.

"He was shot," said Nick.

"What?"

"Maybe he got shot," said Camilla. "The coroner's report said maybe it was a stick or something else."

"A stick?" groaned Mel.

"What's the trooper want?" said Jeff.

"Anything about Fernández," replied Camilla, "where he worked, who saw him last, that sort of thing. They know he left the *Ema Louise* before the first opening. They don't know what happened next."

"That's their job, not yours," said Mel. "Who knows what else they'll do with your notes? It would start with Fernández but it could take them anywhere, illegal fishing, lack of permits, improper trades... If people think you're working for the troopers, kiss your project goodbye."

"I agree," said Jeff. "Did you offer to help?"

"Not formally, not officially. I stalled. But Cooper said he could get our stuff if we refused. I tried to move him off that."

"Don't give squat to Cooper," said Mel. "Those goddamn troopers! Don't give him anything until I get back to you. Don't get messed up in this. Your project is no murder investigation."

"Okay," said Camilla.

But it was an intriguing puzzle, thought Nick. Where had Fernández worked after the *Ema Louise*? How did he get to Round Island? What about the bullet hole?

"Nick? You hear?"

"Uh, right."

No murder investigation.

The call ended.

Camilla stared at the speakerphone.

Nick waited patiently.

Waits never bothered him. Good things came by waiting. Better wind conditions. A cleaner shot. Smoother trails. Kass'aqs didn't know how to wait.

He examined Camilla's face. Angular cheeks, unplucked brows, thin nose, full lips. A tiny scar on her chin. White as death... like a porcelain doll, smooth, fragile. Or maybe a deep-water clam, hard, durable. What was Camilla? Why was she working in a remote Yup'ik village on the Bering Sea?

She was nice to watch.

Camilla saw him looking.

"Another call?" she smiled.

"Yeah?"

"But maybe I shouldn't."

"Hmmm..." hedged Nick.

Camilla jotted down a long number from memory.

"They'll know I made it if I use the state code, right?"

"Yeah."

Camilla bit her lower lip. She looked at the wall clock.

"I've got an old account from Berkeley. It should have money, if it works."

She searched Nick's eyes.

"You want me to leave?"

"Doesn't matter."

She lifted the receiver and began punching the string of numbers. Nick couldn't follow it. But he knew it wasn't local.

"*Hola. Bueno. Puedo hablar con Javier Tampecho? Bueno.*"

"Where are you calling?" said Nick.

"Chiapas," whispered Camilla.

"*Hola, Javier! Esta es Camilla. Sí! No, en Alaska. Sí!*"

Nick listened to Camilla converse in Spanish, easily, comfortably. Somebody named Javier in Chiapas. The dead worker came from Chiapas Trooper Cooper said, a region in Mexico. Nick didn't know Mexico.

Camilla's face shifted from happy to serious. She said the name of Francisco Fernández Muñoz. She was asking for something, a favor it seemed. She nodded, clarified, nodded, clarified more. Listened.

Her face changed again. Saddened. Tears appeared.

"*No, estoy bien. Sí, gracias. No importa. No importa. Estoy bien.*"

Thanking Javier, she hung up.

Camilla turned her dark eyes on Nick's.

Her pale cheeks were wet.

She wiped her eyes with the palm of a hand, sadly smiled, and huskily whispered.

"Okay. Let's go interview."

30

"He's nice," said Winnie Friendly.

Theodore Bavilla, a minister in the Moravian church, had been drawn for the next interview. This was Winnie's assessment... 'nice.' He lived in the old parsonage of the congregation. She pointed it out on the plat map, a house along the route to the landfill, kind of messy after the snow melted.

"Just him today," she predicted.

Bavilla's wife and three children were gone to fish on the Nushagak River toward the mountains where the men chased caribou. Church duties kept Bavilla in Togiak. He'd join the family later.

True to Winnie's prediction, Camilla and Nick found only the preacher at home. The track to the city dump was indeed littered with trash. A large, substantial man, he politely invited them inside, offered them tea, and agreed to be surveyed.

Theodore Bavilla knew little about herring.

"I'm not from here," he apologized.

His bass voice, deeply satisfying, jiggled his neck on low decibels. He slowly worked his thick hands as he spoke, a constant washing in an invisible basin.

"I grew up in the mountains far above the Nushagak."

Sausage fingers fluttered eastward.

"I had dogs for playmates. They finally corralled my grandparents and made us move for school. I remember my first day. I couldn't understand the teachers. They spoke English. I didn't know anything!"

Bavilla laughed at this absurdity.

"Now I preach twice a week."

Ask him about caribou. He was an expert there. Or moose or marten. He knew the mountains.

"We trade for herring," he smiled. "Swaps. You know about that, Nicholas, I'm sure. Things move around."

Nick nodded. People traded on the Yukon River too, especially those without enough family to feed them. The minister still harvested at the camps of his childhood. He swapped with the coastal dwellers. Nick understood the reason. No local kinsmen. The minister was still an outsider.

"I'd love to see your mountains," said Camilla. "You'll be our expert if we study caribou."

"Caribou," agreed the minister, wiping his forehead with a meaty palm. "Moose, trapping, whatever it is you want to talk about."

Nick closed his notebook. He shifted to leave.

Camilla sat firm.

"You're a bishop?"

"No, no," Bavilla chortled, a chesty rumble. "A lay minister. Like a deacon who preaches."

"Everybody is Moravian here?"

"Most are Moravian."

"Quinhagak and Goodnews too?" asked Camilla, naming nearby villages.

"Yes, and Bethel, Kwethluk, Kasigluk…"

Bavilla explained how this happened.

Sheldon Jackson, a nineteenth century Presbyterian educator, convened a consortium of American denominations for schools in Alaska. The Presbyterians got the Tlingits of Southeast Alaska. The Quakers got the Inupiat of the northwest Arctic. The Moravians got the Yup'iks of the Kuskokwim, and so on. Of course, the Russian Orthodox priests didn't appreciate this. Or the Roman Catholics. The Protestants were dividing up Alaska to steal their flocks! But many places had no churches, schools, or stores. The territorial government asked Jackson to organize it. So the Moravians came to southwest Alaska, a hundred years ago.

Nick listened sourly. He knew this history. The churches colluded with the government to undermine the traditional beliefs of the Yup'iks.

"You hold services?" asked Camilla.

"Sunday and Wednesday. Come and visit," said Bavilla cheerily, "and bring Nicholas along. He'll be handy. We conduct them in Yup'ik. Scriptures, songs, liturgy, mostly Yup'ik. We're proud our children speak it."

Nick remembered this part too. In his village, it was the Latin Mass. The Roman Catholics had the lower Yukon. The Vatican finally switched it to English. The people said, 'oh, that's what they're saying.' Now only elders attended. And children weren't proficient speaking Yup'ik, Latin, or English.

So much for Jackson's educational system.

"I'll try," said Camilla.

She offered Nick a chance to say something. He flashed her an irritated look. 'Let's go.'

Camilla sipped her tea.

"Mr. Bavilla, I heard something odd this week. Perhaps you could help me to understand it."

"Yes?"

"The high school dismissed a teacher for having a Ouija board. That's what I heard. My question is this… what's the Yup'ik view about séances?"

Nick's jaw unhinged.

What was Camilla doing? Why was she asking this again? She'd brought up the Ouija board with Jerome Paul. It ended a good party. Nick sat on his notebook. He wasn't taking notes on séances for Fish and Game.

Bavilla's forehead puckered.

"Is this part of the survey?"

"No, no. We're done with herring. But as you offered to talk about other things, you must be an expert on this."

Bavilla measured Camilla. His large hands washed.

"Séances… what we believe as Yup'iks about séances."

He shook his head as if he recalled some sordid episode. The wattle of skin swung like a pendulum beneath his neck. His voice was low and sonorous.

"Ouija board… it's a game, you know."

"Yes," Camilla nodded.

"They sell it in Anchorage. That's where you'll find it, a store that sells games. To them, it's only a game. But you will find, if you travel far, what is a game in one place is not a game in another.

"I'll give you an example. Sport fish guides pass through Togiak in summer. They are gathering up the Togiak River right now, putting up their tents for clients. They fish for salmon and trout with rods-and-reels. They call it sport. Sport fishing. It's like a game to them. The kass'aqs catch a fish, take a picture, and let it go. Over and over. Catch-and-release they call it. They are proud of it.

"But that's not the Yup'ik way of doing things. That's not how Yup'iks are taught. We are taught, don't play with fish. Food should not be played with. Food comes from God. If you touch a fish, you must keep it. If you put it back in the water, the fish decrease, especially if you abused it. That's what the elders teach.

"What is a game in one place is not a game in another."

"I see," said Camilla. "Catch-and-release isn't a game for Yup'iks. It's a serious matter."

"Yes."

"The same with a séance?"

Bavilla measured Camilla again.

He placed a finger upon his palm.

"The Bible, you know, forbids sorcery. It forbids the use of charms and spells. You know the Witch of En-dor? She had a familiar spirit. She conjured Samuel for King Saul at Saul's insistence, bringing Samuel back from the dead. Samuel said to Saul, 'Why have you disturbed me? Why have you brought me up?'"

"Yes, I know the Witch of En-dor."

"And the two possessed at Gadarenes. Jesus cast their devils into swine. They rushed into the lake and drowned. You know that one?"

"Yes, I know that one."

Nick sat dumbly. He didn't.

"California, you are from California," Bavilla fluttered his fingers vaguely southward. "We hear about it. What do they call it… channeling? They do channeling in California?"

"I've never seen it," said Camilla.

"They channel the voices of the dead?"

"People pay for it. I've never seen it done."

"As Yup'iks, we are taught, leave the dead alone."

Bavilla pressed his huge hand downward, pushing the anchor deep into the ground.

"Yes," agreed Camilla.

"Let them rest."

Camilla let the point sink in.

"So that's the traditional view," said Camilla. "The Yup'ik view is the same as the Biblical view? Séances are forbidden?"

Bavilla hesitated. He considered the young kass'aq carefully. His forehead puckered equivocally.

"As Yup'iks, we have always tried to discern the will of God. That is the traditional view."

Camilla nodded and waited.

"The elders tell us that," Bavilla continued. "Even the old times, they worked to know God's will. They did not know it fully then. We do not know it fully now. That is what they did. They worked for the truth applied in their lives. We do this now as they did then. That is our tradition as Yup'iks."

Nick heard the measured evasion.

He won't say it's forbidden. Shamans contacted spirits, sometimes like a séance. What was traditional for Yup'iks was to seek truth. His answer worked hard to value the old and the new. Maybe that's why children in Togiak still spoke Yup'ik.

Bavilla was done.

Nick was too. He tried to catch Camilla's eye.

Tua-i. 'That's enough!'

Camilla sat comfortably in the silence.

Bavilla rolled his hands, watching the young kass'aq.

A 'nice man' said Winnie Friendly.

"I think I understand," said Camilla. "But can you tell me then, was something conjured? I mean, the girls who used the Ouija board, the high school girls. What was conjured by it? I didn't understand that point. Was it a Samuel, like you said? Or like the devils in the swine? I didn't understand that."

Nick's jaw dropped again.

Camilla was nuts! She was asking the preacher about conjuring devils!

"Or nothing at all!" blurted Nick.

Bavilla and Camilla turned to look.

"They were kids, right? Fooling around, scaring themselves. Not shamans, just kids, fooling around."

"Yes," agreed Camilla. "maybe nothing got conjured except the imagination of impressionable teens. Do you know what happened?"

Bavilla worried his thick lip with his teeth. Nicholas John, the silent partner, had joined the conversation, blurting out about shamans and kids who scared themselves, the Yup'ik boy from the Yukon River, the university.

Nick felt the eyes.

To his surprise, Bavilla answered the question.

"It was a person."

"A person was conjured?" said Camilla.

"Yes."

"Who says that?" said Nick.

Bavilla frowned at the obstreperous partner.

"Who would say that? I will tell you. My daughter. It was my daughter who said it. My daughter told me. Somebody who knows, you see. She was one of the girls."

Nick reddened.

"They were playing. Like you say, Nicholas. That's how it began. They were playing the new game. They asked it questions. They said it answered."

"Who answered?" said Camilla.

Bavilla wiped a brow, considering.

"Qeng'aq."

"Qeng'aq," said Camilla.

"Somebody suggested it. Ask questions to Qeng'aq. That's what my daughter said. Ask Qenq'aq. So they did."

Nick had never heard of anybody named that. Qeng'aq? It meant 'the nose.' He looked to Camilla. She hadn't either.

"Who is Qeng'aq?" asked Nick.

"You don't know the story of Qeng'aq?"

"No," Nick admitted.

Bavilla sighed. He reached for a cotton kerchief from beneath his large rump. He mopped his face, blew his nose, and folded it square to sit on again.

"Qeng'aq was an angalkuq. Some call them shamans. They still talk of him. I heard his stories as a boy in Stuyahok where I grew up. There he was a great angalkuq capable of great things. He was a warrior, a healer. That's what is told in Stuyahok. But here it's sometimes told differently. He was a devil, a monster, born without a nose, a hole in his face that released his soul at birth. Some say his enemies cut it off and threw it in the river. He was Qengailnguq, 'the noseless one.' There are many stories about Qeng'aq, good and bad."

"Which was he?" asked Nick.

Bavilla shook his head.

"Which one of us isn't both? Isn't that the way with power when judged by others? A shaman was both loved and feared, depending on who hired him."

Nick nodded. This seemed uncommonly astute. His opinion about Bavilla was quickly moderating.

"Why did they want to talk to him?" said Nick.

"Because of the stories, I expect. Like you say, it began as a game. Somebody said, 'let's talk to Qeng'aq.' That's all. Nothing more."

"Why is he remembered?" asked Camilla. "What did Qeng'aq do?"

"Oh, many things… many things."

Bavilla's gaze turned inward.

"The way it's sometimes told, he started good but ended bad because of grief. He lost his son. He threw his grief into the animals. That drove them away. People died, lacking food."

"What happened?" asked Nick.

"He was killed… killed by a Russian convert more powerful than him. Killed by a rival say others. They burned the body. Qeng'aq had visions. He foresaw his own return. They burned his body and scattered his ashes so he couldn't return, to be done with him forever.

"What the girls did, what my daughter did, that was foolish, whether a game or not. The elders tell us, leave the dead alone. Do not bother them."

Nick nodded.

Bavilla was done. His hands lay still.

"Your daughter… is she okay?" asked Camilla.

Bavilla looked at her with surprise.

"Why yes, yes, she's fine, thank you. She's at our camp, fishing."

"I know that game," said Camilla. "It can be unnerving, watching how the marker moves. I'm glad she's fine. Do you know how?"

"What?"

"How the marker moved. Do you remember what it said?"

Bavilla's brow furrowed. He sat a long while studying Camilla. His deep voice answered.

"Nothing… there is nothing to remember."

His great hands washed again.

31

Nick chased Camilla, growing angry.

"What were you doing?"

"What?"

"Asking those questions! What the hell was that about? That has nothing to do with herring!"

"Yeah," agreed Camilla. "Just a second."

Camilla stopped to consult the plat of village houses.

"I think that way."

She stowed the map and headed off.

"That's allowed?"

"What?"

"We can ask anything once we're in the door? You want me to take notes on Ouija boards?"

"If it's interesting."

"Interesting to you! Why the hell are you asking it?"

Camilla whirled in her tracks. Nick almost planted his nose in her face. He smelled her soap.

Nick didn't flinch. Neither did she.

He stared cross-eyed at her nose.

She's crazy! No, she's...

"You want this job to be boring?"

He couldn't tell what was happening. Her nose was almost in his eye, her lips inches from his.

"You already asked Jerome Paul."

Camilla abruptly disengaged.

"And he didn't answer, did he?" She took off again. "Bavilla gave us something. Why didn't Jerome?"

"He didn't know," he said at her heels.

"He knew. Like the ivory. He wouldn't say that either."

"Because we're Fish and Game," said Nick, surprised by her harsh assessment of Jerome.

"But why not Qeng'aq? Jerome Paul would know about Qeng'aq."

"Maybe he was scared."

"Of what?"

"I don't know... getting laughed at."

Camilla whirled again. She shoved her face into his.

"And you hate that? Right? Getting laughed at?"

Her voice took a sudden hardness. This was no longer funny. Yes, he did hate it. Almost more than anything. He'd walk an extra mile to avoid it. Her smile faded.

She stared at Nick's lips, close to hers.

"Me too," she whispered.

She moved back a step.

"I don't know why I asked about it. The board was on my mind, that's all."

She looked him eye-to-eye, subdued.

"Nick, listen. If I get out of line, stop me, okay? Say something. Butt in. Give the cut sign under the chin. Kick me, whatever. Let's be partners, equals. Don't sit and stew. I can do stupid things. Reel me in. Okay? You be the enforcer. Keep me from doing something totally fucking stupid. Can you do that? Okay?"

There was a plea in her voice.

A trace of tears appeared. She blinked them back.

He was glimpsing something real about Camilla.

"Okay," he said.

She turned toward a yellow house among willows.

"This is it, Florence Smith."

She mounted the wooden steps, rapped on the outer door, pushed it open.

"Keep me good, Nick. Not happy. Just good."

Nick followed, knowing something had just changed with their relationship, but not exactly what.

Florence Smith.

They drew the Smiths. Two women, living together.

Winnie Friendly predicted for her too.

"Too shy."

They stood beside the open door into the living room. Florence Smith stared at the floor. She stole glances at Camilla. She wouldn't look at Nick.

"Florence won't talk to you," said Winnie. "And Estella can't."

Florence never married, in her forties, extremely shy, said Winnie. A little slow. Florence took care of Estella. Or it was Estella who took care of Florence. Maybe both ways. Estella Smith was ancient. Who knew how old that woman was? It was a rare arrangement for Yup'iks, two women living alone with no close relatives. People helped them, shared with them, charity for an elder and her ward. Maybe they had relations somewhere but Winnie didn't know. It was a mystery, a history she'd like to hear, but no one told it. You hardly saw Estella anymore. She was a shut-in visited by the deacons.

"They won't know about herring," said Winnie.

Standing at the door, Camilla fully explained the project despite Florence's downcast eyes. Nick stood behind her, embarrassed. He wanted to leave. He almost gave Camilla the cut sign. Yet Camilla showed no discomfort.

What an actor, playing this as normal.

"Do you want to get interviewed?" asked Camilla, after the introduction.

Florence declined with a headshake.

Nick prepared to leave. But Camilla stayed put. She looked around the small living room, simple and uncluttered, floor free of dirt, windows fringed with yellow curtains.

"What a pretty house!"

Florence stole a quick look.

"Did you make the curtains?" asked Camilla, walking to the nearest, fingering the yellow lace. "Such tiny stitches! I'd go blind doing stitches like this."

"Yes, I made them," Florence said shyly, her first real sentence.

"I love the yellows."

Florence gestured to a sewing kit and materials draped on the end of a sofa.

"Are you making this? A baby blanket?"

"Yes."

"Who is it for?"

"Orphans," whispered Florence.

"Orphans," acknowledged Camilla, fingering the soft cotton panels.

She can't be too stupid, thought Nick, if she sews curtains and makes baby blankets for the church.

A faint rap sounded from the back of the house.

Florence reacted immediately. She gestured at a chair, half glanced in Nick's direction, and disappeared down a hall.

"Have a seat, Nick. I think we're staying."

"How do you do that?"

"Do what?" asked Camilla innocently.

"Get invited to stay by somebody as shy as her."

"I don't think it's me she's shy of."

Nick frowned at this suggestion and found a chair.

"What are you seeing?" asked Camilla.

"What?"

"When you look at the room. What do you see?"

Nick looked around him... a nice, neat room, devoid of clutter, cleaner than most living spaces.

"No photos," he said.

Families tacked photos to the walls, children, grandchildren, nieces, nephews, students posed in graduate robes, soldiers posed in uniforms, black-and-white wedding pictures, grandpa in the coffin. The room had nothing.

"That's what Winnie said. No family."

For Yup'iks, it was almost unimaginable, thought Nick. Everybody had relations. You had two sides to find them. Fictive relations filled the voids. You could hardly survive without relatives. It took exceptional circumstances to grow old and kinless in an Eskimo village. What had happened to these women? Winnie didn't know.

A stutter of knocks sounded.

Supported by Florence and a cane, a shrunken woman the height of a child came slowly down the hallway.

Estella Smith.

She was by far the oldest-looking person Nick had ever seen. Hair completely white. A mass of tiny wrinkles. Moon-slit eyes lost above swollen cheekbones. An almost chinless face. Long narrow earlobes swung as she hobbled. Her cane knocked the plywood floor with each slow step.

To Nick's great surprise, Florence guided the ancient woman to his chair. They stopped directly before him. Florence stared at his shoe. But Estella Smith squinted directly into his face. Her eyes, half hidden by lids, rolled like glinting balls. They didn't roll together. One went one way, one another, examining Nick from several directions at once.

He endured the inspection.

He didn't know which eye to follow.

"Cama-i," Nick muttered, 'hello.'

"Cama-i," the elder croaked.

She reached out a bony fingertip and touched Nick's cheek. Her mouth stretched into a nearly toothless grin. The eyeballs disappeared behind her massive cheeks.

With a lean of a shoulder, the old woman turned. Florence directed her to the couch. Carefully sitting her, she placed a stool beneath feet that didn't quite touch the floor. She covered her with a knitted shawl.

The old woman spoke beside her ear.

Florence translated, addressing Nick's left shoe.

"It makes her happy to see you," muttered Florence in English. She ended with a shy smile.

"What?"

"It makes her happy to see you."

Nick looked at Camilla, puzzled. Camilla said nothing, the anthropologist watching events unfold. He was on his own.

"I'm glad to meet you too," replied Nick in English. He repeated it in Yup'ik in a louder voice.

The old woman spoke again by Florence's ear. Florence left for the kitchen. In short order she returned with tea, dried fish, and pilot crackers. They ate together in silence. Florence helped Estella with her cup.

The elder began to speak again.

Florence leaned closer to hear.

"She asks, where you come from?" said Florence.

She pitched it to his shoe.

Speaking Yup'ik, Nick answered. He named his home along the Yukon River. He told how he came by plane through Bethel, then boat from Goodnews Bay. He came with Harry Coopchiak.

The old woman whispered again.

Florence listened and translated.

"She heard about that. It's been a long time."

Nick sat completely perplexed. The elder acted as if she knew him. But he'd never been in Togiak before now. To his knowledge, he'd never met Estella Smith. She was obviously confused. Or Florence had not relayed the message correctly.

"How long has it been?" asked Camilla.

The old woman considered her.

She spoke again to Florence.

"Are you his wife?" asked Florence shyly.

Camilla smiled.

"I work with Nick. I'm not married."

Florence translated for Estella.

The old woman nodded. She spoke again, whispering something, telling something like a story. It lasted some time. Florence listened. She did not stop her to translate. As she listened, her face fell.

Finally the elder finished.

When Florence spoke, it was barely audible.

"It's sad... to lose someone," she whispered.

She lifted her eyes to Camilla.

Camilla waited, her face unreadable.

Florence said nothing more.

"Yes, it is," said Camilla.

The elder resumed.

Florence listened. Tears flooded her eyes.

The elder finished.

Florence looked at no one.

"They say, wait," she whispered. "They are not really lost."

Camilla said nothing.

"Wait," whispered again, "they are not lost forever."

Estella caught a large breath.

She slid to the edge of the couch. Florence moved to help her stand. She placed the cane in the gnarled hand and took her arm. Locked by elbows, they slowly stepped away, side-by-side, down the wooded hall, two women, alone and together, softly knock-knock-knocking the slow passage.

32

At the slough the houses gave way to rustic sheds, fish racks, and abandoned boats overgrown with grass, a conversion inside a short walk. Camilla and Nick wended along a muddy trail through swarms of gnats. It smelled wonderful, a mingling of fish, smoke, and mud baking in the sun.

Following Winnie's directions, they steered toward a metallic blue warehouse incongruously set like polished turquoise among large racks of salmon that dried in the morning calm. The business squatted at the slough's farthest bend, erected on contested property.

The shop of Ken Robbins, a kass'aq.

"His wife's allotment," Winnie explained.

Nick searched for the property on the village plat map after Camilla drew Ken Robbins for an interview. Winnie pointed to it on the meandering slough.

"Her dad fished here. When he died it became hers. It never got conveyed right. That's why it's contested. She left him," speaking of Ken Robbins. "He's trying to escape."

"Escape? He's a crook?" asked Nick, confused, sipping coffee to wake up as Winnie Friendly prepped them for the day's interviews. She had opinions about everybody in town, freely given with the random draw of names. It had become the morning routine.

"A kass'aq," said Winnie, as if that explained everything. She shook her head. "Della showed me her bruises."

"What do you mean, trying to escape?" asked Camilla.

"That's what they say. He's trying to get out of town."

"What's keeping him?"

"I don't know. Maybe he wants Della back. But she won't. He's stuck with that warehouse and those freezers. I think maybe he's broke."

"What's he freeze?" asked Nick, getting interested.

"Anything."

"What?"

"Anything… seals, belugas, trouts, anything you want and he'll freeze and ship it. Makes people mad."

"Why?" asked Camilla.

"Because everything's for sale. He's a real kass'aq."

The blue warehouse had been built with a back on the slough. A floating pier connected a loading bay to the water. Aluminum skiffs parked along it. Large racks filled with drying salmon peeked from behind its sheet-metal walls. The grounds presented a disorder of fish totes, barrels, 55-gallon drums, piles of fishing nets, outboards, crab pots, and cutting tables. The clutter impressed Nick. Even by village standards, this was a lot of stuff.

Ken Robbins was expecting them. They had called ahead for an appointment. He smoked outside, leaning against the warehouse door, dressed in Carhartts and rugged rubber boots. Nick guessed early forties. Big and chunky. Thick hairy forearms. Peeling face. Balding. A thick scar split his sunburned pate like a seismic fault.

"Come on in," he greeted, snubbing out the cigarette.

The warehouse's concrete floor pressed cool beneath their feet. A bank of white freezer units hummed along a wall. Stainless steel cutting tables with water hookups marched down the center. High stacks of buckets, boxes, and crates crowded every corner. A small forklift waited by a sliding door. The place looked clean and freshly scrubbed. A hint of lemon masked something heavier, a clinging odor of flesh, blood, and guts. A processor, surmised Nick. The guy cuts, freezes, and ships food. Robbins guided them to a small office partitioned along a wall. He offered fresh coffee.

The interview on herring went quickly.

Robbins didn't do herring.

"I don't mess with it," grumbled Robbins. "America's not Japan. Goddamn joint ventures."

He threw his rubber boots upon a desk drawer and punctuated statements with a half-filled cup.

Japan had a lock on herring roe, he explained angrily, throwing coffee like holy water. American boats fished, the

Japanese did everything else. Joint ventures. They processed the roe into kazunoko, traditional salted fish eggs for the Japanese New Year, like expensive fruitcake with precise product standards for size, taste, and packaging. The best traded for a hundred dollars a pound. He could never penetrate that.

To Americans, herring was bait. Americans knew nothing about herring. That was stupid! Herring was super food. The oil prevented heart disease. Sea lions, seals, humpback whales... they all thrived on herring. But Americans?

He had experimented with various herring lines, filleted, smoked, dried, kippered. Nobody wanted it. Herring was as foreign to American tastes as cactus or bugs. It was doomed as a domestic product. So he sold smoked salmon, dabbled in frozen whitefish, Dolly Varden, seals for the urban market.

"That's legal?" asked Nick. A kass'aq could sell a seal?

"Everything I do is legal," said Robbins. "I buy the salmon I ship. I can't catch it. I don't have a fishing permit. Wish I did. Same with seals. The hunters bring the seals to me. That's all legal. I catch the whitefish. Anybody can catch whitefish. Those are whitefish nets outside."

"Why don't more people do it?" asked Nick. His own cash-strapped village had lots of whitefish. Nobody sold it.

"Because there's no goddamn market!" Robbins threw coffee in exasperation. "Americans eat fast-food crap and they wonder why their hearts fail. Nobody eats fish! Americans eat less than fifteen pounds of fish all year and that's mostly canned tuna! But they'll eat sixty goddamn pounds of sugar! Six hundred pounds of milk! It's all sugar and cows!

"Here's what happened to me and whitefish," snorted Robbins. "This really happened. I caught some whitefish and flew it to Anchorage, frozen and boxed, shipped on the last flight out. 'Wonderful fish! Beautiful fish!' Safeway tells me. Oh boy, I get excited. I catch some more. I freeze it and call them for the next shipment. 'Don't send any more!' they tell me. 'We can't move this batch!' Why? Because Americans eat crap! They don't know good food when they see it. My beautiful whitefish sat in their cases till they freezer burned! Safeway had to dump them!"

"Yeah," said Nick, thinking of delicious whitefish, but suddenly missing hamburger. He hadn't had one in weeks.

"I go broke trying to sell healthy foods to a nation of fast-food junkies!"

"What about seals?" asked Nick. "I've never seen that in Safeway."

"And you never will. That's Native food. An Eskimo can't eat fast-food crap all the time. You know that. His body needs seal. Most get it from their families. The goddamn postal service would be shocked to see what's inside those care packages shipped from the villages. I sell a few seals to George's Market. It's for those who can't get it any other way. Small potatoes."

He shook his head.

"Smoked salmon, how does that work?" asked Camilla.

"It don't!" shouted Robbins, warmed up. "It would, but the goddamn government sticks us with ridiculous regulations! You wouldn't believe it. They're killing small business. See those stainless steel tables out there? Stupid! FDA comes through the state and says, 'no smoked salmon cut on wood tables!' It nearly killed me. I bought those to stay afloat, goddamn thousands of dollars in debt, and are they any cleaner? No! Oh, they shine and they sparkle. They look cleaner. But wood's just as clean. Maybe cleaner! There's not a shred of proof that stainless steel is more sanitary than wood."

"Then why did they require it?" asked Camilla.

"To stick us! The government's in bed with the goddamn corporations!"

Robbins launched into a rant about global conglomerates destroying smallholder businesses. Camilla and Nick put aside their notebooks, dodged coffee drops, and listened. It wasn't herring, but it was entertaining. Robbins played by the rules and barely stayed afloat. He'd open a new niche market and the regulators would close it. Without smoked salmon, he'd be dead. It sold at twenty dollars a pound in catalogs. But it would be years to recoup investments in stainless steel tables and water hookups. Salmon prices had tanked from too much farmed crap on the market. He survived only because he constantly tried new things, a dozen failures for one success.

Robbins ran to a cooler and pulled out a package of shrink-wrapped salmon. 'Traditional Alaska Native Smoked,' a white polar bear label proclaimed. He slit the wrap with a pocketknife, gouged out generous chunks, and offered them to Camilla and Nick.

"Now that's a success. Tasty, isn't it?"

"Hmmm, good," said Camilla, licking her fingers.

"Yeah," said Nick, thinking the fish was too dry and had no proper crust. The smoke tasted funny too, like the spray-on stuff. At his home, no one would pay twenty dollars a pound for this. They'd laugh at you. But Nick wasn't going to insult Robbins. The guy had enough troubles.

"You ever do walrus?" asked Camilla, taking more smoked salmon.

"What's that?"

"You said you dabbled. Do you ever sell walrus?"

"God, no," he snorted. "You can't get any walruses here! Everything's shut up tight."

"Shut up? How?"

"You see those fancy ass boats outside?" asked Robbins, getting more agitated.

"The aluminum jobs?" asked Nick.

"I got those to transport visitors to the sanctuary. But I can't do it. I can't get a goddamn permit! Your outfit's screwed me!"

"My outfit?" said Camilla.

"Fish and Game! They've locked it up with one transporter. That's illegal! You tell your boss that. That's an illegal monopoly! Transporter permits got to be spread around."

"The state sanctuary... so that's a problem," said Camilla.

"No, that's good!"

"Good?"

"That sanctuary," he replied, shaking a greasy finger, "without that sanctuary, there'd be no walrus around here. The ivory poachers would clean out those islands. That's what your study's all about, isn't it? Round Island headhunting?"

"By the herring fleet?" asked Camilla.

"Whoever! They'd clean it out."

"So the government's doing something right," said Camilla.

"Not the goddamn feds! It was the state that closed it. But the state has screwed me with their back-ass sweetheart deals."

Robbins grabbed more salmon and angrily chewed. Camilla and Nick watched his blood pressure build.

"Eco-tourism, that's a future! I saw it coming years ago. Tourists will pay big bucks to get out to places like that. They camp up on top and sip their fancy wines and take pictures because that's the last one left. There used to be haul-outs up and down the Pacific coast, British Columbia, Washington. Think about that... Washington walrus. Wiped out! That's the last one. It's got to be a money-maker."

"You don't support opening it up?" asked Camilla.

"Open it up?"

"For subsistence hunts."

"No! No way!" boomed Robbins. "The goddamn ivory thugs would clean it out. No! Never in a hundred lifetimes."

Robbins grabbed the last morsel of salmon and shoved it into his mouth, his face as red as the fillet. Good thing he eats that stuff, thought Nick. His bulging arteries look ready to blow.

"That's not hard on the carvers?" probed Camilla.

"What carvers? Nobody carves ivory around here."

"Some do," said Nick.

"Who?" challenged Robbins.

"Jerome Paul carves."

Camilla shot Nick one of her looks.

Oops, thought Nick. He had disclosed information from another interview. But the information about Jerome Paul hadn't come from an interview, Nick remembered. It came from the party.

"Jerome? He carves ivory? You been interviewing him?" asked Robbins.

"Not really," said Camilla, "we looked at his baskets and..."

"Baskets?" Robbins interrupted, carefully eying Camilla.

"His grass baskets. Necklaces. Ivory. He was teaching me the difference between old ivory and new ivory. But I think he said the new ivory didn't come from Round Island. Right Nick?"

"Uh, yeah," replied Nick, embarrassed that he recalled that conversation with some difficulty.

Robbins waited for Camilla and Nick to say more, but they didn't.

"He said that? Well, of course he'd say that," Robbins huffed. "You work for Fish and Game. Nobody's going to tell you anything. But let me tell you straight, don't believe a word you hear about ivory or Round Island walrus around here. Don't trust nobody there."

He spat out salmon skin.

"Especially Jerome Paul."

With a flourish of his empty cup, the interview ended.

33

The infamous Isaac Nuniq.

Nick jumped at the interview.

Winnie dished out her opinions with the pancakes while Camilla and Nick drew households from the clinic list. They would interview separately today.

"He's a sovereignty nut," cautioned Winnie.

"I know," said Nick.

"He hates Fish and Game."

"Me too."

"He's militant!"

Winnie made a scary face and Nick laughed.

Now Nick wasn't so sure. He stared at an agitated giant across a checkered tablecloth. Isaac Nuniq was huge. He had heft enough to toss Nick through the open kitchen window, one-handed. Isaac was considering it.

Isaac's pretty wife, Patti, worked at the kitchen sink. She declared that wasn't going to happen today. Something like that just wasn't happening. Isaac wasn't going to jail again anytime soon if she had anything to say about it. She was tired of doing all the fishing and boat repairs and childcare, not when she had a husband.

"Next time you land in jail, we're finished," she declared, standing maybe five foot two at the cutting board. She'd go back home to Oregon. That was her home, the Umatilla reservation. She and Isaac met at Indian boarding school.

"A waste of time."

"Just talk to him, Isaac," Patti said, chopping potatoes.

"I've talked to hundreds like him."

"Hundreds?" said Nick.

"Hundreds," Isaac displayed his fingers, laying them down one by one. "Biologists, fish managers, politicians, reporters, students, do-gooders... it does nothing! Changes nothing! You talk and talk and talk and nothing happens. The only way to change anything is to just go do it!"

Nick understood Isaac Nuniq did exactly that. He fished when he wanted. He hunted where he wanted. He took as much as he needed for his large extended family. He lived as they did traditionally, Isaac claimed, before the meddlesome state and federal agencies. He was asserting his traditional rights. This protest had got him ticketed, arrested, fined, and jailed. Nick had heard of Isaac's exploits for years. That's why he wanted the interview, to meet the legend. So far, the renegade lived up to his billing.

"Just talk to him," sighed Patti.

"Okay," he swiveled to Nick. "I'll answer questions if you can tell me why it matters. After this study, will there be fewer boats stealing our herring?"

Nick shook his head 'no'. The study had nothing to do with the number of outside commercial herring boats.

"Will they lower the caps to protect herring?"

Again, Nick shook his head 'no'. The study had nothing to do with herring quotas.

"Will they reopen Round Island?"

Reopen the island? Nick didn't know.

"See? A waste of time! Why talk? What's the point?"

"Document subsistence herring to get it recognized by the state for protection," volunteered Nick, repeating what Camilla said in her introductions.

Isaac roared with laughter.

"Recognized by the state? We don't want it recognized by the state! Keep it hidden! That's what protects it. Keep it secret! When the state recognizes anything, it's as good as gone! Outsiders come and take it! It gets closed, regulated out of existence! They can't steal what they don't know exists!"

"Isaac," said Patti dismissively.

"What are you chopping up?" asked Nick, his stomach feeling empty from mid-morning pancakes.

"Walrus," said Patti.

"You caught a walrus?"

"Afcan Tooluyuk," said Patti.

"They closed that," said Isaac. "Is your study going to get that back?"

"What?"

"Walrus. They took that away from us."

"You got some, right there."

"Bullshit!"

"Isaac!" warned Patti.

"Bullshit! You hear about me and walrus?"

Nick shook his head, smiled, and leaned back to listen. This was a great interview.

"I go out to Round Island to hunt. I go out to get a walrus so the elders can have a taste. I even told them ahead of time. 'I'm going out there to teach my son how we used to do it, the traditional way.' One walrus! I'm going out to get one walrus. And what happens? They send in the state troopers! Jesus! What if I had gone out to take two walrus? They'd have called up the National Guard! It's an Indian uprising!"

Patti began laughing.

"It's true," she said.

"But that rich kass'aq, he can go out anytime he wants!" growled Isaac. "Fish and Game gives him a goddamn permit. He takes out tourists for a ton of money and the elders can't have one walrus just to taste? My son can't learn his heritage? It's bullshit!"

"The island's closed without a tourist permit?"

"Not to me!"

"Yes, it's closed," said Patti. "Can you stay to eat?"

"It's not closed to tourists!"

"That used to be a hunting place?" asked Nick.

Issac yelped, incredulous, like Nick had asked if birds could fly.

"What I mean is, how could that happen, get closed to hunting?" amended Nick.

"You tell me. You're Fish and Game. You tell me how it happened. You work for them. Tell me how something like that could happen."

"You don't know?"

"He knows," said Patti. "Can you stay for dinner?"

"Sure, I never get walrus."

"We don't either," growled Isaac. "Forty years without walrus because of Fish and Game."

"Well somebody got some, if that's a walrus," said Nick reasonably. The slab of meat went into the oven, smothered in onions.

"It's not," growled Isaac.

"Yes it is," said Patti, removing freshly baked bread where the walrus went.

"It's road kill!"

"It's walrus," said Patti to Nick, as if saying, 'just ignore him.'

"Road kill?"

"Road kill. Run over by some goddamn herring boat."

"He doesn't know," said Patti.

"A hunter can't take one walrus from Round Island without them calling in the troopers, but goddamn herring boats can run over dozens."

"Afcan Tooluyuk found it."

"Found it?" asked Nick.

"On the beach," said Patti.

"Oh," said Nick, finally understanding, "it's scavenged."

He instantly regretted it.

Isaac leaped from his chair. He gripped the back of Nick's neck with a beefy hand and squeezed like an industrial press. He whispered into his ear.

"You think we like that? You think we like being called scavengers? Like vultures? Eating road kill scraped off the rocks because Fish and Game closed our island? Huh?"

Nick gave a non-committal grunt.

"Let's go hunting, you and me," Isaac smiled evilly. "Then you'll see. We'll hunt them like we're supposed to hunt them, just like Fish and Game wants us to hunt, on my boat, hunting walrus, just you and me, together!"

"Isaac!" warned Patti.

* * *

The island drifted off the bow like land needing anchor. Isaac Nuniq nosed his boat into the swell. For the first time, Nick saw Qayassiq, called Round Island by the kass'aqs, the Walrus Islands Preserve.

Nick lifted binoculars. He studied the landscape he'd been hearing about. A cliff with a shaggy top rose off a rocky beach. That's where the tourists sit, on the grassy top, Isaac explained. Nick saw no signs of tourists this afternoon. The boat was far offshore. But Nick understood that they sat on top, looked down, and took pictures of the walrus beneath them. They camped elsewhere on the island to laugh and sip wine and celebrate their elite visitor status.

Nick surveyed the bottom of the cliff.

Walrus filled the beach. They were sleeping, hundreds, maybe thousands, closely packed, back-to-back, side-by-side, skin-against-skin, the extreme of tactile existence, buddies crammed among buddies, dreaming walrus dreams. They glowed rosy pink, a great field of sandstone boulders awash with sun. All were males, Nick understood, but he supposed no one was down there inspecting the goods.

These walrus had lost out to the dominant males, Philip Elsberry claimed. They had stepped aside and stayed behind when the females traveled north with the pack ice. As punishment for their submission, they slept with bellies full of clams in the mild summer sun, glowing a healthy pink while the macho males floated north, wearing out their bodies trying to defend harems. The punishment was biologically severe, Nick supposed. Genes wouldn't pass through them. They were biological surplus.

Through the binoculars, the surplus looked content.

"Can we get closer?" asked Nick.

"Not without making Patti mad," said Isaac, smiling into the spray. The militant renegade had turned engagingly friendly once on the water. He pointed to a GPS range finder. "We're at the edge of the buffer. I can't risk my marriage for Fish and Game. And my son's watching."

He winked at his boy, Jacob, an eleven-year-old, who smiled back and surveyed the island with Nick. Jacob decided he liked Nick. He was glued to him wherever he went on the boat. Isaac brought the engine to an easy idle.

"We used to hunt from the other side. That's what the elders tell us. That's where I went to hunt the time they called the troopers. There's a bay inside there. You sneak up and choose the ones you want. You shoot them on the rocks. Then you butcher, load, clean up, and come home. That's how it was done."

"With a group?"

"A group with a hunt leader, like an elder, an expert. He made sure the rules got followed. Nothing wasted. Everything cleaned up."

"Do they stampede?"

"That's what walrus do. They're not going to just lie there to get shot like a cow. They're going to escape. But they always come back. As long as you clean up, they come back. That's what the elders tell us."

"When was the last group hunt?"

"Oh, I don't know. Forty, fifty years ago? There's hardly anybody left who remembers. We should start up again while there are still elders to show us how to do it right. I want my son to be able to teach his son. It's become a memory."

Isaac cranked up the engine and moved off. The sun's low rays cast the ocean in silver. A perfect evening for riding.

"Now you're going to see how Fish and Game wants us to hunt, from a boat on the open water."

"What's wrong with that?" said Nick, though he imagined he knew already.

"You got to find them swimming," said Isaac. "That's not so hard. They feed on the bottom in the evenings, so we may find some tonight. But you got to harpoon them. That's the problem. You can shoot them all right, but walrus go down fast and stay down. If you hit them, they always dive or sink. They go down like stones. You got to get a line and a drag fixed right away. On land, like we used to do it, there's no waste. On the open ocean, it's almost impossible not to lose them. I don't get why Fish and Game wants us to hunt on the water. It makes no sense. That's why nobody does it."

Isaac goosed the boat. Nick looked ahead. Walrus heads bobbed on the surface. Isaac raced to them. At about a hundred yards, the heads disappeared. They didn't resurface. Isaac slowed the boat.

"See? They don't let you get too close. You could shoot at them, all right, but for what? To watch them sink?"

"Can you call them close like a seal?"

"Seals are curious. They aren't seals."

"Maybe there's a call."

"You try."

Isaac brought the boat sideways against the wind and cut the motor. They drifted lazily on the silver water. Isaac coiled line beside several white floats and set a metal point onto a harpoon shaft. Nick and Jacob watched the water.

"There!" Jacob said, pointing excitedly.

A walrus head bobbed in the water about a hundred yards downwind. They drifted closer. It disappeared.

"He smelled us," said Isaac. "They got bad eyes and good noses. Look on the other side."

Nick and Jacob switched sides and stared into the wind and lowering sun. Eventually another head bobbed up. Nick took a fish gaff. He lightly tapped the boat. The head stayed up.

"That sometimes brings in seals," Nick whispered to Jacob. "Look. He's interested. But not enough to come over."

Nick put his hands around his mouth. He blew air to vibrate his lips.

"Brrrrp! Brrrrp!"

The walrus head came up higher.

"Get down!" whispered Isaac urgently. The three hid behind the boat's wale, peering over the edge. "Do that again."

"Brrrrp! Brrrrp!" Nick called.

"I'll be damned," whispered Isaac. "He's coming over!"

Isaac passed the harpoon to Nick.

"You throw. I'll shoot. Jacob, you toss the float."

Nick nodded. His heart began pounding.

Jacob moved back, making room.

"Brrrrp! Brrrrp!" went Nick, gathering his legs beneath him.

The walrus drifted closer... closer... head up.

With a surge, Nick rose.

He heaved the harpoon. A rifle shot blasted. The rope whirred angrily with smoky dust. Nick felt a powerful jerk. His legs yanked! He flipped and slammed the wale. Before he could shout or grab, he went over.

Whoosh! He was swallowed!

He filled his lungs before hitting.

The surface disappeared above him. He flailed, body plunging down, pulled and stretched by a leg. He was caught on the line! The walrus was dragging him under!

Water pressed around him. This was life or death.

Nick twisted. He found his ankles. He groped for the rope. There it was! A loop beneath a kink around his leg. He frantically grabbed and pulled. The line came.

He popped free.

Black rose beneath him.

He slammed into the seafloor. A cloud of mud exploded. He saw the trailing float zip like a fish. Wham! It walloped his head. Sparks flew. His air blew out in a shower of bubbles.

He plowed the bottom.

Nick desperately spread his arms. He flailed for bearings in the mud. His hand touched something flat, upright, like a wall.

It stretched to either side. Green light shimmered from an opening. Nick kicked in, shoved his head into a green bubble, and gasped. His lungs filled with stale air. His knee struck hard. Stairs! He stumbled, found their shape, staggered from the water, and collapsed.

The air-filled space flickered with green light and stank of fish, the odor of an old cutting room. His chest heaved, his lungs starved, his head as light a balloon. He buckled and fell again but hatchery workers, that's what it had to be, a hatchery setup, grabbed his elbows, brought him upright, and walked him. They shuffled into a roar, a commotion, not really a fish canning station, more like an unruly convention.

They hung him over a rail to clear his senses. He stared into a chamber of long tables of mahogany and teak, shimmering like lime ice cream. The room was fully packed, side-by-side, moving with walrus. They complained in loud groans, not contented pink beneath an evening sky but brown-suited and angry in the pit. Two huge males faced off chest-to-chest, their heads thrown back and tusks positioned, defending differences with bellowed threats. A cormorant perched above the faceoff, screaming from a pedestal. Chesty sergeants at arms shoved on the floor, restoring order.

In a far corner, others played, oblivious to the uproar. Bingo cards covered the polished tables. A sea lion brayed numbers. Clamshell markers searched for solutions.

A headset clamped over his ears. An attendant adjusted a knob, scanning across translations to catch the cormorant's final statement.

"...disaster! It will be a disaster! Complete destruction! For us, our children, our children's children! Time is running out! We must act now! Thank you!"

The cormorant soared from the podium. A huge walrus rose above the pit and bellowed through Nick's earphones.

"Order! Order for the keynote speaker! Bingo too!"

The walrus pointed across the floor. The clamor of the chamber immediately fell. Heads moved in unison. They stopped, finding Nick heeled over, gripping the rail, panting the rarified air. Nick stared back. He was the keynote!

A huge male, one of the angry duelers, lunged across the convention floor. He plowed through the mass of walrus, roaring a challenge through the headset.

"He's a spy! A spy!"

"No! He's the keynote!"

212

Pandemonium erupted.

The speaker leaped into the pit to intercept the disruptor. They collided, chest against chest.

A single declaration exploded from the corner.

"BINGO!"

Nick saw the blast wave. It swept across the convention floor. In horror, Nick watched as flesh shuddered and peeled from the walrus heads, most looking up to him, stripping rows of skulls perched on skeletal shoulders, white tusks shining like unsheathed scimitars. The tusks and bones trembled, ripped apart, and exploded into billowing clouds of dust that swirled toward centers that sparkled like stars.

The sound of the blast hit next.

With a great roar, Nick burst into air

Pounding filled his head. His lungs heaved in rank exhaust. A gaff pole shoved at his face. Nick grabbed it two fisted. It dragged him to a ladder. He clambered halfway and got bodily yanked by Isaac's great hands and thrown coughing to the deck. Jacob grabbed his neck. The little boy was sobbing.

Isaac knelt and gently lifted Nick's chin, a quick and sympathetic inspection

He declared simply, concluding the lesson.

"That's why we like haul-outs."

34

Nick speared hash browns at Winnie's table.

She had just heard the news from her brother who had heard it that morning from somebody else who heard it from Isaac Nuniq. Not yet eight a.m. and the story circulated. Winnie was shocked. Her children saw Mom's expression. They followed her around the kitchen, listening carefully, trying to understand.

Camilla observed from the table's end. She sipped her coffee. That's how children learned everywhere, tailing moms.

"Gone! That's what he said!"

Nick said nothing.

"In that black water, just gone!"

Nick again said nothing.

"They looked and looked and looked, and then up you pop like a cork!"

Nick smiled weakly.

"Dumb luck."

"Luck?"

"Popped up by the boat."

"Popped up by the prop! Popped up, nearly chopped up! That's what they said!"

Nick jabbed at a potato.

"How could it happen? You step in the rope?"

Nick blushed an angry crimson.

Yeah, he got stupid.

He didn't harpoon walrus every day. He forgot his feet and stepped into the coiled rope. She didn't have to broadcast it.

His face said as much.

Winnie got the message. She shepherded the children into the bedroom to dress.

"You're embarrassed," said Camilla.

Nick continued to spear potatoes.

"You were almost killed hunting walrus and you're embarrassed? Is this, like, a Yup'ik thing?"

Nick waved his fork in frustration.

"She doesn't have to talk about it in front of them."

"It's not like you were arrested for drunk driving or something. It was an accident."

Nick's look at her suggested he didn't think so.

"That's what I'll tell headquarters," said Camilla.

"Don't do that. They don't have to know."

"We're not supposed to report accidents?"

"What accident? Look at me, I'm fine!"

Camilla was incredulous.

He looked almost anxious.

"Well, if you're not hurt. No property damaged. I mean, they'll want to know, but I guess they don't have to hear it from me. They'll find out eventually, Nick. Winnie knows. Half the town knows."

"There's no way they'll find out if we don't tell them."

He resumed eating. Camilla watched.

"You want to talk about it?"

"What?"

"What happened. They say it helps... talking."

"Helps what?"

"I don't know. Make sense of it. Put it into perspective. Release the demons. You're deep into something. Whatever happened, it helps to talk."

Nick put down the fork.

"There's no way to make sense of it."

"Of what?"

Camilla's brows arched like question marks. Her face was inquisitive, undemanding. She calmly sipped her coffee, waiting.

How does she do that?

"Make sense of what?"

"What I saw."

"You saw something?"

"Underwater."

Camilla nodded and waited.

Nick said nothing more.

"You saw something underwater, something that doesn't make sense. What did you see? The walrus you harpooned?"

Nick shook his head. He had re-lived it, even in his dreams.

"Lots of walrus."

"Lots of walrus."

"The bottom of the bay. I think... I think it was... I don't know... a hallucination, the weirdest I've ever had."

"You have hallucinations?"

"No, not like that. I don't get hallucinations. I couldn't breathe. My air was gone. I got hammered by the float. It seemed absolutely real, not like a dream. It wasn't dreamlike at all. It was like... I don't know, like they say people see their lives pass by, just before death?"

"You saw your life pass by?"

"No, I saw walrus, lots of walrus! And... you're not going to laugh at me, are you?"

"I don't know. I don't think so."

"They talked."

"Hmmm...."

"They talked."

"Like... in Yup'ik?"

"In walrus! I had a headset. They gave me a headset with translations like the United Nations. See, you're smiling, you're going to laugh."

"It wouldn't be nice if I did," said Camilla, her eyes beginning to shine. "What did they say?"

"Nothing. They fought. They argued. There wasn't any time because, well, a cormorant said there wasn't any time left. There was a cormorant. He was warning them. There was some great danger, some disaster coming. They wanted me to say something, to make a speech. Then everything exploded. I think it was the bingo. Somebody won the bingo. And everything blew up. They turned into bones and the bones disintegrated like dust twirling around sparks. That was their souls. They returned into souls that sparkled like stars."

Nick looked hard at Camilla.

She watched him intently. She wasn't smiling.

"Then I was up."

"You surfaced?"

"Yeah."

"By the boat."

"I don't remember swimming up. I was just there, by the boat, breathing exhaust."

216

"Right by the boat."

"They pulled me out."

"Yeah."

"Jesus! I was at the bottom of the bay!"

Nick looked around for his coffee cup. He didn't have one. Camilla pushed him hers. He took a large gulp, reviewing it all again.

"The bottom of the fucking bay," he whispered.

Camilla watched the emotions cross his face.

"And you lived."

"Yeah," said Nick.

She gently squeezed his hand.

"You're a lucky guy."

"Yeah."

"Somebody down there must like you."

35

Theresa Manumik, the Village Health Aide, graciously relinquished her office phone. From the ether, the hollow voices of Jeff Hall in Anchorage and Mel Savidge in Juneau crackled over the speaker. It had been three days since the last conference call. The walrus hunt was not yet a day old.

"Hi Camilla and Nick," said Jeff.

"Hi to everybody," said Mel. "Got to keep this short. There's a meeting in ten minutes."

"Okay, short it is," said Camilla. "We wanted to keep you abreast of developments, uh... about walrus."

"Walrus? Not herring?" said Mel. "Go ahead. Shoot."

"We're getting an earful about walrus," said Camilla, checking Nick for confirmation. "We're focused on herring, but another big issue is walrus."

"Hunting for ivory?" asked Jeff.

"Hunting for food. That's the issue. People can't hunt walrus for food. They blame the State."

"Wait, wait," said Mel. "Okay, I'm taking notes. Give me a quick rundown. That's where I'm going in ten minutes. It's a meeting on buffers around Round Island. Give me what you've got."

"Okay, Yup'iks used to hunt Round Island for walrus. Small parties with hunt leaders killed walrus on the island, butchered, and cleaned up. When the State created the sanctuary, no one here remembers being consulted. They were left out of the decision. The closure caught hunters by surprise. Now the only way to get walrus to eat is to find them dead on the beach. They can't hunt in open water."

"Wait, I'm writing," said Mel. "Okay, why can't they hunt in open water?"

"Struck-and-loss… it's too wasteful. Nobody wants to kill and lose a walrus. That happens in open water hunting. Hunters want to hunt on land again. Some are threatening just to go hunt on Round Island, get arrested, and make their case in court. Others would prefer a negotiated solution. They'd be satisfied with a regulated subsistence hunt. That's it in a nutshell," said Camilla.

"Is that right, Nick?" asked Mel.

"Tourists can go out there and elders can't. How is that right? Tourists look at walrus and elders starve. It's salt in the wound."

"Jeff, you know about this?" asked Mel.

"We do know about this. But we've never had anyone assigned to it. There's a local hunter group pushing with the tribe to open the sanctuary. But they haven't gotten far."

"Why not?" asked Mel.

"It's a jurisdictional mess. The State controls the island, but the Feds manage the walrus. The State lost walrus management in court. You can guess why. It was a case from Togiak. Some sovereignty advocates have used this issue to press for tribal rights, which flips out the State. Add to this ivory and environmentalists who think walrus shouldn't be hunted and it's a mess."

"So they can't get changes?"

"Proposals bog down instantly. Unless something drastic happens to shake things loose, with those powerful interests at play, nothing's going to change anytime soon."

A long silence followed.

"Shit," whispered Mel.

"Mel?" said Jeff. "Check your inbox. I've just sent you a request from the tribe for a hunt on Round Island. I dug it from my files while we talked. It's a couple years old. But it's probably still good for showing what some hunters want."

"Okay, got it," said Mel. "Yeah. Perfect. Hey everybody, I really have to run. Great call! Thanks for the stuff!"

The call ended with a button push.

* * *

To Mel the conference room was déjà vu, same players from the first herring meeting. Derby Peters directed. Dr.

Philip Elsberry, King of Assholes, sat beside him, looking pissed. Jeffery Means from the Fisheries Board idly picked at his thumb. Fred Hendricks and Bud Jerkins from Commercial Fisheries read emails on their laptops, already checked out. But no Sgt. Combs in his blue suit. There were no new corpses to talk about. Filling his place was a new player, Kurt Tromble, head of the Fisheries Board.

Mel had an instant brainstorm. She chuckled gleefully.

Kurt Tromble also chaired the Joint Board of Fisheries and Game! Oh boy! This was perfect!

Derby Peters brought things to order and introduced Tromble. The meeting's topic was the proposed buffer zone around Round Island. The other proposal about a single-period herring fishery had already died a quiet death.

Derby let Elsberry brief Tromble about the need for the increased buffer to protect the walrus sanctuary from marauding herring boats. Bud Jerkins spoke about potential effects on the commercial herring fishery. They could still take the quota but boats might catch more immature fish. Tromble asked a couple of polite questions.

The buffer proposal appeared headed for the Fisheries Board. The meeting drew to a close.

"Anyone else with comments?" asked Derby. He almost crossed his eyes seeing Mel's hand.

"Thanks," replied Mel turning slightly so Kurt Tromble could see her earnest (and she knew, gorgeous) profile.

"As the representative of the Subsistence Division, I'm here for the Director to say we're concerned about impacts on subsistence food by the proposed new buffer. We're concerned that the impacts receive proper consideration by the Board."

Kurt Tromble perked up. No one had mentioned 'subsistence' in relation to the buffer proposal. Elsberry snickered and jumped at the bait.

"Impacts on subsistence in Togiak?" sneered Elsberry. "Togiak doesn't use herring for subsistence."

"Well, of course they use herring at Togiak," replied Mel politely, "though this may not be well known to marine mammal biologists. But I'm referring to other subsistence impacts... on walrus."

Elsberry's mouth froze open. Derby Peters began to squirm. He was losing control of another meeting. Hendricks and Jerkins of Commercial Fisheries smiled and turned from their laptops. They hated Elsberry's buffer. With subsistence on the table, it was their turn to enjoy a show. Elsberry quickly recovered.

"That's a federal issue," objected Elsberry. "The Feds manage walrus hunting."

"Technically, that's true," replied Mel calmly, "but it's a State sanctuary. The State closed access, including access for subsistence hunting. I believe the State's position has been that Togiak hunters can fill their walrus needs by hunting in open water. The proposed buffer closes waters where the State has encouraged Togiak hunters to get walrus in lieu of hunting on land. So of course, the State will want to examine the proposed buffer's potential impacts on food in Togiak. I'm sure the State would not support a buffer that inadvertently jeopardized the diets of Togiak's children."

Elsberry choked.

'Gotcha!' smirked Mel.

"That's a hunting issue, not fishing," said Derby Peters, jumping to plug the breach.

"I agree," replied Mel. "It seems to us that the buffer proposal has both fishing and hunting implications. When I said we hoped it would receive proper consideration, and perhaps mitigation, by the Board, I was referring to the Joint Board of Fisheries and Game. That board can deal with mixed issues. Mr. Tromble, you head the Joint Board too?"

Mel flashed him a perfect smile.

"Uh, yes I do," replied Tromble cautiously. "But I can't imagine what 'mitigation' might be, except not to increase the buffer. Is that what you mean by 'mitigation'?"

"Yes, but also maybe this," said Mel. She passed out a single sheet. "I'm sure you know about this, Mr. Tromble, but I doubt that our herring managers do. This is a request from a hunter group at Togiak. It asks for a small, managed walrus hunt on Round Island. The enlarged buffer may make this request more pertinent. Of course, some hunters claim the courts should allow Natives to hunt on Round Island regardless of State closures. I suspect the State would find a small, managed hunt preferable to that sort of freewheeling solution. Don't you think, Mr. Tromble?"

She gave him another beatific smile.

Kurt Tromble returned it, acknowledging her clever hijacking of the issue.

And to the fish managers' delight and Elsberry's chagrin, based on information from the Division of Subsistence, the herring buffer proposal got referred, not to the Fisheries Board, but to the Joint Board of Fisheries and Game to assess its potential impacts on fishing and walrus hunting. With unanimity, the committee took Elsberry's carefully crafted buffer proposal and tossed it into regulatory hell.

36

Camilla stared at the dead speaker phone. The conference call had ended. She checked the clock.

"I should make another call."

"Want me to leave?" asked Nick.

"Only if you want."

She punched the long string of numbers. Nick stayed, curious, wishing he spoke Spanish.

"*Diga*," a voice answered, still on speaker.

"*Buenas tardes, Javier*," answered Camilla with a smile.

Once again, Javier in Chiapas.

As before, they conversed, and Camilla's smile gave way to sadness. With a muffled thud, Javier did something with the phone. A female's voice came on. Camilla spoke to her for some while in Spanish. The woman asked questions. Camilla responded. From Chiapas, Nick heard crying. He saw tears in Camilla's eyes. The female voice resumed bravely. Camilla listened and replied with assurance. The phone got passed again. Javier was back. He said goodbye and *buena suerte*. The call ended. It had taken less than ten minutes.

Camilla took a deep breath and wiped her eyes.

"Family?" asked Nick.

Camilla nodded. He made his guess.

"The family of Francisco Fernández Muñoz."

"His sister."

The sister of the dead man.

"How did you find her?"

"I didn't," said Camilla sadly. "My friend did, Javier Tampecho, on the phone. I played a hunch. I thought he might know how to find the family. He did."

"That was his sister?"

"They brought her in from her village. His family farms about two hours from that phone."

"You've been in Chiapas?"

"Guerrero, a different region. I worked on a health project for my dissertation, family planning, immunization, nutrition, those kinds of things, four regions simultaneously. Javier did Chiapas. You get to know lots of people doing health surveys, lots of connections. A name like Fernández Muñoz in Mexico is like Smith here. But Javier was able to find them. It was the Alaska connection. Not many from Chiapas take work in Alaska. That was notable, traceable. Fernández sent money to support his parents."

"You told her he was dead?"

"Javier did yesterday. They suspected it after his last package. They never heard from him. Now they know for certain. They've contacted authorities. But they know next to nothing. They don't understand how it could happen. They want desperately to know. They want his body back."

"What? Where's his body?"

"It's still up here."

"He's been dead a month!"

"The body is in Anchorage," said Camilla grimly. "They've been trying to find the family. But he was undocumented. How do you find the family of undocumented workers who have died? It happens a lot more than we imagine."

A tragedy, thought Nick. A family member leaves for work and disappears. Yup'iks worked hard to recover bodies. Whole villages searched to find them.

"What was the package?" asked Nick.

"What?"

"The last package he sent. Money?"

"Money gets wired. He sent gifts. And a note that said he was fine. He had found better work."

"Did he say what?"

"*Con los angeles.*"

"What? In Los Angeles?"

"No. *Con los angeles.* 'With the angels.'"

"The angels?"

"That's what his letter said. It said he found a better job with the angels."

Tears came to Camilla's eyes.

"That's why they knew he was dead."

37

Paul Smart, an elder and long-time subsistence fisherman, provided detailed answers about herring. The whole while, he stared at Nick, the translator.

He seemed to be listening for errors.

That pissed off Nick.

Camilla asked in English. Nick translated into Yup'ik. The elder answered in Yup'ik. Nick translated back into English. Back and forth it went. Slow. Arduously slow. The elder listened to everything. He seemed to follow it all.

Why didn't he just speak English!

A traditional elder, Winnie said.

She didn't have much to do with Paul Smart.

His family and her family were not on speaking terms. They had feuded for generations. Why? Winnie didn't really know. Nobody had ever told her. Paul Smart was highly respected. He knew lots of things. He was active at church. Her contacts with him were in that capacity. Otherwise, she hadn't spoken with Paul Smart more than a few times her entire life.

She sighed.

That's how things went between families.

The interview ended.

Camilla thanked the elder. But she didn't stow her notes. Instead, she sat quietly at the kitchen table on the paint-splattered chair, contentedly sipping tea.

Paul Smart acknowledged her thanks.

He returned to look at the translator.

Nick knew what Camilla was doing. She had noticed the old man's interest in Nick. She was giving him an opportunity to reveal it. They didn't wait long.

"You're the person of the Yukon River," he said in Yup'ik.

"Yes."

"I know of people from there."

This was a question about his family.

Get over the translating.

Nick took a breath. He named his grandmother, his aunt, and cousins. He did not have a large family to list. The old man listened carefully. Nick finished and sat respectfully. Paul Smart was an elder. Elders enjoyed high status among traditional Yup'iks. Nick was an acculturated Yup'ik. Elders made him nervous.

"I heard a boat went hunting for walrus," said the elder.

Nick nodded warily.

"It's hard to hunt walrus with a boat... like a seal," Smart smiled.

So, even this elder had heard the story of the botched walrus hunt. The old man was being polite. He hadn't mention names. And he acknowledged the difficulty of hunting walrus like a seal with a harpoon on open water. He hadn't mentioned Nick's stupidity stepping into coiled harpoon line, yet. By elder standards, Nick was an inexperienced youth. Elders could say just about anything to young kids, especially to drive home lessons. So far, Paul Smart was being gracious.

"I heard someone talking. That's all I know," said the elder.

Nick heard the cautious groundwork. He didn't want to insult Nick with what he was preparing to say if the rumors proved inaccurate.

"They said you called a walrus."

Nick saw a twinkle in the old man's eye.

This was unexpected.

The elder leaned forward.

"Like a seal. They said you called a walrus like a seal."

"Maybe," nodded Nick. "A walrus came to the boat."

"Walrus don't like to come to boats," said the elder. "They want to go the other way unless they must protect a baby. They attack bears to protect a baby. I have never seen a walrus called to a boat like a seal."

Nick pondered this.

He had no reason to doubt the elder. Here was another inexplicable thing about that hunt.

"I don't know walrus," confessed Nick. "I thought it might be like a seal. So I called to it. I didn't know."

"How did you call it?"

The elder was curious to learn something new.

Nick looked at Camilla. She didn't know what they were talking about. Still, he felt embarrassed.

"I tapped the boat with the gaff, like this."

Nick tapped the table with his hand.

Camilla watched, not interrupting.

"He stayed up. Looked interested. But he didn't come."

The elder also did not interrupt.

"So I used a call, like this."

Nick put his hands around his mouth and blew.

"Brrrrp. Brrrrp."

Camilla smiled. She had guessed the topic.

Nick felt his face flush.

"He came to that. I stood. Threw the harpoon."

Nick made the motions.

"That's all?"

"Yes."

The elder digested the account.

"Now this is odd," said the elder. "We know that one. Seals like that call. Not walrus."

The elder considered Nick.

"Maybe that was a seal, pretending to be a walrus," the elder joked.

They both laughed.

Nick translated for Camilla. She smiled too. He felt good, seeing her smile.

"But maybe," mused the elder, "maybe it wasn't the call. It was the person who made the call."

He looked at Nick intently.

"What do you mean?"

"The old people say it. Some people can call a walrus."

Old people say... Paul Smart himself was old. This meant that he had learned this from someone older than himself. It was old knowledge, older than even this elder's generation.

The elder leaned forward again.

"Be careful."

"Be careful?"

"You are not from here. You are a person of the Yukon River. So I am telling you this. Be careful."

Nick frowned.

"Hunting walrus?"

"No, careful how you speak of hunting them. It is a rare skill, to call a walrus."

Nick looked at him puzzled.

What was this old man telling him?

"It is not improper," said the elder. "But be careful. A good hunter does not boast of how he hunts."

Nick sat, troubled.

He knew about not boasting. Boastful hunters lost their luck. But the elder meant something else. Don't boast about calling walrus. Why? Camilla watched them carefully, not understanding the conversation. She knew the topic had taken a turn, but not how. Nick returned to the elder, an old man, a respected elder, active in the church, an expert on many things.

He was teaching him something obscure.

"Why is this dangerous?"

The elder sat quietly, thinking.

"It is not for me to say," he finally replied, "but Tusekluk."

Nick nodded.

Tusekluk? Who was that? The elder had referred him to somebody else. Why should he ask Tusekluk?

The elder sat back, apparently finished.

But Nick wasn't.

Camilla was right. Some things were better talked about.

"Grandfather, I'm a person of the Yukon River. I don't know about walrus. I have another question."

The elder nodded.

Nick worked to phrase it right.

"It's said the animals are gifts. We are grateful to kill them. If done well, the gift continues. The same is true for walrus?"

"Yes," replied the elder easily. "Like real people, animals are made by God. They live under God's sway. They have their homes and their ways as we do ourselves. If we treat them with respect, they come back so that people may continue to hunt and make use of them with gratitude."

Groundwork. Nick asked his question.

"Grandfather, is there some problem with walrus?"

The elder considered the question.

"Some special problem connected with walrus?" said Nick.

"Perhaps," said the elder finally. "People and walrus have become estranged. It began even when I was a child. We used to hunt walrus. Now, people and walrus drift apart. It is said the animals go elsewhere when humans lose interest in them."

Again, this was something Nick knew.

"But that is a problem not just for walrus," clarified the elder.

"Yes, even in my home," said Nick, where teens played computer games instead of learning to hunt. "But Grandfather, for walrus, is there some danger, some impending... disaster?"

Nick used the words of his vision.

The elder stared. He stared as he had during the interview, seeing Nick, and something else. The old man leaned forward. He now whispered.

"Who speaks of disasters?"

Nick checked on Camilla, who could not understand what they were saying. Still, he almost swallowed his answer.

"A cormorant... to the walrus."

The elder's face went blank.

"A cormorant speaks to the walrus... about disasters?"

"Yes," Nick affirmed.

The elder sat back in his seat.

He sat deep in thought, as if remembering older things.

Finally he answered Nick, matter-of-factly.

"Then the walrus should listen."

38

Andrew Sipary, the VPSO, found Camilla and Nick in the aisles of the general store. He shined in his uniform compared to them, unlaundered over a week. Sipary politely smiled, shook their hands, and asked how they were. His manner proclaimed business.

"I've got Jerome Paul at the station."

He said it almost apologetically.

"For what?" asked Camilla.

"Uh... disturbing the peace, maybe assault. He hit his girlfriend, but she hasn't filed a complaint. They partied last night."

"Is she hurt?"

"Bruises on an arm. He's got a black eye."

Fight night, thought Nick.

"I'd like to ask you about something," said Sipary. "Actually, Jerome suggested it, your expert opinion. I'm considering a third charge."

They accompanied Sipary to the station. His small office adjoined a holding cell. Behind his desk, Sipary pulled up cardboard boxes. One held burnt clay pipes that smelled like the inside of Jerome's house. Nick recognized them. They had used the gray one at Jerome's party. The pipes had been in plain sight on the work table.

"I'm deciding what to do about these," said Sipary, setting it aside. "That's not what I want to ask you about."

He picked up the other box, switching on the table lamp. A jumble of bone, stone, and ivory filled it.

"Can we touch?" asked Camilla.

"Go ahead."

They pulled out items. A flint blade from a woman's knife. A bone awl. Chert points for bird arrows. Round grooved rocks used as sinkers for fishing nets. A needle case of coffee-colored ivory, carved to form the head and body of a seal, beautifully made, fully intact. But most items were in pieces, incomplete and unrecognizable, detritus an archeologist might identify after careful study.

"Why did Jerome want you to ask us about these?" said Camilla.

"To vouch for him," said Sipary. "He says they're legal, dug from private lands on St. Lawrence Island, traded to him with other things. He claims it's legal on St. Lawrence. I need to decide whether to charge him for dealing illegal artifacts, or grave robbing, or whatever the federal law is. I'm new at this, you know. I'll check the laws, of course. But as he asked, I figured I'd get your opinion. Both of you are anthropologists."

"I can't help you, sorry," Camilla said, putting items back in the box. "I'm not that kind of anthropologist. I can't tell you where these came from. Can you, Nick?"

"I'm no archeologist," said Nick. "But this does look like the stuff that comes from St. Lawrence Island. It gets sold in shops in Anchorage packed in boxes like this. For fifteen bucks a tourist buys a broken ulu legally stolen from somebody's grave."

"Legally stolen?"

"Legal if it's private land, on that island anyway. I think it's owned by the tribe. At Land Claims they took the island instead of money. Somebody digs this for income."

"Huh," said Sipary.

Nick suspected Sipary was digesting this as a Yup'ik as well as a cop. Digging up graves would be one of the last ways a person would want to make a living. People stayed clear of graves out of respect for the dead.

"It drives the archeologists crazy," said Nick. "The artifacts lose their context. It's difficult to prove where they came from. Jerome can say it's from St. Lawrence Island and it's hard to disprove."

"Yeah," said Sipary.

"Sorry I can't help you more," said Camilla.

"You want to see him?"

"He's here?"

The lockup adjoined the office through a thick door with a mesh-glass window. Half the room was caged. Inside, Jerome reclined on a cot. He seemed surprised to see them. He squinted. His left eye was swollen shut.

"Nick! Camilla! What's you doing, man?"

"Hi Jerome," smiled Camilla.

Nick nodded a greeting.

Jerome danced nervously. He stared through the half-opened door past Sipary.

"Anybody else out there?"

"Just us," said Camilla. "Officer Sipary said you wanted us to look at artifacts."

"What'd they tell you, Sipary? It's legal, right?"

"You're still here for disturbing the peace."

"Oh, you don't want to do that," whined Jerome. "Shit, it was a party. That's why I live way out there. We didn't mean to bother nobody."

Sipary nodded noncommittally.

"Good to see you, man!" Jerome said again to Camilla and Nick. "How's that study going?"

"Okay," smiled Camilla. "Getting some answers. We've still got a couple of puzzles, but we're getting there."

"Yeah? What puzzles?" asked Jerome eager to repay favors.

"Well, maybe this isn't the best place."

"Go ahead," said Sipary. "Bring in chairs. You can talk through the screen. Leave the door open. I'll be at my desk."

Nick sat uncomfortably. He'd never been in jail before. It was something he'd imagined all his life.

Camilla sat unflustered, chatting up Jerome through the screen. The topic wasn't herring.

"We learned more about that Ouija board," said Camilla. "We learned who the girls talked to."

"Yeah?" asked Jerome cautiously.

"Yeah," said Camilla.

Jerome waited. Camilla waited with him.

Finally, she went on.

"You know any stories about him?"

Jerome reached for a non-existent pack of cigarettes in his shirt pocket. He scowled not finding any, sat on his fingers, fidgeting. Nicotine withdrawal, care of Sipary, noted Nick. Sipary's punishment for disturbing the peace.

"There are lots," said Jerome, confirming what Camilla expected. Jerome knew about Qeng'aq.

"Like what?"

Jerome looked out the open door nervously.

"You heard how he lost his nose? They cut it out when he was little. Chucked it in the river. He became the noseless warrior."

"Yeah, we heard that one," said Camilla, grimacing.

Jerome grinned at her reaction.

"And you heard about the prophecy? He said all the animals would die… a big famine."

"I didn't hear that one, exactly."

"All the people too," said Jerome. He looked mournfully at Nick. "You don't have a cigarette, do you?"

"Sorry, I don't carry them."

"Damn. Sipary does, but he won't get me any. He's one cruel bastard. But I like him. Sipary! I like you! But he's cruel."

"He prophesized a famine?" asked Camilla.

"Not just that… he caused it!" said Jerome. "That's why they killed him. He was causing it. They killed him, all his children, tried to. He sent the animals away."

"He could do that?"

"He had power over animals. He could call them, send them away."

"He could call them?" asked Nick.

"Right out of the water."

"Fish?" asked Camilla.

Jerome laughed hysterically.

"No. No. Not the fish! Seals, sea lions, walrus… he could call them right out. Send them away. So they killed him. They burned him, scattered the ashes so he wouldn't return. That's what they did, tried to do."

Camilla glanced at Nick. He looked like he had swallowed a worm.

"They did or didn't?" asked Camilla.

"What?"

"Burn him."

"No, they did. Least some say they did. Others tell it different. Somebody stole the body away before they could burn it. Hey! That sounds like Jesus, doesn't it? They stole the body away, just like that!"

Jerome giggled. He shouted out the half-opened door.

"Sipary! Can these guys get me some smokes?"

"No!"

"Damn! He's cruel. But I like him. You sure you don't have some in those packs?"

"No, sorry, I don't carry them," said Camilla. "Someone took the body?"

"Yeah," said Jerome, looking glum.

"What did you mean by, 'killed all his children,' or 'tried to'?"

"Huh?"

"What did you mean, 'tried to kill his children?' The way I heard it, Qeng'aq lost his son and threw the grief into the animals. That's what caused the famine. He lost his son."

"No," glowered Jerome. "That's not the right way to tell it. They tell it that way so little kids don't get scared. Yeah, he lost his son, but not his daughter!"

"Not the daughter?"

"She got away. They tried to get her, but they couldn't find her. That's why he can come back anytime, you know? If ever they have a child again, anytime. If ever that family has a child and they name it for him, he'll come back, try it again."

Jerome's smiled evilly. He hunched.

His voice grew sinister.

"So that's why they watch. They always watch the children. Watching for when he comes back. Is it that one? That one? That one?"

He jumped at an imaginary child.

"You!"

He laughed hysterically.

"That's how to tell it to kids!"

39

Trooper Hyde Cooper found Camilla and Nick over lunch at Winnie's house. He declined an offer of food, stood stiffly, jaw muscles exercising the sides of his bullet head. He'd hurried from Anchorage to Togiak after learning who had located the family of Francisco Fernández Muñoz.

Camilla Mac Cleary.

Cooper wanted to talk.

They all went to the station. Cooper sat at Sipary's desk, putting Camilla before him. He seemed agitated. Sipary and Nick stayed by the door.

"How did you find that family in Chiapas?" growled Cooper.

"Playing a hunch."

"A hunch?"

"I called a research associate I knew who worked in Chiapas. He found the family through a health network."

"We agreed to share information."

"Yes, if we learned something."

"Why didn't you tell me?"

"Because of the sequence," said Camilla. "I called Javier Tampecho, my associate in Chiapas, on the chance that he might know how to find the family. He did, the next day. The family called authorities in Mexico City who called Anchorage. I only learned about that later when I called Javier back. So, in the sequence of events, you learned about finding the Fernández family before I did, at least a day before because you're in Anchorage."

Cooper was pissed.

Nick saw why. He'd been left out. He didn't get credit for finding the family. Nick decided he didn't much like Trooper Cooper.

"You have a contact like that, you let me know," said Cooper.

"I see," said Camilla.

"Then we can get a statement."

"You've questioned them?"

"What?"

"The Fernández family."

"Not me," grumbled Cooper. "We get all that from the Mexicans."

"It's not helpful?"

He scowled. The Mexican investigators were on Cooper's shit list too. Fuming, he had Camilla go over the sequence again. Sipary approached when she was done.

"Camilla, can you look at something I have in my truck?"

Once gone, Cooper turned on Nick.

"Is what she says true?"

"What?" Nick said warily. "Yeah."

"How do you know?"

Nick saw what was happening. Camilla removed so Cooper could pump him.

"I was there when she called."

"What do you mean?"

"When she phoned Chiapas. It's like she said."

"But it was in Spanish," said Cooper. "How do you know it's like she said? You speak Spanish?"

"I asked what had happened. She told me."

"But you didn't understand anything she was saying on the call to Chiapas, right? You couldn't hear the other end. Actually, you're just guessing it's what she says, because you couldn't understand or hear most of it."

"Sure," said Nick, irritated.

"What?"

"If you say so."

"What got said on the other end? What did she say that Javier Tampecho said?"

"I don't recall, ask her," said Nick, finished with Cooper.

Cooper scowled.

"Don't you think it's a little coincidental? Thousands of families named Fernández in Mexico and with one phone call, bang! She finds the right one. Instantly finds him, his family, three countries south, the guy behind her project."

"What do you mean?"

"Francisco Fernández Muñoz dies. She shows up. She finds the family."

Yes, a coincidence decided Nick.

"What do you know about Camilla Mac Cleary?" Cooper challenged.

Nick said nothing.

"Did you know she worked in Mexico?"

"Yes," said Nick.

Well, not until this week, he remembered, and not until the phone call.

"Do you know why she came to Alaska?"

"No."

"Do you know anything about her? Her family? Recent activities? Her problems?"

Nick said nothing.

"Would it surprise you to know she was in debt a year ago so deep she couldn't get student loans, and the debt vanishes with a large cash deposit in a Mexico City bank?"

Nick watched the man work.

He was painting a sinister picture of Camilla.

True, he knew nothing about her past. But so what? Nick had told Camilla nothing about his own past either. They were mutually ignorant partners. He remembered her saying, 'Keep me good, Nick, not happy, but good.' She had tears in her eyes. That suggested something. But he knew kindness when he saw it. And he knew meanness too, this jerk investigator.

"You'd do well to distance yourself," growled Cooper. "You know what an accomplice is? An accomplice is somebody who knows and won't tell. And we'll find out."

He pointed his thick finger.

"Don't move."

Cooper left.

They never ask, stewed Nick.

"Hey man!" a voice called out.

"Jerome?"

"Yeah!"

The door to the holding cell was ajar. He looked inside to find Jerome Paul sitting on his cot behind the screen.

"Who's that asshole?" asked Jerome.

"Have you been listening the whole time?"

"I mean, man, there's not much I can do about it, you know? Stick my head under the mattress? You and Mac are in deep shit! Got a cigarette?"

"You know I don't."

"Damn."

"Does the Lieutenant know you're here?"

"Lieutenant? Is that what he is? No, he doesn't know shit. What an asshole."

"Yeah," agreed Nick.

"This is about that guy who drowned?"

"He's investigating it."

"Camilla found the family?"

"In Mexico."

"By making one phone call? That sure pissed him off!"

Jerome started laughing.

"Yeah," said Nick.

"She's in trouble now. Never help those fuckers. You see how it comes down? They screw you. You tell her. Don't ever help those fuckers."

The outside door opened. Camilla entered with Sipary, who sweated uncomfortably though the day was cool. Camilla looked flushed but calm. Nick left the cell.

"Exciting," Camilla smiled.

"What's going on?" asked Nick.

Sipary raised his palms outwards as if to say, 'I can't say anything.'

"I just got questioned again by Lt. Cooper," said Camilla. "He's not a happy camper. He thinks we're hiding something, me and you. He doesn't trust us anymore. He says we're supposed to call headquarters. We can use the office phone."

Sipary politely exited. Camilla dialed and hit speaker.

"Hello?" came Mel from Juneau.

"Mel? It's Camilla and Nick in Togiak."

"What the hell's going on there!" shouted Mel. "I've got a formal request from Public Safety for your fieldnotes! Immediately! For criminal investigations!"

"What?" said Camilla.

"On my desk from Public Safety. No warning. It's just short of a subpoena. It wants the fieldnotes of Camilla Mac Cleary and Nicholas John from the Togiak Subsistence Herring Study, dated yesterday, signed by their commissioner. Why's this here?"

Camilla gave Nick a mournful look.

"Nick! Are you okay?" shouted Mel. "I just heard you almost got killed! How come I hear you almost got killed from fucking Sport Fish?"

Nick returned Camilla's look.

"And Nick! What's this invoice for a drum of gasoline at Goodnews Bay? Paid with a state TR! That doesn't work! What the hell were you doing in Goodnews Bay?"

High squeals of laughter came from the cell.

"Hey Mac! Got any smokes?"

40

Dillingham was hopping, three thousand people at the peak of the salmon runs. The lucrative sockeye attracted outside boats from far places, Kodiak, Petersburg, Bellingham, and beyond, all hoping to strike it rich in the high-roller fishery. The world's largest sockeye runs raced up the Kvichak and Nushagak rivers. Between periods, the fishing town bustled.

Camilla and Nick mingled with off-duty fishermen downtown. The seasonal cafes overflowed with rowdy lunchtime crowds. They followed a guide, an ex-pat Scandinavian anthropology instructor from the university. After staid Togiak, Dillingham felt like an amusement park. It smelled like money. The sockeye cooperated. Big returns. Lots of fish. The state managers opened. The boats caught. There was raw energy, a buoyant expectancy that this was the year to retire the debt, remodel the house, refit the boat, and winter in Hawaii.

Last night, Nick and Camilla flew into Dillingham. Claude Richter met them at the plane, a huge rosy-faced archeologist and personal friend of Mel Savage. This morning he personally ushered them through their errands. At the Bristol Bay campus they spent hours duplicating notebooks and field materials from the herring project, labeled and annotated for the lawyers and notarized with an official letter. These were complete copies of the materials requested by Public Safety. They sealed everything in heavy envelops and dropped them in the snail mail for Juneau.

"We'll fight this request," Mel had told them.

Meanwhile the materials would sit unopened, ready to send if the department lost. Camilla assured Mel that nothing in the fieldnotes should jeopardize respondents. Public Safety would not be writing citations in Togiak. She and Nick had carefully written them without names. They used a numbering system for sources.

"Who has the key?" asked Mel.

"I do," said Camilla.

"No you don't," said Mel. "You say, 'there is no key.' What that means is, 'there is no key in the Fish and Game materials.' They'll be asking you as a state contractor. As a state contractor, you have no key. What you might possess privately is your own business. If you declare a key exists, they'll argue it belongs to the state and you'll have to produce it."

"Okay, I understand. There is no key."

"Perfect."

Mel didn't seem particularly upset that, contrary to orders, Camilla had dabbled in the trooper's murder investigation, landing the division in a legal tussle. Mel seemed to love it. She smirked when she learned that Camilla had one-upped the detectives. "They should hire anthropologists," she laughed. She seemed more upset about Nick's gasoline purchase with a state TR because it created an administrative nightmare paying the vendor. As for Nick's ill-fated walrus hunt, Mel listened and grunted appreciatively. Good story. She didn't say 'don't hunt' or 'watch your feet,' only 'tell me next time!' She hated hearing things from the idiots in Sport Fish.

Nick wondered what Mel looked like.

He imagined a tattooed bulldog.

Mel told them that the buffer proposal would go to a Joint Board committee. The committee would decide whether to advance the proposal to a scheduled meeting as a special request. Final action required public notice. Mel and Jeff Hall would attend the committee session.

She added Jeff to the phone call. They both wanted an update on walrus and herring.

So Camilla and Nick gave them an hour's worth at Sipary's phone. They went over their findings. Sipary, bored waiting outside his own office, came inside and listened to the update. Jerome Paul did too from the adjoining cell. In a village, few things remained absolutely private. Villagers became experts on a surprising range of topics.

With Claude Ricter's help, they mailed off the fieldnotes. The business at the college was officially completed. They had time before the flight to Togiak. Claude invited them upstairs for a commanding view of the harbor packed with the salmon fishing fleet. Before this panorama was a worktable with materials from his archeological projects. The college ran a summer dig with the tribes at Lake Clark. Students earned credits and got employment. The Lake Clark site was producing an interesting complex of tools, many related to caribou hunting by an inland cultural adaptation. Claude unrolled a regional map of archeological sites. He pointed to the Lake Clark site on a peninsula near its outfall. The people at Nondalton village still fished there seasonally.

"Could you look at something I have here?" Camilla asked, opening her backpack. To Nick's surprise, out came several artifacts taken from the box that Sipary had confiscated from Jerome Paul's house.

"St. Lawrence Island," said Claude immediately.

He examined them.

"This one is a beauty," he said about the coffee-colored ivory needle case with the seal's head.

"How do you know it comes from St. Lawrence Island?" asked Camilla.

"The elements are very characteristic of needle cases made there about 100 to 500 years ago. You can't tell precisely with some of these other artifacts. The slate ulu could come from many places. But the needle case is a clear tip-off. I can even say with fair confidence where on St. Lawrence Island. It's a site producing most of the artifacts for the tourist market. These are part of that dig, I would bet."

"Nick thought they were St. Lawrence Island," said Camilla.

"A guess," said Nick.

"It's a good guess. You can see how different they look from the materials at Lake Clark."

"Nick says this drives archeologists crazy, the legal grave robbing."

"Well, some," said Claude. "I must confess, in this case it doesn't bother me too much. I understand that families are poor out there and need money. One can argue these artifacts are their patrimony first. After all, their great great grandparents made them. They are serving a new purpose now, giving something back to their descendants. As long as the digging is concentrated at a few sites, it doesn't hurt the island's archeological record greatly. Of course, that history is also their patrimony. So it's controversial. I don't fit in the mainstream of archeologists on this. Maybe that's because I live here and work with the tribes. I see both sides of it."

Nick studied the map of numbered archeological sites. He examined the area around Togiak.

"Looking for something in particular?"

"Whether there are sites on Round Island."

"You can't tell that from this map," said Claude. "It shows major survey sites. But I can tell you that there are numerous sites on Round Island. In fact, I believe the tourist camp is located at an old hunting site. It's never been properly excavated. Small sites like that won't show up on this map."

So Philip Elsberry's crew was camped on an archeological site, thought Nick. He pointed to a cluster around Cape Newenham.

"Yeah," said Claude. "Lots of old sites at Newenham. That area is an important place. People have been hunting around that cape for thousands of years. Much of what we call the Bering Sea Small Tool Tradition may have developed in that area. Some of the earliest sites in western Alaska are there, going down to Kulukak Bay just south of Togiak."

He pointed out the cluster of sites at those places. Nick saw most were coastal sites. Others lay inland. One of the dots sat near the location of the Coopchiak's camp.

"Are all these being excavated?" asked Camilla.

"No," said Claude. "Hardly any. Most sites are inactive at any point in time. No funds. Low priority. They get listed here because of past surveys. But they are rarely completely excavated. If you went out you'd find no signs of anything beyond a few test pits. You'd be the only one there. You and the bugs."

Well past noon, they abandoned the college for lunch. Claude guided them into the crowd of commercial fishermen. Nick wanted a hamburger. Claude found the seasonal café that served them. Camilla had grilled sockeye, Claude a salad. Slightly nauseous from the burger, Nick suggested beers. Camilla agreed. They found the Hungry Bears Bar.

The Hungry Bears was dark and clouded with smoke. Fishermen drank shoulder-to-shoulder at a short bar, downing beer drawn by a blond with wide hips and deep voice.

"Hey, Claude!" she greeted.

Claude secured a table.

Something odd caught Nick's eye on the smoky ceiling. The ceiling was festooned with miniature stalactites.

"Spit wads," said Claude.

"Spit wads?" asked Nick.

"Look harder."

"Money!"

"Flick 'til they stick."

Thousands of crewed up bills hung above them, hardened and blackened with cigarette smoke.

"Fishermen and money," said Claude.

"Hey! Hey! Mac Cleary! Nick! Hey!"

Ken Robbins stumbled across the room, the fishmonger with the turquoise warehouse on his estranged wife's contested land, flinging coffee at government regulations. He was in Dillingham. He dragged a man in a bright white cap. Robbins was drunk. White Cap was not.

"Hey Mac Cleary. How's it going?"

"Fine," smiled Camilla. "How are you, Ken?"

"Busy. Busy. Mac Cleary, meet Ronald Schaffer, Silver Seas Seafood. Schaffer, Mac Cleary, Nick John, Fish and Game."

"Claude Richter," said the red-faced Swede.

Hasty handshakes went all around. A colorful swordfish leaped on Schaffer's cap. Pretty logo, thought Nick. Was he handing out free caps? The wide-hipped barmaid arrived. She took orders.

"Schaffer's buying fish," declared Robbins. "I'm telling him about traditional Native smoked salmon from Togiak, the best smoked salmon in western Alaska."

"Yeah, it's good," said Camilla to Schaffer.

"See?" Robbins grinned. "Ask Nick, he'll tell you."

"Uh, yeah, it's good," said Nick.

Never argue with drunks.

Beers arrived. Schaffer escaped.

Robbins collapsed heavily at an adjoining table.

"Those bastards," he scowled.

"Did we say something wrong?" asked Camilla.

"Those rich bastards," snarled Robbins. "They work for the big boys now."

"What's he buying?" asked Claude.

"Sockeye. Bright fresh sockeye. That's all. Not even frozen. Iced. He flies it out for some goddamn sushi market in San Francisco and Seattle."

"No smoked salmon?" asked Camilla.

"Fuck 'em," growled Robbins. "Not even lox is good enough anymore. Working class Jews in New York? Not good enough! It's sushi for the goddamn effete lawyers in Seattle! Well, I say fuck 'em."

Robbins saw the tall frosted mugs. He realized he didn't have one. He remembered something else.

"Hey, Jerome Paul's in jail. That true?"

"Yeah," said Nick.

"What for?"

"Partying."

"Partying?" snorted Robbins.

"So far," said Nick.

Robbins watched drips zig-zag down Nick's mug, reliving his encounter with Silver Seas Seafood.

"Why are you guys here?" asked Robbins abruptly.

"Subpoenaed fieldnotes," smiled Camilla with foamy lips.

"Huh?" asked Robbins.

"The trooper investigating Fernández wants our fieldnotes on Round Island. Claude helped us copy."

"Fernández?" muttered Robbins. "The dead guy?"

"Yeah," said Camilla, licking her lips.

"You with the college?" Robbins asked Claude.

"Yeah."

"We're learning about his dig at Lake Clark," said Camilla.

"And grave robbing on St. Lawrence Island," laughed Claude.

"Grave robbing?" sputtered Robbins, confused by the transitions.

"The stuff Jerome had," said Nick.

Robbins looked completely lost.

"Sipary got stuff from Jerome's place during the party."

"Got what?" asked Robbins.

"Artifacts. Stuff from St. Lawrence Island."

"Oh," said Robbins

His eyes strayed.

"Excuse me."

Robbins abruptly lurched from the chair and out the exit. He waved at somebody he needed to talk to.

"Sounds like Robbins' traditional Native smoked salmon doesn't make it this year in the seafood trade," said Camilla.

"Fine with me," said Nick.

He didn't like the cheesy knockoff.

"Why's this place called the Hungry Bears?" said Camilla.

"Good story," Claude smiled. "Want to hear it?"

"You bet," said Camilla.

"Bristol Bay sockeye… you know it's fiercely competitive, especially the upper borders of the fishing districts. Fishing is best there, very lucrative. Boats jockey for position. They do nasty things to each other, bump other boats, cork nets, cut buoys.

"Well, one year this particularly aggressive captain did all that. He muscled his boat into the best place. He sat at the line blocking everybody, not letting anyone in, making huge hauls. He stuffed his hold with fish.

"He fished so hard he lost track of the clock. He looked up from his hold. Where was everybody? He was all alone. The tide was leaving fast. So had the boats. Too late for him. His heavy boat stuck hard on the flats. It wouldn't shake free, glued to the mud. He was cursing and swearing over the radio. He couldn't get off to sell his fish.

"Serves him right, everybody said. Pretty funny.

"Night fell. That's when they began to hear other things over the radio.

"'A bear!' they heard him yell. 'Another bear!'

"He's grounded on the Kvichak flats with a boatload of sockeye. The bears smell him. They walk out on the flats to investigate. One bear. Then another bear. Then another. A mob of grizzlies. Big grizzlies. They smell the fish. They surround the boat. They're really hungry!"

Camilla began to laugh.

"What happened?" asked Nick.

"He begins to chuck fish over the side. He doesn't want them climbing aboard! He's chucking fish. They hear him on the radio, cursing and swearing and tossing. It's like throwing money. And he's throwing for all he's worth!"

Camilla covered her mouth.

Her beer jiggled dangerously.

Nick raised his mug to the spit-wad ceiling.

"To the Hungry Bears."

"The Hungry Bears!"

41

They flew into Togiak with a low sun on the northwest sea. Flecks of gold accented a watery horizon. A storm was forecast, but this evening the water was flat and peaceful. Nick saw Round Island poke like a gray wart in the distance. He searched for the place he went to the bottom of the bay. It was now like an odd dream. Nick had come to terms with it. Exploding walrus and bingo boards! Anoxia did strange things to the human brain. He shook his head in disbelief. How could that ever be real?

Camilla dozed beside him. The monotonous drone had lulled her to sleep. He remembered how he first met her. She stepped off this very flight, shook his hand, and puked by his left foot. He watched her sleeping profile. They had shared a hotel room last night. He slept on the couch, she on the bed. He worried about snoring but she said he didn't. He wondered if she lied. She smelled good, like the tiny cake of soap that came with the room. Like she smelled with his nose planted on her cheek.

The plane touched down with a whisper and grind.

Camilla woke, stretched, and grinned at Nick, making pretty Yup'ik girl eyes, happy moon slits. It was no hardship working with Camilla.

They deplaned into a cool evening. He had to pee. Too much beer. With the bags coming off, he walked to the edge of the runway. He unzipped his fly, heard a pop.

"Brrrrinng!"

The bullet screamed past his ear.

Nick dove for a rut.

It was shallow, pebbly, and damp.

He hadn't finished!

He rolled, stuffed, zipped, and carefully lifted his head. At the plane, passengers grabbed bags and walked to their rides. No one had noticed a thing.

Nick lay in the dark cursing, looking this way and that, seeing nothing.

"Nick!" shouted Camilla faintly by the plane. "Nick, where are you?"

This was really stupid!

"Nick?"

Camilla began walking toward him.

"Stay there!" shouted Nick.

"What?" shouted Camilla, still coming.

"Stay there!" shouted Nick.

Too late. Camilla came to where he lay. He lifted his head higher and looked around.

"What are you doing?"

"Somebody shot at me!" he said angrily.

"What?"

"Somebody took a shot at me!" He brushed crumbly mud from his pants and shirt. "The bullet missed my ear!"

"Are you sure?"

"I'm sure."

Camilla did a three-sixty.

"I don't see anyone," she said.

"Let's go," said Nick, taking her elbow and walking fast toward the plane. They grabbed their bags, dashed to the airline agent's truck, and climbed in the back with the freight. The truck rumbled and bounced toward town in a dusty cloud.

Nick scanned the terrain behind them. He touched Camilla's shoulder and pointed. Off on the horizon walked a silhouette with a rifle on its shoulder, moving away from the field. It disappeared into willows.

"Who is it?"

"I can't tell," said Nick.

"A hunter," suggested Camilla.

"At the strip?" growled Nick.

"A stupid kid?"

Nick was a hunter.

He had scoped lots of silhouettes in his life.

"That was an old man," he grumbled.

Nick said his goodnights to Camilla at Winnie's place. He rode alone in the truck bed toward the old water tank. A strange feeling moved in his stomach. For the first time, the tank felt bad. He jumped from the truck with his pack at the tank's door and the driver sped off.

Had he locked it? He couldn't remember. Sometimes he did, sometimes he didn't. This trip he couldn't recall.

With a mental effort, he worked the fear.

He had beaten the old man to town. There would be no one waiting in that water tank. It was an accidental shot by some idiot hunter, popping at hares or birds at the edge of town, an old man with bad eyes.

He strode to the door and turned the large knob.

It opened. A hot breath of air hissed out, stinking with creosote. He reached inside, found the switch, and gave light to the naked bulbs ascending the staircase. The security lock on the downstairs storage door was closed and fixed.

"Anybody there?" he shouted up the stairs.

He felt like a fool.

No one was there. What idiot would lurk in this stinking oven for him to return? Only someone as stupid as him would stay in a place like this.

With a laugh at his paranoia, Nick climbed the stairs. His feet found the familiar dents in the rough wood. He reached the top and pushed open the door with his boot. He gave the light cord a yank and froze.

Ragged shadows moved beneath the swinging bulb. The room was a wreck. Every box emptied, contents strewn around. His food and clothes and gear lay in disordered heaps. The room was ransacked.

He found his sleeping bag, jammed between cot and wall. He draped it over his neck, shouldered his pack, and jumped down the stairs into the twilight, pulling shut every door behind him, lights burning. He double-locked the outside door, went straight for the beach, hopped a log, and crouched in the dark.

The sounds of Togiak came to him from the mid-distance... a rumbling pickup... barking dogs... a group of teens laughing.

Gulls called faintly.

The waves shushed on the short beach.

Nick sweated in the chill wind, listening for the quiet steps of an old man who carried a rifle.

His bladder complained.
He watched a long time.

42

Nick arrived wet at Winnie Friendly's place.

The forecasted storm blew in during the early morning, hammering the beach with pellet rain. Nick slept beneath the abandoned wooden skiff. The rain's pounding woke him but he was too sleepy to vacate the hiding place. He rolled over in the bag and returned to his dreams, hissing waves and swimming walrus waiting offshore for something to happen. The boat roof held tight and dry. Runoff seeped beneath.

Nick didn't care. He'd slept in much worse conditions.

"She's sick," Winnie said sadly.

"Sick?"

"Headache."

Nick found Camilla in her alcove. She lay in the semi-dark with a pillow covering her eyes.

"Hi partner," she whispered, lifting a limp hand.

Nick took it. Strangely long fingers. Cold. The first time he'd really touched her. The hand seemed only half alive.

"You okay?" asked Nick, worried.

"Nope, not today. Bad head. Bad stomach."

Nick sat silently with the hand in his.

"I think you're on your own today," she whispered.

Nick wondered at the change. She was lively and fun at Dillingham. This morning, she lay comatose. The pillow came off her head so she could look at him. Specks of light glinted in the dark. She had been crying.

"That okay?" she whispered.

"Yeah, it's okay," said Nick. "I'll interview from the list."

"Or take a break," whispered Camilla, shutting her eyes to the too-bright dark.

Nick dropped her hand and reset the pillow over her face. Patting her bare shoulder, he left the alcove.

"Thanks," he heard her say. "You're a great guy."

Winnie served dried fish and seal oil. After the night's disquiet, he was grateful for something familiar.

Winnie looked at him critically.

"Where were you?"

"Outside," Nick answered, dipping fish in oil and stuffing his mouth. He must look pretty bad for Winnie to comment.

"Why?"

"Didn't like the tank."

"The Laundromat has showers."

"I need to steam."

Saying it, he realized it was true. He felt gritty, dispirited. He needed to sweat.

"Check my brother," said Winnie, waving vaguely, sounding downcast too.

"When did she get sick?"

"Last night, I guess."

"She's been crying."

Winnie nodded.

"It hurts that much?"

"Something does," said Winnie. "She won't say."

Nick read the sadness in Winnie's face.

"She doesn't tell me either," said Nick.

"Something bad happened to her."

"Yeah," said Nick. Something in Mexico. Something involving debts and cash deposits. Something eating her up.

"She won't say," sighed Winnie.

"Maybe she needs a steam too."

Winnie looked askance at Nick.

"Not with you!" she huffed.

Her tone caught him by surprise. He hadn't been thinking that. Winnie grabbed a jacket for the rain, going out the door.

"Or my brother!"

Nick retrieved his rain gear from the tank to walk the town. Its locks were as he had left them the night before. He cleaned his space and repacked food, clothes, and personal items into a single duffle. Then he carefully closed up. He doubted the burglar had a key. But a good crowbar would be enough.

By mid-afternoon, Andrew Sipary found him wandering in the rain from an interview. He invited him inside the VPSO office and poured him coffee. He presented to Nick a pair of small binoculars.

"Just recovered them," said Sipary.

Nick turned them over for his name etched in the plastic. His field glasses... he hadn't missed them.

"Thanks."

"A kid had them at the Teen Center, showing off. He couldn't give straight answers. He said he found them on the ground. But they're not wet or muddy, are they?"

"Nope," said Nick.

"You know how he might have gotten them?"

Nick idly fingered the glasses. So the 'break-in' was just kids in the unlocked tank. All they found worth taking were the binoculars. The connection of the bullet at the airstrip and the ransacked room seemed less likely.

"I left the tank unlocked."

Sipary nodded. He didn't need to say, 'you should lock it up.' This was a reason Nick liked VPSOs. The good ones didn't lecture. They assumed you had a brain. And they didn't feel a need to bust kids for acting like stupid kids.

"How was Dillingham?"

"Good," said Nick. He described what he and Camilla did there, sharing the funny stories. As he talked he realized he spoke to Andrew Sipary as a friend, not a cop. At some point, they had become friends. He wasn't sure exactly when that had happened.

"We got in last night," said Nick, deciding about the next event. "I saw somebody with a rifle by the airstrip, maybe an old man."

"Yeah?"

"Shooting."

"Shooting?"

Nick nodded and flipped his thumb by his ear.

"Zing! This close."

Sipary looked unhappy.

He glanced at the clock, then back to Nick.

"You know who it was?"

"We hardly saw him as we drove away."

"You want to file a report?"

Nick shrugged.

"I'll tell you, I got spooked. First that bullet, then my room messed over. I slept on the beach."

"In the rain?" asked Sipary.

"Under a boat," said Nick.

"Then you were pretty spooked," said Sipary, half smiling.

"I'd like to know who that old man was, but I don't need to file anything, I think."

"We're always telling people not to shoot near town. But they hide in the willows, kids and old men who can't walk far. We told them when the birds came in this year. Somebody's going to get shot."

Nick nodded. Somebody like him.

"Did Camilla bring back that stuff?" asked Sipary.

"The artifacts? They're over at Winnie's."

"What did she find out?"

"The university said they're from St. Lawrence Island, alright. Hey, Jerome! You hear that?"

"He's not there."

"He's not?"

"I released him. I had him long enough. His girlfriend wouldn't file."

"When?"

"Day before yesterday, just after you guys left."

"Huh," said Nick, rethinking the break-in. Jerome knew he and Camilla were off to Dillingham. But would Jerome break in to search his things? Why would he do that? Besides, a kid had the binoculars.

"I've got to get his stuff back," said Sipary. "I was going to check on him."

"Camilla's sick. I could bring the rest."

"Okay," said Sipary, tucking the box of artifacts under his arm. "Don't steal his stolen goods."

With a smile, he left Nick to watch the office.

Camilla hadn't moved all day. She sprawled in the alcove, drifting in and out of pain. Nick sat with her by the bed and reported the day's work. She grunted in appreciation and took his hand to squeeze it. She waved at her pack. Nick found Jerome's artifacts. He transferred them to his own.

The rain had stopped. The clouds split, revealing a silver evening sky. Nick wandered toward Harry Coopchiak's place. He found the steam bath by its smell, tucked behind the fish rack and sheds. Sparks shot from the stovepipe. He had timed it right.

He stooped through the weathered door and entered a narrow cooling room. The bench held folded clothes. Nick undressed, folded his own, and shoved his sneakers beneath it. He found a washing towel on a hook, dipped it into a barrel of cool water and liberally wetted his hair, face, and bare soles. He took a deep breath, opened the inner door, and plunged into the sauna.

The heat was thick.

Nick squinted for bearings. Two occupants hunched above a sunken firebox. An oil drum piled high with volcanic rocks breathed red heat from an open end. The men looked partially melted. Nick wrung the washcloth on the blistering plywood and sat before the puddle evaporated. He draped his hair and ears. Then the sweat began and the long slow bend of the penitent, seeking absolution near the floor.

His pores opened.

A hot lake slowly spread beneath him. This was what he needed, a good purging. The runoff carried every knot and strain. The washcloth on his head dripped, scalding his thighs. He squirmed and repositioned, squinted and sucked through tightened lips, trying to strip the air of pain. His lungs cooked. His eyes grew rubbery. The room blurred.

Harry Coopchiak hunched nearest the firebox.

In the gummy blur, he grabbed a long-handled ladle. He dipped into a deep pan soldered at the stove's mouth. Reaching atop the volcanic rocks, he poured.

SSSSSShhhhhhhhh...

Steam erupted from the pit. In white waves, it descended.

SSSSSShhhhhhhhh...

He poured again. And again.

SSSSSShhhhhhhhh...

The pain hit. Nick sank lower. There was nothing else to do. Hunker down. Absorb the scalds.

"Ik'ikika!"

Nick heard his companion whimper. 'So much!'

"Ii'i," Nick agreed. 'Yes.'

Time crawled. Moments dragged. Nine... ten... eleven... Nick counted. He felt his skin cooking. He felt his body's systems struggling to dissipate the agony, the swell of his vascular network, the capillary expansion to near bursting... twelve... thirteen...

Enough!

Nick dove for the door. He slapped the scorched wood, shoved through, and tumbled to the floor. Somebody followed. They sprawled in the narrow space, naked bodies smoking.

The door slammed shut behind them.

"Ahhhh… ho ho ho!"

The muffled gloat came through the door.

Harry Coopchiak had won.

Nick didn't care. The cold earth absorbed his fire.

So it went.

Rounds of pain.

He lost every time. He hit the exit first, even when he poured. Nick was the perfect guest. He never embarrassed his host by winning. By the end, Nick sprawled in the cooling room with Harry Coopchiak and Matthew Tusaya, the other combatant. Steam rose from them like the tropics. Nick felt drunk, every part wonderfully loosed and relaxed.

At home he once took his temperature after a round… one hundred and four degrees, a self-induced fever. A public health student at the university had challenged the accuracy of the reading. 'Do it rectally,' he snipped. 'Do it yourself,' Nick shot back. But he conceded the point. His internal temperature was probably one hundred and three.

Harry Coopchiak was an addict. Sauna marks covered his torso, a mottled black and red patina from broken capillaries and subdural oozing, a flesh of permanent burns and bruises. He wore the damage proudly. In his own steam bath, Harry reigned. His companion tonight was Matthew Tusaya, a youth, 'almost a cousin' to Harry, whatever that meant. They were glad when Nick crawled through the door. It was always more fun.

"They do it like this where you live?" asked Matthew Tusaya.

"Just like this," said Nick truthfully, relaxed on the cooling room floor.

"Just as hot?" asked Harry.

"Maybe not this hot," said Nick, lying to please his host.

In fact, idiots back home did steam this hot. But most bathers didn't. Only the crazed competitors punished their bodies night after night.

Nick observed Harry did this for other reasons too. Sitting beside the firebox, he whipped his wrists with a swatch of Artemisia, a tundra plant, an ancient remedy for painful joints. Harry was a commercial fisherman. He had ruined his wrists pulling nets. The switching introduced the plant's analgesics into the swollen capillaries.

"How's that study?" asked Harry.

"Almost done with interviews," said Nick.

"When do I get mine?" asked Matthew nervously.

"I don't think we pulled your name."

Matthew looked relieved.

"Who is that trooper I saw?" asked Harry.

"From Anchorage. He's bothering my boss."

"Why?"

"Because she found that family and told them where they had the body."

"He's not buried yet?" said Harry.

"Not yet."

"Why do they keep it?" asked Matthew. "Evidence?"

"That's not right," declared Harry. "They should give him back."

The talk moved around.

Nick described the buffer proposal to prevent headhunting, maybe now on its way to the Joint Board of Fisheries and Game. Harry said he didn't like that proposal. It could mess up the fishery. Some years it could take boats off the ripe herring. Green herring couldn't be sold. The catch got wasted. Harry didn't like waste. And he didn't like fishermen getting blamed for headless walrus.

"You don't think they're getting ivory?" asked Nick.

"A herring captain could lose his boat if his crew got caught headhunting. Nobody would risk his boat for a couple thousand dollars of ivory."

Seemed logical.

"You'd be seen," said Harry. "That hunting place is shallow. Too shallow for a herring boat. You'd have to anchor offshore and use a skiff."

"You've been out there?"

"Once or twice."

"Who's doing it?" asked Matthew.

"I never saw anybody do something like that," said Harry.

"Guys for drugs?"

"I never saw anything like that."

The conversation shifted to sea lions, belugas, and killer whales. Harry said he once estimated how many salmon those animals killed. He took a biologist's population count and multiplied by the number of fish he figured each needed to eat.

They ate more salmon than the total subsistence catch by several factors.

Matthew heard that killer whales trailed halibut boats out of Dutch Harbor. The whales had learned to eat the halibut off the commercial long lines. Whales had favorite boats. They ate the halibut from that boat's hooks. The boats with pet whales had to give up fishing.

"I got to go," said Harry.

He slipped into the steam room, now just pleasantly hot. The sounds of soaping and splashing came through the door.

"I heard you went for eggs," said Matthew Tusaya.

"Puffin beaks," said Nick. "His nephew took me."

"The cliffs by his camp?"

"Yeah."

"You met his aunt and uncle at camp?"

"And lots of kids."

"There are always kids out there," laughed Matthew.

Nick thought about the Coopchiaks. And Lydia.

He hadn't thought of her recently. This embarrassed him. Why wasn't he thinking about Lydia? Maybe it was Camilla being sick. Lately, he worried about Camilla. He recalled his intense attraction to Lydia. And his peculiar unease.

"Uh, that girl out there," asked Nick.

"What girl?"

"That older girl at camp with them. Is she a granddaughter to Harry's aunt and uncle?"

"Oh, yeah... uh... sort of."

"Sort of?"

"You didn't hear that story?"

"No," said Nick.

Matthew Tusaya closed his eyes, relaxing. Cool air filled the room. Harry came out to dress. The bench got crowded.

"I'm going in," said Nick.

Matthew quickly joined him. The steam room's temperature was perfect for bathing. Nick grabbed a pan from a corner, ladled water from the firebox, and began to lather. Matthew did likewise with another pan. They heard Harry leave. After the second rinse of his hair, Nick leaned against a warm wall to dry in the heat. Matthew did the same. Nick's body felt boneless. They sat in relaxed silence for a while.

"So what's that story?"

"What?" murmured Matthew. He was almost asleep.

"About that girl at camp. What's her story?"

"Oh," said Matthew. He seemed to be remembering, eyes closed. "I don't know. Maybe I can't tell it right."

"Yeah," said Nick.

"Somebody else could tell it right."

"Yeah."

"Kind of spooky, you know."

"Yeah?"

"What I heard."

"Okay," said Nick, wondering what this could mean.

There was a long silence. The heat licked the water from their bodies.

"What's the short version?"

There was another long silence. The heat covered and soothed. Matthew wasn't going to do it. He'd fallen asleep. Nick leaned back and relaxed completely. His body wanted sleep too and drifted toward it. He seemed to hear a voice, the rhythm of a story, or maybe Nick dreamed the cadence, his heartbeat, the pulse of blood, resting in the warmth of the room, drifting on the edge of sleep.

A story about shamans.

A spooky story.

Lydia's story.

43

The room pressed hot about the new mother, thick with pungent smells of stove oil, sealskins, and baby powder. The newborn rested on the mattress beside her, bundled in a rag-tied comforter.

Waves of people ebbed and flowed like the tides in the bay. Loose and fluid, they came and went, gatherings that formed and reformed what would become the society of the child. They came to greet the young mother and meet the newest arrival, asleep from nursing, inert from the satisfying effort.

The old woman of the house made tea on the cast-iron stove. Others laid food on the rough table. Small knots of women spoke in whispers. The cool of winter moved in and out with each opening of the door.

By eight, the wind began to rise outside the pitted glass, harbingers of night changes. By nine, a gale built off the bay. By ten, doors struggled to shut. The baby woke and fussed. The young mother nursed. The women patted and cooed and rewrapped the child, cocooned within the comforter.

A raw wind howled in the eaves. Sear fingers searched for entry. Walls shook. The storm struck with a blow. With a violent kick, the outer door banged. They heard hard footfalls ascend the entry. Without a knock, the inner door blew open.

A bulky shape filled the door, a wolf ruff pushed back. The angalkuq. He stood at the entry, grinning with a weathered smile hard as ice below a dripping lip. His eager eyes swept the room. None spoke. None dared to move. Each watched frozen.

Satisfied, the angalkuq lurched across the floor, his sweating boots marking a path to the bedchamber. The mother gasped to see him.

She lunged for the child. The old man was quicker. He snatched and held it to his leering eye and laughed, a piercing cackle. To the mother's horror, he swung the baby. Once around the room. Twice. On the third terrifying turn, he shoved it beneath his parka. He howled like a beast, stomped, and shouted unintelligible commands.

The mother attacked. They wrestled. She pulled the child free, clutched it, and turned from the nightmare.

The old woman swept into the chamber.

"Gone!" she shouted. "Gone!"

She came at the enemy with a broom. The angalkuq yielded before the crone's fury, hooting and dancing across the floor and out the door. She slammed and leaned upon it.

Cries came from the bedroom.

A mother's wail and an infant's squall.

Deviltry!

The women rushed to the chamber.

The mother rocked on the bed.

"What's wrong?" they said.

"It's over."

"Shush."

"It's over."

They hugged her and laid the baby down.

"No, no, no," the mother cried, reaching for her child.

"Hush. Hush."

"It's all right."

"See, it's all right."

The old woman, resolute, bent low, unwrapped the comforter, and released the wet diaper. She lifted the tiny child.

All fell back in shock.

In the old woman's grip, the baby howled, its body stretched in back-bending protest, bandied legs, muscled rump, short cleft, firm mons.

All witnessed it, none believing.

Only the mother still reached out.

'No, no, no,' she cried.

The day had turned to stormy night.

The newborn, once a boy, was now a girl.

44

Nick woke in the steam bath.

The fire had died. He had overslept and squandered his heat. He dressed slowly, his brain wooly, clothes clammy against his skin. His muscles felt loose, every knot smoothed, every strain removed. The bath had purged him. A walk would restore the heat. The dressing room clock pointed at midnight when he crawled out, backpack on his shoulder.

His tired mind replayed it. Had he been asleep? Was it a dream? The story wasn't just spooky. It was unnerving.

Lydia's story.

She was the baby.

In the grass at Cape Peirce, she had told him she was adopted. Matthew Tusaya hadn't reached that part, or Nick had slept through it. He covered the birth, before the adoption, an incredible account.

Transformed.

Boy to a girl.

Matthew Tusaya told it reluctantly. He worried he might not get it right. He had heard it from others, Lydia's beginning, the elemental rumor, the dark whisperings, the undercurrent of her existence.

A shaman and a mother wrestled for a newborn. She retained the child, but transformed, boy to a girl!

Nick drew up short.

The lopsided cabin sank into the sodden earth. Nick had mindlessly found it, Jerome Paul's lair at the edge of the village. Light glimmered through foil-shrouded windows. He negotiated the listing stairs and rapped on the hoary door. It opened with blasts of sound and smoke.

A heavy-lidded girl swayed on the doorframe.

"Who's it?" a voice shouted behind her.

"Don' know," the girl replied.

She looked Nick over and smiled, rows of broken teeth.

"Who're you?"

Jerome Paul appeared, staggering drunk.

"Nick! Buddy! Come on in!"

Nick grudgingly entered. Music pounded. The atmosphere was thick with hash. Jerome introduced his girlfriend, Kitty. 'Catherine' she said angrily. Jerome laughed. He recovered the pipe he'd stashed at the unexpected knock. He relit and offered it. Nick politely refused.

"Just steamed."

"Already there, eh?" laughed Jerome.

Jerome took a hit and flopped on the couch. Half asleep, a beer in her hand, Catherine sat on the floor in a clutter of paper plates. Nick had missed the party.

"I brought these back," said Nick. He opened the pack.

"My treasures!" laughed Jerome. "Kitty, my treasures!"

Jerome waved the slate ulu beneath her nose.

She swatted it away.

"Fucker!" she muttered.

"Hey! It's treasure! Treasure!" complained Jerome.

He flung the ulu across the room. It shattered on a wall.

"Fucker!" said Catherine.

Jerome turned to Nick.

"You... you see... how they don't know..." he said, fluttering fingers toward Catherine. "They don't know... but we do, eh? We do."

He staggered to a corner, opened a beer, and took a long swig, stumbled, and doubled up laughing.

"He sure thought he had us... fucking locked me up for two days... and what does he get? Nothing! He got nothing! Know why? Cuz he knows nothing... he knows shit!"

He grabbed at Nick affectionately, turning to Catherine propped on the floor.

"But this guy, he knows! Nick, he's my man! My good buddy, Nick and Mac, they got me out! But they didn't get me no smokes. They got me out, didn't you!"

"Yeah, we did."

"Why didn't you get me smokes?" he asked, perplexed.

"Don't carry them. You know that."

Jerome nodded sagely.

"But you do the dirty, eh?" he laughed.

Jerome released him, grabbed the pipe and lit again. He started to hand it to Nick but jerked it away.

"You just steamed," taunted Jerome.

He took a long hit and coughed up smoke. The fit ended with a dark scowl.

"Those fuckers! If they knew... if they knew..."

Jerome plopped on the couch hacking.

Nick frowned.

"Knew what?" asked Nick, against his better judgment.

"What's... what's going down," coughed Jerome. "They'd be... shitless! But a little ivory and... what? Busted two fucking days!"

"You got busted for that?" asked Nick, surprised.

Sipary had said nothing about holding Jerome for ivory.

"That fucker! He's pointing the fingers, that fucker!"

"Who? Sipary?"

"You tell him... you tell him he knows shit about walrus. Mr. Hotshot Walrus Man... he knows shit! Well here's my finger, pointed back at him!"

He jabbed the middle one.

"You mean Elsberry?"

"You ask him... yeah! You ask him this... what killed that walrus? Huh? Ask him that."

What was Jerome raving about? Philip Elsberry... was he the 'hotshot walrus man'?

"Just ask him... what killed that walrus? No! No! Ask him this... what about bullet holes? Huh? What? No bullet holes? Then Dr. Shithead, what killed them?"

Jerome squealed a high laugh.

Bullet holes?

Nick finally worked it out... the walrus on the beach! He was supposed to ask Philip Elsberry about bullet holes. Did the walrus have bullet holes? Had anybody even checked that out, whether the headless walrus had bullet holes?

Was Isaac Nuniq right after all? Had the three headless walrus on the beach been run over by herring boats? They were road kill, not poached?

"Those fuckers!" gasped Jerome. "They're after one thing. Two things!" He clumsily laid the fingers down. "Money!

Money! That's two... and... Oh! Oh! Oh! King Shithead of Round Island! Your majesty, may I? May I? Oh, thank you!"

Jerome fell on the couch. He morosely stared into space, watching some personal drama... invisible actors... inaudible lines... unwanted endings. His face ran with anger, remorse, and repulsion.

"You got to know when to stop!" he choked. "You got to know when to just stop!"

What was Jerome raving about?

"Stop what?"

"Before they fucking kill us all."

Jerome shut his eyes and grimaced. Tears came down his cheeks. Nick now listened hard.

"Jerome, somebody tried to kill me."

"Yeah?" moaned Jerome, eyes still closed.

"At the strip, some old man shot at me. Last night. The bullet blew by my head."

Jerome cracked his eyes, regarded him without surprise.

"You see how it is? They'll get you too. Watch out. Watch your fucking back."

Nick was stunned.

That's what Paul Smart had said to him. This was the same warning he got from the elder about his accident in the boat, killing walrus on open water. In so many words he warned, 'watch out, be careful.'

"Who? Who will get me?"

"The Man... the fucking Man," groaned Jerome. "They learn who you are... that new guy, oh yeah, he shows up, he's Yukon River. Oh yeah... snoops around, asks questions. They watch... they freak... get really freaked..."

"Shut up," growled Catherine from the floor.

"You shut up!" said Jerome angrily, slapping the side of the couch.

"Get me a smoke."

"Fucking get it yourself."

"You get it!"

Nick left the sorry exchange.

He pushed through boxes of junk, shoved his shoulder against the heavy door, and climbed from the pit.

The last he heard from Jerome was angry.

"I'm not your fucking slave!"

The silver sky had clouded over. The village had turned dark.

Nick wandered, trying to make sense of it.

Jerome Paul was not just angry about his two-day lockup... he was frightened. They were getting 'freaked,' he said. Who were 'they'? Who was 'the Man' who watched? Trooper Hyde Cooper? Yes, Cooper watched, pissed at Camilla and Nick. Philip Elsberry? Jerome called him 'King Shithead' of Round Island. The shadowy old man at the airstrip? Who was that?

Jerome as much as admitted that some of his ivory came from the headless walrus on the beach. Ask Elsberry what killed the walrus, Jerome insisted. What other walrus were there but the headless walrus on the beach? Jerome challenged Elsberry to show that they had been shot. Had Jerome cut off the heads and seen they weren't shot? That meant Jerome had been on Round Island.

No, not necessarily. He could have found the walrus on the beach after the storm and cut off their heads for the ivory. That was even legal.

Nick had never talked to anyone who actually inspected the walrus for bullet holes. He hadn't read the refuge report about the carcasses. Isaac Nuniq said they were road kill, killed by propellers of herring boats. How did Isaac know that? Had he seen them too? Did he talk to Jerome? Nick didn't think Isaac and Jerome ever spoke. Even in this small village, they lived worlds apart. Patti said Isaac just guessed about the herring boats. But somebody must have seen what killed the walrus.

Of course! The hunter who found them would have seen it. The hunter who shared the meat with Patti and Isaac... Afcan Tooluyuk, an elder. Nick remembered his name on the list drawn for interviews. It sat near the bottom. They could just ask him. What killed the walrus? Tooluyuk would know. A hunter only salvaged carcasses considered safe to eat. The cause of death would have been the first thing Tooluyuk looked for.

What did Jerome mean, 'before they kill us all?' What did he mean, 'you got to know when to stop?' Jerome wasn't surprised that somebody shot at Nick. 'They watch ... they get freaked.'

Nick swore. It had happened, just as he feared. Some druggies or black market dealers were getting freaked about him and Camilla snooping around the village. They think we're spies. Mel Savidge was right too, telling them to stay clear of the trooper's investigation. They had talked with the trooper about Fernández and his death. They had asked about ivory. Now Nick was a target.

Or, maybe it wasn't black markets. Maybe it was Elsberry, pissed that the herring study might obstruct his proposals to close off Round Island. Was Elsberry involved somehow? Jerome obviously hated him. King Shithead of Round Island… that implied Elsberry wanted to control it personally. Harry Coopchiak believed that too.

'Watch out,' Jerome said. Paul Smart, the elder, said 'be careful.' But Smart had said it about boasting. Don't boast about calling walrus. Why? 'Ask Tusekluk,' the elder said. Who the hell was Tusekluk? Why couldn't Paul Smart just tell him what was bad about it?

Because it wasn't his place to tell, that's why, decided Nick. Smart was traditional. He followed traditional protocol when it came to dispensing information. Nick should hear it from the proper source. Smart was so traditional, he wasn't surprised by cormorants talking to walrus about disasters.

'The walrus should listen,' he advised. He whispered it, like you shouldn't say it loudly. The very idea was dangerous, the seed, a beginning.

Be careful.

Nick neared the tank.

The story played back to him… boy to a girl…

Nick froze.

Something moved. Something in the dark moved at the edge of Nick's vision. A stack of crab pots rose between the road and the shoreline. Somebody owned that parcel. They rented it to crabbers to store their pots. The crab pots were piled two stories high. Something had moved in the dark between rows.

Nick cautiously maneuvered behind the chassis of a rusted truck. He knelt behind a knobby tire and watched the shadows between the crab pots. He remembered his purloined binoculars. He quietly removed them from his pack and focused on the dark cracks. Something long and narrow glinted. It could be anything. Metal scrap. Wire catching light.

It withdrew into the crevasse.

Nick swung the glasses to the tank's door. It looked shut, just as Nick left it, latched, probably locked. He swung back to the crab pots. Somebody sitting in the crack would have a clear view of the tank's door.

Nick's skin crawled. He lowered the binoculars.

Somebody waited for his return, hiding in the crack, holding something long and metallic. Somebody freaked.

Nick carefully replaced his binoculars.
He shouldered the pack.
Melted into the shadows.
That stinky tank was the last place he ever wanted to sleep.

45

When Nick arrived at Winnie Friendly's house, Camilla was eating oatmeal. Winnie's children sat with her. Winnie's husband, Aloysius, was there too. Usually he was out early, working. But today he ate the morning meal, laughing at the table with his family. Winnie gave Nick a critical look. He had slept in his clothes again, this time inside Harry Coopchiak's steam bath wrapped in towels to stay warm. His back hurt from the hard plywood. He hadn't yet gone to the tank to change. He wanted company first, some assurances of normalcy.

Camilla smiled. She looked worn and subdued. A small line marked the space between her bushy brows. She still endured pain. Nick ate with her, also subdued. Winnie watched them both, wondering what was happening to her guests. Aloysius did the talking. The money he had just earned made him chatty. He told Camilla stories about trapping weasels.

"We should call headquarters," said Camilla at a break between weasels. "We need to find out what happened at the Joint Board committee."

Nick nodded. He had forgotten about the committee meeting. It had convened two days ago when he and Camilla worked in Dillingham, looking at archeological maps and drinking beers at the Hungry Bears. That seemed an age ago.

"We're near the end of the household list," she said. "With your interviews yesterday, there are just a few left, plus a couple we missed the first pass through."

Nick examined the list.

Afcan Tooluyuk was on it.

"Why are you here?" Nick asked Aloysius. He ate dried salmon instead of oatmeal. Oatmeal was tasty but hardly sustaining.

"Already finished my work today," he said, implying Nick was a sleepyhead.

"He finished the charters," said Winnie.

"The charters?"

"The Round Island charter boats," said Aloysius, "for tourists, over and back. I tune the motors every week."

"Oh," said Nick, recalling the disgruntled Ken Robbins. Robbins had invested in boats but lost the charter bid. He blamed Fish and Game of collusion, a sweetheart deal with the winners.

"They go out when the crew arrives, first plane."

"What crew?"

"The research shift. Elsberry takes them out."

"Elsberry? He's here?"

"He trains them."

Nick pointed to Camilla's list.

"Pencil him first."

Nick and Camilla beat Elsberry's team to a small floating dock near the slough's mouth behind town. Three aluminum boats shined in the mid-morning light. They were the same model as the boats Nick saw tied behind Robbins' blue warehouse, designed to ferry people in open water. They sat wide and deep, ample space for people and gear, powered by large inboard jets. They looked fast. Nick wondered how they performed in heavy seas.

A truck arrived from the airstrip with the student researchers excited about their Alaska adventure. With endless chatter, they began unloading gear for the boats. Dr. Philip Elsberry, King of Round Island, svelte in his Australian bush hat, supervised. The king was not happy to find Camilla and Nick waiting at the dock.

"What do you want?" said Elsberry in greeting.

"Just checking out your operation," replied Camilla, squinting into sun. She forced a smile.

"Yeah, well, this is it," said Elsberry brusquely. He shouted instructions to the charter captains. "As you can see, we're kind of busy."

"Yeah, heading out to the island, nice group," agreed Camilla. "How'd the Joint Board go? We didn't hear."

"Just ducky," said Elsberry, not bothering to face Camilla.

"They approved the buffer?" asked Nick, surprised.

"No, they didn't approve the buffer," said Elsberry with irritation. "It was a committee. They voted to pass it along to the full board," he paused and turned to Camilla, unable to resist the jab, "despite your boss and her chubby consort."

"Oh, were Mel and Jeff there?" asked Camilla with innocence.

Elsberry grinned at Camilla's performance.

"Oh yes, they were," he replied with undisguised sarcasm, "alert and annoyingly prepared."

"I'm glad to hear you say it."

"You're training this outfit?" asked Nick.

"Yes," replied Elsberry flatly. "They'll soon be experts observing walrus."

"Instant experts."

"Yep."

"Speaking of experts, I had a question for you. I was told I should ask you, because it's about walrus."

"Yes?" asked Elsberry, adjusting the bush hat.

Nick waited for Elsberry's full attention.

"I was told to ask you, that you would know the answer. This is the question. Did the walrus have bullet holes?"

"What?"

"The walrus, the ones without heads, the walrus the storm washed up. Did those walrus have bullet holes?"

Elsberry stood transfixed. His eyes bored into Nick. His face reddened and expanded.

"What kind of game are you playing?" Elsberry growled.

"No game. It's just a question I'm supposed to ask you. Did they or didn't they have bullet holes?"

"Whose question?" Elsberry loudly demanded. "Who's asking?"

"I'm asking. Were there holes?"

Elsberry's eyes flared between Nick and Camilla.

"Fuck off!" he exploded.

Complete silence followed.

Every student froze at their tasks and stared wide-eyed at the instructor. Camilla gently pulled on Nick's shoulder, guiding him away.

"Thanks, Philip," said Camilla sweetly.

She cheerily waved to the students.

"Hey! Have a nice trip, guys!"

As she pulled, Nick noticed Camilla's other hand. It moved to her mouth, suppressing a convulsion.

"Ow!" moaned Camilla. "God, it hurts to laugh!"

At the willows Camilla stopped short. She jerked around, yanking Nick with her. She squinted into the pain.

"Look!" she whispered.

The students were back at work, stowing gear.

"The boats... their names!" said Camilla.

Aluminum flashed as the boats rocked.

Angel One.

The others flashed too, black decals on their sides.

Angel Two. Angel Three.

"Fernández... his last letter!" said Camilla. "Things were looking up, he said. He had a better job!"

Nick remembered.

Con los angeles.

With the angels.

ROBERT J. WOLFE

46

Camilla and Nick called Juneau from the clinic. Mel was glad they called but she had to run. Yes, the buffer proposal got moved along to the Joint Board, not as expected.

"The committee was set to kill it," said Mel. "Commercial Fisheries got the message to the Big Boys on the committee. 'The buffer's bad.' They had the votes to kill it."

"Why didn't they?" asked Camilla, shielding her eyes against the fluorescent lights.

"Because of us, the walrus connection. They would have killed it except for your report on walrus hunting. That kept it alive. So we actually helped Elsberry. But it's pretty clear that it won't pass the full board. They have the votes to deep six it."

Camilla lowered her head to the desktop. Her arm covered her eyes. She looked green.

"How did we keep it alive?" asked Nick, taking over for Camilla.

"Alexie Encelewski, a new Board member. He's from Prince William Sound, an Alutiiq Eskimo with ties to Kodiak. I don't know him, but he's sharp. What we said about walrus hunting bothered him, that hunters have to hunt wastefully in open water. He wants to hear more. In deference, the committee passed the proposal along."

"Huh," said Nick, thinking about this unexpected twist. "So, is that good or bad?"

"It's not what we expected," said Mel. "But in this business, I'd guess 'good,' based on one thing."

"What?" asked Nick.

"Elsberry was pissed!"

With a hearty laugh, Mel clicked off.

Theresa Manumik burst into the office.

"Theresa?" asked Nick.

"You hear?" said Theresa, a voice of resolve and fear.

"What?"

"Jerome Paul... he's dead! And Catherine Manumik..."

Theresa's face screwed up.

"She tried to kill herself."

"How awful!" said Camilla, rising from her agony.

Theresa fell into Camilla's arms and buried her face.

"Is she going to be okay?" whispered Camilla.

"I got her sedated at her mom's. She went crazy."

Jerome Paul... dead?

"Nick, they want to talk to you, right now."

Theresa didn't say who 'they' were.

She didn't have to.

They were coming through the door.

47

Trooper Cooper was clearly unhappy.

He chewed a pencil and glared at Nick in the hot seat. His jaw muscles worked beneath the buzz cut. He was entirely dissatisfied with Nick's answers. So he went over them, again and again. Sipary sat to the side listening somberly. Cooper had not asked Sipary for anything during the interrogation. Sipary liked Nick. So Sipary couldn't be trusted.

"You left them when?" said Cooper.

"About one," said Nick.

"How do you know that?"

"Like I said, the clock said midnight when I left the steam bath. I walked to Jerome Paul's place. I stayed about half an hour. That makes it one, more or less."

"The Manumik girl, she remembers you coming in but not going out."

"She was pretty wasted."

"Drugs?"

Nick shrugged his shoulders.

"She was wasted on drugs?" pressed Cooper.

"Like I said, I saw her with a beer. That's all I saw."

"Wasted how?"

"Half asleep. Eyes barely open. She sat on the floor, almost asleep."

"She didn't see you leave because she was sleeping."

"Because she was wasted," said Nick. "She and Jerome were arguing about cigarettes when I left. She wasn't paying attention to me."

Cooper tapped his pencil.

276

"Why did you go over there?"

"I told you, I brought back his stuff for Camilla and for Sipary."

Cooper gave Sipary an irritated look.

"Artifacts," stated Cooper.

"That's right."

"We'll find them at his place?"

"He smashed one against a wall… the ulu."

"Smashed one. Why?"

"He got mad about something and tossed it, not to smash it but just tossed it. It hit the wall and broke."

Nick was tired and frustrated and getting mad. No one had told him anything about Jerome Paul's death yet. Cooper was purposively keeping him in the dark, trying to trap him into an admission. Cooper looked frustrated too. Nick was giving him nothing useful.

"Where was Paul when you left him?" asked Cooper again, for the fifth time by Nick's count.

"In his living room. He was arguing with his girlfriend."

"He wasn't in the bathroom?" Cooper had asked this before too.

"No," replied Nick again.

"And you never went into the bathroom?"

"No."

"But you've been in his bathroom."

"I used it on a different visit. Not last night."

Cooper tapped his pencil, stuck it in his teeth, and chewed. The muscles on his bullet head worked. A rap on the door preceded a uniformed officer, someone Cooper knew.

"The team's here," said the officer.

Cooper nodded and got up. Nick figured this was an investigative unit from Dillingham. They were headed for Jerome's place, which had been sealed. Cooper was going with them. Nick's interrogation was over.

"I'll need to talk to the Mac Cleary girl," said Cooper.

Sipary nodded.

"What about me?" asked Nick.

"You?" Cooper pointed rudely and growled. "Stick close."

Cooper exited. Nick frowned, looked to Sipary.

"You're not going?"

"I'm not invited," said Sipary. He finally moved to sit at his own desk, stewing at Cooper's arrogance. "But I've already seen it. I was there first. I looked it over. They'd be mad to know."

Nick waited. If Sipary was going to tell him anything, he'd tell. Nick wouldn't have to ask. Sipary pushed aside the papers in front of him, one clean space in a messy world.

"He died in the bathroom."

Nick nodded, waiting.

"His face was in the toilet."

Nick grimaced. He wasn't sure he wanted to know. But he asked anyway.

"Under water?"

"Under water," said Sipary. "That's how I found him. Maybe he drowned. I don't know. He had vomited and missed. It looked to me that he'd hung himself over the pot and passed out. He fell into the toilet face first."

So ended Jerome Paul, a life that began in a small village, drifted around the world, and finished face down in a toilet, a life of dislocation and dissonance, a life like his own.

Nick shuddered.

"Yeah," said Sipary.

Sipary poured cups of old coffee, handing one to Nick.

"What was he using?"

"Hash, beer," said Nick. "That's all I saw."

"That's all I noticed too."

Nick thought about it.

"Maybe that's enough," said Sipary.

"Yeah."

"She found him there and went nuts," said Sipary. "She ran screaming to her place, screaming the whole way that he was dead. She got lots of company but she locked herself in a bedroom and cut her wrists before they could force the door. Theresa got her sedated and patched up. But she had to run to the clinic and back. There was plenty of blood before they were done."

Nick nodded.

"So is that it?" Sipary asked.

He drank coffee and waited. It was Nick's turn.

"I don't know," said Nick, recalling snatches from the previous night. "He was drunk, angry, scared. He talked a lot, real drunk stuff. He said things like, 'they'll kill us all' and 'you have to know when to stop' and 'we're fucked.'"

"What did he mean?"

"I don't know. I tried to get him to say but he was rambling crazy drunk. He told me to 'watch my back' because they'll get me."

"Who?"

"The Man. That's what he said. I thought he was talking about you because he was pissed about jail. But it wasn't you. He was pissed at you but not scared. It was something else. I thought maybe Cooper was the Man, but I don't know how that makes any sense. I figured it was the black market or drug dealers, whoever they are. You know he deals lots of stuff. Whoever it was, he said they were getting 'freaked' and that you 'got to know when to stop.'"

"Stop what?"

"I don't know. Dealing?"

Sipary waited, but Nick was finished.

"So now he's stopped," said Sipary.

He appraised Nick.

"Where'd you sleep last night? The tank?"

"Coopchiak's steam."

"The tank's still too spooky?"

"I thought I saw something. So I slept in his maqi."

"What'd you see?"

"Something inside those crab pots. But you know, maybe nothing."

They sat together in silence.

"You should have come to my place," said Sipary.

"Yeah?"

"The couch isn't great. But it's better than Coopchiak's maqi."

"Yeah, okay," agreed Nick, feeling instantly unburdened. He had heard that a big storm was coming. He didn't relish another wet night under a boat.

"Am I supposed to stay here for Cooper?"

"I heard him say 'stay close.'"

"Then I will... close enough."

Grabbing his pack, Nick escaped outside. He felt a strong urge to find Camilla. The gray sky threw sprinkles. Finally, something fresh and good.

It had clearly happened.

This project had hit bottom.

Nick found Camilla suffering in the alcove. She hid in the dark with a washcloth over her eyes. Nick sat beside her. She immediately took his hand.

"Thanks for coming, Nick," she whispered.

They sat for a while in the dark.

"Squeeze here," she whispered.

Camilla put Nick's hand to the side of her head. Nick applied pressure. He squeezed one-handed, two-handed. He kneaded. He lightly rubbed. He gently tapped. He repeated everything, several times. Finally, worn out, he rewetted the cloth and draped her eyes.

"Thanks," said Camilla, taking his hand again.

"Did it help?"

"Yeah."

Nick doubted it did. He held her strangely thin fingers, wishing he could do more. Against her constant pain, he felt useless.

"Need to lie down?" whispered Camilla beneath the washcloth. She scooted over a couple of inches.

Lie down? Next to her? There was no way to fit.

What was Camilla thinking? Nick decided she wasn't. She was in too much pain to think clearly. She moved on autopilot. Her nature was to give. She had only a couple of inches.

"Thanks. But I'm going."

"Okay."

Nick wandered into the living area. Winnie washed greens in the sink, looking sad.

"It's raining," she sighed.

Nick looked out to the gray world. The rain fell hard. He knew the herring project would be on hold for the next few days. Death in a village brought life to a halt. No hunting. No fishing. People grieved, supported the grievers, reflected on the dead and death, and covered it all in small mounds at the edge of the village. That's what would happen here. He had never been to Togiak. But he knew, that's what would happen.

"Did he have family?" asked Nick.

Winnie knew who he was talking about.

"Cousins. His mom died five years ago. Maybe he has a brother somewhere. He came back after his mom died. He hadn't been home for years."

Nick thought about families. Some flourished, others withered. There were families who had five, six, seven children, all of whom survived to have children of their own, living, working, sharing, increasing. For Yup'iks, that was success. Other families lost them, an accident here, an estrangement there, unexplained exits, suicides, a slow dwindling until at the

280

end only neighbors remained for the burials. Nick's family seemed to be doing neither... not diminishing but not growing, just holding on. Nick's aunt had two kids and no husband. Back home, she represented his grandmother's best hope for the family's future. Himself? Nick didn't know what she hoped for him. He was a dead end, like those walrus on the beaches of Round Island baking in the sun, foraging in muck, growing old, dying, sinking to the seabed to feed the clams.

"Those drugs are bad," said Winnie.

"Yeah."

"Kids shouldn't use them."

Winnie was right. It was the drugs after all got said and done. The drugs killed him. The paranoia that gripped Jerome that final night, that was drugs too. No one was after him. No one cared enough. Jerome killed himself. He was just a lonely Yup'ik who had lost his way and come home too late. He never really made it back.

Nick headed for the door.

"Where are you going?" asked Winnie.

"To sleep."

"Where?"

"The tank."

And its spooks, thought Nick.

Tonight he didn't care.

48

Nick dreamed.

Camilla and walrus and creosote.

In his dreams, he smelled it, the acrid stench.

Nothing to do with Camilla or walrus. It came from the tank. Roll over and sleep… it's just a little creosote.

Something prodded. Almost hurt. Move!

With a great effort, he rolled.

He came off the cot and hit the floor.

Blistering hot!

Nick woke to smoke. It rose from every seam, swirling in the half-light of the room's bulb.

The tank was on fire!

Nick grabbed his shirt and pulled it over his nose. He stumbled to the door and placed a palm upon it. Searing hot! He pulled on sneakers, threw on his duffle and pack, and found the ladder. Climbing the rungs, he pushed into the night. Four stories up, he stood. The flat roof was wet with rain. A seething wall of smoke encircled it. Black boiled every direction he looked. A firebox. The tank's bottom was aflame.

Nick stumbled toward the edge he guessed held the ladder. Crackling flames lapped over the lip, belching cinders with blasts of smoke. Oily explosions drove him backward. The side was engulfed. He staggered back to the center, heart pounding, dragging in ragged breaths of sooty air, knowing with a certainty his life was now measured in seconds.

He frantically swung around trying to gain a solid bearing. The top was featureless. Wavering gray shapes came through the barrier of dense smoke. There was no clear direction.

Nick looked up. The marine layer pressed down. It presented no breaks, no moon, no stars, no streams of clouds.

He had to get off. When the roof collapsed, he was dead. He frantically surveyed the encircling wall of smoke and flame. Where was it? He turned full circle again. Where would it be? He had one chance to find that spot. Sirens wailed. They drew closer, too late for him now.

Nick looked up again. The clouds covered like a pot lid.

There! On the watery veil, a fuzzy spot glowed. It blinked, on, off, on, off, the runway's beacon reflecting off the low ceiling. He closed his eyes... felt his heart pounding... imagined the beacon, the circular tank, the hatch in the roof. He turned, placing the reflected glow at his shoulder. That way!

Nick trotted toward that edge, bent back, and heaved the rucksack into the wall of fiery smoke. He stripped off the backpack and heaved it too. They vanished into black. He trotted back to the center.

Flames shot up through the hatch. The puddles beneath his feet steamed. The sirens blasted. This was it. He set his shoulder to the red sky, pumped his lungs with hot air, thought of living, and sprinted toward the smoking edge.

He set his foot at the flaming rim and vaulted into blackness.

He kicked once, twice...

With a crash and a rip he stuck the nets feet first. His body tore between pots before the nets grabbed. The crab pots wobbled and tumbled. He fell too, over and down, collapsing within the cascade of net-covered frames. He rolled with the spidery mess and came to rest.

"Here!" someone yelled.

A flood lamp hit him.

Hands grabbed and hauled him from the nets. Nick looked into several faces. One was Andrew Sipary's.

The roof of the tank erupted with a roar. They scrambled back to watch it implode, releasing a fountain of red cinders. They stood at a far periphery with the whole village to watch the conflagration, the greatest fire in memory.

Camilla found him in the crowd.

"Oh God, Nick!"

She hugged him, not letting go.

Sipary stood on his other side.

They watched the walls of the tank collapse.

"I told you," said Sipary.

"What?"

"My couch is better than that tank."

In the dull flicker, two kids approached. They had the duffle and backpack. Nick thanked them both. They shyly grinned.

"Nick," whispered Camilla by his ear, drawing him closer.

"Yeah?"

"You're staying with me tonight."

"I am?"

"Yeah."

Her cheeks were red with fire.

"Someone's trying to kill you."

49

They holed up at Winnie's for the period of mourning, on-and-off-again rain, suffering, sleeping, conferring, editing, licking wounds. The funeral happened the afternoon of the second day after the fire. Elders of the Moravian church conducted the services, mostly in Yup'ik. Nick and Camilla attended, sitting side-by-side on the hard pew. In a homily, an elder talked about the giving that brings joy, the sharing of life to family and community. Nick whispered translations into Camilla's ear. Jerome had done this, Nick supposed. Merchants dispensed things that gave joy.

Much of the village attended. Nick saw some they had interviewed. Theodore Bavilla, the minister whose daughter had played the Ouija board and gotten a high school teacher fired... he presided among the elders up front. Paul Smart stood there too, the elder who warned Nick about calling walrus, or more precisely, boasting about it. 'Watch out,' he advised. Since the fire, Nick was watching.

Aloysius and Winnie Friendly sat in a center row with their children. Her brother, Harry Coopchiak, sat nearby. His son Cornelius and his nephew, Herbert Small, were missing. Isaac and Patti Nuniq occupied a bench together. The giant militant wore a tie and dress shirt. Ken Robbins, the fishmonger, hugged a side pew, looking downcast in faded dungarees. Florence Smith, the simpleton recluse, sat on a back pew, her eyes fixed on stained glass. Her ancient great grandmother, Estella, was absent.

Nick saw Lt. Hyde Cooper standing at the back, perusing the crowd. He wasn't there for Yup'ik homilies. Jerome's

285

girlfriend, Catherine, wasn't present, but her cousin, Theresa Manumik attended, the practitioner who had patched her wrists, occasionally looking Nick's direction. He saw old women he remembered from the bingo match. But most in the church Nick did not know, people from the good village of Togiak burying an unfortunate young man from a poor family, not a kinsman and barely a neighbor, but one of God's children, one of theirs. About thirty reassembled to watch the rough wood coffin lowered into the ground beneath a misting sky, then the shoveling of earth, putting to rest the goodness and grief of Jerome Paul.

Andrew Sipary sidled to them as the dirt fell.

"Come to the office?" he asked.

Under the frown of Lt. Cooper, the three left the cemetery in Sipary's truck. Nick had hardly spoken with Sipary since the fire. He declined sleeping at Sipary's place, bunking instead with Harry Coopchiak, Winnie's brother, and spending days with Camilla. Nick liked Sipary, but he didn't want to be associated with 'the Man.' Sipary understood.

"Where are we going?" asked Camilla as they passed the VPSO station.

"Health Clinic."

Theresa Manumik waited with a stranger, a tall kass'aq in casual dress fresh off the afternoon plane.

"Dr. Howell, this is Nicholas John and Camilla Mac Cleary. Nick and Camilla, Ted Howell, State Epidemiology, Anchorage. You've met Andrew Sipary."

There were handshakes all around. Dr. Theodore Howell, a thin man with large teeth, took charge and dropped the bombshell.

"We know what killed Jerome Paul... botulism."

Nick looked at Camilla, shocked. Camilla's face registered nothing.

"His blood serum tested high for botulinum toxin," said Howell.

"Not the toilet?" asked Nick.

"That's just where he fell. He likely went to vomit. He collapsed and died."

"And not from drugs," added Sipary.

"Marijuana and alcohol may have compounded effects," said Howell. "But it was the toxin that killed him... paralysis and respiratory failure. This is why we'd like to interview you, Mr. John. We want to identify the source so we can prevent additional cases. I'm told you may know what the victim ate the night he died."

Nick sat stunned... botulism, one of the world's deadliest poisons. Since the advent of public health in rural Alaska, most villagers knew of botulism and the toxin that caused it, a tasteless poison lurking in wrongly-preserved foods. The spores of Clostridium botulinum, a bacterium, lived naturally in dirt. The bacteria excreted a toxin so deadly, a spoonful evenly distributed could devastate a city. Potent, undetectable, it killed by attacking the nervous system, disrupting nerve impulses, paralyzing breathing, swelling the brain. Blurred vision, dry mouth, and nausea were early signs. As with snakebites, antitoxin could neutralize the poison. It could save a victim if given in time.

Nick knew the bacteria's weakness... oxygen. This was taught in village schools. Clostridium botulinum grew in airless environments. This meant that wild foods handled in traditional ways were usually safe. Foods air dried, stored in porous containers, even buried in the ground, were usually okay. Foods preserved in sealed airtight containers were the problem, especially uncooked foods fermenting in glass or plastic, especially the sealed plastic bucket. If contaminated with soil, the airless containers could grow the bacteria, producing the toxin. Botulism was a curse of modern storage.

"I'd like to make a list of foods you remember Jerome Paul eating that night," said Howell.

"The house got cleaned," explained Theresa. "The cleaners threw out leftovers."

"We've interviewed the cleaners," said Howell.

"We'll do Catherine too," said Theresa.

"That's important, because she didn't get it. The victim ate something she didn't."

Howell turned to Camilla.

"Were you there too?"

"No, I wasn't. I don't know anything."

"I don't think I do either," said Nick, stretching his memory to that night. "They ate before I got there. I came about midnight. I just remember empty plates."

"You didn't see what they were eating?"

"I didn't see them eating."

"They didn't complain about being sick?"

"Jerome's girlfriend was sleepy. They were drunk. No one complained about feeling sick."

"Blurred vision? Droopy eyelids? Slurred speech?"

"Well, they were drunk."

"Do you recall the dishes? Anything you remember might help."

Nick thought hard. He conjured up images of their empty plates.

"I guess I did see some things on their plates. I remember dried fish on Catherine's plate. And potato salad."

"They made potato salad?" asked Howell, marking a form.

"Probably from the store. It comes in small containers."

"Okay. What kind of dried fish?"

"Salmon. I don't know what kind. I didn't eat any."

"What about the victim's plate?"

"I saw a plate on the work bench. I guess that was his. It had fish skins from the salmon. Potato salad. And he had beluga."

"Beluga? You saw beluga?" asked Howell.

"Oil soaked the paper plate. A couple of chunks were left. Half the plate was soaked with oil."

"Cooked?" asked Howell.

Nick knew why he asked that. Cooking destroyed the toxin.

"Raw," said Nick.

"Was beluga on her plate too?"

Nick thought hard and became frustrated.

"I don't remember."

"I'm impressed you remember so much," said Howell.

"Well, I notice food."

Camilla smiled and covered her mouth.

"But you didn't eat?"

"I wasn't hungry."

He had just steamed. He had no appetite. He had overslept in the maqi and come late to Jerome's house. He was upset about Lydia's story, the rumors of her birth. These things had saved him.

Dr. Howell produced a food list. He read from it, systematically covering food groups a respondent might overlook. With the help of the list, Nick recalled bread rolls, margarine, mustard, potato chips, and two brands of beer. This same list had been administered to the housecleaners, but not yet to Jerome's girlfriend.

"What does all this suggest?" asked Camilla.

"At this stage, I'd say the beluga is the prime suspect," said Howell.

"Why is that?"

"We've seen it before. If stored in a plastic bucket or a zip-lock bag, anaerobes can grow. Botulism doesn't like acids. Beluga isn't acidic. Fermented beluga, bowhead, sea lion flippers… these are risks if stored wrong. Clean plastic containers look sanitary, but they can be deadly."

"Where did the raw beluga come from?" asked Camilla.

"Not from here," said Theresa.

"How do people get it?" asked Howell.

"Dillingham," guessed Theresa. "Levelock, Clark's Point, and South Naknek through Dillingham. Those places hunt beluga."

"Somebody gave him beluga?"

"Or he traded for it," said Theresa. "He did lots of trading."

"We'll want to track this down," said Howell. "I don't recall beluga in the list of foods in his storage."

"It wasn't," said Theresa.

"It got thrown out by the housecleaners?" asked Camilla.

"It wasn't identified by them."

"He has one cache," said Theresa. "There was no beluga there or in his house."

"We'll want to find out where it came from," said Howell. "Let's interview Catherine. She might know. If she didn't eat any, we definitely should put out a general alert about beluga."

"Let's put it out anyway," said Theresa.

Poor Jerome, thought Nick.

What's more appealing than fermented beluga whale, creamy pink in glistening oil? If tainted… death in twelve hours.

Looks were more than deceiving.

They could kill.

50

"A big storm is forecast."

"A storm?" asked Camilla.

"Forming over the Aleutians and heading this way, tomorrow afternoon," said Sipary.

Nick listened with half an ear as they drove to Winnie's... 'storm,' 'Aleutians,' 'tomorrow afternoon.' He shoved the information with the rest, a growing accumulation of facts and impressions, a messy puzzle.

Since the fire, Nick worked its pieces.

'Someone's trying to kill you, you're staying with me,' Camilla had concluded. Nick had stayed close, as if that protected him. Of course it didn't. How could staying close to Camilla, a skinny girl with headaches, protect anyone?

They drove past the station. Was the asshole Cooper inside? Surly Trooper Cooper had frowned when they left the cemetery for the clinic to learn that botulism killed Jerome Paul, not drugs or alcohol.

Cooper had interviewed Nick after the fire. He was unhappy, almost angry. Why was the burned-out tank the place where Nick slept? Why Nick, of all people? Nick worked with the anthropologist who located the family of Fernández with one uncanny phone call, the undocumented worker killed while poaching ivory in a storm, the anthropologist from Mexico who refused to give up her fieldnotes without a fight. Nick escaped with all his gear.

'How did that happen?' Cooper wanted to know.

'I repacked. I was set to leave.'

'Why?' pressed Cooper.

'The tank stunk.'

Nick withheld the details… the shadowy cracks of the crab pots, the warnings of a church elder, Jerome's rants about the Man. Nick said nothing of the bullet that almost clipped his ear at the airstrip. Sipary knew these facts. Let Cooper ask Sipary. But the arrogant bastard would never consult Sipary.

Faulty wiring. That's why the tank burned. That was the popular explanation. The fire burned so hot there was little left to see. Everybody knew the wiring was not to code. The owner stored drums of flammables on the ground floor. The wiring shorted in the rain and the drums ignited. That's why the tank burned so violently. It should have happened years ago.

Nick miraculously escaped with all his stuff.

Cooper treated it like a personal affront. The trooper didn't like miracles.

Nick did not mention 'the angels,' boat names that possibly linked Fernández and the Round Island charters. Jerome's death and the fire had pushed it from the forefront of his concerns. The interviews brought it back. But Cooper was unpleasant and adversarial.

'Screw him,' thought Nick when he remembered the omission. Had Camilla told him?

She said she hadn't when Nick asked her. The migraines had laid her low. Other things intruded. Did Nick think they should?

'I don't know,' he said.

'Maybe we should,' she said.

Camilla disliked Cooper too. They were told to stay clear of his investigation. Mel fought to keep their notes from being subpoenaed by his department. Cooper had broken the deal about informal sharing.

After the fire, Nick tried to contact Lydia. He tried several times. The awful rumor nagged at him, the malicious shaman, the unnatural transformation. He wanted to hear her voice.

He got static on the CB.

'It's down again,' said Harry. The camp's CB was notoriously unreliable. Some connector was loose, bad wiring, or the antenna. It worked half the time. No mobiles worked out there.

Nick endured the rumor.

Did the Coopchiaks know about the storm?

Assuredly, said Harry. They had a radio and a generator. They listened to Alaska Weather. It was sheltered. They'd be fine at camp.

He wished he could talk to Lydia.

Nick caught Camilla watching him brood.

He still couldn't read her. She wore a theatrical mask. Naïve optimism... that's what she usually projected. But beneath was something more complicated, more conflicted. Under that controlled optimism was something troubling, some emotional scar or neurological torture. She didn't share it. He didn't fault her for that. He didn't share his troubles either. Camilla and he were alike in that. He wondered about her past and its agony. But he didn't pry. Nor did she... much.

"Working things out?" she asked exiting Sipary's truck.

"Yeah," said Nick. "Well, no."

"So who's after you?" said Camilla calmly.

Like asking about the weather.

"I don't know."

She took Nick's arm in hers, drawing him closer as they walked. Winnie watched through the kitchen window. She shook her head.

Screw her, thought Nick.

This afternoon, he was glad for Camilla.

"We have an interview," she said.

It was the first scheduled survey since Jerome's death.

"A VIP of sorts."

"Who?"

"Afcan Tooluyuk."

51

The scheduled interview put Nick on edge.

Philip Elsberry had reacted explosively to his question about the headless walrus on the beach... 'we're they shot?' 'Fuck off!' Elsberry had shouted. It was Jerome's question for Elsberry. Jerome was now dead.

The herring proposals from Elsberry for Round Island presumed the walrus had been killed for their ivory. Trooper Cooper's investigation did too. Fernández had died poaching ivory in a storm... that was the presumption.

But what if the walrus weren't shot? What if propellers from herring boats had killed them? Elsberry's proposals would be groundless. And if propellers killed them, how did Fernández die? What had he been doing?

Something to do with angels?

Elsberry's charter boats were named for angels.

Afcan Tooluyuk might be key to answering these questions. The old hunter had found the headless walrus. And he found the body of Fernández.

The modest home of Afcan Tooluyuk sat near the beach. Camilla and Nick walked the shore to find it. Wind from the incoming storm whipped sand. Nick saw Sipary's truck parked on a rise. He sat in it watching the bay. Where was Trooper Cooper? Probably flying back to Anchorage, angry and frustrated. Spoiled food had killed Jerome. That was Public Health, not Public Safety.

"Remember, herring... that's why we're here," said Camilla. Nick concurred.

Of course, herring came first, but then...

Afcan Tooluyuk welcomed them, a short wiry elder with a big smile. He would do his best to help them learn about herring. He said it with modesty in Yup'ik and English. His wife, Agrafina, sat them at the rough kitchen table. Hot tea was waiting.

Every Yup'ik community had people like Afcan and Agrafina, unassuming, hardworking, and generous, the core of successful families. Afcan knew herring well. He had acquired his knowledge from day-to-day experience, living off the land, guided by generations of oral tradition. Without any advanced degree, barely a grade school education, Afcan knew as much about local ecology as a university scholar. Agrafina knew the storage and preparation of wild foods like herring. They were living libraries.

Afcan answered questions in careful detail, translated by Nick to Camilla. Agrafina hovered nearby and added details. She filled their teacups with tea from the tundra, a bitter brew that burned going down, perfect for loosening the gutturals required by proper Yup'ik.

Afcan described the multiple runs of herring that came to spawn in Togiak Bay, the dynamic cycles of fish tied to sea ice, their connections with seals, sea lions, and beluga, and the processing of herring by drying, smoking, and fermenting. Nick felt privileged to hear it. Afcan looked pleased. Youngsters rarely visited to listen and learn.

The interview stretched three hours. By the end Camilla reached to the ceiling and arched her back.

"I'm stuffed. We've been at this a while, eh? It's great. Thanks so much for this good information!"

She smiled warmly at Afcan and Agrafina.

"How about it, Nick? Are we getting done?"

Done? They still had questions about the headless walrus. Camilla had worked slowly and meticulously through the herring questions, never interrupting, rarely redirecting. Why was she doing it this way? It was almost like she stalled, like she didn't want to ask about walrus. The old man would grow tired. He'd ask them to leave.

Beyond the room's dusty panes the sun edged along the horizon, dusk on a sea whipped by the first winds of the forecasted storm. It was getting late.

Nick's stomach growled.

Everybody heard it.

The old man laughed. Agrafina instantly reacted. Could they stay a bit longer to eat? She had stew on the stove. There would be plenty. Nick checked Camilla, who nodded. Agrafina beamed.

She served up bowls of stew with fresh baked bread. There was enough for a small expedition. The rich fare soon had them sweating. Camilla's pale cheeks glowed a ruddy red.

Nick fretted. He had agreed that Camilla should take the lead in the interview. But it was getting hard to wait. Should he shoulder in and ask the questions?

Camilla scraped the bottom of her bowl.

"This is good! Is it seal?"

"Asveq," said Agrafina smiling.

Walrus... Nick worried a bone in his mouth. She had built the stew around the backbones of a walrus. Come on, Camilla. Here's the chance. Ask about walrus.

"Kass'aqs sometimes don't like our Native food," said Agrafina. "Except ice cream, kass'aqs always say they like Eskimo ice cream."

"It's good. Do you like it, Nick?"

"I could eat it all night," he said, frustrated.

He couldn't wait. He'd give this a push.

"But I think I've tasted it before," Nick gently teased, pulling the bone from his cheek.

"Where?" asked Agrafina round-eyed, staring at the bone between his fingers. How had Nick eaten her stew?

"Patti Nuniq. Isn't this that walrus?"

Agrafina looked to her husband. He nodded.

"That old man gives away all our food!" she laughed. "Look at him. Look how thin he's getting!"

Afcan grinned.

"I heard about that walrus," said Camilla. "It washed ashore, the storm last month. You're the hunter who found it?"

Nick relaxed, his trust in Camilla restored. She had taken the push and flawlessly maneuvered to the beached walrus. Nick listened to see if he needed to translate.

The old man smiled modestly. He had not become a good hunter by bragging, or by being stingy.

"I'm glad I got a chance to taste it," said Camilla. "Now I can say I've tasted a walrus from Round Island."

Afcan made a playful look of mild concern. He spoke in Yup'ik as Camilla scraped a final spoonful.

"What? I shouldn't say I ate this?" asked Camilla.

"Not that," said Nick. "He just says 'maybe'."

"Maybe what?"

In Yup'ik, Nick clarified. Afcan answered.

Nick considered how to translate.

"Maybe that's Round Island walrus, maybe not," Nick said. "He says walrus ride on the sea ice. Their nature is to go with the pack ice. Walrus aren't tied to any one place."

"Hmmmm…" said Camilla, turning to face Afcan.

"I read a report about it. Let's see, uh, Darryl Thomas, his report. He interviewed you, yes?"

Nick translated. Afcan nodded. He remembered.

"Three walrus came up on the beach after the storm," said Camilla. "Thomas measured them and took tissue samples and interviewed you."

"What do they do with it?" Afcan asked in English, not waiting for a translation. "I wondered when I watched that boy put them in jars. I wondered, what will they do with that? They never said."

"They didn't say? They were testing genetic signatures for stock analysis. Someone in Oregon is doing it. The report said they are testing for discrete walrus stocks, looking for genetic differences within the Bering Sea. Are eastern Bering Sea walrus related to the western Bering Sea walrus on the Russian side… questions like that."

Nick translated. There were no Yup'ik words for 'stock analysis' and 'genetic signatures.' Afcan and Agrafina listened carefully. Nick wasn't sure either knew much about genetics. But they listened respectfully to the explanation.

"They planned to test for contaminants too," said Camilla, "heavy metals like cadmium and mercury and some other things I don't know much about, polychlorinated biphenyls from pesticides, I think. Is that right, Nick?"

"Uh, I don't know."

"Pesticide residues," said Camilla.

Nick translated again, using the English words for the contaminants. Agrafina looked worried.

"The walrus isn't good?" she asked.

"No, no, it's good," said Camilla. "They're looking just in case. I guess they have found contaminants on the Russian side. Traces. Small amounts. Well, maybe not with cadmium, that's in the gall bladders, I think. They're checking to see if there are contaminants here."

Nick translated. Partway, he complained.

"That's the problem with these studies. They do tests, but nothing gets back to the hunters. They've tested on the Yukon. We never hear what they find."

He repeated the complaints in Yup'ik.

Afcan responded at length. Nick translated.

"He says animals pick up things from what they eat. He gives the example of bears. Bears that eat seals begin to taste like seals. That's why they're careful to not spill gasoline and kerosene. It gets picked up and makes the animals sick. The animals know it's bad. The smell drives them away."

Afcan continued. Nick translated.

"He says to check the liver. If the liver has white spots or if it's too big then that animal is sick. Don't use it. But the liver on this walrus was okay."

"Yeah," said Camilla. "The liver looked okay. That means it was healthy. So what did kill those walrus?"

The key question!

She asked it like one of a hundred others. Camilla could work on stage. Nick's heart pounded as he translated to Yup'ik.

Afcan answered as he had the others, confidently and carefully. The answers astonished Nick as he translated.

"He says he looked at the carcasses. The first two were on sand. He considered using them. He might have tried on the way back to Togiak but he found the third walrus on rocks. That's the one he butchered. He looked at each for the cause of death. The first walrus had one bullet hole through the shoulder. It passed out the other side. It was not a good shot, whoever made it. The second walrus had no bullet hole that he could see."

Nick put up his finger to Camilla. His throat was dry. He gulped tea. He found his hand trembled.

"The third walrus, the one he used, it had no bullet hole either. None had cuts from propellers. But it would be odd for three walrus to be killed that way together, he said. He looked anyway. No cuts. So he wondered, what killed these walrus? So as he butchered, he looked carefully for the cause."

Nick took another sip.

"And?" asked Camilla.

She's hanging on each word, saw Nick. She's feigning indifference, but she's almost falling over.

"I don't know yet," said Nick.

Afcan spoke more at length. Nick listened carefully. He hesitated before translating.

"This is hard for me. There are words I don't know, technical terms for walrus parts. He's described to me in detail the major steps of butchering a walrus. We should have had the recorder going. The upshot is that the walrus was not diseased. The lungs, liver, heart… all the organs looked fine. There was no bullet coming in from the other side. But inside he discovered internal bleeding, a large bruise on the underside of the walrus. On that side, the ribcage was crushed inward. He didn't use meat or fat from the bruised side. He didn't use the crushed ribcage."

Camilla digested this.

"Then what killed it?"

Afcan instantly replied. Nick translated.

"He doesn't know," said Nick. "He's never seen injuries like that on a walrus. It was like something powerful hit the walrus on the side. He doesn't know."

"And the others?" asked Camilla.

"He already said, he didn't open them up. He doesn't want to speculate about what was inside. But it could be the same."

Camilla sat thinking. Nick was stumped. Three dead walrus. Only one shot.

Nick asked something. Afcan replied. Nick translated.

"I asked if they all died at the same time. He said the signs are that they all died at the same time."

Nick asked more, received a reply, and translated.

"He says the one walrus was shot, but he doesn't think the shot killed it. It was a lousy shot. The walrus died from something else."

Afcan spoke again. Nick translated.

"He wonders, what could kill three healthy walrus at the same time with no external marks except a blow to the side? Could a fast ship go through a group and hit three at once? Maybe, but walrus don't fall asleep like that in open water. He doesn't know. He's never seen it before."

"But it had no head, right?" asked Camilla. "The report said they had no heads."

Nick began to translate but Afcan already understood. He answered, this time in English, directly to Camilla. He seemed amused.

"Darryl Thomas asked about that head. He kept looking over this way at my boat. I didn't know why he kept looking at my boat. He talked to me but his eyes were looking over that way. Only later did I guess why he was looking like that. He was looking for that head! He wanted that head and those tusks!"

Afcan laughed. He spoke in Yup'ik. Nick translated.

"He says that Darryl Thomas thought Afcan had salvaged the ivory. Thomas kept saying he'd tag the tusks. Afcan couldn't figure this out. He wasn't making sense because anybody could see that the heads had been missing for a couple of days."

"From the condition of the cut," agreed Camilla. "The heads got cut off at Round Island before the storm hit."

Afcan quickly spoke to Nick. He turned to Camilla.

"Not Round Island," Afcan said in English.

Camilla waited but he said nothing more. She looked for help from Nick. He didn't know what Afcan was getting at.

"Not Round Island," Camilla repeated. "But then I'm confused. Philip Elsberry said they drifted to Rocky Point. They were walrus killed during the herring closure by commercial fishermen on Round Island."

Nick translated. Afcan listened, dubious. Agrafina frowned behind him, concerned about the confusion.

"Elsberry said they washed over from Round Island, so he wants to lock up the sanctuary," repeated Camilla tentatively. "But they didn't, did they? They didn't come from Round Island."

Nick translated. Afcan said nothing, waiting, allowing Camilla her time.

"They drifted from somewhere else," said Camilla, reasoning aloud, looking at Nick, Agrafina, and Afcan. "They came from a different direction... of course, because of the storm, and the winds."

"And currents," added Nick, thinking aloud with her.

The elder smiled broadly at his clever students.

Afcan immediately pushed plates and bowls and flatware around on the table. He formed an arc around a cleared area. He placed the sugar bowl by his elbow.

"The bay," Afcan said, waving his palm over the spread of dishes. He pointed to the sugar bowl. "Qayassiq."

The sugar bowl was Round Island.

"The winds and the currents go this way, this way," he said in English, pushing with his hands from the island to the shore to demonstrate. He lifted a finger. "But that one, the winds came this way."

Afcan gestured with an opposite motion, a clockwise swirl around the bay. He swirled his flat hand over the cleared space. Nick and Camilla watched it pass over Round Island moving from shore out to sea. They understood what Afcan was teaching. Certain storms changed the winds. Things carried away from shore.

"Currents too," said Nick.

Afcan nodded.

"So something on Round Island gets carried away from land and out to sea," said Nick.

Afcan nodded again.

Nick stared at the makeshift map. He pointed at a spot near the sugar bowl.

"Rocky Point."

That was the place Afcan found the walrus. Nick looked at Afcan with the next obvious question. Afcan said nothing. Nick reached across to the other edge of the bay and pointed to a cup.

"Cape Newenham. They came from Cape Newenham."

"Big tides go by that place to Kuskokwim," Afcan said in English.

Afcan placed a fork near Cape Newenham.

"Hagemeister," he said.

He pointed to the space between it and the cups, the strait between Hagemeister Island and the mainland.

"Winds go this way. Currents go this way."

He moved his hand to demonstrate again.

Nick stared at the new fork in the makeshift map. He looked at Afcan again with the silent question. This time the old hunter leaned forward and pointed to a spot to the side of Newenham, just before the mouth of the strait where the storm winds and tides funnel in a clockwise gyre.

"Cape Peirce," Afcan said.

Nick and Camilla stared dumbfounded at the finger and everything it indicated.

Cape Peirce.

The walrus haul-out.

The Coopchiaks' camp.

The Fish and Wildlife lookout.

"Cape Peirce," whispered Camilla. "The walrus came from Cape Peirce because of the storm. The storm carried them across the bay and left them at Rocky Point. The headless walrus came from Cape Peirce."

Afcan smiled at his brilliant protégé.

He nodded.

"Then… so did Fernández," she whispered sadly.

Afcan nodded again.

This time, he did not smile.

52

The sun disappeared in ominous clouds.

Nick and Camilla walked in the breezy dusk, pondering the implications of the interview with Afcan Tooluyuk.

If the observations of the old hunter were correct, the headless walrus did not come from Round Island. The walrus came from Cape Peirce! They had seen walrus when they visited the Coopchiak's camp, hauled up at Nanvak Bay and the base of the cliff. The dead walrus had floated from there, pushed by the storm across Togiak Bay to the rocky point where Tooluyuk found them.

A gunshot had not killed the walrus he butchered. A blow killed it, something so powerful it broke ribs and ruined meat.

Fernández too?

What had killed them?

A dark shape floated at the edge of sight.

It moved with the storm clouds above the beach ridge. Nick noticed it... a shape, a silhouette.

It stopped. The clouds didn't.

Nick dove.

A bullet screamed and slammed the ground.

"Damn!"

He tripped Camilla down.

The old man!

Nick angrily tore from the gravel and up the slope. He ran in a mindless fury. He crested the ridge. A shape dodged among houses. Nick tore after it. Food sloshed in his belly. He'd puke when he caught him. Serve him right!

Nick passed the houses. Where?

302

He spotted him struggling up the stairs of a complex for elders. Nick came at him, huffing and puffing. He vaulted the stairs, grabbed the man's middle, and ploughed into the lobby.

Residents scattered with astonishment.

Nick twirled him around, a thin old man, no rifle.

"Why are you shooting at me!" Nick demanded in Yup'ik.

The old man shrieked hysterically.

"Qeng'aq! Qeng'aq!"

Over and over he screeched like an owl.

"Qeng'aq!"

Elders gathered around them. One took the little man by a shoulder. He tried to calm him, speaking in the soothing way of a friend.

"Hush. It's nothing, Tusekluk. Hush."

Nick let go, stunned.

Tusekluk!

Paul Smart's interview...

'Ask Tusekluk.'

Is calling a walrus dangerous?

'Ask Tusekluk,' said the elder.

Tusekluk was the sniper!

It took some time to calm him. He'd cast fearful looks at Nick and screech again. The lobby filled with residents drawn from their rooms by the commotion, others through the front door called by observers. Pot-bellied Wasky Evon arrived, the head of the traditional council. He glared at Nick and attended Tusekluk. Andrew Sipary arrived from the station. The giant Isaac Nuniq joined the crowd.

Camilla found them. She placed herself near Nick.

Wasky complained to Sipary. He angrily pointed at Nick. Eventually, Sipary approached them.

"So what's happening here?"

"That old man shot at us," said Nick angrily.

"Where?"

"The beach. Blasted by gravel."

Sipary looked to Camilla.

"Somebody shot at us," she said.

"Where's the gun?" asked Sipary.

"He ditched it," said Nick.

"Okay. Wait. I'll talk to him again."

Sipary went back to Tusekluk. The old man now sat placidly. Sipary spoke with him. Wasky angrily objected. Sipary spent time placating.

He returned to Nick, trailed by Wasky and Isaac Nuniq.

"He's hard to follow," said Sipary. "He's scared and confused. He says it wasn't him. He didn't shoot at you."

"He's a troublemaker!" growled Wasky, jabbing a finger at Nick.

"Please. A moment," said Sipary.

Wasky wouldn't wait. He scolded Nick directly.

"You're scaring that old man! Chasing him! Grabbing him! Go home! You're not wanted here! Go back home!"

Isaac Nuniq gently pulled Wasky's arm, directing him toward a corner. Sipary shepherded Nick and Camilla outdoors. The wind whipped around them.

"This is what I'm going to do," said Sipary. "Based on everything, I'm going to take the old man to the station. You both come too. I'll take statements. I could hold him overnight but I'll probably release him to some residents. We'll look for a gun. Then we can decide about charges."

"What did he say? Why is he shooting at me? This is the second time. He's the guy at the airstrip, I'll bet on it."

"He says he didn't do it. But you can see, he's pretty confused. He's really not all there."

The group walked to the station. Sipary took statements while helpers searched for a gun in the blowing dark. Two hours later, no gun had been found. By midnight, the group had dispersed. Sipary released Tusekluk into the care of other elders at the apartments. Tusekluk left considerably calmer. He looked askance at Nick, giggling uncomfortably between his attendants.

Nick and Camilla departed soon afterwards, accompanied by Isaac Nuniq.

They walked in silence, a biting wind blowing off the bay.

"Wasky wants you evicted," declared Isaac.

"Evicted?" said Nick.

"He says you're a troublemaker. I told him he has no authority to say anything like that without convening the tribal council. I sit on the council. I told him he's speaking for himself. So he might call the council."

Nick couldn't believe it.

"To kick me out?"

Isaac shrugged.

"Why is that old man shooting at me?"

Isaac said nothing.

"When I grabbed him, he began to shout, Qeng'aq! Qeng'aq! That's what he shouted. Qeng'aq!"

Still, Isaac said nothing.

"Why was he shouting that?" insisted Nick.

"He's an old man. Who knows what old men think?"

Nick stopped. He wasn't moving until Isaac provided more reasonable answers. Isaac teetered uncertainly.

"Maybe he thinks you're him."

"He thinks I'm Qeng'aq!? A dead angalkuq?"

"Shhh!" said Isaac, peering around in the dark.

"Why would he think that?" asked Camilla.

Isaac didn't look at her. He hadn't acknowledged her presence. He wasn't going to talk to a strange kass'aq.

"We interviewed Paul Smart after our walrus hunt, after I called the walrus," said Nick "He's an old man too. Do you know what Paul Smart told me? Don't talk about calling walrus. He told me to talk to Tusekluk."

Isaac said nothing.

"He told me to ask him something. If calling a walrus was dangerous. He said, ask Tusekluk. He would know, if calling a walrus was dangerous."

Nick waited obdurately.

The winds flapped their clothes.

"Well, I guess you know," growled Isaac.

"What?"

"It is."

The giant stomped off.

Camilla took Nick's arm and guided him away. She let him stew in silence, his mind grinding. When she finally spoke, her voice was calm and reflective.

"Jerome Paul, back in lockup. Remember the stories he told us? The stories about Qeng'aq?"

"Of course I remember them," grumbled Nick.

"And Theodore Bavilla, the minister. He said he was shaman. He could send away animals. Call them back."

"I remember," Nick growled.

"They blamed him for a famine. They killed him and tried to kill his children. They watch for him. That's what Jerome said. To stop his return."

"Yeah, so?"

"Nick, that old man. He thinks you're Qeng'aq?"

"Isaac said that."

"Because you called a walrus? Is that what you're thinking? Because you called a walrus?"

He refused to answer.

Another story occupied him, a different story.

He forced the pieces, trying to make them fit… boy to a girl, boy to a girl.

The lights at Winnie's house glimmered in the wind.

Nick veered away. He took the path to the beach. He collapsed on the sand between the log and the derelict skiff. Camilla flopped beside him. She tried to take his hand. He wouldn't let her. He seethed in silence. The wind howled.

"That old woman, Estella Smith," said Camilla, thinking aloud for them both. "And her granddaughter Florence. Remember what that old woman did? She looked you over head to foot and said, 'it's been a long time.'"

He was done with it.

"She acted like she was happy to see you, like she recognized you."

He was done with failed memories, insane accusations, threats to expel him, just like home.

"That's how she acted, like she recognized you from before."

Nick turned angrily.

"So what! She was old and crazy too!"

Camilla flinched back.

"She was old, Nick… not crazy."

"Crazy! To you too! Remember?"

The wind pelted with sand.

"Remember?" he demanded.

"What?" she whispered.

"Losing somebody! Oh how sad it is to lose somebody!"

He mocked her.

"She said that to you! I saw it. Not to me!"

Camilla turned away and shrank against the boat.

"Not lost forever. That's what she said. You screwed up tight. Didn't you!"

He shouted angrily.

"But so what? It's crap! I'm through with it!"

Nick hammered the hull.

"Like the calls to Mexico when you cried. That pissed off Cooper. He thinks you're some kind of monster! Watch out for her. She's a monster. But I say, so what! Who cares! I don't!

Because I'm through with it! This fucking project! I'm through with it all!"

She gave a painful sob.

He instantly felt sick.

He slumped with self-loathing.

I'm an asshole. I'm getting thrown from the village and I attack her? None of this is her fault.

Camilla wept.

The wind moaned above the boat.

Eventually the sobs quieted.

"He's right," she choked.

"What?"

"I am a monster."

Nick winced.

"You're not," he said sadly.

"Yes, I am."

"I'm the one who's fucked... not you."

He took her hand.

"We're both fucked," she whispered.

They sat in silence. Camilla wept again. A frayed rope slapped the empty hull, an aimless, hollow sound. The sea wind thrashed the shore, building toward the storm.

Nick could barely hear her when she finally spoke.

"I was broke," she whispered.

Nick nodded, said nothing, thought nothing.

"More than broke. But that's not why I did it."

The winds quieted.

"I did it for her. And him, I guess. I was a fool."

The frayed rope renewed its hollow knock.

"They found me. I was connected with the networks, the clinics in Mexico. They came to me. I was broke and they were desperate. It was their last chance, their last hope. She'd given up. Surrogacy. She begged me herself, begged me to do it. And I thought, I was such a fool, I thought, I could do this. You can convince yourself, you know, a thing in your head. I can do this for them, to save her life and her marriage."

Camilla wiped her eyes.

"So I did."

"What?" asked Nick.

"Got pregnant for them."

The wind sighed around the buried hull. Large drops of rain began to fly.

"I carried to term in Mexico during the fieldwork, came back for the birth. God, I never knew, I didn't imagine it. How hard. How wonderful. How horrible it would be. The awful feelings, the changes, those goddamn fucking hormones... I'd read about it, how it happens with some women, but I didn't really believe it, never imagined it could ever happen to me."

Camilla turned to Nick.

"I couldn't give her up. I couldn't let her go."

"Couldn't..."

"No."

Nick waited.

"I couldn't give up my little girl."

"Yeah," whispered Nick.

Camilla wept again.

"They took her."

She choked back sobs.

"Where?"

"I don't know. They can take your baby and there's nothing you can do. Except die."

Camilla fell against his neck and openly cried. Nick felt sick. He held her close, not knowing what to say. The rain began to fall. It drenched them.

He spoke against her hair.

"So she's gone?"

Camilla nodded weakly.

"You don't know where?"

Camilla wept.

"So you'd be like my mother is to me."

Camilla stilled. She didn't understand.

"I never knew her, my mother. The only thing I knew was her grave, not in town, far off at camp... that's where they put her. They said she drowned, a drunk. So they put her where they found her... off, out, away."

Nick paused, bitterly remembering.

"They treat me the same way... like that grave."

"Why?" whispered Camilla.

"You won't believe it. When I tell you this, you won't believe what they say about me, what they've always said, why I'm like that grave."

Camilla sat back to see Nick's face, her dark swollen eyes unmasked.

"I was born a girl."

"What?"

"That's what they say about me. I'm a freak, an unnatural freak. I was born a girl to an alcoholic teen and somehow, no one knows how, no one ever says exactly how, became a boy. Somehow at camp, the baby became a boy. And then they pulled her body from the river."

"No."

"Like I had killed her. That's my story. Back home they whisper it. It scares the children."

Camilla surveyed Nick's face.

"What does it mean?"

"I don't know. I think no one knows, except nothing good. With me it's never been anything good."

Nick looked toward the village.

"The same as here, they think they know me too, the stranger from the Yukon. Oh yeah, they've been figuring it out, pulling out their old stories, watching, waiting, starting the rumors. I'm becoming somebody here, just like home."

"Yeah," said Camilla.

She leaned against him and whispered sadly.

"We're fucked."

53

Camilla and Nick stumbled into Winnie's kitchen wet and cold for breakfast. They looked horrible. They saw it on Winnie's face. They slept beneath the boat, explained Camilla. They fell asleep when the hard rains began.

Winnie was glad to see them. Her husband and brother had flown to Dillingham for meetings. They'd be stuck there for three days. She was lonely for company.

"Theresa Manumik came looking for you."

"When?" asked Nick.

"Last night."

"What did she want?"

"To tell you her cousin didn't eat the beluga. She didn't know where he got it."

Nick understood. Theresa had interviewed Catherine about Jerome's last deadly meal. She hadn't eaten any beluga. Nick had seen it on Jerome's plate. It now became the prime suspect. What was its source?

"She left you her notes in case you remember something more."

Nick flipped through them during breakfast. He saw nothing new. She left copies of everything. The cleaners had tossed the plates found in the living room but nothing from the refrigerator, freezer, or outside cache. Nick read through the inventory of Jerome's food stores. Theresa's handwriting on the forms was tiny and precise. There was no beluga anywhere. Jerome must have eaten it all. Nothing else jumped out, nothing obviously bad. But something bothered Nick. He studied the inventory looking for bad food. Bad food...

"Let's find Theresa," Nick said abruptly to Camilla, hurrying to the door.

"It's pouring," complained Winnie. "It's not even eight."

Camilla gave Winnie a hug.

"Thanks for breakfast!"

What's happening with those two?

Winnie stirred her coffee, lonely again until her kids woke.

They found Theresa Manumik in her small kitchen. She welcomed them inside. Nick opened her notes on the table and pointed to entries. He began to read off the list of food stored at Jerome's.

"Smoked chum salmon, four packages, frozen."

"Yes, smoked chum," Theresa replied. "I found them in his freezer."

"And here you wrote, 'Smoked sockeye salmon, two packages, frozen.'"

"Yes, smoked sockeye."

"And here again, 'Smoked pink salmon, two packages, frozen.'"

"Yes. So?"

"What kind were they?"

"What do you mean what kind? Chum, sockeye, and pink salmon, smoked and frozen. Can't you read?"

"But were they subsistence salmon or store-bought salmon?"

"Oh," Theresa thought for a moment, recalling the shrink-wrapped packages of frozen fish. "Not subsistence."

"What brand?"

"I don't remember. Does it matter?"

"It might."

"Then let's go look," said Theresa, grabbing her rain gear. "I still have his key."

They drove in hard rain to Jerome Paul's cabin, still sinking into the soggy earth. Theresa unlocked the heavy door, bringing them to a freezer humming beside the entryway. She flipped on a light, opened the lid, and extracted a package of smoked sockeye.

"Arctic Fresh, Traditional Alaska Native Smoked," she read the blue label.

It was shrink-wrapped in clear plastic and frozen. A polar bear crouched on the corner. Theresa grabbed a package of smoked pink salmon. 'Arctic Fresh, Traditional Alaska Native Smoked,' it read. So did the chum salmon package.

"Robbins," said Nick to Camilla. "Arctic Fresh… that's Robbins' label."

"I remember," said Camilla.

"Does the store sell this?" Nick asked Theresa.

"They sell it. But I don't know who buys it. It's not very good and it's too expensive."

"Is that how Jerome got it? He bought it?"

Theresa looked doubtful.

"Robbins gave it to him," guessed Camilla.

"Swapped it for something else," said Nick.

"A trade," said Camilla. "He's a trader."

"What other foods did Robbins give him?"

He looked at Theresa, thinking of beluga. Theresa was too.

"Well, let's go ask him," said Theresa.

The rain flooded the paths to Robbins' warehouse, challenging Theresa's truck driving skills. Fishtailing through runoff, Nick saw the turquoise warehouse rise above the slough. Another truck parked at its entrance. A man worked to secure tarps blowing above fish drying on racks behind the building. He came around to greet them.

Oscar, said Theresa. One of her cousins.

"Pretty early for work," he teased as Theresa slogged from the truck.

"Same as you. Fixing tarps?"

"Before the big storm hits."

Nick examined the operation behind the warehouse. Large racks held drying salmon. The tarps kept off the downpour. The salmon glistened in the blowing rain.

"Robbins' fish?" asked Nick.

"Yeah, Arctic fresh," said Oscar, laughing at his joke. Togiak was not in the arctic. This morning, the fish didn't look too fresh.

"We're looking for Robbins," said Theresa.

"He's gone," said Oscar. "Took off yesterday."

"Where to?" asked Nick.

"Nick, this is Oscar," said Theresa. "Oscar, Nick and Camilla."

"Yeah, Fish and Game. Is this Fish and Game business?" asked Oscar.

"Public health business," said Theresa.

"Where'd he go?" asked Nick. "We'd like to talk to him."

"I don't know. He took a boat."

Oscar gestured to the docks at the rear of the warehouse.

"Is the place open?" asked Theresa.

"No, but I can open it," said Oscar.

He pulled out keys and unlocked the front door. Here was the advantage of kinship. Cousins unlocked doors without questions. They pushed inside. Oscar flipped switches, bringing light to the open two-story warehouse. Nick remembered its smell from their last visit, fish guts and disinfectant. The stainless steel tables gleamed under the fluorescent lamps.

Theresa began walking a wall, opening freezers and inspecting wrapped and canned items. Oscar trailed behind her.

"Arctic Fresh, Traditional Native Smoked Salmon," Theresa read.

"That's the end product. The shrink wrap machine is over there," said Oscar, pointing to a corner.

Nick pulled a white package from another freezer.

"What's this one?"

"I don't know. What's it look like?"

Nick opened the wrapper and peeked inside.

"Caribou?"

"Yeah, caribou," agreed Oscar.

Nick reached in further and pulled out a long whole fish wrapped in freezer paper.

"Pike?"

"Maybe," said Oscar. "I only do the salmon. He does lots of other stuff."

"Do you work alone for Robbins?" asked Camilla.

"He's got lots of help."

"How about Jerome Paul? Did he work here?"

Oscar stopped to consider Camilla's question. He looked toward Theresa and decided to answer.

"Yeah, I saw him around."

"With salmon?" asked Camilla.

"I don't know. I never asked."

"Do you get paid with money or fish?" joked Nick, holding up the rigid pike.

"Both," Oscar laughed. "I always wish it would be more money and less fish."

Theresa opened another freezer unit.

"Are you looking for something special?" asked Oscar.

"Yes, beluga," said Theresa.

"Beluga?"

"Beluga."

"You won't find any there," laughed Oscar.

"Why not?"

"Because he took it with him."

Theresa, Nick, and Camilla froze in unison.

"What do you mean?" asked Nick.

"He took it with him," said Oscar. "I helped him load the boat. I saw it in the boat."

"What was it?" asked Theresa.

"You know, a six-gallon bucket. What's this about?"

"That beluga may be bad," said Theresa. "Jerome died of botulism. He ate beluga."

"Oh," said Oscar, no longer smiling.

"You didn't eat any, did you?" asked Theresa.

"No, I just saw it in the boat."

"Is there more?"

"He'd have it outside if there was," said Oscar, leading them to the back exit.

He pulled open the doublewide door. Several plastic buckets sat in a vestibule beneath an aluminum awning, their lids slightly cracked and opened to the cool air. Theresa inspected each in turn. The buckets held seal meat submerged in oil. None contained beluga.

"I guess he trades them," said Oscar.

"Nick!" shouted Camilla from the end of the dock.

Nick trotted over. She stood beside an aluminum boat, one of the craft Robbins had bought, unsuccessfully, to charter tourists over and back from Round Island.

"Look," said Camilla, pointing.

On the prow of the boat was a name stenciled in black letters.

Angel Five.

Nick looked stunned.

"Oscar!" shouted Nick. "Did Robbins take one of these boats?"

"Yeah!" Oscar shouted back.

"Was it *Angel Four*?"

Oscar joined them and looked at the moored craft.

"Yeah, he took number four."

"They have the same names as the charter boats operated by Philip Elsberry," said Camilla. "He has Angels one, two, and three."

"They started as one outfit. But Robbins got pissed and left. He got two of the boats."

Nick and Camilla looked at each other. More boats named after angels!

"Oscar," said Camilla, "did Robbins ever hire a guy named Francisco Fernández Muñoz, a Mexican national?"

"That's the guy who drowned?"

"That guy."

"I don't know. I never met him. No one ever heard of him before that big storm. But it's funny you ask," said Oscar, leaning out of the rain.

"Why?" asked Camilla.

"Because that guy drowned during the herring run."

"What's funny about that?" asked Nick.

"Because that was the other time I helped Robbins load the boat with his stuff, right before that big storm hit the herring run."

"You helped load his boat before that storm?" asked Nick.

"Yeah, right before the storm, just like yesterday," said Oscar.

"With a bucket of beluga?" asked Camilla.

"No, no, not with beluga, with his equipment."

"What equipment?"

"You know... tent, lanterns, ropes, shovels, and some other stuff... a winch, pulley, chainsaw."

"A chainsaw? For what?" asked Nick.

"I don't know... cutting driftwood?" said Oscar. "I don't ask. He's kind of cranky, you know? I just helped to load. Like yesterday, he took the same stuff."

Nick found his heart suddenly pounding.

"Where?" asked Camilla. "Where does he go?"

Oscar shrugged. He didn't know.

But Nick did.

Because of last night's interview with Afcan Tooluyuk who talked about storm winds and currents, Nick knew where Robbins had gone during the last big storm with a chainsaw and probably two riders, Jerome Paul and Francisco Fernández Muñoz, a place where walrus heads get sawed off for ivory and carcasses left floating in the sea. The same place Robbins left for last night before the new big storm carrying the same gear, this time with a bucket of poison that had killed his last partner.

Cape Peirce.

The walrus haul-out... where Fernández died.

Near Lydia Coopchiak's camp with a busted radio.

Nick sprinted for the truck.
Camilla came behind.

54

The storm surged into the Bering Sea from the North Pacific gaining power over the Aleutians. It rose swift and furious, stealing the light. Alaska Weather predicted high winds and seas for the Cape Newenham region. Bush airlines canceled flights. Fishing fleets took cover. Factory ships battened down for the ride. Only the foolhardy or desperate ignored forecasts of high seas.

Camilla Mac Cleary felt both foolhardy and desperate as she pounded in the open skiff. Theresa Manumik jolted beside her. They were drenched and bruised riders of a wild sea, gripping the boat's towrope against the vicious rolls. They raced into the storm toward the specter of a camp with a dead CB and a batch of deadly food.

"I'll go with antitoxin," Nick declared. He could sneak in beneath the storm.

"I'm going too," insisted Theresa. Antitoxin reactions could kill, so preliminary shots were administered, monitored, and assessed to adjust the dose. Nick wasn't trained.

Camilla had never seen Nick look so sick or determined. Of course, she came too.

They raced in Harry Coopchiak's skiff loaded with supplies from the clinic. Winnie would look for Andrew Sipary. He was missing somewhere around town. Searching for Tusekluk's rifle, Nick presumed.

After two hours of pounding, spray plastered their hair. Their foul weather gear gleamed slick black. At the stern, Nick wrestled the outboard. It fought like something alive as he pounded through waves at full throttle. High surf caromed off the shore. Whitecaps swept past at eye level. Winds howled from the north. Nick hugged the coast to cheat them. Blasts lifted the boat from the water, dropping it hard onto swells, hull booming like a drum.

"How soon?" yelled Camilla.

"Soon!" shouted Nick.

A dark shape rose beside them. It grew by the minute, a massive wall that drew alongside. Sheer rock leapt from the water into clouds, the high cliffs before Nanvak Bay.

"Look!" shouted Theresa. "Walrus!"

Nick saw them. They had hauled up on a strip of beach beneath the cliffs. A rocky shoal was swept of water, exposed by winds and falling tides. Walrus clumped here and there like mounds in a cemetery.

"A boat!" shouted Camilla.

Beyond the walrus, the boat sat at the foot of the cliff, a dull slip of silver against the dark rock wall.

"Robbins!" Nick shouted.

"Yeah?" shouted Camilla.

"One of his jets!"

"You were right!" Theresa shouted. "He's here! What's he doing?"

Good question, wondered Nick, angling the skiff through more waves, making the dark connections.

He and Camilla guessed right. Robbins had snuck under the storm's cover to Cape Peirce. He'd done so during the last big storm. He had done it again. Two men who went with him the first time were dead. Robbins' jet boat was parked on the cobble beach near hauled-out walrus. A few more hours might find that place completely submerged, though maybe not. Nick was unsure of the tides at Cape Peirce.

"Ivory!" answered Camilla, almost toppling in the effort, declaring what Nick was thinking.

Robbins snuck to Cape Peirce to shoot beached walrus for ivory. He took off heads with a chainsaw. That made Robbins a trafficker as well as a trader. Did Fernández die because of black markets and drugs, as Trooper Cooper suspected? And Jerome Paul?

"Can you see him?" shouted Nick.

"I can't see anybody! Too far!" Camilla shouted, staring at the receding cliff.

"Nanvak!" shouted Nick, pointing ahead.

They had made it. The Robbins puzzle must wait. The Coopchiaks took priority.

Nick swung the boat toward shore and carefully watched the channel. The wind that had pushed the water from the cliffs also pushed it from the salt chuck. The entrance to Nanvak Bay presented a confusion of gray shallows. But Nick had traveled it twice before. He remembered the twisting entrance and found it, driving the boat through the narrow slot and into the bay without slowing. He gunned for speed, hauled up on the outboard, and scraped through the final shoals.

Nick leaped to the sand.

Things looked wrong. No smoke. No barking dogs. In the stormy gloom, tents sat dark and lifeless. The canvas shuddered ominously in the wind.

A death camp.

Nick sprinted for the main tent. He burst inside.

Bodies stretched upon cots. Nick's heart almost stopped.

Fred and Millie Coopchiak.

He knelt beside them.

"He's still alive!" gasped Nick.

Theresa shouldered him aside. She addressed the old man and woman, ear close to their mouths. They replied feebly.

"They say it's getting worse," said Theresa.

"What's getting worse?" asked Camilla.

"The paralysis."

Camilla uncovered a pot atop the cold stove.

"Stew," she announced.

"Beluga," said Nick.

"They cooked it," said Theresa. "Thank God, they cooked it. Heat kills toxin. Maybe they didn't get a full dose."

It smelled fishy. Botulism had no scent or taste.

"I'm dumping this," Camilla announced.

She hauled the pot into the storm and emptied it at tideline.

Theresa feverishly opened vials. She inoculated Fred and Millie, the first shot. She monitored vital signs, a syringe of adrenalin at hand.

"They're freezing," said Theresa.

Camilla found blankets, tucking them tightly.

Nick worked the stove, priming oil and fighting drafts. Eventually it caught. The tent began to warm. He lit a lantern. Camilla filled the teapot from the rain barrel.

"I'm giving the antitoxin now," declared Theresa. "I'm going to give them moderate doses because of their small frames."

"Where's Lydia?" asked Camilla.

"I don't know," said Theresa.

Nick spoke to Fred. He put his ear by his mouth.

"Lydia went for help," said Nick. "The CB's down."

"Did she eat any stew?" asked Theresa.

Nick asked Fred, who whispered the reply.

"They all had some. They got sick, not Lydia."

"Where did she go?" asked Camilla. "The boat's still outside."

He spoke again with Fred.

"Maybe three places," said Nick. "Miners are camped up the bay. Maybe she went there. Or the Fish and Wildlife camp on the backside. She might go there, but it's farther."

"What's the third?"

"To find Robbins. He came and went last night. He brought the beluga."

"Why?" asked Camilla, shocked. "Why would he poison them?"

"He didn't know," said Theresa. "He left town before we announced about botulism."

"He could have brought them anything. He brought the beluga!"

"But that would mean he meant to kill them. Nobody would do that."

"Where is he?"

Nick asked Fred.

"On the hill," said Nick, "right above us, the hill we climbed last time... Cape Peirce."

"That doesn't make sense. His boat is on the beach."

Nick asked Fred again.

"He's up on the hill," repeated Nick, looking sick. "Fred doesn't know why. Maybe he's prospecting. Robbins has gone up before. Fred's worried. Lydia should be back."

Fred spoke and Nick translated.

"He's worried she can't move."

55

Nick hiked the shoreline in a growing violence. He carried rope, flares, a dry jacket, and antitoxin. Despite his lack of training, he had insisted. He swung a large flashlight. With a similar pack, Camilla hiked another direction toward the Fish and Wildlife camp on the backside of Cape Peirce. Each went to find Lydia. If she wasn't along these routes, they were to check the top of Cape Peirce. Theresa stayed to watch Fred and Millie. They had improved somewhat after the injections. The CB remained down.

The miners camped up the bay. The boggy trail that Nick took skirted the shore. They moved around, Fred had said. More prospected last fall, just three this spring. Nick said nothing. He remembered the special forces soldiers on the plane to Cape Newenham. These weren't miners.

The Coopchiak camp had firearms. Under protest, Camilla accepted a .22-caliber rifle. Nick carried the bear gun.

Rounding willows, Nick looked upon the camp, a single wall tent lit by a lantern. Shadows flickered within. It turned darker. Rain began pounding. The forecasted deluge had arrived. A man came through the tent flap. He walked to the edge of the clearing to piss. A man without worries. Lydia wasn't here.

Nick weighed options. Surely they had a radio.

"Hey the camp!" he shouted.

The man jerked around.

"Hey the camp!"

A light blinded him.

"Who's that?"

"From the fish camp! Have you seen Lydia?"

They surrounded him, storm gear dripping. One carried a holstered sidearm. Another held a rifle. The third waded in closer, the giant from the plane, the sour-faced, tight-lipped commando who upbraided his mate for talking to Nick about Newenham. None smiled.

This was a mistake, Nick saw.

"Who?"

"Lydia Coopchiak, the fish camp. Did she come here?"

"No one's come here." He spot-lighted Nick's face. "Don't I know you?"

"I came up from Togiak to help. There's been trouble. Botulism… the old couple at the camp. Lydia's gone. She didn't come here?"

"Botulism?" frowned Sour-face, confused.

"That's a poison," said another.

Uh oh, Nick thought hard.

"Bad food… they ate some bad food. You got a radio?"

"Wait," ordered Sour-face.

The men conferred in agitated whispers.

It's going wrong, Nick realized. They're going to screw me up. Sour-face turned back to Nick.

"Who got poisoned?"

"Fred and Millie Coopchiak, the old man and woman at camp, but they're recovering. I'm looking for Lydia."

"Who's that?"

"The granddaughter. She went for help."

"You said you came to help."

"I did. She tried to call by CB."

"You just asked for our radio."

"The CB is broken," said Nick. This was sounding contrived. It was contrived. He'd left Camilla and Theresa out, by design. "The Coopchiaks are better. Lydia's gone. She didn't come here. I'll look someplace else."

Nick backed to leave.

"Wait! Where?" barked Sour-face.

"The Cape."

Nick gestured up.

Sour-face shook his head fiercely. Searching Cape Peirce seemed abhorrent.

"I've got a better idea," he sneered.

"What?"

"Let's all walk back to your camp and check things out."

An order, no suggestion.

"You go ahead," growled Nick, feeling for the bear gun. "I'm finding Lydia."

Nick turned. A rifle blocked him, aimed at his gut.

The hairs rose on Nick's neck.

"Wait! Wait!" shouted Sour-face.

Sour-face consulted and returned to Nick.

"The old couple is better."

"Yeah," said Nick.

"The girl that's lost, how old?"

"My age."

"Okay, then we all search," he pointed toward Cape Peirce. "We'll help you look. Four's better than one."

"Suit yourself," growled Nick.

The men shouldered packs. Nick cut inland. The men trailed, flashlights scoping the storm. Nick's heart pounded with adrenalin. Who are these idiots? They act like pumped up fanatics on a mission. What have I landed in?

* * *

The biologists' camp bustled when Camilla arrived. It was placed above Nanvak Bay for viewing birds. Biologists in foul weather gear milled outside the tents. She sensed turmoil. They conferred breathlessly with her.

Yes, they knew the Coopchiaks. They hadn't seen Lydia.

"Should we radio town?" asked the camp head.

"Yes, please," said Camilla. "Call Andrew Sipary, the VPSO, or Winnie Friendly. Tell them Theresa Manumik gave antitoxin to Fred and Millie. They're improving. Theresa Manumik doesn't want a medevac. Too dangerous, the ceiling is too low. We're mostly worried about Lydia."

"We haven't seen her."

"What's going on here?" asked Camilla.

"The walrus!" said a biologist excitedly.

"They're moving!" blurted another.

Camilla had seen none hauled out on the trail to the camp. What did walrus do during storms? Ride them out at sea?

"Moving out the bay?" asked Camilla.

"No, inland!" said the biologist.

"We've never seen it before," said the camp head, "nothing like this. Maybe the wind, confusing them."

"Confusing them?" asked Camilla.

323

"Pushing."

"Pushing them up!" said another.

"They're going up, groups of them."

Camilla remembered how they moved, a shuffling on flippers, shuffling inland, pushed by wind?

"Up the valley?" said Camilla.

"No! Up! Straight up!"

The biologist pointed skyward, bewildered.

"We've never seen it before."

"They're climbing the cape."

"Lots of them."

"Climbing? The walrus?" said Camilla.

"Going straight up."

"Groups of walrus."

"Into the clouds."

56

Nick struggled upwards in the storm. He'd found a path going up, a narrow trail over tundra and ground-hugging shrubs. He was uncertain, everything darker and muddier than his climb two weeks before. He could see only steps ahead. But it seemed right. The others followed. He remembered the steep slopes falling to sheer cliffs with the beach far below.

"Stay close!" he warned them. "Drop offs!"

Like soldiers, they did.

Every so often he shouted for Lydia.

The wind scattered his voice.

This seemed futile. Cape Peirce stretched for miles. She could be anywhere. But he took a route close to the fish camp. If Lydia went up, it would be this way or near to it.

Nick paused to catch his breath. He shouted again.

"Lydia!"

This time, faint and above them, came a reply. The soldiers heard it too. They redoubled their speed up the slick hillside.

"Lydia!" called Nick.

"Here!"

Nick stumbled ahead and found her. She huddled in a shrubby depression, drenched by rain. A pack lay beside her. Her ears shined red, her lips white. Nick sighed with relief. He hugged her, the soldiers at his back.

"My leg's twisted," she said in Yup'ik.

"Is it broken?"

"Twisted. I can't walk. My grandparents?" she pleaded.

"Better. Theresa Manumik is with them. She's given them antitoxin. They'll be okay. They were worried about you."

Lydia began to cry with relief. Nick held her as the soldiers watched. Screw them, he thought.

"What's she saying?" asked Sour-face.

"Bum leg," said Nick. "She can't walk."

"Broken?"

"She says it's twisted. She's relieved about her grandparents. We need to get her down."

"Okay," said Sour-face. He barked instructions for ferrying the girl downhill.

Nick spoke in Yup'ik.

"Have you seen Robbins?"

Lydia's eyes got wide.

"He shot at me!"

"What?"

"He yelled to stay away. Then he shot at me!"

"Where?"

"On top where we hiked. I called him for help and he shot at me! I slipped and twisted my leg."

"The bastard!" cursed Nick in English.

"Bastard?" growled Sour-face.

"Just leave him!" said Lydia in English.

"Leave who? What's she saying?"

"Robbins," said Nick, reluctantly. "The guy she came to find for help, he's up on top."

"Robbins? Who's that?"

"A white guy from Togiak."

"Why leave him?" he demanded of Lydia.

Nick answered for her.

"He took a potshot at her."

The soldier instantly hardened.

"Why? With what?" he demanded.

The sky released a downpour.

"We're ready!" shouted a soldier, set to lift Lydia in a fireman's carry, straps fashioned from pack materials.

"Wait! Why? Shot at you? With what?" he demanded.

"A rifle," said Lydia, looking scared. "He had ropes and packs. He yelled to stay away. Then he shot. He wasn't trying to hit me. I ran, twisted my leg."

"Ropes and packs? For what?" he growled.

"I don't know. I couldn't see."

"Captain, the trail!" shouted a soldier.

In the deluge, the trail had become a brown river. Hail began falling. Huge ice chunks pounded like rocks.

"Captain! We've got to get her off!"

A captain, confirmed Nick. They are soldiers.

Sour-face grimaced and gave the order.

"Take her down!"

The men positioned Lydia for the carry.

The captain grabbed Nick's arm.

"Not you! We're going up!"

"What?" yelled Nick, shielding against the pounding ice.

"You and me… we're going up to find him!"

"Leave him!"

"You show me where!"

"That's crazy!"

The captain shoved Nick away.

"Wait!" he ordered the carriers.

Nick looked down at the nose of a .45 automatic.

"She stays unless you take me up," the captain growled. "Or they come with me and you take her down by yourself."

Nick snarled at the gun. Rain and hail obscured Lydia. Nick angrily threw on his pack.

"Take her to camp!" the captain barked. "Radio base! If this guy shows up alone, stop to find me, you got it?"

The soldiers started the downhill slide above a cascading flood.

"Nick!" shouted Lydia.

She disappeared into the storm.

Nick led the mad captain. His mind raced furiously. This was insane! Threatening civilians at gunpoint! What were these maniacs doing? He looked back. They were rescuing Lydia.

"Damn it," muttered Nick.

"Stay close behind me!" he yelled. "Don't turn right off this trail! That's the quick way home!"

"Check!" Sour-face shouted, almost enthusiastically. He holstered his pistol.

'Idiot!' fumed Nick.

He wasn't thinking of the captain.

57

Camilla climbed into clouds.

She took strange paths twisting this way and that, going upwards on the mountain slope into drenching clouds. They looked freshly plowed, tundra torn by a legion of wild hogs, brush compressed by heavy machines.

Walrus paths.

Like a dream.

She moved among the braided trails going ever up, on guard, her rifle before her. She did it for Lydia and the promise to Nick. Her heart pounded. She knew what she tracked, something new, inexplicable, two-ton behemoths tearing trails up a mountain.

Stay calm, she told herself. Stay alert.

"Haroommfff!"

Camilla froze. Thick clouds boiled on her right, caught in a swale. A bristled face materialized, eyes glinting, pale tusks hanging.

"Hi," whispered Camilla calmly.

She cautiously stepped to her left.

The fog swallowed the walrus.

"Ooooffff! Ooooffff!"

A shape hurtled from the left. Camilla leaped up the slope like a cat. The beast lunged, chest on the ground, its hind flippers pushing. Tusks swiped at her heels.

"Ooooffff! Ooooffff!"

The huffs dwindled behind her.

She crested a rise and fell gasping.

The rain eased. Cold clouds swirled about her. Wet gusts pushed the fog into great billows. The hillside cleared.

Camilla gasped.

Walrus filled the swale, grayish red with rain. Dozens, maybe hundreds, sprawled like her, resting before the next effort. Smoke blew from bristled nostrils. Some saw her. Necks arched. Tusks displayed below expressionless eyes.

"Just me," she whispered.

A walrus moved, coming on her left. So did another. They converged, a heavy pincer of flesh. Camilla plunged ahead. The clouds resettled, blotting them out, erasing all but the next step. Camilla wove. A shape appeared right. She deflected left. Walruses on the left, a shoving match. Camilla went right, never stopping.

"Harrommff!"

A walrus charged from the fog.

She swung the rifle, hit his nose.

He stopped short and bellowed.

Leaping, she frantically clambered.

"Lydia! Lydia!" she called.

"Ooomph!"

The answer came from her left.

"Hummff," came another on her right.

The skies opened. Hail hammered the slope.

Camilla leaned into the ground and covered her face.

"Lydia!" she cried. "Lydia!"

A chorus of moans replied.

A hundred monsters moved with her into the sky.

58

The hail stopped. Powerful gusts from the sea swept from below, slamming the cliffs, driving the clouds skyward.

Nick moved carefully.

Don't step into updrafts. Updrafts meant death.

He tracked a trail encrusted with hail wending along a high falloff. The captain followed closely. The ice melted with rain. Nick traced its darker shade.

The slope lessened. The footpath leveled. The split was coming. Nick stopped. He remembered this place from the climb with Lydia and Herbert, a divergence of trails. He shouted above the wind and pointed.

"See that path? It's another way down!"

"Where's it go?"

"Other side of the cape, the biologist camp, Fish and Wildlife, a longer way out."

"How much more?"

"I don't know. This is crazy! I say leave the bastard!"

"You just show me where he is," sneered the captain. He touched his holster.

"You going to shoot him?" scoffed Nick.

The captain shoved. "Go!"

They climbed again. Nick skirted the edge of the cliff. He recalled this part of Cape Peirce. A misstep could be fatal, a slide down a steep, hail-covered slope ending in a sheer drop. In the thick fog, he nearly tripped on it.

"Stake!" he yelled.

He knelt and inspected. The stake was set at the peak of a hummock with a smooth slope. The ground held footprints filled with ice. Somebody had worked around the stake. A steel eyelet held a three-quarter-inch line that disappeared down the incline, falling into the clouds. The wind blasted beneath them into their faces. It was a sheer cliff below. Nick pointed along the ridge of undulating hummocks.

"There are slide paths from this point on!" shouted Nick. "The slopes start gradually, then increase, then... whoosh!" He pushed his hand into a vertical drop. "You can walk them dry, but in this stuff they're slick as snot."

"Okay," agreed the captain. "Where's Robbins?"

Nick touched the ice-filled footprints and pointed at the rope. The captain grinned evilly. He tested the stake. It was firmly set. He pulled his .45.

"Down!" he waved the pistol.

Nick couldn't believe it. The rope descended into roiling clouds. The slope ended with a vertical cliff.

"That's crazy!"

"I said down!"

Slide blindly down a wet line? This maniac behind him? Enough was enough. He was through taking orders.

Nick whacked the handgun.

CRACK!

Shit! No safety!

Nick grabbed the arm and fell back from the edge. He grappled for the gun. WHOOSH! New hail fell, pounding like steel shot. They rolled. The commando came on top. A burly hand found Nick's chin. It gripped and squeezed. A knee jammed into his side. His face pushed into the ground. Nick felt the handgun under his stomach. He was pinned, couldn't reach it. He stared down the rope. It fell to oblivion.

The captain suddenly froze.

A rifle barrel shoved his neck.

Camilla stood above him, a spire in the storm, hood thrown back, black hair flying. Her deadly voice cut the icy wind.

"Want to hear mine?"

"Don't shoot!" the captain yelled.

She jabbed the barrel harder into his neck.

"Why not?"

"Special Forces!"

"Then let's be special and roll off, slowly!"

She pushed his face aside with the ice-crusted barrel.

His hands and knee released. He came off slowly.

"There's a gun here!" warned Nick, rolling the other way.

She jammed Coopchiak's rifle into the captain's belly.

"You okay?" she asked.

"No," growled Nick.

He found the handgun and aimed it at the captain's nose.

"Don't shoot!" the captain yelled.

"What's your game, Special Forces?" demanded Camilla.

"No game!"

"He wants Robbins," said Nick, feeling his throat.

"Why?" said Camilla.

The captain said nothing.

Camilla shoved the rifle hard in his gut.

"Why!"

"The bomb!"

Gritty ice blasted her full in the face.

The captain kicked, whacked Nick's arm.

"HARROOMFF!"

With a bellow, the walrus struck, galloping full force.

The monster bowled through them like a truck.

They flew off the path and hit the slope.

The captain slid into clouds.

Nick reached in desperation and found the rope. Grabbing hard, he ground to a halt.

"Camilla!" he shouted.

She was gone!

Gripping two-handed, Nick went down the line, skidding on his heels, slipping into the clouds.

"Camilla!"

He slid faster, panicked.

"Here!" he heard faintly.

He ground to a stop. More stakes poked from the hillside. The rope continued down. Another stretched laterally across the face of the slope.

"Camilla!" he yelled again.

"Here!" she called from below.

Nick held the line tight and followed the sound. The hill grew much steeper. Nick felt his heart pounding. Robbins, you idiot, where's your rope taking us?

It went vertical, straight down a chute.

And there was Camilla, holding on fast.

Nick slammed out his foot and caught the downward lip, halting the slide. Camilla grabbed to steady him. They hugged atop a crack in the cliff.

"You okay?" gasped Nick.

"Barely," said Camilla.

"Where's the captain?"

"Down there, I think," she pointed into the hole.

Braced by his heels, Nick whipped off his pack. He found the flashlight and swept its beam into the crack. It was a rock chamber, a fracture that cut into the cliff, a cave like those he'd explored on the bird roosts with Lydia's cousin. Debris filled it, eroded grit, old bird nests, an accumulation from a hundred seasons. There was no sign of the captain.

"What do we do?" said Camilla.

"Get the hell out," said Nick.

"What about Lydia?"

"Lydia's okay."

"What?"

"We found her! Back up there, up on top, on the trail. She's on the way down."

"She's okay?"

"Bum leg. They're helping her down… his men."

"Botulism? Paralysis?"

"None of that."

Nick moved to climb. Camilla grabbed his leg.

"What about him?"

"What?"

"We can't just leave him."

"Oh yes we can."

"He might be hurt."

"Look," said Nick. He flashed light into the chamber. There was no sign of the captain.

"He said he was Special Forces."

"So?"

"Nick, that's the military."

"He's a fucking madman captain. He shoved a gun in my face."

"Why?"

"Because he's an idiot."

Or I was an idiot, thought Nick. We both were idiots.

"I wouldn't go down the rope," growled Nick, "so he pulled his gun."

Camilla chewed on that for less than a second.

"He said 'bomb.' What bomb? What's he talking about?"

Nick didn't know. He didn't care.

"Where's Robbins?" pressed Camilla. "Are these his ropes?"

The ropes were staked to give access to the bird roosts high on the cliff. Nick found he did care about that.

What the hell was Robbins up to?

Why did he poison the Coopchiaks?

"He shot at Lydia," growled Nick.

"What?"

"Robbins took a shot at her."

He was fed up with snipers.

"Nick, something's wrong."

Nick sat on the edge, angry at everything.

Camilla put her white face inches from his, ice stung and raw. Her eyes glowed strangely in the fog.

"Nick, you know something's really wrong."

His anger suddenly released.

The puzzle filled his mind... inexplicable deaths, charters, angels, artifacts, ivory, monsters...

"What was that, up there?" croaked Nick.

"You won't believe it. A walrus! There are hundreds climbing the cape!"

Hundreds of walrus?

Nick suddenly felt lightheaded.

Underwater, pressure, all around.

Wind roared like a noisy convention.

"That's how I found you! I knew where you'd be."

Camilla put her nose against his cheek.

"I followed the walrus."

Nick drew back, trying to break the spell.

Hundreds of walrus?

Walrus climbing Cape Peirce?

You know something's wrong. Wrong enough for Special Forces. Wrong enough for sniper shots and poison. Disastrously wrong, shouted the cormorant above the pandemonium when the walrus turned expectantly, turned to him and shuddered, vaporized in the horrific blast of a...

Without a word, Nick grabbed the rope. He slid to the chamber's floor. In a moment, Camilla stood beside him, her own flashlight shining. She scarcely breathed hard.

The chamber felt cold and dry beneath the inside lip. Above them, a muffled storm raged. They stood on springy refuse that crunched beneath their feet. The inner space was pitch black. Its outer edge received moisture that dripped from the entry. It trickled into the debris heap and disappeared. The air smelled musty like decayed feathers and droppings.

Nick flashed his light across the chamber.

"Ow!" he cried as his head hit rock.

His vision danced.

A ghoulish face grinned in the dancing beams. Through the shimmering blur, it leered from a black crevice.

"A mummy!" whispered Camilla.

A desiccated corpse glowed in their lights, a mummified body topped by a grinning skull. The skull's skin stretched like leather, a papery mask of death, its lips shrunk to a rictus of shining teeth. Square orbits emptied of sight stared at them. And in the center, a hole pierced the skull, a ragged black gouge that once held a nose.

Or... maybe not, saw Nick.

The mummy sat in a niche draped with furs, a bow and spear across his lap. He was postured like royalty overseeing an eternal domain. An exceptional man, thought Nick, to be buried this way, hidden at the top of an inaccessible cliff. A leader... a shaman.

"Pardon us," Nick apologized in Yup'ik. "We're looking for somebody else."

The skull grinned.

"What did you say?" whispered Camilla.

"I excused us."

"Is this what Robbins is after? He's robbing graves?"

"Then where is he?"

Camilla swung the light down the chamber. His beam joined hers. The space extended further. It was a narrow, roofed crack eroded along the face of the cliff, born by some geologic fracture or corrosive flow. Following the light, Camilla edged carefully forward. Nick came behind, leaving the grinning mummy. The crack opened into a succession of linked chambers. Rain came through the roof, pocked with holes, entries and exits for birds. By the wind, other holes lay beneath their feet and the layers of debris. They walked lightly, carefully placing their feet.

"A turn," whispered Camilla.

Nick squeezed through the tight corner. Camilla came too. They entered more chambers, raggedly roofed, grottos noisy with water. A strobe flickered at the far end, eerily flashing green and white.

"The captain!" said Camilla.

A flashlight flickered within a wall of water. The captain fought beneath a waterfall. He seemed trapped in debris.

"Help me!" he screamed.

"Nick, look!" said Camilla.

She swung the light across the chamber's floor. Metal and plastic flashed beneath the running beam, shattered and glistening, wreckage embedded among the feathers and bones of ancient nests like the remains of a silvery bird, glittering from a dozen cascades. Words gleamed off fragments... U.S. Air Force... Grumman... numbers.

"What the hell?" muttered Nick.

A missile... or a missile-shaped drone.

"Things fall," he remembered.

"What?" shouted Camilla.

"Things fall from the planes!" shouted Nick. "Fred Coopchiak said it! At the camp he said things fall from the planes above Newenham!"

This one fell hard and shattered, probably last summer when 'miners' scoured the land to find it. But it wasn't lost on land or sunk at sea. The wreckage was caught in between. It struck the cliff and washed into the bird roosts.

A cruise missile or drone.

A delivery system for a heavy payload.

"Help me!" screamed the captain.

"Stay here!" said Nick.

He squirmed against the inner wall, ducking through cascades. Holes perforated the ragged roof. The storm's deluge fell in noisy cataracts off the headland's crest. It splashed off walls and disappeared into the floor. A stiff breeze flew up from his feet.

"No bottom!" he shouted to Camilla.

He pressed his back to the wall, edging past debris toward the far cascade. The captain struggled beneath it. He flailed with a knife above a metallic cylinder shaped like a six-gallon drum. It was trussed within a sling, gathered by cables and brackets where a thick rope disappeared through a ceiling crack. Water poured through the hole.

The captain futilely sawed beneath the downpour.

Nick could hardly believe it.

A warhead.

That goddamn Robbins! Here was a madman's treasure, the ultimate lucre. Something more valuable than artifacts. It was a nuclear bomb!

What would that fetch on the black market?

Robbins was crazy!

How did they work? Nick wracked his brain. He knew warheads were electronically armed and could be preset to explode on contact or certain heights. Was this one armed? The missile had hit the headlands without an explosion. Did that mean the warhead was safe? What if it fell the rest of the way? What if it hit at sea level? Was it stable? If it went off, could it destroy the cape? This was mad!

"Cut the rope!" screamed the captain.

"Is it safe?" yelled Nick.

"Cut the goddamn rope!"

Cables groaned. Brackets wrenched. The grotto lurched beneath his feet. With a cracking jolt, the sling suddenly ripped from the floor. Nick pitched backwards.

The outer wall exploded.

The floor disintegrated.

Nick slammed the inner wall. He blindly grabbed for holds.

The floor fell into blackness. A hurricane blasted, a swirling detritus of grit and nests. Nick held and squinted to see. The warhead lifted. It disappeared through the ceiling. The captain was still there, dangling and screaming. His legs thrashed and kicked. He disappeared with it.

Nick braced against the wind, his flashlight swinging wildly. He clung to the wall, rough and pocked. The blinding debris made purchase hard to find. He worked his way back along the wall by feel, inching along it. His foot slipped. More floor collapsed, falling to oblivion. He dangled, painfully set a knee, and pulled himself up.

Somebody grabbed his wrist. Camilla!

She guided him around an outcrop and through a crack. Walls and a sturdy floor. The winds muffled. They had made the first chamber.

"Where's the captain?" yelled Camilla.

"Through the roof," gasped Nick. "He's riding the sling!"

"Sling?"

"A warhead in a sling! It's off the wreckage. Robbins is stealing a nuclear bomb!"

"My God!"

Nick found himself alone. Camilla's light moved down the rock chamber. He scrambled behind her, blinking back grit. Camilla kicked up the rope. He gripped the dangling line and followed, the light beam swinging.

It caught the mummy's face.

The rictus smile shouted goodbye.

The storm roared its greetings. Nick pressed his feet into slippery muck and ascended the wet rope. Camilla waited at the middle stakes. The winds blew fury.

"Where's your pack?" Camilla shouted.

Nick felt. He had lost it in the grotto's collapse.

"Wait here!" she shouted.

She disappeared up the rope. Nick recovered. He wiped his eyes in the downpour. His vision cleared. Camilla reappeared with Coopchiak's bear rifle.

"Mine's gone," she panted. "So is the handgun. They must have gone over. How are you doing?"

"Better."

"Where's this go?"

The rope stretched across the face of the slope.

"Let's find out."

Nick shouldered the bear gun. He grabbed the lateral rope and worked across the headland. Camilla followed. The slope was dangerously slick, saturated by the storm. Unstable mats of grass separated and slipped beneath them, oozing mud like thick blood. They came to a hump with more stakes. Electric lanterns glowed in the murk ahead. A motor rumbled.

Nick swept his light. So did Camilla. Their beams caught a figure in foul weather gear, perched on a narrow shelf, flitting between ropes and dangling lines. It froze in their beams.

"Robbins!" Nick yelled.

"Wha…?" came a faint retort.

"Robbins! Crank up!"

"Who's there?" he shouted.

"It's Nick! Crank up! He's on your line!"

Something disengaged. The motor fell to a low murmur.

"Nick? Nick John? I can't hear you! What'd you say?"

"I said, crank up! There's a man on the line!"

Nick swung his beam down the slope. A rope taut with weight fell into boiling clouds. Nothing could be seen, hidden by the storm. But Nick knew the rope held a heavy sling and nuclear warhead with maybe a man, clinging for life.

Cantilevered above was an improvised pulley and winch.

Nick recognized the setup. A chainsaw, staked above the slide path, provided power. Safety ropes went up the hummock, secured at the top. Instead of a cutting chain, the chainsaw's motor drove a winch. Robbins wasn't using the chainsaw for cutting off walrus heads. He had it powering a pulley for moving loads. Looped through the winch, a burden line carried the sling. A parallel line dangled slack, providing the extra rope, the end of the pulley.

Nick knew this system. Hunters used it to haul moose from bogs. Loggers used it to drag trees through clear cuts. With three-quarter-inch line, staked to the ground, it could easily move half-ton loads. It was cheap, simple, and lightweight, everything fit in packs.

Robbins also had a block and tackle. He had been dragging the load line along the cliff. He was re-positioning the line before dropping the warhead to the boat. Nick couldn't see, but he guessed they perched on the cliff above Robbins' skiff. He had moored on the beach at the foot of the rock wall.

"Crank up!" shouted Nick.

Robbins just stood. He made no move toward the winch.

"He's not going to do it," said Camilla.

Nick pulled the rifle from his back.

He aimed straight at him.

"I said crank up!"

Without a word, Robbins scrambled. He went straight up the safety line behind him. The gear sat idling and abandoned.

"Damn!" growled Nick.

Camilla jumped around him. Like a cat, she scrabbled the final distance to the ledge. Nick shouldered the rifle and followed. The storm roared.

"How's this work?" shouted Camilla, baffled by the jury-rigged setup.

Nick immediately engaged the winch. He gunned the chainsaw's motor. With an angry groan, the burden line began to move. Camilla directed her flashlight down. Water blew like swirling bugs. Sections of rope slowly dragged up the slope. It was long and heavy.

"Come on!" swore Nick.

The load finally materialized. A large gray cylinder trussed in a sling dragged into view.

An inert body hung below it.

"He's there!" shouted Camilla.

Nick brought the sling almost to the ledge. He cut the motor to idle. Camilla slid to the captain, tangled in webbing.

"He's unconscious! His arm's pinned!"

Nick scooted beside her. They looped a rope inside the captain's belt and secured it to a stake. On the ledge, Nick engaged the chainsaw. He gradually lifted the sling. Camilla yanked the man's arms.

"He's out!"

Instantly, the blow struck.

Robbins came feet first, sliding full tilt. He hit broadside.

Nick flew off the shelf. Camilla upended.

She screamed and was gone.

Nick frantically grabbed. His hand found a boot. Robbins teetered and came off the shelf too. They slid grappling. Robbins' safety cord yanked them to a halt. He kicked violently. Nick lost a grip. A heel came down hard. Nick screamed in pain. Robbins kicked him free.

Nick hit the slope and slid. The ledge vanished above him. A cascading slurry greased the descent. He blindly grabbed for anything to halt the slide. There was nothing but slick turf and mud. To his horror, he gained speed. Wind blasted beneath him. He frantically clutched this way and that. He slipped toward the invisible cliff, an inevitable void, and heart-stopping plunge. Suddenly, his fingers touched rope. It was the pulley's loose end, wet, long, and dangling. He snatched and squeezed to a stop, belly down on the steep incline. His toes touched something.

"Careful," rasped Camilla. "That's my head."

"Jesus!" gasped Nick. "Where are you?"

"The cliff," groaned Camilla. "I'm on the rope."

Nick settled carefully beside her. His foot felt emptiness. They clung at the brink of a vertical drop. Wind whistled. Nick's mind whirled.

"Jesus!"

"Is it water down there?" yelled Camilla.

"I don't know," he gasped, thinking hard.

"The boat's there, right?"

"Yeah, the boat."

And a stormy sea?

"Slide down?" shouted Camilla.

"What?"

"The bomb's at the top! This rope should touch bottom, right?"

Nick did a blurry calculation.

"What if he's short?" shouted Nick. "What if there isn't enough rope to touch bottom?"

"We fall."

Neither moved.

"Me first," declared Camilla, positioning for the plunge.

The rope jerked in their hands.

"He's dropping the bomb!" gasped Nick. "Hold on!"

Nick held tight, Camilla below him. The rope moved skyward. They dragged with it up the slick incline. Water sluiced around them. Wind howled. Without warning the heavy sling passed going down, the warhead at the end of the burden line. It disappeared into clouds. Nick winced. Would it blow when it hit sea level? A faint whine came from above. The lanterns glowed through the fog. The winch abruptly jerked to a stop.

"There you are, damn it!" shouted Robbins from above.

Nick frantically looked around him. Where was Camilla? She had vanished! Where had she gone? Did she slip off? The slope inclined less steeply here. Muddy rivers ran down it. It felt slick as greased glass. He didn't dare release the rope.

"You pest!" screamed Robbins. "You freaking pest! You're messing me up! You're messing up everything!"

"Me?" Nick yelled. "Robbins! It's a goddamn bomb! A nuclear bomb! You're going to blow us up! What are you thinking!"

"You're messing me up!" screamed Robbins, kneeling at the ledge, fumbling with ropes.

"Robbins! Don't do it!"

"He slipped!" shouted Robbins. "He fell! And so did you!"

Robbins viciously shoved the captain.

The body came directly at Nick.

Nick pulled up to his knees, wrapped a leg around the rope, and set his feet. The captain hit. Nick almost came off. But he snatched at the captain's belt one-handed. The two swung sideways on the line and stopped. Nick pinched the body between his legs, transferred the captain's belt to his other hand. The slope took much of the weight. The line held both.

Robbins danced in a rage on the ledge.

"You freaking bastard!" screamed Robbins. "You freaking bastard! I don't care! I don't care! You freaking bastard!"

Robbins unhooked his safety. He vanished. In moments he reappeared with Coopchiak's bear rifle.

"I don't care if they find you shot!"

Robbins aimed down the slope, Nick in its sights.

"Don't do it! Robbins! Don't do it!"

Nick frantically checked left and right. There was nowhere to hide! The blast exploded from the sky.

"HROMPH!"

Robbins whipped around.

"HROMPH!"

A gleaming monster hulked at the crest above him, slick with the storm. It swayed, slowly moving side to side, surveying the slope. Long tusks flickered in the ghostly glow. The beast searched and stopped, eyes fixed on Robbins.

Robbins yelled enraged.

With a roar, it lunged!

Down it came at the ledge. Robbins dodged.

The walrus missed him and launched onto the slide path.

Nick pushed aside hard holding the captain.

The creature passed and vanished into clouds.

"HROMPH! HUMPH!"

Challenges exploded from the storm.

CRACK! CRACK!

The bear gun replied.

Another walrus came over the crest. And another. And another! They came shoulder to shoulder. There was no place to dodge. They slammed into Robbins. The gun went flying. The walruses soared and landed on the slide path. So did Robbins, tumbling between them.

Two passed on Nick's right, another on his left. Robbins came last, screaming and flailing.

Nick gripped the line with his leg and made a desperate grab. He missed. Robbins reached out and found the captain's leg. He ground to a stop.

Nick's fingers strained with the extra weight, hooked through the captain's belt.

"Grab the rope!" yelled Nick.

Robbins grabbed the line beneath the captain's body. He planted his boots and clambered upwards. He scrambled over the captain and swung hard. His fist slammed Nick's head.

Nick's ears roared. He desperately clung to the rope and the captain's belt. Robbins pummeled him again and again.

"HROMPH! HROMPH!"

Bellows shattered the air.

Nick squinted upwards.

Jesus!

Walruses fell over the crest, one after another, tons of falling flesh right at them.

A walrus smashed Robbins.

Nick lost the rope.

They slid. He gasped for air and scrabbled with his feet, still gripping the captain, trying to slow the descent. It was too slippery, too steep.

A strangled scream came off his shoulder.

A walrus passed gaining speed.

Robbins came with it, his eyes round with surprise. A tusk impaled his chest. They vanished into clouds.

Nick felt something slide along his fingers. A rope... the burden line! It sat hard and wet upon the slope. He sluggishly clutched. It slipped on his palm. He couldn't get his fingers around it. The winds howled from beneath. The cliff...

They fell.

Nick desperately hugged the rope.

The blow almost knocked him senseless. Wind whipped. His ears rang. They swung in open space, caught in the sling. He dangled above a crashing sea sitting atop the captain and the warhead. Things began to disintegrate.

Suddenly, the sling jerked.

It rose slowly, then faster. Nick held on.

With a quick skip he was on the slope again. He moved with increasing speed. A huge walrus slid past, looped to a rope by a tusk. The sling burst into a halo of light. It stopped just short of the winch.

"Nick!"

"Camilla!" gasped Nick.

"You've got the captain!"

"Yeah?"

With Camilla's help, Nick crawled to the shelf. He sprawled by the disengaged winch.

"How?" gasped Nick.

"I jumped to the sling rope and climbed up. You were busy with Robbins."

Nick weakly stared at the disabled winch. A line stretched taut to the bottom of the cliff.

"Nothing worked," said Camilla. "So I snagged one going over."

A falling walrus had pulled them up.

Blinding light flooded the hilltop. They covered their faces. Engines pounded. Wind and grit from rotors blasted. A helicopter beat in the storm above them. Men in combat fatigues jumped to the crest.

Nick and Camilla crawled the safety rope to the top of the cliff. Nick recovered in the buffeting tumult. He watched first the captain and then the warhead dragged up the cliff's edge in a fury of wind and storm and placed in the chopper.

A familiar face appeared, smeared with mud, one of the original soldiers.

"How's the captain?" asked Nick.

"Coming around. He's tough," said the soldier.

"Lydia?"

"Back at her camp. She asked about you."

"Good," said Nick.

"You okay to get down?"

"You guys going somewhere?"

"Yeah, somewhere. Here's your lady."

Camilla stepped into the floodlights. She carried a new pack. The soldier shook Nick's hand, ran a few steps, and hopped in the chopper as its engines revved.

"Look out for monsters!" he yelled.

The chopper disappeared into the storm.

Camilla wrapped an arm around Nick, shoved a flashlight in his hand. She spoke by his muddy ear.

"Let's take the long way."

59

Nick sweated in the steam bath at Coopchiak's camp, waiting and brooding. Where was Camilla? The fire had fallen, the temperature perfect if she wanted to bathe. She surprised him, asking to steam. Rain pounded the plywood roof. The storm raged outside building toward its peak.

Nick poured water on the hot rocks for the last time. The steam enveloped him. His body's soreness melted in the wet heat. Bruises covered him. His palms were chafed and swollen. The corners of his eyes itched. But otherwise his body was whole, cleansed by the steam. He had miraculously survived. As had Camilla. Where was she? She should come to rid herself of the day's horror.

Walking off the stormy mountain, they found Coopchiak's camp deserted. Theresa Manumik had penned a note at the main tent alongside a replacement CB radio, one that worked. 'We got medevaced,' her note read. A floatplane braved the storm, landing beside the camp. Everyone had left... Fred, Millie, Lydia, and Theresa. The Coopchiaks had improved, Theresa wrote. Lydia wanted to stay but her leg looked broken. 'Call Sipary,' the note ended.

Nick called immediately.

"Good to hear you!" Sipary said through a storm of static.

"You too," said Nick.

"I was getting worried. You're at Coopchiak's?"

"Me and Camilla."

"You both okay?"

"We're fine. She's here too."

"We heard about the accident," said Sipary.

"Accident?"

"From Fish and Wildlife. They got it from the miners."

Nick looked at Camilla, perplexed, not knowing what to say.

"What did you hear?" asked Camilla, taking over.

"The miners brought Lydia down."

"That's right," said Camilla.

"She's gone to Dillingham. They said her leg is fractured."

"A fracture."

"And we heard about Robbins," said Sipary

"What did you hear there?"

"He fell off a cliff in the storm. His body is missing at sea, right? Is that right? He fell off a cliff. It's just him?"

Nick and Camilla said nothing.

"I can't hear you. There's a lot of static. Is that right? Robbins fell into the sea? It's just him?"

"Yeah," said Camilla. "That's about right."

"What the hell was he doing up there?" asked Sipary. "How did he fall?"

"They didn't say?" asked Camilla.

"Who?"

"The miners."

"No," said Sipary.

"Where are they?" Nick jumped in, sourly.

"I don't know that either."

The radio crackled.

"Nick? Camilla?"

"We're still here," said Camilla.

"There's nothing we can do for Robbins, right?"

"Yeah," said Camilla, eying Nick.

"Nothing right now, Sipary," said Nick.

"I've told Cooper. He's in Dillingham trying to interview the Coopchiaks."

"Trooper Cooper," said Camilla.

"And Nick, Camilla…"

"What?"

"He seems pretty mad."

Coming from the sauna, Nick found Camilla sprawled on a cot in the wall tent under a wool blanket, a jacket over her head. When he sat beside her, she took his hand and squeezed it weakly.

"You didn't come for the bath," said Nick.

"No," whispered Camilla. "I washed up in here."

He saw her wet clothes hanging.

"Headache," whispered Camilla.

Nick lifted the jacket. Her face was wet with tears.

"Shit," Nick cursed sadly.

"It's killing me."

Nick rose to get a washcloth. Camilla held him down.

"Just sit with me," she whispered.

Nick sat, stroking her head, listening to hard rain pelt the canvas. The storm caught its breath, a lull in the roar of wind. The pressure lamps softly hissed. They pulsed like living things, casting yellow light into the dark corners. The humid air smelled of wet wool, seal oil, and kerosene. He felt used up, defeated.

"I'm thinking of him," whispered Camilla from the cot.

"Robbins?"

"Yeah."

The rain blew in heavier gusts.

"There was nothing we could do, right? Nothing to save him."

"He didn't want our help," said Nick flatly.

"No, he didn't," whispered Camilla.

Nick smoothed Camilla's brow, streaked with grit. Her voice edged above the hiss of the lamps.

"And I'm thinking of that poor guy, Fernández…"

"Yeah?"

"…how he died too."

Nick thought on events, the mystifying deaths, putting them in order, imagining it all. Francisco Fernández Muñoz had worked with Robbins and Jerome during the last big storm. They must have worked above the cliffs like tonight when he died. Fernández was crushed… by a falling walrus.

"So it's happened before," whispered Camilla.

"I guess once before, at least."

"During the herring run, they fell then," whispered Camilla. "A walrus killed Fernández."

Hard rain rattled down the stovepipe, hissing in the cast iron box.

"Why didn't they bring him out?"

"What?" asked Nick.

"Why didn't they bring out his body?"

"I don't know. Tides… tides carried it off."

"Jerome took heads afterwards," whispered Camilla. "At the bottom of the cliff, after they fell... he took ivory. Why didn't they bring his poor body out?"

"I don't know... tides," said Nick.

"I would have brought him out," whispered Camilla.

"Yeah, me too."

The wind quieted. The distant surf voiced its low roar.

"They were hunting for artifacts," whispered Camilla. "They didn't know about the bomb."

"I think so."

"They stumbled on it."

"Jerome didn't like it," said Nick, recalling the drunken tirade. "He didn't want anything to do with it. 'You have to know when to stop'... that's what he said. That was the warhead. It went too far for him."

"Maybe Robbins knew it had crashed. They looked for it."

"I don't think so."

"Fred Coopchiak knew something fell. Maybe he told Robbins."

"They stumbled on it, like you said. They were hunting for artifacts."

"Yeah," groaned Camilla, painfully. She grabbed Nick's hand and pressed it hard against her temple.

"They'll never admit it, will they?" said Nick dully.

"Special Forces?"

"They've got everything, the warhead, the sling, even the ropes. I saw them take the rope and stakes. That cave is gone. They spread a phony story with Fish and Wildlife... a cover."

"Yeah," groaned Camilla.

"They leave us with nothing, no evidence, no names. They'll never admit it happened."

"Nick, can you find something for this pain?" she whimpered. "It's never been so bad. It's getting worse and worse."

"How can it happen so fast?"

"I'm fucked, Nick. My goddamn hormones from the baby, they're all fucked up. I'm all fucked up."

Camilla began crying.

Nick searched the tent for its first aid box. He checked the side tents, buffeted by the fierce winds. Returning, Nick found Camilla crunched painfully beneath the blanket.

"Camilla," he whispered, brushing her head again. "I can't find anything."

Camilla wept.

"All we have is Theresa's kit, what's left of it."

"What's there?" choked Camilla.

Nick said nothing.

"What's in there?"

"Leftovers... antitoxin, adrenaline... and morphine," said Nick, reluctantly.

Camilla gripped his arm.

"Give it to me."

Nick said nothing.

"Give me it. Shoot me."

"I don't know," Nick protested. "It's morphine sulfate. I don't know anything about morphine. I don't know the dose."

"It's an ampoule, right? That's the dose. Shoot me."

"Camilla, I could kill you."

Camilla pulled Nick's face into hers and hissed.

"Who cares!"

The tent shook violently, the storm at its peak. No more medevacs, nothing for Camilla, bunched in agony, her thin body beaten and bruised, the woman who rushed into death with him on the cliffs, who saved his life.

"Please," she whimpered.

Nick broke open a syringe. He loaded it from the vial marked morphine. He swabbed with alcohol and hit the plunger. Pulling out, Nick felt sick.

Camilla relaxed immediately.

"It's hot," she whispered.

Nick strode from the tent. The storm howled against him. He threw the syringe and vial as far as he could and screamed, awash in its great fury, swinging his fists. Finally, worn out and spent, he fell back into the tent and collapsed by Camilla's cot. She found his dripping hand. The pressure lamps beat like hearts.

"How is it?" he muttered.

"Better," whispered Camilla, her voice sleepy. "Much better."

Nick sat in silence, watching her eyes flutter beneath half-closed eyelids thick with lashes, searching for dreams. He thought of the first time he saw her, pack on her back, coming off the plane. She had accepted him completely... hardly a question. Her 'partner.' Who had ever done that? Camilla stirred from her dream. She squeezed his hand.

"You missing her?" whispered Camilla dreamily.

"What?"

"Lydia."

Nick said nothing.

"Cuz she's gone?"

Nick released Camilla's thin hand. He reached inside his jacket and withdrew a thin packet. He undid rubber bands, unwrapping layers of cellophane.

"Wallet," he muttered self-consciously.

He searched with his fingertips and extracted a small photo. He held it above Camilla's eyes, positioned to catch the lantern's yellow light.

"Lydia," Camilla weakly smiled. "The ears."

Nick looked at it long.

"It's not," said Nick, dully.

Camilla waited.

"It's my mother."

The gas lanterns hissed. The storm winds shook the canvas.

"Lydia's mother," whispered Nick.

The lantern sputtered, dimmed to brown, flared back to life. The rain muttered endlessly.

"How can that be?" whispered Camilla finally.

"I don't know," groaned Nick, tired and sick. "The rumors, I told you about them, what they say about me. Well, I just learned this… here they say the same about her! Lydia was born a boy, turned into a girl! I couldn't believe it. Boy into a girl! Like the rumors about me, reversed! A shaman did it. Then her mother died… like mine. Somehow the Coopchiaks adopted her, raised her in camps away from town."

"Adopted," whispered Camilla, fumbling for the picture.

Nick held the picture for her to see again.

"It's the same as me but reversed," groaned Nick, "born a girl, became a boy. It killed my mother. That's the only picture I have of her."

"She looks like Lydia," whispered Camilla. "Just like Lydia."

"We were switched," declared Nick with finality, putting his face into his hands. "My mother is really Lydia's mother. Lydia… she's my mother's daughter."

"Nick," said Camilla, putting a hand on his lap.

"I know it now," groaned Nick. "We were switched somehow. When I look at her, I'm looking at my mother."

Camilla lay relaxed, the drug taking her. She could barely see the pulsing light.

"Nick," she said again, dreamily, moving slightly over.

She pulled on Nick's hand.

"Nick, lie down."

Nick saw her drifting away, pulling him toward her on the cot, a narrow camp cot with room for one. What was she thinking? She wasn't. It was the drugs.

"Lie down," she repeated.

"You've got two inches," said Nick.

"Take 'em," she murmured.

And then Nick was alone.

60

Alaska's Joint Board of Fish and Game convened at the Captain Cook Hotel in downtown Anchorage, fourteen members, seven from Fisheries and seven from Game. They convened convivially, a rare meeting of the combined body. Few issues required joint action. Fish management differed from game management. Usually the boards worked separately.

The Joint Board finished a morning of mundane administration. Kurt Tromble, the chair, called for a recess. But he announced the agenda's next item, a special request for a buffer extension around the Walrus Islands State Game Sanctuary.

Mel Savidge, practicing anthropologist, watched from the sidelines, her usual place at board meetings. At the break, clots of board members formed around the silver coffee urns. The groups socialized and (unofficially) strategized. On this break she watched the newest board member in action, Alexie Encelewski, the Alutiiq from Prince William Sound, the reason the buffer proposal had advanced this far. He flitted from group to group, smiling, small-talking, teasing, a young man dressed smartly, casually working the factions.

Mel had prepared for the meeting, checking facts and people. She learned that Alexie Encelewski held a commercial salmon fishing permit, a commercial herring permit, and a sport fish charter license. He was an up-and-coming Native businessman, a leader within his region, and a strong subsistence advocate. The scuttlebutt said his family was a key provider within their village. He hadn't said much so far at the meeting. But the next issue was his. He mixed like a seasoned politician. 'I care about this one,' his relaxed manner proclaimed.

The public also strategized. To one side of the room a small group of Yup'ik hunters from southwest Alaska conferred. It was the walrus hunter contingent. They wore jeans and old jackets and caps, the rustic attire of the country. They grouped around the head of the Eskimo Walrus Commission, a hunting leader who had flown in from Nome to offer support. At breakfast, Mel saw this same cadre of hunters meeting with Encelewski, getting acquainted, sharing information. Tromble had briefly stopped to chat with them. So had several federal bureaucrats. At this break in the meeting, federal interests conferred in another section of the room. This cluster included representatives from Fish and Wildlife Service, the Bureau of Indian Affairs, and their solicitors.

Mel was the consummate outsider, the anthropologist observing from the margins. The Division of Wildlife Conservation biologists sat in their own corner conferring around their deputy. She was not invited there. In their midst was Dr. Philip Elsberry, his big mouth flapping. It figured. Her own department was in cahoots with that asshole, part of them anyway. The commercial herring managers sat off in another group, checking their smart phones. They were a different faction. Round Island wasn't their problem.

It was a foregone conclusion how the Joint Board would vote on the herring buffer. That proposal was dead. The fish managers were wasting no energy on it. But the game biologists sweated.

"This is fun, eh Nick?" said Mel.

Nick John didn't think so. He sat at the edge of the meeting with Mel watching the strange event, feeling inordinately uncomfortable. Camilla Mac Cleary sat beside him, looking very different from Togiak. She wore a long dark green skirt with an elegant, colorfully-embroidered blouse that accentuated her neck. She looked tall. 'My power clothes,' she joked. 'Feminine. Deadly. They worked for my dissertation defense.' Nick felt shabby in his jeans and black shirt, washed so often it was nearly gray. Jeff Hall sat beside Camilla taking careful notes of the proceedings. This clot was the Subsistence Division. Nick yearned to sit with the hunters. But he chose to sit with Camilla, feeling sad and nostalgic. This was their last day together. She was leaving for home.

The meeting came back into session. The herring buffer proposal was read into the record with its rationale... the buffer might help the enforcement of the closure of Round Island against unauthorized boats for reducing illegal takes of walrus.

Tromble recognized the deputy director of Commercial Fisheries, speaking for the Alaska Department of Fish and Game. The deputy director's carefully-worded presentation politely blasted the proposal. The proposed increase in the buffer introduced economic risk into the fishery, he read. It drove commercial fishermen off prime fishing areas, increased the likelihood of harvests of immature herring eggs, and lowered the value of the catch to fishermen, buyers, and the state.

"It's the 'Buffer is Bad' report," whispered Mel to Nick. "The department is officially against it. The proposal is dead on arrival."

Nick grunted assent. This was all new to him, his first fish and game management meeting. It seemed to unfold like a choreographed performance, a scripted stage play with predetermined outcomes.

Nick glanced at the fisheries side of the audience. The commercial fish representatives and fish managers looked bored. By comparison, the game side of the room looked energized. The fidgeting game biologists listened with rapt attention. So did the federal agency representatives. The Alaska Native hunters also sat on the sidelines listening carefully. The hunters leaned, cupping their ears, their hearing ruined by lifetimes of firing guns. Nick jabbed Camilla.

"They're all deaf," he joked.

"What's funny about that?"

Camilla scowled at him cross-eyed.

Appropriately chastened, Nick returned to watching the meeting, chuckling at the universal ear cupping.

The department's presentation concluded. A member of the Joint Board called for the question. But Tromble followed his own script. He wasn't ready for a vote.

"Before I hear any calls for the question," said Tromble, "I'm giving time for clarification about the proposal, or for discussion among board members. We have a lot of experts in the room. We have the flexibility to call them to the front."

The Joint Board sat silently.

"This will be short," muttered Nick.

"Yes, Mr. Chair, thank you," said Alexie Encelewski, sitting straighter in his chair.

"No it won't," grinned Mel.

"I'd appreciate more information about the hunting side of the proposal," Encelewski began. "I understand an increased buffer might impact subsistence takes of walrus by hunters from Togiak. I must confess, I'm new to this issue. I'm new to the whole history of Round Island. I understand there's a hunter association at Togiak. Members are here today. For many years now they've submitted proposals for opening a managed walrus hunt on Round Island. We've just heard an analysis of effects of an increased buffer on the herring fishery. But the impacts of buffers and closures on the traditional walrus hunt seem very unclear, at least to this board member. Again, I apologize, because I'm new. But I'd appreciate hearing more on that, after which I may be prepared to offer an amendment to the original buffer proposal."

The room's whole dynamic shifted. The fish attendees groaned. Some began exiting to smoke. But others sat at full attention, in particular the state's game side, especially Philip Elsberry.

"This is great!" whispered Mel.

"Okay," said Tromble. "Have you got specific questions?"

"Yes," said Encelewski. "I'd like some additional background about walrus hunting on Round Island."

And with that, Nick watched a succession of presenters invited to sit at a low table before the Joint Board. Board members listened attentively. Alexie Encelewski was not the only one new to the issue. None of the current members knew the history of Round Island. Its management regime predated them. A quarter of the board members were Alaska Natives. Three-quarters were not. At some point in Alaska's history, Natives got kicked off Round Island. The tension was palpable. That history was going to be recounted.

Except it wasn't recounted, at least in any detail.

The history presentation fizzled.

A biologist from the state's Game Division gave the history of the Round Island Sanctuary. The closure to Native hunters occurred around statehood, he reported. No one in the department could find information on subsistence walrus hunting on Round Island, he claimed. Certainly, protecting the haul-out was the reason for closing the islands to the general public. But no one recalled the details about how Round Island got closed to walrus hunters.

"Were the Native hunters consulted?" asked Encelewski.

"I don't know," the biologist replied.

"Were impacts on villages assessed?"

"I don't know."

"What do the reports say regarding walrus hunting by Togiak hunters when the sanctuary was created?"

"The reports don't say anything about walrus hunting."

"Nothing?"

"I'm not sure the drafters of the sanctuary regulations knew about it."

The federal agencies, invited next to speak, cleared up little. They described an entanglement of overlapping management jurisdictions. The Fish and Wildlife Service managed walrus in the waters of the United States, they said. This included walrus on Round Island, even though it was state lands. The state managed access to the island. The state closed access to hunters, but hunting was technically still open. In fact, the federal solicitor sitting at the table doubted that his agency could limit the take of walrus by Alaska Natives on Round Island, if the area was opened to access.

"We regulate the take of herring," said one surprised Fish Board member. "You're saying your agency can't limit the take of walrus by Natives?"

"If it's a non-wasteful, traditional harvest, we can't, in my opinion," said the federal lawyer. "If the harvest hurts natural and healthy walrus populations, then we can."

"Are the walrus populations healthy?"

"A biologist should answer that question, not me," said the lawyer.

Nick saw Philip Elsberry grinning.

Encelewski asked for information about walrus hunting on Round Island. Camilla, Nick, and Jeff Hall came to the front table. They described walrus hunting patterns based on their recent interviews at Togiak. Jeff promised the Joint Board that a written report specific to subsistence walrus hunting would be produced by his staff.

The hunter contingent was called next. They came en masse, shoulder-to-shoulder at the table, facing the board. Native elders testified on hunting patterns. They described how Yup'iks used to hunt walrus on Round Island. There were seasonal hunts guided by hunt leaders. The room was hushed during the testimony. The old men said no one consulted the villages about the sanctuary. Hunters were surprised by the closure.

"Did subsistence hunting hurt the haul-out?" Encelewski asked the elders.

"The walrus always came back," said an elder.

"If you clean up and respect the walrus, they come back," said another.

"If Round Island were reopened, would you be amenable to a managed hunt with rules?" Encelewski asked the group.

"The traditional hunt always followed rules," said an elder.

Nick looked over at the Game Division side of the room. Elsberry looked like a volcano ready to blow. Encelewski had tipped his hand. He was talking about reopening the island to a managed hunt.

The hunter association representatives then spoke about their efforts to reopen the island. Past proposals always got stalled in jurisdictional entanglements.

"Some think we should just go hunt," said the renegade, Isaac Nuniq, the only hunter wearing a tie for the occasion. "But the elders say to cooperate, to work things out first."

"Would the hunters agree to voluntary restrictions in harvest numbers?" asked Encelewski.

"Yes, the hunters would consider this," responded a spokesman.

"How many?" asked another board member.

"That would be negotiated."

"But about how many, just so we get a sense," asked Encelewski.

Nick watched the hunters at the table nervously whisper together. Here was a difficult point. Encelewski was forcing an answer on something they hadn't resolved when he spoke with them that morning at breakfast. The hunter association's head finally responded, looking very uncomfortable.

"Maybe ten," he said, "Maybe, you know, as a start."

"Ten walrus a year?"

"Yes."

Nick saw board members whispering. There was a buzz in the room. Ten walrus seemed like a very low number to Nick. But maybe that sounded outrageous to others.

Tromble called for a short break. The hunter group left the table. The expert biologists were up next. Nick glanced toward

Elsberry. His face was flushed, his eyeballs white, his mouth working among the state's game biologists.

"God, Elsberry," groaned Mel.

Isaac Nuniq showed up at Nick's shoulder, excited.

"He's doing a good job, eh?" stated Isaac, speaking of Encelewski.

"Real good," said Mel.

"Where's he from?" Camilla asked.

"Prince William Sound," answered Isaac congenially. "But he's got ties with Kodiak, maybe even Togiak. He told us about some old stories over breakfast. They were his family's old stories about Kodiak. I couldn't hear it all. But the elders are trying to figure it out, if anybody's related to anybody."

"Encelewski has ties to Togiak?" asked Nick.

"His family's got a story about going up there, a great great grandfather or something."

"From Kodiak?"

"They've got a story about him. Uh oh, we're starting."

Dr. Philip Elsberry approached the table. He carried a stack of folders. As an expert on marine mammals in the Bering Sea, the department's game staff was deferring to him to present the information on walrus populations. He spoke as an independent scientist from the university.

"What bullshit," muttered Mel, sinking in her chair. "He's the sponsor of the damn proposal."

Elsberry came prepared with an overhead presentation on walrus. The lights fell. Graphs and tables and color photographs flipped across a large screen. Research methodologies were described with funding sources and publications. Elsberry traced out the Bering Sea ecosystem, a natural system pressured from multiple quarters, illustrated by arrowed flow diagrams. Pacific walrus populations showed a downward trend as evidenced by counts on Round Island, the last remaining haul-out. He begged to differ with the good elders who had not been to Round Island in several decades, but seasonal counts showed substantial yearly variability and lower overall trends, a statistically significant decline and a cause for considerable concern among managers, particularly regarding unrestricted hunts (mentioned by the federal solicitor) and ivory trading (on the black market). The lights came up. Elsberry coolly waited for questions.

"He's good," said Camilla.

"Asshole," muttered Mel.

The questions began about the charts and photos. Elsberry gave quick, efficient answers. Every question, answered. Yes, the federal standard was 'natural and healthy' populations. Was it difficult to count walrus on ice? Yes, which is reason for being conservative in management, as the Joint Board knew. Margins for error were less forgiving. Yes, there was evidence of population stress. Under such conditions, individual walrus mattered more and more. Yes, undisturbed trend counts on Round Island were essential. Without them, who even knew what might be happening with walrus populations on ice? Elsberry eagerly scanned the board for more questions.

"So in your expert opinion," asked a board member, "given the data presented, is the Round Island population natural and healthy?"

"I can't say I have information to support that it is," said Elsberry.

"The weasel," muttered Mel.

"So, given that, what about opening a hunt at this particular moment in time on Round Island?"

"Even with natural and healthy populations, I think any informed manager would feel very cautious about opening a hunt on Round Island, the last haul-out," replied Elsberry, "but particularly at this moment."

"Thank you."

"That was a set-up," growled Mel. "He's handed them the excuse to do nothing."

The Joint Board sat quietly. Tromble assessed its mood. Encelewski looked troubled. He raised a finger. Tromble recognized him.

"So, Dr. Elsberry," began Encelewski, "you're saying the biological numbers can't support any harvest on Round Island. Putting aside just how a hunt might be regulated, you're saying, biologically speaking, the numbers can't support any additional harvest?"

"In the face of trends like these, I guess I like to err on the side of the resource," replied Elsberry.

"So no additional harvest. Not even ten, like the hunter association mentioned? Ten walrus?"

"I don't know what to say," said Elsberry, acting embarrassed. "The population trend is downward. I guess I can say as a biologist, killing more walrus will make it go down faster."

"How many walrus are there in the North Pacific again?"

"Well, there may be different stocks, but monitoring suggests, perhaps, a reasonable estimate of, say, two hundred thousand."

"I've heard reasonable estimates up to 250,000 walrus," said Encelewski, "but accepting yours, that's ten walrus out of two hundred thousand. That's a biologically significant number, ten walrus?"

"It's the trend we should be looking at," explained Elsberry kindly. "Down is down."

"I see," said Encelewski.

The board sat quietly. Encelewski put up another finger. Tromble recognized him.

"I may have missed this in your report," said Encelewski, "but how about the walrus killed at other haul-outs? How do they fit into the trend, biologically speaking?"

Elsberry looked momentarily confused, his first hesitation of the afternoon.

"Other haul-outs?" asked Elsberry, taking a sip of water.

"I know you said the Round Island sanctuary is the 'last haul-out,'" said Encelewski, "or maybe you said the 'last major haul-out,' but I'm thinking of the haul-outs at Cape Peirce and Cape Newenham. Let's just say Cape Peirce. You know, the haul-out there."

Elsberry again looked confused.

"Of course I know Cape Peirce," said Elsberry, cautiously. "I'm sorry, what was your question again?"

"In your graphs and charts on trend counts, I didn't see anything about Cape Peirce, the haul-out there."

"Well, that's because that's not a real haul-out," said Elsberry. "Yes, a few walrus do occasionally beach themselves there for short periods, but compared to Round Island, it's insignificant. You can hardly call it a significant haul-out."

"I see, it's insignificant in the general scope of things," said Encelewski, "so you treat what happens there as not significant. That's why I guess I didn't see it in your charts. So the kills there, I take it, they're biologically insignificant too, that's why they're not in your presentation?"

Elsberry again sat confused. He quickly glanced over to the game biologists for help. None of them offered any.

"Or maybe you don't know about those kills?" asked Encelewski. "Can we get some help up here to talk about that? Maybe someone from Fish and Wildlife? I understand they have a research camp at Cape Peirce to monitor this, uh, 'place.' I guess we shouldn't call it a haul-out."

"Okay, okay," said Tromble, sensing confusion in the meeting. He saw a hand go up among the federal contingent. "Yeah, okay, come on up."

Two staff on the federal side of the room scooted in beside Elsberry, who momentarily looked uncomfortable but then smiled graciously, sharing his space at the front table. They introduced themselves as staff with the Togiak National Wildlife Refuge, which included Cape Peirce.

"Do you call it a haul-out, Cape Peirce?" asked Encelewski.

"Well, yes, we do," they said.

"However we choose to call it, I'm curious about the kills there," said Encelewski.

The refuge staff looked extremely uncomfortable. Each stared at the other to see who would answer.

"Well, there haven't been any kills there lately," said one finally. "We, uh, well, by watching from our camp, we think we discourage, you know, the ivory hunters from stopping there."

Elsberry's breath released perceptibly. He smiled.

"Boat traffic goes around Cape Newenham," said the other. "Since we've been observing, we've not noticed any boats bothering the walrus at Nanvak Bay or Cape Peirce."

"It's insignificant," reiterated a smug Elsberry.

"Thank you," said Encelewski. "But I guess I'm not asking this right. I'm referring to kills more generally. I'm asking about the walrus killed falling off Cape Peirce. Also, a related question. As Cape Peirce is part of the refuge, perhaps you can also say what steps are being taken by the refuge."

There was complete silence from the table. Elsberry looked again toward the state's bench of game biologists. The federal staffers appealed to their side. No one answered the questions.

"Is there someone we can get up here to talk about the falling walrus and the refuge efforts?" asked Encelewski.

No one moved. Discomfort filled the room. Encelewski turned to Tromble.

"Mr. Chair, I understand there was a video clip taken," said Encelewski.

At this, the solicitor on the federal side of the room began whispering excitedly among his staff.

"I'm just reporting what I have heard," said Encelewski, "but I understand that the Native Corporation at Dillingham requested a copy of the video clip from the refuge and that, if we can't get an answer, I guess we can view it ourselves and..."

"Uh wait, please wait just a moment," said Tromble, seeing a hand waving from the federal group. "I see someone coming here. Have a seat and introduce yourself."

A federal staff member in a brown uniform scooted next to the three at the table. Elsberry found himself almost shoved off the end. The newcomer introduced himself as a federal refuge biologist. He apologized for being nervous. He said he didn't plan to talk at the meeting.

"It's the guy at the camp I met," whispered Camilla to Nick, "the head field biologist when I was at the camp."

"That's okay," Tromble reassured him. "Can you enlighten us about 'falling walrus'?"

A twitter of laughter rippled across the room.

"This is great!" whispered Mel to Nick.

"This past month," the refuge biologist said, clearing his throat, "during the big storm, there were walrus that fell."

"From the top of Cape Peirce?" asked Encelewski, taking the lead again.

"Yes."

"What were they doing up there? Isn't that a good sized mount?"

"We don't know," he replied.

"You don't know?" asked Encelewski. "The biologists don't know?"

Encelewski stared straight at Elsberry with the question.

Elsberry sat red-faced in silence.

"Well, I think they got confused," the refuge biologist replied. "This is my personal opinion, you understand. They got pushed by the strong north wind, sort of uphill. Once there, they tried to get down. It looks like you could slide down. But you can't. Once you start, you can't stop."

"During a big storm?"

"Yes, that's right."

"But how is there a video clip? You filmed it during a big storm?"

"No, no. It lasted several days. The event. The falling. We started filming during the second and the third days."

"After the storm," said Encelewski.

"That's right."

"Then how did they get confused by wind?"

"Well, like I said, we don't know why they did this. It looked to me like follow-the-leader. You know, you follow the animal in front of you."

"Off a cliff?"

"Yes."

"For three days. Two of them clear and sunny?"

"Well, yes. But they shouldn't have been up there, you know. They're marine mammals. They got confused way up in the air. Maybe they saw walrus below on the beach. Some haul out there. They tried to join them and started sliding and, you know…"

"And you have this on film?" asked Encelewski.

"Yes," said the biologist.

"You've shown it to other experts, like the hunters, the media?"

"No."

"Why not?"

"It's… it's new. And it's… kind of horrible to look at, you know, sliding down, smashing on the rocks on top of one another, one after another… bouncing…"

"Yeah, I see," said Encelewski.

There was a general muttering in the room, a low-level buzz. The biologist looked embarrassed, like he was being forced to talk about some prurient event. The chair rapped his gavel. The room hushed.

"But," said Encelewski, "I understand you've tried to stop this walrus sliding, yes? That is, the refuge staff."

"Well, when it wasn't stopping, we went up the third day. We tied stakes with ribbons and rope along the slide paths. You know, to try to keep them from going over. But, you know, it's a big hill."

"So they may still be doing it?"

"Well, maybe, yes."

There was another general murmuring in the room.

"Natural populations behind ropes and ribbons," Mel whispered to Nick, cattily.

"I see," said Encelewski somberly. "So, if you can say, how many walrus fell off Cape Peirce? You know, climbing up and falling off, before you put up the ribbons and stakes."

"Uh, well, we don't know for sure."

"Why is that?"

"The storm probably carried off a lot, you know, before we even started counting. The ocean goes up to the cliff twice a day."

"Okay, so they float off. But knowing this is a low count, how many fell off Cape Peirce that got counted?"

"Uh, maybe forty, maybe fifty…"

The twittering rose in the room. Board members began whispering.

"Thank you," said Encelewski, "maybe forty or fifty, with others washed away by the storm? So, maybe sixty or seventy or, probably we'll never know. Does this count the times it's happened before?"

Here the refuge biologist looked confused.

"What do you mean?" he asked.

"This has happened before, correct?"

"I don't know," he said, looking to his staff for help.

"Well, we could ask them to come up, but I believe Nick John and Camilla Mac Cleary with Subsistence can report that this has happened at least once before, earlier in the season during the herring fishery."

The buzz in the room continued.

"So, coming back to you Dr. Elsberry," said Encelewski, turning to the end of table. "I'm comparing numbers here… the ten walrus that the hunter association has asked for under a managed hunt, so they don't have to scrape meat off the rocks to feed their families, compared with the sixty or seventy or who knows how many walrus that fell off Cape Peirce, which, as I understand you to say, is so 'biologically insignificant' the event and the haul-out aren't mentioned in your report, uh… though really you don't know about this walrus phenomenon at all, do you? And the federal biologists really don't have a good count of the kills anyway, so they can't understand the significance of such events over time, if any… uh, I apologize. I'm rambling a little. Uh, I guess I don't have any more questions that you can answer, Dr. Elsberry. Thank you. Mr. Chair, I guess I'm done with these experts."

"Okay, break time!" shouted Tromble.

Nick and Camilla sat in the hall outside the meeting room. A newly-constituted walrus committee was just finishing up an hour-long session, readying its report to present to the Joint Board. Mel hurried out, flashed a big grin, and rushed past with her cell phone, saying she had to make a couple of quick calls. Isaac Nuniq came out next, stretching his great frame, walking toward them in the slow, side-to-side fashion of a Yup'ik hunter on sea ice.

"What did your guys come up with?" asked Nick.

"A start," said Isaac, smiling.

"Yeah?" asked Camilla.

"Yeah," said Isaac, sitting comfortably beside her. "A good start. A good framework. It's going to pass out, probably to the Game Board next. We're going for a small, managed hunt, a three-way co-operative deal… tribes, feds, and state. Yeah, it's all good, but…"

"What?" asked Nick.

"The other villages want in," Isaac whispered. "We're talking by phone to them now. I always thought of this as a Togiak hunt. But they want in too. But we can work this out. We can work this out."

"Yeah," smiled Camilla. "I'll bet you can."

"I got to get some air," complained Isaac, standing up stiffly and lumbering down the hall.

The room disgorged more committee workers, among them Alexie Encelewski. He came over to Nick and Camilla's couch.

"Almost done," he said congenially.

Encelewski sat and offered his hand to each of them.

"Thanks," he said.

"Uh, what for?" asked Nick, embarrassed.

"For being out there, sitting out there in Fish and Game, presenting that report, it makes a real big difference."

"Well, you guys did the work," said Camilla, smiling. "The hunter association, the tribe… they've been fighting for this for years. It wouldn't have happened otherwise. And you were great."

"Yeah? Thanks," said Encelewski.

"I'm just happy to watch," said Camilla.

"Hmmm…" said Encelewski, looking from Camilla to Nick.

"Really, I'm… I'm not Fish and Game," grumbled Nick.

Encelewski laughed jovially at Nick's joke.

Two elders emerged from the room, the elders who had described traditional walrus hunting at the front table. They drifted over.

"You know Frederick Bavilla and Jackson Henry from Togiak?" asked Encelewski, introducing them. "Nick John. Camilla Mac Cleary."

"Ah," exclaimed the elder Bavilla, shaking Nick's hand as if to say, finally we are meeting. Jackson Henry smiled warmly at each of them too. The two old men, in their eighties or more, looked very happy.

"I have something here," said Bavilla, sitting down, opening a rumpled paper sack he carried. "They gave us some things I'm supposed to give away."

Encelewski stood up to leave.

"No, you should stay," said old man Henry.

Encelewski sat again.

Bavilla pulled out a handful of tissue paper. He slowly unwrapped it. To Nick and Camilla's surprise, he uncovered an ivory disk. He held it out on his palm. It looked old, an ivory pendant elegantly carved. A walrus motif circled the disk. At its center a harpoon point had been cunningly embedded, surrounded by the walrus.

"They found this," said Henry vaguely.

"At that boy's house," said Bavilla, nodding at Nick and Camilla. "You know, that boy with all his stuff."

"Oh... Jerome Paul?" asked Camilla, sadly naming the dead.

"Yes, that one," said Henry. "They found it at his house."

"We discussed this thing at council," said Bavilla, hefting the old pendant. "Throw it away! Just throw it away! Somebody said that. But we decided, we voted, it's better to give it back."

"Who decided this?" asked Camilla.

"Us oldsters," laughed Jackson Henry.

"Yeah," smiled Camilla.

"We decided, uh... to give it back," said Bavilla, "you know, that it's best to give it back... to you!"

He nodded at Nick respectfully.

Nick sat dumbfounded.

He'd never seen this ivory disk before. He knew nothing about it. What kind of a mistake was this? They were giving the ivory pendant to him?

"But, then... well, then we met this other guy here at the meeting," said Bavilla, nodding at Encelewski. "So if you say it's okay, we think it's even better that we give it back... to him."

Bavilla pushed the pendant toward Encelewski.

Encelewski looked stunned.

"You know," said Bavilla to Nick, "even before, it belonged to him, that lucky hunter."

"Cuniq," whispered Encelewski. He held the pendant as if it were fragile treasure. "It belonged to Cuniq when he lived at Kodiak, from his grandfather. It was Talliciq who made it. He gave it to Qeng'aq and lived."

"You know about that one?" asked Bavilla.

"I heard the story many times when I was a boy," whispered Encelewski.

Tears formed in his eyes. Stories of his own family's history. Here was the ivory pendant given by Cuniq to Qeng'aq. The maker of this was like a great great grandfather, many generations back.

"Okay by you?" old man Henry asked Nick.

Nick saw pure joy in Encelewski's face.

"Yeah, okay," nodded Nick.

"Good!" said Henry, slapping Nick's knee. "We're rid of it!"

Bavilla dug into the sack. He pulled out something larger.

"We talked about this one too," said Bavilla. "We decided not to throw it away too, like that other one. They said to give it to you because… well, you're a kass'aq and asked about it and you know what to do with it. And because of what you did for us."

To Camilla's great surprise, Bavilla handed the gift to her.

It was a flat cardboard box secured with a rubber band.

Camilla's eyes shined. She knew what it was.

The Ouija board.

"Thanks," she whispered.

"Good!" exclaimed old man Henry. "We're rid of that one too!"

Bavilla turned to Nick, sitting next to Camilla.

"I guess that leaves you with nothing!"

Bavilla chortled at his rude joke.

Jackson Henry laughed with him.

He gave Nick an impish pat. They were two old men having a very good day.

"Nick," said Camilla with sympathy.

She drew closer and placed the Ouija box on his lap.

She put her nose almost into his cheek.

He smelled soap.

"You can play with me, anytime."

POSTSCRIPT

The Alaska Board of Game approved access to a walrus hunt on Round Island in response to years of effort by Yup'ik hunters to reopen it. The island had been closed to subsistence hunting for almost two generations. The *Cooperative Agreement Governing Subsistence Walrus Hunting on Round Island, Bristol Bay, Alaska* was signed by the Qayassiq Walrus Commission (representing Yup'ik hunters), alongside the Alaska Department of Fish and Game, United States Fish and Wildlife Service, and the Eskimo Walrus Commission. Its first year, hunters from Togiak traveled to Round Island and took two walrus under the guidance of hunt leaders. Through the agreement, crews from six other Yup'ik communities also returned to the island to hunt, taking eight more.

The co-managed hunt continues to the present day, a model of cooperation, one of the earliest co-managed marine mammal hunts in Alaska.

The walrus continue to return to Round Island.

Because of persistent problems, the federal refuge through the Fish and Wildlife Service erected a 250-foot-long, wooden-slatted fence near the base of Cape Peirce in an effort to prevent walrus from climbing the cape to plunge to their deaths. Though counts remain uncertain, at least one hundred and fifty walrus fell the first year of the big storm.

The fence has been only partially successful.

Biologists say they don't know why the walrus fall.

ROBERT J. WOLFE

ABOUT THE AUTHOR

Robert J. Wolfe is a cultural anthropologist, author of "Playing with Fish and Other Lessons from the North" and other works on traditional hunting and fishing practices in the Far North.

CPSIA information can be obtained
at www.ICGtesting.com
Printed in the USA
LVOW13s1711160217

524503LV00012B/1325/P